LOVE AFFAIR

LOVE AFFAIR

Seymour Epstein

DOUBLEDAY & COMPANY, INC., GARDEN CITY, NEW YORK

FOR JENNY

LOVE AFFAIR

1

Gabriel Michelson stepped out of the Air Terminal building at Kennedy Airport and hailed a taxi. The driver put his two pieces of luggage in the trunk and then quickly pulled into the stream of traffic.

Gabe noted the wire-reinforced glass shield between himself and the driver. It brought to mind those opaque, filthy slabs of glass used as siding in the old subway entrances. This one was not quite so opaque or filthy, and it was, Gabe supposed, some kind of protection; although what would—he leaned forward to inspect the license and photograph of *Rafael Ramirez*—what would Rafael Ramirez do if the nose of a .38 tapped on the other side of that glass? Gabe smiled to himself. Here he was already confronted with evidence of the condition of his onetime city, city of his birth, but he was feeling no anxiety, only this nervously happy excitement as familiar sights came into his view.

All his life—except the past ten years. All of memory that counted, for memory is made magic only by experience that doesn't know its future. Gabriel Michelson pretty much knew the future of his experience by the time he had moved with his family from the city. All of experience was well on its way to becoming a sometimes interesting, sometimes dull tabulation of events that filled his days as rewardingly as any he could imagine, but devoid of the chemistry of magic.

The glass panel suddenly slid open, causing Gabe a start of alarm.

"You know whether it's on Forty-fifth or Forty-sixth, the entrance to your hotel?" Rafael Ramirez asked.

"No, I'm sorry, I don't," Gabe said. "Damn it, no, I just don't remember. Haven't been back in five years."

"Well, is not important," said Ramirez. "I thought maybe I save some time for you. You come in the right way, you save maybe fifteen minutes, depending on traffic."

"Oh, I know," Gabe said, pleased by the driver's friendliness. "You can spend fifteen minutes just circling once around the block." It was a silly impulse, one he thought he'd be able to resist, but suddenly he didn't see why he should resist it. "I'm a New Yorker by birth," he said. "Lived here all my life except the last ten years."

"Where you live now?" Rafael asked. His w's had the Puerto Rican guttural . . . "Hchwhere you live now?"

"Denver . . . Denver, Colorado."

"Yeah? Hey, I bet that's nice. You got mountains there, hah?"

"Lots of mountains," Gabe said smiling.

Rafael's head went up and down. He turned his head slightly each time he spoke, passing the words over his shoulder. He had a mustache, the droopy kind, and his long black hair flowed over the collar of his leather jacket.

"You know how much it cost me to buy a medallion to operate this cab?" he asked.

Gabe assumed he had been asked because the figure was impressive and Rafael wanted to show it off like a trophy or diploma.

"Ten thousand," Gabe said, making the figure larger than he imagined it could be.

"How you like *fifty* thousand?" Rafael said.

"What!"

Rafael repeated the figure, and Gabe believed him. He wondered where on earth someone like Rafael would get fifty thousand, and immediately labeled the thought racist, although the puzzlement remained. He asked where one would get fifty thousand, and Rafael explained it was part cash, mostly loans. Gabe listened only partially as Rafael went on to tell him about the profit and danger of operating a taxi in the city. He had only been hit twice by bandits. Not bad, considering. Gabe agreed, thinking that if Rafael could gather together through payment and promise the stupendous price of one of those medallions, it was probably because it was worth it.

A surreal vision of the new city came to Gabe: a place of separate fiefdoms where each bought his castle, moat, and drawbridge —singly or collectively—coming out by day to trade, closing up by night, afraid. . . . A nightmare fortress is our city. . . . Would Rafael appreciate such sentiments? Probably not.

Rafael chose the Long Island Expressway into the city. Gabe prepared himself for the assault of sensation he anticipated around the Kew Gardens section. It came with the appearance of those massive apartment complexes. Built in the fecund fifties. He and Jean had lived in a three-room cage in one of the less expensive warrens, having those Saturday-night parties with Brie and politics, almost all newly married, the men almost all ex-servicemen, almost all hanging on for dear life to a job or a grinding, government-paid education. Partially paid, anyway.

Gabe recalled walks he and Jean had taken in some nearby park on autumn Sundays, after one of those Saturday nights, the weather brisk, the sun bright, the trees carrying on their gold-and-vermilion carnival. Jean walking with her arms folded across her breasts. Jean with her touchy skin already mottled by the cold air. Jean wearing a heavy sweater, saying, "I'm not going to wait to have my first child, Gabe, and that's that!"

That was that. They had their first child. Sweet Pam, who would be starting college next fall. Colic, of course. Soybean gunk instead of milk. Lord, the nights of howling! Gabe shut off thoughts of that time like the light in a film projector. Blank wall, darkness. . . . The point, of course, was that they had all survived. He had burrowed like a mole through years and books and starting pay, and he had become moderately successful. Jean had burrowed through years of diapers—Pam's and Andrew's—and meals and tears and the long, awful, endless chrysalis of growing up, and she had become, more or less, a free woman.

God bless them, every one!

And now here he was back in New York, representing a Denver client, instead of the New York client whose western interests had instigated the Michelson move to the Rockies. This deal would go

4

through, of course. There would be the usual minuet of hand-
shakes and opposite numbers and niggling questions, but each side
had predetermined the limits of their give and take, and they
would make a contract. The New York franchise interests would
buy the Denver restaurants owned by his client, Harry Curtis, because the New York people had looked the properties over and
had decided they could be easily converted to their franchise operation. Harry Curtis would sell because he wanted into the building
business with his son-in-law, and part of the deal would be first
bid on new properties developed in that area by the franchise people. There would be a contract because there was willingness on
both sides. First rule of contract law and life: desire. . . . "Do
you take this *gonif* to be your lawfully wedded party of the first
part?" . . . "I do." . . . "I now pronounce you. . . ."

Rafael Ramirez drove his taxi into Manhattan and turned north
on the avenue—First or Second, Gabe wasn't sure which. Then he
turned west, sliding open the glass panel to announce, "I remember now, it goes west, the entrance."

The taxi pulled up to the hotel. Gabe paid and tipped Rafael
Ramirez, wishing him good luck.

"You too, mister," said the man with the fifty-thousand-dollar
medallion, and drove away.

Gabe carried his own bags into the hotel.

2

By the time lunch was over, Evelyn White felt as if that famous smile of hers had been nailed into place by a dozen rusty spikes. Big asset, her smile. Everybody loved to see Evelyn smile. It made people feel warm and wanted. All she ever did was stretch her mouth, and what happened happened. No, that wasn't true. She knew she had a smile. She had been flashing it purposefully ever since her child's mind had made the connection between that exercise and happy consequences. Personally, she had always thought the rewards for having a large mouth and even teeth a bit incommensurate; but life, as no less a favorite of fortune than John F. Kennedy had observed, was not fair.

Not that it had been all *that* much a boon. The Evelyn White smile helped, but it wouldn't have gotten her very far without a few other, very definite assets. Like a brain. Like a large helping of what her grandfather had called *Geduld*. This wingding for distributors had become the annual crisis of her life ever since she had taken on her lady-executive role, but this year's gethsemane was somehow more taxing than any she could remember. Hotels, of course, had become unspeakable. There was no such thing as a promise. And as the hotels became more inefficient, the distributors became more demanding. Almost a hundred of them this time! Some with wives, some without, and in the case of the latter the demands became as fidgety and obvious as a little boy who has to go to the bathroom. And some not so fidgety . . . like Mr. Sandy Bethune.

Evelyn began gathering the order sheets and memos she had accumulated on the long reception table outside the dining room. Thoughts of Mr. Bethune made her angry, but she wasn't sure whether the anger was directed at that sexual quarterback or herself . . . Sandy Bethune . . . "Call me Sandy." . . . Evelyn slipped all the papers into her portfolio. His name was John, she had learned from the roster, but she called him "Sandy," as he had requested, because not to would have been ridiculous. She called others by whatever name they wished to be called. But there was something insinuating about Sandy Bethune's request. There was something altogether insinuating about John "Sandy" Bethune, but she just wasn't sure if the insinuation originated entirely with the man, or whether Evelyn White might not have turned on a few switches. Unconsciously, of course. It had happened before. There had been occasions when a reflective Evelyn had been able to see the whole subliminal number she had done without being aware that she was doing it: things with the eyes and the voice and, of course, the smile, the Evelyn smile, which had its own inner thermostat, ranging from living-room sociability to bedroom heat.

If there had been nothing to Sandy Bethune but his loud plaid and smiling bullishness, there wouldn't be this retrospective fussing now, but Evelyn, at last and categorically, made the admission to herself that there *was* something else. There was the leonine head with its surprisingly long hair—for a Cleveland business man, that is—and his smile, and his wit, and his heavyset shoulders, and the way he had looked at her, and, altogether, something that reminded her of someone else.

"Do you think this jacket is too loud?" he had asked her, sitting down next to her when people had begun to move from table to table in the valedictory way of ending conventions.

They had spoken before. She knew his name and the name of his business. His was a big operation in Cleveland. He handled not only Academy Publications but all other publications that went to bookstores, airports, drugstores, supermarkets, hotels, etc. Don Marshall, her boss, had tipped her off on the man's importance. "I suspect all is not kosher in Mr. Bethune's far-flung empire," Don had said. "I shudder to think of his making a misshipment of some of his other stuff to one of our customers. But he is a power. He can get us the distribution—and not only in Ohio." So she had been especially "nice" to Mr. Bethune, and the niceness seemed to have settled into his heavy but handsome features like some delicate emollient. It was absorbed. It was appreciated. It was, she suspected, expected.

"No, I don't think that's too loud," she had said.

"I've been told it's a bit too loud."

Evelyn checked herself just in time from asking, "By whom?" Instead she said, "I believe that's what's called a bold pattern. On you it looks good."

"Are you Jewish?" he asked.

"Why do you ask?"

"Because I'm invariably attracted to Jewish women. I'm told by my Jewish men friends that they're invariably attracted to *shiksas.* Nature's great mixing talent. Your name is White. That's not Jewish. But I figure it might have been Weiss at one time. Weiss is white in German, isn't it?"

"Well, I didn't change it," Evelyn said. "I was born White."

Sandy Bethune grinned.

"That sounded funny, didn't it?" she said.

"I'm sure our black brothers and sisters would make something of it," he said. "I like the traps language sets for us. But you didn't answer my question."

"I am Jewish," Evelyn said. "The family's name was Weiss. It was changed to White by my grandfather, who was a very adaptable man. Now you know all about me."

"No, I don't know all about you," Sandy Bethune said, resting his bold-patterned arms on the table and shifting his big body slightly so that, adjacent as he was, he somehow created the illusion of surrounding her. Perhaps it was only his physical idiom, perhaps only her radar, but there did register the notion that Sandy Bethune had effectively announced that this table was private for the time being. She was alerted. "I don't know you at all," he went on, "but I'd like to. May I say something to you?"

"I thought that's what you were doing," she said.

Sandy closed his eyes briefly and smiled. Something smooth and sinister in that smile. He was not a man to be put off easily.

"I mean say something serious," he said.

"Serious?"

"Serious."

"Dear me," she said. "That sounds serious."

"Do I have your permission?"

"To say something serious? Yes. Of course."

By a movement of his shoulders, or something, Sandy Bethune seemed to tighten his encirclement, and then, with no change in voice or demeanor, he proceeded to launch one of the oddest verbal sieges Evelyn had ever undergone. This Ohio distributor of many publications told her that he was an interesting man, an unusual man, but that these special qualities could only manifest themselves in any man-woman thing after the vital question had been settled. He detested, he said, the silly, time-wasting game of sexual maneuvering. He was an entertaining man. He had read extensively. He was one of the few people he knew or had heard of who had read the complete Gibbon's *Decline and Fall*. He had gotten an undergraduate degree in business administration, and then had gone on, just for the fun of it, to take a master's in history. "I would like very much to go to bed with you," he said. "If we could settle that matter now, we would avoid the whole dull business of gamesmanship and spend our time really enjoying ourselves." And when she said that she couldn't quite believe what she was hearing, Sandy replied that that might be true but not because the idea was so strange, only because its utterance was. When he said that, she experienced a dizzying little lurch of agreement. She wasn't agreeing to his purpose but to the clinical observation he'd made to support his purpose. She recognized the feel of this subsoil of truth, worms and all. Perhaps there wasn't the *immediate* sexual speculation Sandy suggested, but after a certain point of interest there was. She felt a small-girl giggle of subterfuge bubble in her, as she had once felt when she and a girlfriend had sneaked into the foyer to listen to an uncle of hers tell a dirty joke.

"Well—?" said Mr. Bethune.

She laughed, but she wasn't pleased with her laugh. It was a nervous laugh. "I'm curious," she said. "How would we spend our time really enjoying ourselves?"

And Sandy seemed all ready for this, too. He said he had two orchestra seats for *Equus*. Had she seen *Equus*? As a matter of fact, she hadn't. They would have dinner at The Four Seasons. A bit splashy, but he liked it. Best of all, they could talk with ease.

They wouldn't waste their valuable minds on the stupid games men and women play.

"And all because you'll be quite certain that I'll go to bed with you after?" Evelyn said.

"Exactly."

"I have another idea, Mr. Bethune," she said, suddenly inspired. "I won't say it's a better idea, but it's mine. Let's do everything you say except the last. If it's only a question of *certainty,* then be certain that I won't go to bed with you. In that way nothing will interfere with our pleasure. We can enjoy the evening. We can avoid the whole dull business of gamesmanship. You can tell me all about Gibbon's *Decline and Fall.* You can really test your theory, Mr. Bethune. See if it's really a matter of mind."

Almost instantly, Evelyn felt a slight lifting of the siege. Sandy slid his arms back from the table and leaned back in his chair, putting his hands in his jacket pockets. He nodded, then stopped, then nodded again, more affirmatively.

"That's good," he said. "That's very good. You overlook one thing, though."

"What's that?"

"The question has to be settled favorably, for all good things to happen. If the answer is no beforehand, then I'm left too sad to put on a really good performance."

"Ah, that's too bad. But that's your problem, isn't it, Sandy?"

"Yes, Evelyn, that's my problem."

The siege was lifted entirely. Sandy Bethune began to look around the room in the vagrant way of a man measuring out some courtesy seconds before departure.

"Are you leaving for Cleveland immediately?" she asked, to ease the separation.

"No, I have some further business here," said Sandy.

"Well, a pleasant journey, whenever you go."

Sandy nodded vaguely and looked at her. "No hard feelings?" he asked.

"None," she lied.

"That's good," he said. "Personally, none on my part. You needn't fear there'll be any repercussions as far as our business connection is concerned. I don't operate that way."

"I'm glad to hear it," Evelyn said.

She was. Glad to hear it. It had passed through her mind that Sandy might operate differently. A little vindictiveness to smooth his feathers. But all right. Good-by, Mr. Sandy Bethune.

The annoyance she was left with reached in so many directions that all she could do was stand frustratedly at its center. She admired the colorful *chutzpah* of the man, and she resented it. She had very definitely experienced a throb of sexual excitement, and, worse, a quick, murmurous conspiracy toward capitulation; and then, again, the slow burn of resentment. *Did he really think he could get her into bed with that trumped-up garbage?* Gibbon, indeed! And yet hadn't she wished on occasion for someone to simply step up and announce his intentions without all the ridiculous sashaying around of cuteness and cleverness and schmertzy, doglike appeals of the heart? And yet hadn't she plaintively thought to herself that she must really be over the hill if a man like Sandy was no longer willing to take the usual chances for so nice a prize? Or wasn't the prize so nice? Or does no one take such chances any longer? Evelyn clicked shut her portfolio and swept out of the room.

The hell with it!

She met Don in the lobby, as arranged. It was getting on to three o'clock. Don took her by the arm and marched her into the bar. He moved a table so that she could slide into a cushioned wall seat. He took the chair opposite.

"Thank you," he said. "You were, as usual, magnificent. The whole thing was, as usual, a great success. Thanks mainly to you. You must be beat. What can I order you?"

"It's so early," she said.

"Depends on the day," he said. "For us it's late."

"Gibson," she said.

"Gibson."

Don flagged a waiter and ordered their drinks. He was such a nice man. He was bald and brown and harriedly successful. He had a son going to medical school in Boston and a daughter who had made it her life's work to torment him, running off with one hairy nerd after another, then coming back and promising a new life. His wife, sad Hilda, gathered debilitating diseases as another woman might gather flowers. The latest was some indefinable blood thing that kept her more in bed than out of it. No doubt the illnesses were real, and it was callous to be impatient with another's infirmities, but there seemed to be such congruity between fate and temperament that one couldn't help suspecting they had sought each other out.

Evelyn knew that Don had a woman somewhere in the Riverdale section of the Bronx, but for some unimaginable reason poor Don tried to hide his visits there from her as carefully as he did from his wife. Countless times, she had been on the point of telling him to drop the nonsense, that knowing his life as she did he had an ally not a spy in her, but it occurred to her that Don's need for secrecy might have motives other than concealment. Let him play it as he wished.

"But tell me what *you* think," he said.

"An unqualified success," she agreed. "The great majority were happy with the arrangements. They seemed to be having a good time."

"And they should!" Don exclaimed. "Let me say it right now before I forget: that suggestion list of yours was a stroke of genius. I lost count of the number of people who said to me that it made the convention. Places and prices and that very clever *de gustibus* thing. Truthfully, Evelyn, it didn't occur to me how much work you must have done on that. It was thorough. It told people where to go according to their tastes, and how much they could expect to spend, and all in all it was a very useful thing. And I guarantee you this: it will translate into dollars. The company thanks you. It will do more than thank you come Christmas. I can tell you that right now."

"I'm overwhelmed, Don," Evelyn said. "Thank you for the pretty words. I thought I was doing my job."

Don twiddled a deprecating hand. "We all try to do that. The one who brings something special to the job deserves something special."

"Well, you're very sweet."

Don nodded. He suddenly looked sad. Evelyn could tell that something had crossed his mind, and she could almost guess what. The wish for a different life, with different people. But that was as evanescent as breath on a window pane. He looked at his watch. "My son is driving in from Boston today," he said. "I expect him at the house by five. I also have to stop at the office first and get two very important letters on the machine. If you're in the office before me on Monday please see to it that Gladys gets on them right away, will you? And kick me out of here on time. What are you going to do?"

"What do you mean?"

"I would like to think of you having a smashing time this evening," Don said.

"Oh, that's already been proposed to me."

"Has it? Tell me."

Evelyn told him about Sandy Bethune. Not everything, but enough.

"That sonofabitch!" Don swore indignantly. "I told you there was something shifty about that man! He can take his business—"

"He doesn't operate that way," Evelyn said. "He made a point of that."

"I don't care how he operates. The hell with him!"

"Don, you make it sound as if I were some kind of virgin queen. Does it shock you that a man would make a pass at me?"

"No, that's not the point," Don replied. "It was a pretty raw proposal. A man should know who and who not to pull that stuff on. That he'd try to pull it on you confirms my feeling that he's half a gangster."

Evelyn smiled. "Am I too high-class for that kind of stuff, Don?" she coaxed him.

"You're quality," Don said, looking her straight in the eye to underline his conviction.

Evelyn bit her lip to check her laughter. Don was shrewd and Don was practical, but there was a streak of Old World courtliness in him that he would put out on occasion as a patriot puts out flags. Evelyn reached out and put her hand on his arm.

"You know how to make a lady feel good," she said. "And I promise you I'm going to have a smashing time tonight."

Before leaving the hotel, Evelyn made a telephone call that established pretty certainly that she would have *no* kind of time that evening, let alone smashing. She phoned at four, after she had sent her boss on his way, and the phone at the other end rang the usual half dozen times before it was ripped off the cradle and a "Yeah!"

snarled into it for greeting. She said hello, and then could visualize Frank nodding his head rapidly as he adjusted himself to this particular human contact. "Hi," he said, more humanly. "How're you? Christ, four is it? How'd the thing go? The whatchamacallit? Convention. Big success?"

"Tremendous."

"Good girl. You're a killer. I hope Squire Marshall gives you a fat bonus. Where are you, anyway?"

"At the hotel."

"What are you going to do?"

"I don't know," Evelyn said. "What do you think I should do?"

"Oh, Christ, this is Saturday, isn't it?" Evelyn heard him grunt disgustedly. "Listen, we can have dinner and that's all, I'm afraid. I'm terribly sorry. Do you mind, darling? Darling, do you mind? I'm sorry as hell. I have *got* to get a decent amount of work over to Sam by Monday or my name is shit. Worse than that, I doubt I'll get the rest of that advance if I don't, and as you bloody well know I need that advance! I've made too many promises. That's about the size of it. Sam stopped yelling last week. He just plain stopped yelling, and he said to me, 'Get it in by Monday, Frank.' Just like that. Very cool, very ominous. So I figure I'd better get three chapters in by Monday—and if we have a nice, leisurely dinner with four cocktails and a bottle of Pommard and all the nice sexual blessings that flow therefrom, I'm just not going to get those three chapters in."

"Stay where you are," Evelyn said. "We don't have to have dinner."

"No, no, no! I *want* to have dinner with you. I want to tell you what I'm doing and get your reaction. I want to talk to you about what I'm doing. I tell you what, let's go to that fish place on Third. You can't linger in a place like that. We'll have an early dinner . . . okay? Let's see—it's four now—how about five-thirty? We'll spend an hour, an hour and a half, no booze, not even a beer, and then I'll have the whole evening to work. Do that for me, will you?"

"All right."

All right? . . . Well, what could she do? Pose a need as great as Frank's? Tell her writer-lover-friend that his needs need not always have top priority in their two-year-old, more-than-a-little-manic love affair? She could do that. She could say, "To hell with your book and your editor and your career. You get over here and be very, very charming and attentive to me this whole evening, because I need it very badly. I don't know why I need it, but I do!"

No, she couldn't say that, because that was not the understanding, the arrangement. Their relationship had started on the basis of her respect for his work, and it had continued—grown!—with that for soil and rain and seed. Frank Moore was a good writer. Not the best, but good. He was a journalist turned novelist. He wrote novels about the city that were half documentary, half fiction. They were about the poor, the ethnic, the angry. They were about drugs, squalor, and crime. They revealed the life that most taxpaying citizens would rather not think about, and Evelyn admired the courage and compassion that went into Frank's books. But they were not first-rate. They lacked the dimension that would lift them out of their journalistic base and make them art. His people were revealed in their predicaments but not in their hearts. She knew it and found them nevertheless praiseworthy and fine. Frank knew it and it tortured him. There was ample evidence in the world that the Jews held no patent on such self-inflicted anguish, but it was still a small surprise to witness the universality in its Irish-American form.

Evelyn glanced at the clock above the registration desk of the hotel. It was a quarter to five. An hour earlier in St. Louis. There wouldn't be time to get to her apartment and make the call from there, and then get to the restaurant and meet Frank in time. For some reason, she could never reach Jay in his dormitory room around five o'clock. He studied, he claimed, in the library or in the rooms of classmates. He went, he claimed, to evening lectures on campus, to concerts, to movies, to plays, to any of the many stimulating activities going on at the university. She hoped to God it was true. Even half. It wasn't that Jay was deceitful but that he so often counted intention as accomplishment. She realized that someone else might ask what was that if not deceit—her former husband had called it deceit, and much worse—but there *was* a difference. It was *not* deceit. To her mind, deceit argued a deliberation that was simply not present in Jay's consciousness. He strove toward approval so ardently that at times his imagination reached out and gathered in the means of it. That was not deceit, and anyone who insisted that it was was a fool in his heart.

Evelyn made the phone call collect—she paid the bills anyway—and this time she was lucky. She heard Jay's voice say, "Yeah, sure, I'll accept the charges. . . . Mom?"

"How are you, Jay?"

"Fine. Anything wrong?"

"No. I just wanted to say hello. How are things going?"

"Pretty good. We had an exam in bio on Wednesday. I think I did all right. I'm pretty sure of a B, maybe a B+. How're you?"

"I'm fine. We just finished the big convention."

"Oh, yeah. That's good. . . . I mean, you know, how was it, okay?"

"Yes, I think it was quite successful."

"That's good. How's Mr. Marshall?"

"He's fine. . . ."

The conversation went on in the usual, skitter-bug fashion, darting here and there across the surface of their lives. Evelyn understood that it was the sacred convention of Jay's age to make a slightness of conversation with one's parents. She remembered it from her own life. It had nothing to do with love or a lack of love. The new identity growing each minute of each day was too swift and too amazing to convey to another living soul, especially one's parents, who seemed suddenly to have developed the wrong emphasis in everything. So Evelyn had learned not to wish more from word exchanges with her son than was given to her. She listened to the words, but only as clues to something beneath or beyond. She listened for categories, and when Jay would discuss classes and grades so quickly it meant that things were going fairly well in that department. If they were not, the order would have been changed. And she listened just for cadences, the falls and lifts, spaces, judging from them the state of his frustration or contentment. And she listened in order to orchestrate for herself the visual image from the sound of his voice. She hadn't known how acutely that would work until Jay had gone half across the continent to attend college. It did work. She listened to his voice, and she could see so much more clearly his dark eyes, so much like her own, and his terribly overgrown, springy hair, and that configuration of nose and mouth and chin that had astonishingly lost precise definition for her in the few months of his absence.

"Hey, Dad got in touch with me . . . Friday, I think . . . yeah, yesterday. . . ."

"Good," said Evelyn.

"He said I should send him the bill for the . . . you know . . . tuition."

"But, darling, that's been paid," Evelyn reminded him.

"He meant for next quarter."

"Oh . . . all right."

"He said he was going to California on Sunday, and he would stop off here for a couple of days."

"Oh, that's nice. Good. . . . Are you getting enough sleep?"

"Come on, Mom."

"Just a reminder."

"Thanks."

"Oh, listen," Evelyn said, quickly changing the subject, "I've still got those sweaters and flannel shirts, the ones I had cleaned. Do you want me to send them out now?"

"Yeah, I guess you'd better. It's getting pretty cold now."

"I'll get them together on Monday and send them out."

"Okay. That'll be fine. Thanks. Okay, Mom, so . . ."

"Take care, Jay."

"Sure. . . . Talk to you."

"Good-by, darling."

"Yeah . . . okay."

Evelyn stepped out of the phone booth and almost immediately spotted two men from the convention at the registration desk. Their backs were turned to her, so she quickly crossed the lobby and left the hotel, walking out into the wet, darkening day. She just couldn't serve up another helping of cheerful vacuity for the customers. She wanted to stay in the messy, familiar kitchen of her own thoughts, putting together into some kind of hash all the emotional ingredients that had slopped over during this trouble-some day.

What time? Five. Good! She would find a taxi, get over to the fish restaurant on Third, and then listen to Frank tell how this time—*this time!*—he had really gotten a purchase on character and story, and how he would squeeze out of his soul the one goddam quintessential drop of greatness!

3

Once settled in his room, Gabe Michelson wondered why he always came back to this moldy old place every time he returned to New York. The rooms were large and the price reasonable, true, but the place was definitely getting flaky with age. He noticed how the paint was peeling off the water pipes that ran through the closet. He was a little repelled by the mouse-gray bedcover. Probably quite clean, but it *looked* seedy. And the carpeting, with that stain near the stone-dead fireplace, whose marble frame gave out more chill than cheerfulness. And there was that pervasive *smell* everywhere, as if it needed all the windows and doors torn off and a hurricane of fresh air blown through the place. Well, someone had once recommended it as being close to everything and relatively cheap; after the first stay, it became a habit.

He took a shower, changed clothes, and went to meet his friend, Jeff Singer, at the arranged restaurant, the Italian place that made veal scallopine like nowhere else.

His first impulse was to take another cab down to the Village, but he decided on the subway instead. Jean had warned, "For God's sake, stay out of the subways!" "Why?" he had asked. "You know why," she had said. "From what I hear, they've got a murderer planted in every car." He had laughed and shaken his head, asking, "How about the millions who use the subways every day?" "Well, then, stay out of them in the evening." . . . Was this evening? Six o'clock? He supposed it was. Certainly it was dark outside. But, whatever the statistics, he borrowed on a mythic sense of safety where the subways were concerned. He harbored no nonsensical ideas about his invulnerability, but he allowed himself a small superstition of place. The streets, yes, but not the subways. Subways were not his nemesis.

He entered the Forty-second Street station on the Independent line. It seemed no more dirty or clean than he remembered it. An F train rolled clamorously into the station, and Gabe noted with a mixture of shock and amusement the official graffiti defacing the cars. His amusement may have been only a recognition of his ambivalence. When he had first heard about the practice of city-sponsored defacement, he was reminded of the kind of neurotic who rushes to tell you his faults before you discover them for yourself. . . . *Yes, yes, we recognize the impulse toward destruction, and since we're powerless to prevent it, since we're powerless to compel any other kind of impulse, we'll smear our own face and lampoon our own dignity, and hope that you'll think poorly enough of us to calm your rage.* . . . Of course it was easy for him to take a lofty attitude, not being involved in the daily nightmare of keeping this city together. On the other hand, perhaps it needed this distance to see how far things had fallen.

The people were the big difference, not the subways themselves. They were not the same people who had ridden in the cars when he was growing up, when he was going to school, when he was making his interborough voyages of discovery. They didn't look menacing, but they did look different.

Gabe stood. He had only a few stations to go. Standing gave him a better vantage for observation. He watched three young blacks, a girl and two boys, talking excitedly about something. He caught snatches of their conversation. The girl seemed to be in command, the boys listening to her with a sidelong attention that was at once sullen and respectful. They were not enjoying her authority, but they were damned well *listening*. Gabe heard her say, ". . . don't *deny* it to their faces, Chrissake. They know you said it. You tol' me yourself they got five witnesses that *heard* you say it. Now don't go ahead and tell 'em you *didn't* say it. That's *dumb!* You tell 'em you said it, but that it was just the dumb-ass thing a man say when he angry. You didn't *mean* it. . . ." Gabe turned quickly as the girl lifted her eyes and swept the immediate vicinity with a disdainful look. Gabe thought he had removed the eavesdropping evidence just in time, but he wasn't sure.

That girl would make a good lawyer, he thought. He was struck by the cold, deliberate articulation. There was something studied in her speech, not the English but the vernacular, as if her pride was not in having mastered the proper diction but in having retained the black tonalities.

The way those three discussed their concerns snagged in the loose texture of Gabe's mood. He had been trying to define for himself the difference between the city he remembered and the city he was now seeing. He could point out the many physical changes —the buildings on Sixth, the bad dream that Forty-second had become—but such landmarks only obstructed a clear view. The real difference was in the people. The city had become a holding action. Everybody seemed to be waiting for something, not just another external change but a change of state: cold, colder, ice; hot, hotter, fire—the change toward which all changes were tending. And this gave a suspended look to everything. Waiting. Waiting. Some to bug out, some to take over, but in either case the separation of self from the vast transience the city had become.

He described this feeling to Jeff over their delicious dinner, and Jeff nodded thoughtfully, then said, "I think you're right. You put it very well. The change of state. Everybody's waiting for that. It doesn't surprise me that you're getting such a strong reaction. How many years since you've been back?"

"Five."

"Why five years? You used to come back regularly."

Gabe said he wasn't quite sure himself how five years had gone by without a visit back East. Of course, it wasn't literally true that he hadn't been back in five years. He had been back three years ago, at the death of his mother, but that was hardly a visit. Airport to chapel to cemetery to airport. Perhaps part of the answer was that Jean no longer had any great desire to come back East. She had taken root in Denver. They had spent one summer vacationing in Mexico. One summer, they had done the European thing. And the kids were at that in-between stage where taking them East would have been an expensive conflict of interest, and leaving them to fend for themselves would have been just too worrisome. Somehow five years had gone by.

"But doesn't it make you sad?" Gabe asked Jeff.

"The state of the city?" Jeff said. "No, not particularly."

"Why not? You're a native. Aren't you made sad to see the end of something you knew?"

Jeff regarded Gabe with those worn, creased, ironic, slightly protuberant eyes. He was losing hair, presenting a fair sketch of what age would do to him. The young eagle, Jeff Singer. The imperial look. Gabe felt a clutch of sadness, but not for the city, for Jeff, who was going to be *the* poet, *the* voice of postwar America. One volume of poetry—*Game with Mirrors*—and then sidling into the academy. . . . "Just for the present, you see. I've got to have some money." . . . Gabe had always wondered where else Jeff had imagined his future. Where else was there for a poet to go? Surely Jeff hadn't expected to make a *living* on his poetry? No, he was too practical for that. Then, what? Grants? How many could you get? Perhaps he had expected some patroness, some female incarnation of the nation itself, all devotion and sex, to appear and take him under a downy, all-providing wing. Instead he had married Laura, who was neither beautiful nor rich. And now here was Jeff, apparently stuck in his Associate status, lacking the publications and the luster that would move him up.

"I'm not sentimental about the city," Jeff said. "You always were, weren't you?"

"If that's the word," Gabe said. "Yes, I guess so. Yet here I am living two thousand miles away, and here you are still living in the midst of it."

"Don't tell me you're longing to return to this mess," Jeff said.

"Don't tell me you're longing to go elsewhere," Gabe returned.

Jeff shook his head. He said, "I'm neither longing to stay in this city nor to go to another. It isn't place I'm longing for. It's what you described before: a change of state."

Gabe waited, half a smile on his lips, as if he were almost on the wave length of Jeff's thoughts. In fact, he wasn't. He had no idea what Jeff meant. A different teaching job? No teaching job at all? To grow younger? Gabe looked at Jeff's hands, which were engaged with knife and fork. They were dry-looking and spotted with the marks of age. Gabe recalled that Jeff had about three or four years on him. That would make him close to fifty. Christ, *fifty!* That terrible tolling! And who will not be fifty? Only the unlucky.

"What do you mean?" Gabe asked.

"What do you mean, what do I mean?"

"About 'change of state'?"

"Your phrase."

"I know, but how are you using it?"

Jeff broke off a chunk of bread, impaled it on his fork, and sopped up some of that great gravy. "I'm using it metaphorically, as I use all my plagiarisms. . . . I keep forgetting that you've been away for five years. And I don't suppose I've written very much. I never do. . . ."

"No," Gabe confirmed, "you haven't written very much. You never did. Although one of the few times you did write, you expressly promised a visit. So far, no visit."

"I know," said Jeff. "I'm sorry. I don't know why I never did take that trip out West. I really would like to."

"Laura?" Gabe asked.

"What Laura?"

"Is Laura reluctant?"

"On the contrary."

"Well, then. . . ."

Jeff finished his meat and placed his knife and fork neatly parallel on the smeared plate. He pushed the plate slightly forward with the tips of his slightly withered fingers. "Things have happened, Gabe," he said.

"Laura?" Gabe asked again.

"Only collaterally Laura. Or maybe directly Laura. I don't know. In any event, Laura and I are splitting."

"Ah!" Gabe sighed sadly. "I'm sorry to hear that."

"Sometimes," Jeff said, "I think the true anguish of the mortal condition is not death but the pathetically few choices of the living. Well, old buddy, here are the sad, happy facts. . . ."

A graduate student. Her name was Cynthia. It was not as absurd a May-December folly as it might appear. Cynthia was herself divorced, in her early thirties, had come back to school to begin her life again as well as to complete her studies, which were broken off when she married. Nothing remarkable in it, nothing at all. She was pretty, had blue eyes, a lovely skin, and *enthusiasm*. Dear God, *enthusiasm!* She was enthusiastic about the food in this place, here, this very place. She was enthusiastic about sex. . . .

"I hope to God, Gabe, that you are enjoying a decent sex life with Jean. I don't see why you shouldn't be. Jean always struck me as a woman of sexual means. Don't take that the wrong way. I just want to point out how much of a dead letter sex had become in the lives of Jeff and Laura Singer. Not that we didn't fuck. We did. But each such encounter was a kind of morbid checkup to see if the whole business was really as disappointing as we remembered. It was. I had always thought that sex was separate from other aspects of the man-woman relationship. I'd heard that people who hate each other can go on having a ball in bed. Maybe they can. Laura and I did not. Tenderness, the desire to give pleasure, that was out, had been for years. Turn the whole thing around and you get—sometimes, at least, I would imagine—the kind of savagery that gets its kicks *precisely* because the object under you is so detested. Screwing as revenge. You can yell, 'I hate you,' just as orgiastically as, 'I love you.' But that wasn't the case with us. Neither love nor hate but the pathetic sag between. The turgidness of feeling. The inward turning away even as you enter. It takes a long time for that blood knowledge to work itself down to your cock, my friend, but when it does you are finished!"

Gabe waited to see if there was going to be any more. Jeff just shook his head and was silent.

"So. . . ." Gabe said softly.

"So."

"I'm sorry to hear it."

"It's something to be sorry about," Jeff said. "There's always the other life, no matter how much you divorce it."

"And Emily?" Gabe asked, thinking of Jeff's much-loved daughter.

"Emily is making her life in Washington State, curse the luck!" Jeff said. "She's twenty-four now, so who am I to say no? She's not married, but she's living with this guy. I've never met him. I don't know, she's got some *fashlugganah* job in the school system there. Testing kids. That bullshit. God, how I wish she'd come back! But—who am I to talk? Is my life any less screwed up than hers, with all my discipline and values and sense of responsibility? I tell you, Gabe, this may not be a brave new world, but it sure as hell is a *new* one! And I, for one, will not sit in a corner weaving the cobwebs of my heart and soul. . . . Incidentally, do you know who Cynthia reminds me of, a little?"

"Who?"

"Evelyn White."

"Evelyn White?"

"Don't tell me you've forgotten. Of course you haven't. . . . Same eyes. . . . Really the same manner, the zesty approach to life. If I remember correctly, Evelyn White was very much that way. . . . You know, I met Evelyn—when was it? . . . about two years ago—at some sort of convention—not the M.L.A.—something else—anyway, she was there. Divorced, she told me. You met her husband at one time, didn't you?"

"Yes."

"Well, Evelyn is apparently doing very well," Jeff went on. "She works for some publishing outfit that specializes in educational material. Grade school. High school. She's a *macher* there. Has some kind of executive job. I wouldn't say she looks *exactly* as she did twenty years ago, but she sure as hell doesn't look worn twenty years' worth. Lucky bitch! Attractive." Jeff glanced at his watch. "Let's order coffee," he said. "Do you want coffee? No dessert for me. I'm off desserts. Got to keep my figure. It's my mind that Cynthia loves, and my deathless talent; still it's a wise policy not to draw youthful attention to time's ugly jokes. . . . Listen, I hope you won't mind, Gabe, but I'm going to cut out a little early tonight. You say you're going to be in the city for about a week anyway, so I'm sure there'll be a chance for us to get together again. I promised Cynthia I'd meet her right after dinner, and I don't want it to get too late. . . . Christ, I've been doing all the talking. Tell me something about yourself. Tell me about Denver."

"What would you like to know?"

"What on earth is it like living in Denver?"

"It's like living on earth," Gabe said.

Jeff hailed a taxi as soon as they stepped out of the restaurant. He gave an address somewhere in the West Seventies. Gabe calculated it to be somewhere near Lincoln Center, and he felt a silly pride in having the map of the city so accurately fixed in his mind.

Jeff asked Gabe if he could give him a lift somewhere, but Gabe said he'd prefer to stroll around for a while.

"You will be in touch with me again before you go?" Jeff asked.

"Yes," Gabe promised, although he wasn't absolutely sure he would.

It was only eight o'clock. The uncertain rain that had been on and off all day had finally decided to quit. Gabe walked through streets whose features and names had lost precision, but still he retained a general knowledge of where he was, where he would have to turn to come out on Sixth Avenue, or Eighth Street, or Washington Square Park. He was feeling stomach full and a little sleepy. But why should he feel sleepy? It was actually two hours earlier in Denver. Six o'clock. They'd just be sitting down to dinner. . . .

They were mostly young people he was seeing. Frizzy-haired girls in denim jackets and denim pants. Bearded young men in denim jackets and denim pants. Not much different from the kids he saw around Larimer Square or in Boulder. Gabe yawned. He felt hurt. Would *he* have gobbled a quick meal with an old friend after a five-year interval, rushing away like impetuous youth to meet his love? No! Goddammit, no, he wouldn't! As if Jeff couldn't meet his blue-eyed, sex-enthusiastic Cynthia every day and night of the week. After all, Jeff was a teacher. Teachers had plenty of free time. The split between Jeff and Laura was being openly announced, so there was no need for the sexual logistics of a clandestine affair. . . . And, after all, it was none of these things. He could forgive Jeff his other foolishness, but he was finding it difficult to forgive the careless way he had tossed out Evelyn's name. Gabe wondered if Jeff Singer was on his way to becoming one of those egomaniacal poets who, having learned the language of sensitivity, feel they've earned the right to a life of callousness.

He walked around in the Village until the sum of his impressions drove him away. He could see where the young would still find this geography the land of dreams, but he could also see to what degree the dreams no longer matched his own. Wilder? Dirtier? More depraved? Or the change of state whose leading edge was even now altering the climate? Gabe suspected the latter.

Berlin in the years between the wars must have tried for this style. . . . *The apotheosis of moral garbage.* . . . Gabe smiled to himself as he recalled Professor Murray's phrase in that course in criminal procedure. Murray the Messiah! The appropriateness of some of those nicknames! But also how well that phrase applied here—and elsewhere. . . . *The apotheosis of moral garbage.* . . . It suddenly struck Gabe that pre-Hitler Berlin and this raunchiness could not have come about had there not been a morality to mock. Those two muscle-bound fags who had passed him a moment before had to have something to defy in order to achieve such a wide-eyed, imperious gaze.

Thoughts of morality brought Gabe around to Jeff again. Was he finding something morally objectionable in Jeff's behavior? Maybe. A little. Not the sex and the hunger for another helping of high emotion, but something else, something Gabe couldn't quite define. He had sensed in Jeff a kind of capitulation, as though he had seized his new life as much in despair as in love, and in this there was something morally questionable.

It was not even nine o'clock when Gabe got back to his hotel room. He wouldn't be able to sleep for hours. He hadn't even thought to buy a newspaper. He hadn't taken a book with him this time, thinking the city itself would provide him with all the distraction he could handle. Television was more than a bore; it was a depressant. And he felt cheated of the human company he had so looked forward to enjoying on this first evening of his return.

Impulsively, Gabe put on his raincoat again, went downstairs, left the door key with the desk clerk, walked the few blocks to the Algonquin, and entered.

This, at least, hadn't changed. Everything familiarly brown and muffled. Gabe turned into the lounge and looked around for a place to sit. He saw a couple who looked like a hundred other couples he had seen sit in hotel lounges. Older man, gray-haired, red-faced, wearing a fawn-colored vest beneath a classy brown sport jacket. Younger woman sunk in sofa, listening to words of wisdom, of opportunity, of utmost sincerity. Gabe turned to another corner of the room and looked directly at a woman who was looking, apparently, directly at him.

He knew the woman before his mind was willing to establish

the identity. Instantaneous with his recognition of the woman was his recognition of the heavy shoulder of coincidence butting him loutishly in the back. Coincidence is always a little funny and a little victimizing. Instead of going forward with his best self, Gabe felt like enforcing a stop-action on the scene so that he could reconstruct the exact order of things said earlier in the evening that made this meeting so ridiculously foretold. The only thing he had time to recollect, though, was the little pulse of satisfaction he had felt when he learned from Jeff that Evelyn White was divorced.

But he had had too many years of professional practice to allow himself to be paralyzed. He moved forward, smiling, knowing he would say some proper conventional thing while waiting for the whole complex of past and present emotions to catch up with him.

4

Evelyn listened—and listened. She wondered if Frank was going back to the bottle. Everything seemed to have been turned up to a slightly higher pitch, but that may have been due to the literary crisis developing. There was always a crisis, of course, but time would undoubtedly make a difference in the intensity of each one.

Frank's cross was the familiar one of wanting to be better than he was. He was *convinced* he was better than he was, needing only the theme that would reorganize his talent into a constellation of high art. There were examples he could point to . . . well, he couldn't think of who at the moment, but he remembered reading about this one or that one who had shuffled along doing ordinary things, then suddenly broke through on a sixth or seventh book. . . .

This time he was onto a natural. He could feel it in his bones. The story involved two college friends, both engaged in the campus furor of the sixties, both go on to study law, pass the bar, go into politics, one remaining true to the radicalism of reform, the other buying the philosophy of expedience. Of course, he wasn't going to make it a black-white thing, a goodie and a baddie, but, rather, a natural progression toward ideals based on temperament. . . . "Do you see what I mean?"

"Clearly," said Evelyn. "I think it's a beautiful idea, Frank. Exciting."

Frank nodded. She could see that he was breathing pure oxygen. He was creatively high. His eyes were shining. He could be so nice when he was happily immersed in his work. He brought his hoping heart to her like a giant rose, petals flaring. Then she loved him. That somewhat elfish Irish face (detested by its owner) becoming luminous with ideas, becoming pugnacious lest someone think him too elfish, the unflagging intelligence, all that was good and unusual about Frank touched her in a special way. No doubt part of it was the Jewishness in her finding all that she had always valued wearing such a face. There was a secret eroticism in it. It was as if all the world of charming strangers wanted to take her to bed when Frank signaled lust.

"Have you . . . ?" she began.

"Have I what?" Frank pounced.

Evelyn shook her head. "Nothing, I just. . . ."

"Just *what,* my dear Evelyn?" he insisted, his voice gentling, his expression that of a man who dared her to continue, and dared her not to.

Well, fuck him! I will not live afraid!

"Have you worked out the characters?" she asked.

Frank grinned and rubbed the lower part of his face with the palm of his hand. "Have I worked out the characters?" he repeated, his voice taking on the hint of a brogue, which brogue was the little verbal jig he performed before going into his big routine. "Have I worked out my *characters?* God love you for asking me that. How do you think I could begin to write about two men whose friendship and subsequent antagonism is, as I've told you, the blood and bowels of my book if I hadn't worked out the characters?" He shook his head in feigned wonderment. "Why, do you fear that I *haven't* worked out my characters?"

"I don't fear anything, Frank. I'm only remembering what you yourself said."

"What was that?"

"That unless you had an absolute grip on character, you were in deep trouble by the fourth chapter."

"Did I say that? Wise of me. It should be struck off in brass and mounted above every writer's desk. But tell me, if I said it, and if you remember it, what makes you think I would lose sight of it?"

"Well, then, you haven't lost sight of it, and I'm glad, and let's drop it."

Frank sighed. Frank slumped in his chair and tilted his head and used one long finger to push bread crumbs into a pattern. "Perhaps I'm wrong," he said, after a lengthy delay, "but I have a feeling that you're warning me instead of asking me."

"You are wrong."

"I have this sneaking feeling that you're warning me that I have in the past thought I had worked out my characters, only to find that time, critics, Evelyn White, and the sales of my books had all contributed to the conclusion that I *hadn't* worked out my characters, that my characters are always missing a dimension, that when you scrape away the thin veneer of a few freckles and a grimace or two, you have the face of Frank Moore shining through—"

"Stop it, Frank!"

"Stop what?"

"This nastiness."

"Nastiness is it? To whom?"

"To both of us. Stop it."

"But you haven't read word one of this new thing. How can you be so bloody sure I haven't worked out my characters?"

"Now you're being deliberately perverse, Frank. I said nothing of the sort. I said—"

"I know what you said. You just *asked* me, right? Well, people *ask* things when they have reason to fear habitual lapses. . . . 'Did you go to the john, Johnny?' . . . When Johnny has a habit of wetting his pants, a good mother thinks to ask."

"I'm not your mother."

"Indeed not. Mothers have such divinely dumb confidence."

And then, of course, there were the other times, those that followed on his sweetness as swiftly and venomously as a snake's bite. Then she hated him—no, not hated, she never hated Frank—felt *sorry* for him, because she knew that this anger was directed mainly against himself. His fear of not being good enough. His fear that each work in progress had inadvertently, without his being aware of it, stepped once again into the trap of mediocrity. It was a dangerous thing for her to feel sorry for a man with whom she was sharing her life, even a small part of it, even a tentative sharing. She knew it would be the end, once pity became the predominating feature of their relationship. She could give pity in oceanic quantities, but to marry it would mean to drown in it. That was why she turned against Frank's conscious or unconscious appeal for pity with such ruthlessness. No doubt she over-did it, came on tougher than she felt, but she could deal with the danger in no other way.

"Frank," she said, "we've talked enough about your book. I remember you saying that letting too much of it out robbed the thing of its essence. For God's sake, your books are published, aren't they? Why should you care what I say, what anyone says? Write the damn thing as best you can, and it will be better than 90 per cent of the garbage being published."

Frank gave her a big wink and a congratulatory smile. "Now, that," he said, "is what I call zipping a man's balls back into place."

"They shouldn't be detachable," Evelyn said.

"I love you, Jew girl."

"You have a funny way of showing it."

"I must go," he said.

"That was the understanding."

"I'm not wholly convinced you like my new book."

"I'm wholly convinced I haven't read it," she said. "I'm wholly convinced you haven't written it yet."

"I want your blind approval," he demanded.

"You can't have it," she said.

"God, how I know it! All right, I've got to get over to the Algonquin."

"The Algonquin? Why?"

"Because an aunt of mine—ahnt!—from Boston—she's in for a few days. Always stays at the Algonquin. Says it reminds her of old Boston. She telephoned me to say she was coming into town, and I asked her to bring a family album of photographs she has. She had her own dinner engagement this evening, so I told her to leave it at the desk and I'd pick it up."

"How fascinating!" Evelyn said. "What do you want it for?"

"My business."

"Tell me! Please!"

"Well . . . actually, one of the characters in the new novel is modeled after my father. I really don't have a good picture of him at the age I'm writing about. I think there's one in that album."

"But what do you need it for?" Evelyn asked. "I mean, why do you have to know what he *looked* like at that age?"

"Because the human face is the message to which we respond, is it not?"

"Oh, it is. . . . Did you like your father?"

"I don't know. Yes and no. Loved him when I was a kid. Adored him. He did all the right things. Took me to ball games, the circus, chucked the football with me in Van Cortlandt Park on gorgeous autumn days. Then I grew up and he grew down. He was personnel manager of some large, reactionary outfit. He didn't exactly agree with their views, but, you know, Jews *were* pushy, Negroes *were* dumb, Spics *were* dishonest, et cetera. The thing that bothers me was that he *was* an intelligent man, *and* a compassionate one, but he let his imagination be suffocated by those bastards."

"But he had to make a living," Evelyn said. "You can't completely blame him."

"I can and I do!"

"Oh, well—are there pictures of you in that album?"

"I suppose."

"May I see?"

"You'd have to come along with me."

"All right."

"But I can't stay long."

"So you won't stay long."

They took a taxi to the Algonquin, and Frank picked up the large manila envelope that had been left at the desk. Then they went into the lounge and found what looked like the brightest corner. The photographs of Frank's father were the usual obscurities made by squints in the sun and an unsteady camera hand. One shot was the studio kind—touched up, stiffly posed—but Evelyn thought she could see a resemblance. "The smile," she said. "I think I can see him in your smile. Or maybe the other way around." Frank grunted. "And that's my mother," he said. "Plain as any name can be." Another posed photograph, but not quite so lifeless. She wore her hair high. Evelyn was reminded of an aunt of her own who had that swept-up look, a faint aureole of filaments behind the ears. Mary Moore was a lovely woman, the kind of beauty Evelyn would have preferred seeing in the mirror instead of her own *gamine* image.

"And you?" Evelyn asked.

Frank found some pictures of himself. He seemed to know exactly where to look. That touched a sympathetic nerve. She, too, had looked at Evelyn photographs, wondering at the lost, smiling creature who was once herself. It could have been a total stranger for all she knew of the moment of life caught on that bit of paper. *Her* life. And there was Frank with a baseball cap and a bat on his shoulder. And there was Frank with a cast crisscrossed on a broken nose. And here was a little boy trussed in a puffy winter outfit, looking apple-cheeked and happy.

"Please don't hate me, but you were adorable," Evelyn said. "Were you really the angel I see here?"

Frank flopped the album closed and slipped it back in the envelope. "Great hopes were reposed in me," he said.

"And why not?" said Evelyn.

"Great hopes should never be reposed in a child," he said. "The poor little bastard is just liable to take it seriously. . . . I gotta run."

"Run."

"What are you going to do now?" Frank asked, getting up.

"Stay here a little and have a glass of sherry."

"That's a good idea. Just don't get picked up by some literary type with a soft secret in his eyes and a hard secret in his pants."

"Like you?"

"Yeah."

"Good night, Frank," Evelyn urged. "You have work to do."

Frank nodded, picked up her hand and kissed it, then departed.

Evelyn ordered her sherry. One of the nice things she remembered about this hotel was that no one looked askance at a woman sitting alone and having a drink. It was assumed that everybody was waiting for somebody, which was usually the case. But she was waiting for no one. She would have her glass of sherry and leave. It was—she looked at her watch—twenty minutes of nine. She felt neither sorrow nor satisfaction at being alone on a Saturday night. She recalled the long string of perfectly matched Saturday-night parties, at her home, at other homes. Lord, those Saturday-night parties! The arty talk, the motherly talk, the football talk, the political talk, and as midnight came and passed, the bar-ing of wounds, the uncontainable leakages of unhappiness. The unfaithful husbands and stymied careers. The unbelievable dailiness of bringing up children. The sexual boredom and the conversational boredom. The terrible fear of aging and the terrible fear of missing out. . . .

Thank God, no more of that! There was nothing good to be said for it. At one time, Lew had claimed that he liked them no more than she but that there was no substitute for these social clusterings. She had believed him, *made* herself believe him, went on cultivating dozens of people she didn't care for, thinking it her duty to maintain affinities with her husband at any cost. Well, that wasn't a workable arrangement. That hadn't saved the marriage. What on earth *was* the ideal arrangement? Or was there none? Had the ideal arrangement been lost when men stopped hunting in packs and women stopped waiting for their handout of meat?

Evelyn smiled to herself, imagining her own reaction if she had heard some man make that suggestion. Or what she would have to face if some flaming fem-libber had tuned in to her thoughts. She would have to reverse her field entirely to counter either challenge —and there wouldn't be any necessary inconsistency in her doing so. Blessed be the privacy of thoughts! She didn't have to explain it to, or for, either. She knew what she meant. She knew in what dense, uncompassed part of the forest her thoughts were wandering.

She was as resentful as any woman living of the subjugations and roles thrust on women since the beginning of time, but she was temperamentally disinclined to damn and undo the whole of human history. There had been a time when men had hunted and women had huddled, and there wasn't a damn thing anyone could do about that. A lousy time it must have been, but the race survived in that hunting and huddling. What she had in mind was the time that followed, the many, many times and the many, many ways in which the man-woman portrait had been posed without any real feeling that *this* was the nearest thing. It seemed to her that even now, when the air was ringing with victories, the portrait was as much askew as ever. She knew that her relationship with Frank Moore was as much made up of getting things straight as it was of love. She metered his ego trips and little forays into sadism as carefully as a nurse administers drugs. So much and no more.

She was sure that Frank understood that any insistence on larger helpings of the painkiller would end the regimen entirely—no drugs, no nurse, nothing! And she would! She would leave it, *him,* in a minute, if he began to demand addictive doses or if she felt herself weakening to the point of giving them . . . and wasn't . . . that man . . . wasn't that Gabe Michelson? . . . It couldn't be. Gabe no longer lived in New York, hadn't for years and years. Jeff Singer had told her that Gabe and his family had moved to Denver. . . . It couldn't be Gabe, because that big, plaid-coated Casanova from Cleveland had *reminded* her of Gabe, and coincidence doesn't work in such jackpot fashion. . . . But of *course* it was Gabe Michelson! Nature doesn't hand out such duplicates either. . . . He looks the same. He's put on weight. . . . He's definitely looking at me. He's smiling. He's smiling because he knows it's me, and he's asking do I know it's him. . . . How extraordinary that he should look exactly like himself! . . . He always looked a little like an Indian chief. . . . Dear God, what shall I do? Whom shall I be? I hurt you, Gabe, didn't I? . . . Here he comes. . . . Be yourself, Evelyn. . . . Yes, but, oh, who *is* myself? . . .

"Hello, Evelyn."

"I thought it was you, Gabe. How nice to see you! You're looking wonderful."

"So are you," said Gabe, smiling down at her. "You know, this is really an extraordinary coincidence—"

"That makes two," she said.

"Are you waiting for someone?" he asked.

"No."

"That makes three," Gabe laughed. "May I sit down?"

"Please!"

"What are you having?"

"This? Sherry. . . ."

"That seems like a good thing to have. May I join you?"

"Yes. Please. I didn't think men liked sherry."

"I love good sherry."

"Just hit that bell and the waiter will come," Evelyn told him.

"Oh, God, yes," Gabe said, hitting the bell. "I remember that."

Gabe had taken an armchair adjacent to the sofa where Evelyn had seated herself. She had chosen the sofa, thinking it would assure her "waiting" status, and now she was glad she had done so. She felt less exposed sunk back this way in a large piece of furniture. She felt more observing than observed. If she could somehow manage it without seeming like an idiot, she would go on talking about sherry and the crazy Algonquin bells while taking in all the details of this big, friendly ghost. Like his suit. He was wearing a blue suit. Small herring-bone pattern. She hadn't seen a suit on Frank once in the two years she'd known him. Frank didn't wear suits. He wore "combinations." Gabriel Michelson wore suits. Had he always worn suits? She couldn't remember. He must have. A lawyer wore suits. Did he always sit so, elbows on the arms of the chair, a nice smile on his broad, Indian face? What nonsense! He didn't look like an Indian. Dark eyes, dark complexion, black hair . . . but was his smile always so warm and natural? No doubt. Why should something like that change? . . . As she sat and waited and watched Gabriel Michelson, the image before her began to merge with memory, and the younger, slimmer man she had known took shape out of this incredibly present presence. . . .

"What's your coincidence?" he asked.

"I was at a convention today, and there was a man there by the name of Sandy Bethune who reminded me of you. What's yours?"

"Guess who I had dinner with tonight," he said.

"That's not hard. Jeff Singer."

"Yes. He told me about meeting you some three years ago—at some other convention. Shall we give that half credit? I don't think I could take another full coincidence."

"I remember meeting him," Evelyn said. "It was then that he told me you had moved to Denver. How many years have you lived there?"

"We're rounding out ten."

"Children?" she asked.

"Two. Girl and boy. Pamela and Andrew. And you?"

"A son. Jay. Jason. I just spoke to him this evening. He started this fall at Washington University, in St. Louis."

It was easy now to go on in this fashion, trading a flurry of facts, like two boxers holding each other off with feints and jabs. Evelyn would have settled for no more than this, an evening of talk with Gabe Michelson. The first, nervous palpitations over, it was becoming a treat. Gabe had always been so pleasant to be with. She should have known better than to fear his approach, but, still, one never knows what changes might have come about. But here he was—here *they* were, each with an unknown life and a warrant out of the past to ask and ask.

"Why are you here?" Gabe asked.

"I accompanied a friend who had something to pick up at the desk," Evelyn explained. "Then he left, and I decided to relax with a glass of sherry."

"Did you ever read *The Bridge of San Luis Rey?*" Gabe asked.

"No. Why?"

"It has something to do with tracking down some fateful design in the death of a group of people through the collapse of a bridge. Why were just those people crossing at just that time?"

"Do you feel we were destined to meet here this evening?" Evelyn asked.

Gabe laughed. "No, I don't believe anything is destined, but sometimes the chances are fascinating to behold. Like, why *here?* That's a bit much, isn't it?"

Evelyn tried to think of the specialness of "here." They'd never made love here. All *that* happened in those rooms with a very narrow view of the Hudson. Not here. They'd *been* here, of course. That time with Jeff Singer, and that woman he married. But that was only for drinks. To celebrate something. What?

"There was something we celebrated here," she said. "What was it?"

"Jeff took us here," Gabe told her. "He'd found out that day his poems had been accepted for publication."

"Of course! Around Christmas time, wasn't it?"

"Nearer to Thanksgiving, as I remember."

"Was it?"

She wondered why that occasion would have significance in Gabe's bridge of destiny. She could scarcely remember it. Afternoon, was it? Or evening? She wanted to know, but she was a little afraid to ask. She was afraid she might have forgotten something. But if anything important had happened between Gabe and herself that afternoon or evening, she *would* remember it, wouldn't she? She did remember important things. But she mustn't ask now.

So they went on talking about jobs and children and the differences between New York and Denver. More sherry and more talk. Twice she caught Gabe glancing at his watch. He had business elsewhere, a different life he must pursue. She felt a faint pinch of resentment, of jealousy.

"But you must be wanting to go," she said. "I'm keeping you."

"Not at all. I was just wondering how much time we have left."

"I was assuming you must be in New York on business."

"I have business here, but I'm not *busy*," Gabe said. "Look, I'm going to be in the city for the better part of a week. Tomorrow is Sunday. I have nothing to do. Are you busy? Do you think we could have lunch, dinner, go to a museum? I think I need a guide after all these years."

"I'm free in the afternoon," she said, immediately wondering why she had implied limits on her day. Frank would be hammering away at his typewriter all day. She had nothing to do tomorrow, but nothing, and spending as many hours as he would wish with Gabe Michelson would be the most hauntingly nice thing she could imagine.

"That's good," Gabe said. "I'm glad. Shall I pick you up where you live? Meet somewhere?"

They decided to meet at the Plaza—and Evelyn regarded with amazement the ridiculous spectacle of her excitement.

5

Gabe awoke early. He always awoke early, but now he missed his guess of the time by hours. At home, each morning, he would guess at the time upon awakening and then check it out on his wrist watch. His guess was usually within five minutes of the actual time. But the windows in this room faced a side street in Manhattan, where the sun would have to work itself over the warehouses and cemeteries of Long Island City, vault the range of the East Side of Manhattan, get up good and high before it even approached the refulgence that flooded through the east windows in Denver. This was a six o'clock autumn light he was seeing, but his watch reported a scandalous eight. They would have to get those light-proof drapes installed. It was really light that woke him up in the morning. Jean said it was his internal clock, and that might be partly true, but his internal clock took its setting from the splendor that rose out of the plains each morning.

He lay in bed, now thinking that it was *only* eight o'clock . . . nine, ten, eleven, twelve . . . at least three and a half enormous hours before he could even start out for the Plaza. What the hell could he do with that Sahara of hours! Well, he could walk over to Times Square and pick up a Sunday *Times*. He could find a place to have a leisurely breakfast. He could read the Sunday *Times* while having a leisurely breakfast. There, if you please, was the myth made flesh! The means and the time to claim this run-down Alhambra at last! Or was there something else behind this late-found sovereignty? Gabe grunted, shook his head. Damn right there was! Something other than time and place had been restored.

Anticipation! An hour in the day when another human being would join him and make real once again the undiscovered possibilities of Gabriel Michelson!

And could he still feel that way about Evelyn White? Apparently. Her smile and her eyes could still touch off in him that stupidly causeless current of anticipation. His reaction to last night's encounter was still out of focus, but blurred as it was he could make out several familiar sensations. Astonishment? Certainly that, but not exclusively that. Nervousness and confusion that could hide themselves in the presence of the woman who had given him such an emotional reaming. Also there had been a little spiteful satisfaction for him that he found her sitting alone in a hotel on a Saturday night, while he was only a visitor from a high, bright place, a successful professional man briefly back to the ruined city to conduct his profitable business and then depart. Of course that last was as juvenile as a balloon, but nevertheless his imagination had sucked in a breath and blown it full for the quick fantasy of it. And always that dumb shiver of sexual possibility—always that!—the family heirloom every adolescent bequeaths his future self. Also a dilation of pure pleasure, and a contraction of remembered pain. Everything, in short, a man could possibly feel when he had made a noontime date with his own past.

Gabe got out of bed and went into the bathroom. He took off his pajama top. He examined his face, his torso. . . . Well, the face, what could he make of that face? Nothing. It was, he had been assured, a nice face. Handsome? He doubted it. Even in his best, narcissistic moment, he doubted it. A friendly face, a swarthy(?) face, more round than long, hints of ancestral wander-ing around the Mediterranean littoral, maybe Lapland . . . who knows? But a good body! Let no man, or woman, deny that he had kept in shape. Look at that muscle! He made a muscle. He held the safety razor aloft in his right hand and felt his muscle with his soapy left. A muscle, by God! A creditable muscle! He then placed the razor on the wash-basin rim and grabbed two handfuls of excess around his waist. And how, pray God, do you get rid of that? He was, in a sense, on a perpetual diet. That is, there wasn't a meal he ate, not a *nosh* he *noshed*, but he was lighting penitential candles made of the fat he was sorrowfully, deliciously making. Not *fat*, for God's sake! Would you call one

ninety-two fat? Consider his six-foot-one. Consider his bone
structure, these muscles. Just this money belt of years around his
middle. But his hair remained black and plentiful, and his eyes retained their clear, brown luster . . . and he didn't have the dignity
or good sense of an ape, standing in front of a mirror this way,
taking inventory of himself, as if these things mattered, as if, dear
God, he were preparing a line of merchandise for a sales display!

Later, Gabe walked over to the Times Square section to pick up
a Sunday *Times*. The side streets were filthy, and the Broadway
area not much better. All of it changed except for the famous
shape of the street itself. The movie marquees were all different.
So were the stores and the restaurants and the buildings. New sky-
scrapers that were well accommodated to the tawdriness. Broadway had never been one of Gabe's favorite places, but he had
never minded it. Now he did. He couldn't say for sure what it was.
There had been obvious attempts at improvement, and these attempts had only made the contrast between form and spirit
greater. It was the spirit that prevailed. There weren't even those
old newsreel theaters he remembered, small indication that even
this place was part of the world. Now the spirit of the pornographer predominated. There was a rankness here like the rankness
in a zoo house, but it was a rankness of spirit rather than smell.
Everything belonged to the pornographer. . . . *The apotheosis of
moral garbage*. . . . Gabe felt another twitch of resentment
against Jeff Singer, remembering in that instant a remark Jeff had
made aeons ago, somewhere on the other side of the time gulf that
separated this moment from the Michelsons' move to Denver.
Late sixties, probably, that long historical fuse that fizzled out,
and Jeff had made some remark approving all the new freedoms.
"Like a tank of high-octane gas," he had said. "Burn the crud out
of the national engine. Everybody should do his thing." Gabe
remembered pointing out to Jeff that Hitler had done his thing, as
had Dr. Mengele, and Ilse Koch, and all the sweethearts who had
made the world a charnel house. "Different," was Jeff's response.

Was it? Yes, of course it was. There the government itself had
gone insane. Here not. But Gabe's resentment was more diffuse.
As he continued his morning walk north on Seventh Avenue, carrying his bulky *Times,* vaguely considering a place for breakfast,

he was remembering that time, and the time leading up to that time. The Eisenhower years. Law school. Passing the bar. Working for that Wall Street firm. Being in love with Evelyn White and feeling that each day was a crazy ascent up some mountain slope, air thin, inadequate equipment, destruction below, and the top impossibly out of reach. . . . And where the hell would he have breakfast? Every place was closed. He had reached Fifty-seventh Street. . . . There! That ham-and-eggery. Just the place for lost out-of-town wanderers like Gabriel Michelson.

He went in and sat down, ordering more food than he wanted, to justify occupying a table instead of sitting at the counter. He placed the newspaper on the chair beside him, slipping out the magazine section, since that was a little more manageable. He thumbed the pages, but he couldn't give his mind to the words. His thoughts had closed in around that particular time. Not *thoughts,* really—more like a groping toward a lost flavor. It came to him strongest in the swelter of August heat . . . and remembering that, he remembered that it had begun in June, at a cousin's wedding, out at the shore, in a hotel fronting the beach.

Evelyn was a friend of the bride. The mingled sweetness of gardenias and perfume. They had danced. He was not a good dancer. The scene reconstructed itself with astonishing vividness. They had danced past the bandstand, where the five-piece band honked away at "Some Enchanted Evening," and Gabe recalled that the young drummer's black bow tie had slipped its clasp, dangling downward, bouncing to the beat. He had asked his cousin's girlfriend, who had been seated at the same table (on purpose?) if she would like to dance, and she had smiled assentingly, and he had put his arm around her, taken her hand in his, and begun his lumpish one-two-three maneuvers around the floor. He danced, at best, carefully, counting it a success if he inflicted no damage.

He had asked the girl to dance out of politeness. There had been no eagerness in it. Actually, had he been immediately attracted to Evelyn White, he wouldn't have asked her to dance. He would probably have engaged her in conversation, perhaps have taken her for a stroll on the hotel's porch, which offered a view of the ocean and some comfortable rocking chairs. But he wasn't all that taken. She had a wide mouth, a small nose, and little bruise marks of fatigue beneath her eyes. (Later she confessed that she had begun her period the night before, practically hemorrhaging, as she usually did in her first efflux of menstruation, and, naturally, the next day, the day of the wedding, she looked like death warmed over.) But as they passed the bandstand, she remarked on the drummer's tie, saying that it suited the music perfectly. He had laughed at that, because it was so true, and she had tipped back her head to look at him, and although nothing had changed, everything was transformed. How to account for that miracle? Very easily. At that moment, he was to learn later, *she* had become interested in *him*. His laugh. It was such a nice, open laugh, she claimed, a *generous* laugh, giving her full credit for the humor in her observation. She had looked at him with interest, and that made her do a little something with her eyes and that smile of hers, and that made for all sorts of sudden lights. Did she know she could do those things? Of course she knew. Every woman knew to what extent she could do that.

How quickly had he fallen in love? Looking back, it seemed he had fallen in love with Evelyn that same June day. The hour in which she had appeared an uninteresting stranger had separated itself from true time like some joke or oddity, but time had resumed as soon as they had become aware of each other. The wedding party had begun to break up by four in the afternoon, and he had offered Evelyn a ride to wherever she was going. That would be nice, but she had come in her own car—rather, her brother's car, which she had borrowed for the day. Well, where was home for her? The city. Manhattan. Riverside Drive. She was finishing her undergraduate work at Barnard. English major. She was unmarried. She was not in love with one of her professors. Yes, she would see him again if he liked. . . .

He had tried to explain it once to Evelyn, when she asked how he could have fallen in love so quickly. Love at first sight? Surely that was a courtly fable. Surely it was, he agreed, and always had been. One needed some time. But just think how much time elapses between a Saturday-afternoon wedding and the next Saturday's dinner date. First sight? The other person is taken away and lived with in the hermetically sealed, deeply oxygenated, sun-heated greenhouse of the imagination. Time takes on an entirely different value there. If the other person is suited to the soil, the growth is like time-lapse photography, with whole seasons unfolding under racing clouds. In fact, the other person is more lived with apart than in sight.

Evelyn agreed. It was true. She hadn't thought of it that way. And had she thought of him? Of course she had. Would she have agreed to see him again if it were possible not to give him a thought? Yes—but how hot was her greenhouse? She couldn't recall. As a matter of historical fact, she had been given an extension to finish an end-term paper in a course on "The Bloomsbury Group," and she had spent most of that week like a mole digging into a dozen different texts. Perhaps if she had had the time she would have arrived at their next date as full of imaginary leaves as a summer tree. So it was really a question of *opportunity.* . . .

Gabe had always doubted that. In this life, things shove each other aside, and the future looks back on sudden passions and undone papers in the light of inevitability. But all that came later. If she hadn't fallen in love between the first and second meeting, or the second and third, something surely must have happened between a June wedding and the languors of August. My God, weren't they seeing each other every week? . . . several times a week!

They were. They went swimming at Jones Beach. They went to air-conditioned movies and air-conditioned plays. They had fish dinners on Fulton Street and Armenian delights on Twenty-eighth Street . . . and one evening (the mysteries of decision) Evelyn had asked why he lived in that room on upper Broadway, and he told her he had taken the room while going to Columbia and had simply stayed on. Why not? The rent was reasonable, and there was a small view of the Hudson. . . . "Come on, I'll show you."

In the fifties, the assumptions were not the same. It may have been just the beginning of what was to come, but sex was not yet taken for granted. All right, *he* didn't take it for granted. He didn't want to risk the awkwardness of her having to say no, and that's why he had made no move on his own. He didn't want to risk the awkwardness, and he was more than a little afraid of the implications of "No."

They went to his room, craned to see the Hudson with its emerald and ruby lights, and then Evelyn walked over to the table lamp and switched off the light. "Do we need this?" she asked, and later, when she heard him fumbling for something: "You don't need that."

He wasn't sure how she knew that he wouldn't need that, but she knew a great deal. She knew to have patience with him that first time. She knew how to rescue them both from embarrassment. "Talk to me," she commanded cheerfully. "About what?" he asked. "Your ambitions," she said. And he had talked to her, and somewhere in that talk, a moment she had calculated with divine intuition, she touched him, and then laughed at her success.

They talked about that second time for as long as they could talk about such things. They discovered their partnership in pleasure, and they hugged each other in triumphant glee.

"I didn't think you were supposed to laugh," he said.

"Why not?"

"Because it's not supposed to be funny. It's supposed to be better than fun."

"Nothing," Evelyn said, "is better than fun."

Gabe looked at his watch. It was only a little after ten. This was ridiculous. He had planned it all wrong. He was to meet Evelyn at noon, for lunch, and here he was filling up on ham and eggs. How on earth would he be able to eat at twelve? Run around Manhattan for the next two hours? It was probably beautiful in Denver. He could be playing a couple of sets of tennis under a cloudless sky. He had been observing that young couple sitting at the counter, noticing how pale and conspiratorial they looked, probably having spent the night in some cheap hotel, plotting how to outwit their parents. Would his Pam? Yes, his Pam would, given the right guy. As who would not? All did. And there was that old gent sitting at the curve of the counter, eyes all gummy . . . thick amber. . . . A shiver started at Gabe's neck and splayed out across his shoulders and down his back, a real old-fashioned *frisson* of fatigue and mortality. Was it the prospect of meeting Evelyn? Of course. Partly. It was also this perfect setting of big-city isolation. A raw, autumn morning, sitting in a Fifty-seventh Street coffee shop, something illicit coursing in his blood like a flu bug, the beginnings of a febrile condition that would change the order of reality. We all want that, don't we? A little change in the order of reality. But what change?—what reality? Would Jean really mind if she knew? How many years was it? Twenty, about. No, Jean wouldn't mind, as long as he didn't mind. That is, if there was nothing to mind, she wouldn't mind. But was there nothing to mind? As far as he could tell, no, there was nothing. He had nothing in mind to mind . . . and yet he felt that the best and safest thing he could do would be to go back to his hotel and spend the day checking over the things he must take up at the next day's conference.

He would not go back to the hotel. He knew that. The thought of Evelyn standing at the Plaza waiting for him—thirty minutes, forty, how long would she wait?—filled him with sacrilegious horror. He was not made that way. When he made a date, he kept it. But would he have kept it if it was with someone who hadn't put him through the wringer, who still, after twenty years, touched off in him the soft, sinister possibilities of love? Damn her face anyhow! He had met dozens of women who were prettier than Evelyn White, who had sent out unmistakable signals, but who had implanted no virus in his blood. Why Evelyn White? Because . . . because . . . because the goddam mechanism was set way back when one didn't have the wit or experience to regulate it sensibly, and what turned it on turned it on—period!

Gabe stayed in the coffee shop as long as he decently could. Then he paid and left. He hailed a cab and drove back to the hotel. In his moldy room, he removed topcoat and jacket, lay down on the bed, and read the *Times* until eleven-thirty. Then he washed, put on his clothes once again, and went out into the streets for a second time.

He chose Fifth Avenue this time, walking north toward the Plaza, feeling much calmer, more mature, more secure behind the formidable facts of his life.

6

The phone rang at ten, and Evelyn, who was in the tub but had had the foresight to bring the long-wired phone into the bathroom with her, picked it up, fully expecting to hear Gabe Michelson's voice expressing regret. The anticipated disappointment was a measure of the eagerness. But it wasn't Gabe. It was Lew.

"I hope I didn't get you up," he said.

"No, I was up."

"I realize it's early, but I have to catch a plane at noon. I'm going out to the Coast, and I'm going to stop off to see Jay."

"He told me," Evelyn said.

"Yes—well—do you have any idea what I can get for him?"

"If you haven't got whatever it is you're going to take, how are you going to get it on Sunday?"

"I plan on staying over through Monday. I'll get it tomorrow."

"Oh." She should have known better. Lew Pressman was anything but absent-minded. "I really don't know, Lew. He has everything he needs. He can always use sport shirts. He goes through them like—"

"I don't want to get him sport shirts," Lew broke in. "That's the sort of thing he buys for himself. Or you buy for him. I'd like to get him something different."

Yes. Of course. Leave the dull to me and you supply the dazzle.

"Well, there is something you can get him," Evelyn said. "He's finally admitted that he's going to need a typewriter. He said something about an electric portable."

"Good," said Lew. "I'm surprised he's gotten along this far without one. I thought college teachers insisted on having their papers typed. Mine did. But all right, that's fine, I'll get him one. If you happen to talk to him, don't say anything about it. I'd like it to be a surprise."

"I spoke to him yesterday," Evelyn said. "That's my quota. I call him at most once a week. He resents anything more than that."

"Freshman independence," Lew said. "It's largely a fake. He's getting all that peer support. Do you miss him?"

"Of course."

"I do, too—but I'm very pleased he's making it so well. You have a conference around this time of year, don't you?"

"Yes. It's over. It went very well."

"Good. I've got to get going. It takes forever to get out to Kennedy."

"Give my love to Jay," Evelyn said.

"Yes, I will. Stay well."

"Thank you. Have a nice trip."

She hung up, got out of the tub, and wrapped herself in a large towel. An image of Lew appeared vividly in her mind. Odd that it should appear now. There had been no image to deal with while she had been talking to him. Just the voice, that low, sincere voice that stirred so many things at once that it was impossible to say just what effect it had on her.

Right now she was recalling the last Pressman image, at least the one she had last seen, about six months ago, in a theater lobby, after the show, theatergoers and cigarette smoke pouring out of the open doors, and there was Lew in a claret-colored turtleneck, navy blue jacket, and an amazing bouffant of ginger-and-gray hair. *What on earth had he done to his hair?* Just let it grow, apparently. And it didn't look bad. Nothing ever looked bad on Lew. He had an uncanny knack of adapting the most diverse styles to the Pressman personality. He had smiled his quick, concerned smile, somehow maneuvered her away from Frank, pressed her hand in both of his, and for one full minute gave her the fullness of his concern . . . *and he could do that after living together for fifteen years!*

How was she? Did she enjoy her job? Was she able to manage

with Jay? Was the money he sent enough to cover expenses for Jay? She wasn't to hesitate if she needed more. That was a nice coat she was wearing. New one, wasn't it? Did she get along with Frank Moore? He'd read one of Frank's books after learning he was a novelist. Not bad. A bit on the wild side but not bad. They must all get together for dinner sometime. . . . All that in sixty seconds! All that and more! Lew Pressman's laser beam of attention! When he concentrated, he concentrated! Whether one liked it or not, there was no escaping the overwhelming realization that one had been *addressed!*

She chose the knitted dress. It was quality old and very dependable. She had received more compliments in that than anything she had ever worn. The color was perfect for her hair and eyes. Of course Lew *would* phone this morning and upset her. She heard nothing from him for months at a time—not that she particularly wanted to hear from him—but the rules of irony had to be observed.

Gabe would ask about her marriage—as she would about his—and what would she say? She didn't know what she'd say. There was no use preparing a set piece for the occasion. So much would depend on what she felt—on what Gabe made her feel. She could say her marriage was a mistake and let it go at that. That was a facile truth that covered a multitude of tortured reasons. . . . *"Well, the truth is, Gabe, that it took fifteen years to reveal the stranger I had married. . . ."*

Was that true? Yes, it was. The Wharton School graduate who had quickly become a minor executive in a major motion picture company. The East Coast representative. How he loved the life! Dealing with writers, with actors, actresses, properties. Flying between L.A. and New York. A man who was happy in his work was a happy man. And Lew was happy. Lew was more than happy; he was totally engaged. He seemed never to get tired. When tired, his deeply recessed eyes would recess a little more, that was the only clue, but that merely supplied a dimple of introspection to the general handsomeness of Lew Pressman's versatile presence.

He was not a fraud. A fraud must have some awareness of alternatives, and as far as she could tell there were no alternatives in

Lew's life. Is a chameleon a fraud because it changes color? Lew adapted. Sometimes he was wrong, but preponderantly he was right. With executives, he became cool, precise, and marvelously practical. With artists, he became witty, inventive, and raffish. With recalcitrants, he became smooth, diplomatic, and insightful. With adversaries, he became clever, agile, and tough. With gays, he became amusing, loose, and somehow, insidiously, *knowing*. She had asked once what the hell went on, and he had laughed at her, asking how *she* could have any question in her mind. He was right about that, in a way. There was no question of his virility and the direction of it—but there did develop a large question, a tremendous question, about its source.

Evelyn closed her eyes and shook her head. The scene, the terrible scene, came back to mind. The night she had wriggled out from under him in a spasm of horror, having witnessed it once too often to doubt it, knowing at last and for all time that she had very little to do with his erections. He could have them all right, and as far as she knew she was the sole recipient; but she had been able at last to piece together the curious disjunction between his stimulations and his performances. She had seen too many stimulations that had started earlier in the evening, in an entirely different part of the Pressman forest. He could be at her seven nights a week, and some mornings as well, when he was scoring elsewhere. The business score, the social score, the sense that the day had been a total Pressman success, and then he was Pan rampant. At other times, weeks would go by without his even being *aware* that their sexlessness was contrasting strangely with other weeks.

"*It has nothing to do with me! I might as well appear out of a lamp!*"

"*Don't be stupid. Does it surprise you that a man's sex life has something to do with his state of mind?*"

"*Oh, Lew, that's such crap! You only come at me with that thing when you've gotten a mental hard-on elsewhere. I won't be made love to on those terms. It's despicable. I won't let you touch me. Why don't you masturbate and complete the private act that it is!*"

"*Be careful, Evelyn. You're saying things that will be impossible to retract.*"

"I don't intend to retract them! Ever! I KNOW, for God's sake! I've been watching it for years! And I don't know if I'd mind so much if it were not the crowning act of all your other acts! I don't know who you are, Lew! I don't know who it is I sleep with every night, who has fathered my child! Do you?"

She marked the end from there, although there were five more years of crises and reconciliations—and the reconciliations were a spawn of the other nightmare. *She* became a score, a human problem to be overcome. He must have cared for her in some way to have taken the trouble. He tried to become what he had been in the early days, since the need for conquest had shown up in this most unexpected of places; but of course you can't be as successful the second time, particularly when the other person has seen it all, every approach, every permutation. The only real thing she had taken from their marriage was the rages that swept everything else away and left Lew Pressman as cornered and dangerous as a savage animal. It wasn't that she had exposed him as a fraud; it was much worse than fraudulence, it was *natural*—and her reaction had been to cancel the privilege of human response until she was given some evidence of honesty, honesty that *she* could recognize. The only honesty he was driven to was the honesty of violence. His lips became white welts. His voice shook so badly that he couldn't form words. He embraced her once and squeezed so ferociously that she almost fainted. He said, "I can destroy you before you destroy me! I beg of you not to let it come to that!"

After that, he took to other women, and more or less left it to her to leave when she was ready.

Lew had married again. Strangely, he wanted to be married. Evelyn had met the girl. Very attractive, at least fifteen years younger than herself, an actress. Perhaps that's what Lew needed: a permanent borderland between artifice and reality.

But how awful it had been to part with so much relief after having been so much in love!

Evelyn smiled at the perfume flask as she tipped the mouth against the ball of her finger. Je Reviens. Gabe had made no promise to return, and she never had expected him to, so Je Reviens was more a surprise token than an appropriate one. Was this a perfume Gabe would like? Was he familiar with it? Not from her. This was a fairly recent fragrance for her. What had she worn when she knew Gabe? Patou? Schiaparelli? Not that it mattered. Women, Evelyn felt, chose their perfumes as they chose their clothes: for themselves.

She made a sad face, recalling Joanna's latest heartbreak. God, the foul luck that woman had with men! A marriage that had lasted only three years, and all the rest a roller coaster of hope and despair. And why? It was incredible. Joanna was so intelligent, so interesting, so *good-looking,* with those gray eyes, and that lovely hair, and that little cleft in her chin. If she were a man, she'd grab Joanna and hold on for dear life. But that was an old story, the one of misjudgments between men and women: what a woman thought a man should like, and what he did like.

All right, Joanna was a little heavy, but did that *really* matter? Apparently it did. Or something mattered. Perhaps the tidal flesh (it waxed and waned, waxed and waned, according to the moon of Joanna's moods) was only the outward excuse for all the inner qualms. Joanna could fall in love like a shot bird plummeting from the sky, but as soon as she landed she was reincarnated into the old Joanna, with eyes to see and a mind to judge. She simply did not fall in love with men who would measure up on her awakening. Then she would try the Procrustean-bed trick on them, and that was the beginning of the end. But it didn't work that way this last time. Not with Misha What's-his-name, the Russian émigré musician who had told her that a woman's perfume was a barometer of love. When a man was in love with a woman, he was also in love with her perfume; when he fell out of love, that same perfume became the very odor of disenchantment. "Joanna, I do not like your perfume," Joanna had said he had said, her gray eyes thick with tears.

It was extraordinary the things Joanna would say about herself, things Evelyn would never dream of divulging to another human being. What Evelyn thought of as vanity, the necessary dissimulations, the necessary concealments, were either omitted or placed entirely elsewhere in Joanna's ego. And that was part of her constant surprise, her charm. At least for Evelyn White it was. Perhaps it wasn't so charming for men. She could well see that most men wouldn't care for that kind of frankness. Men didn't want to know all that much about women, really. And the same was not true of women. Women *did* want to know about men, as much as they could find out. No doubt it had something to do with illusion. How much was necessary for a man, how much for a woman.

Evelyn smiled to herself again when she recalled Joanna's rueful cry for a third sex, some third gender that a woman, or a man, could turn to when the great arrangement had gotten hopelessly out of synch. "But aren't there all sorts of in-betweens?" Evelyn had asked her. "Gays and neuters. . . ." "I don't mean freaks," Joanna had said, hitching her left shoulder in that way of hers. "I mean a creature with some sign of God's imprimatur on it. Neither man nor woman nor a caricature of either, but something entirely different. A creature of mind and sensibilities and no sex, just for those who've had it with sex and whatever is attached to sex." Evelyn had speculated that perhaps the species would mutate to accommodate the need. "Amen!" prayed Joanna.

Evelyn glanced at the little travel clock on her night table. It was a quarter to eleven. It would take her less than ten minutes to get over to the Plaza. She'd probably take a cab. Loads of time. And if Joanna wasn't up by this time, she should be. Evelyn picked up the phone and dialed.

"Did I get you up?" she asked.

"I'm not sure," Joanna said. "I don't think so. I'm reading this ocean of a novel that's supposed to be so good, but I keep slipping under the seaweed. Christ, I don't know. I think it must be me. I guess I'm losing patience with novels. I keep wanting them to get to the fucking *point!*"

They had met at Barnard, she and Joanna, both of them English majors, and Joanna had always been the more brilliant one, the one who would write the book. She was going to be a writer. . . . *"Evelyn, I'm not going to be just another lady novelist. I'm going to be the American Tolstoy, or Proust, or at least Colette. . . ."* Now here she was, sole proprietor of a successful employment agency—"body snatching," she called it—specializing in media—copywriters, account execs, artists, secretaries—making enough money to live comfortably in this fabulously overpriced city, and wanting novels to get to the fucking point.

"Why go on reading it if you don't like it?" Evelyn asked.

"Because I must finish every novel I start. You know that. Point of honor."

"You'd do yourself and the world a favor if you wrote a good one instead of wasting your time reading bad ones."

"Yeah, yeah. Then you'd have two on your hands. Wouldn't that be nice for you, giving suck to Frank Moore with one tit, and Joanna Hopkins with the other."

"Joanna!"

"Well, it's true about Frank, isn't it?"

"Certainly not," Evelyn said. "I encourage him, of course. Why wouldn't I? I'd encourage you, too."

Joanna laughed her throat laugh. "You're lying," she said. "I can just see Frank walking away with his little pail of encouragement. Don't kid me! Frank isn't looking for encouragement. He's looking for blood and mother's milk."

"And would you be?"

"You bet! . . . And why on earth are you calling at this hour on a crappy Sunday morning?"

"Guess who I met last night?"

"I don't like guessing games. Who?"

"Gabe Michelson."

There was a pause at the other end, which Evelyn understood to be Joanna's consideration of a curious item of chance.

"Good old Gabe," she said. "Is he fat, bald, and boring?"

"No, he's amazingly like he was. He's gotten a little heavier, but still Gabe. Nicer, somehow. More mature. I don't know. The same yet different."

"My, my! Sounds interesting. *Is* it interesting? Is that why you called?"

"It's all a bit eerie. You don't know the whole story. . . ." Evelyn told Joanna about the incident with Sandy Bethune, how Sandy had reminded her of Gabe, although she didn't realize it was Gabe she was being reminded of until she got out of Sandy's clutches. . . . "And then to meet Gabe that same evening! That's a little shattering!"

"Did you act shattered?"

"I don't think so. I was nervous and he was nice. He brought back another time so gently. I've been trying to think why I should feel that Gabe wouldn't turn out the way I saw him last night."

"Because you had deprived him of your life-giving presence,"

Joanna said. "Why should he have turned out *any* way without you being around to do the turning?"

"Are you being sarcastic?"

"I am. Please don't mind, dear. Sunday kills me. It's pure death. I know: Sunday is awful for everybody except football watchers. But, for me it's worse. It produces the exact atmosphere I expect to find in my tomb."

"God, you're morbid today!" Evelyn said.

"I've got to be. Active morbidity is the only antidote for Sunday's natural poisons. So what about Gabe Michelson? You've got a date with him today, haven't you?"

"How did you know?"

"Because you're talking to me now. You've got a date sometime between twelve and one, and you figured talk to Joanna and get a reading on whether you're doing the right thing or not."

Evelyn felt both pleased and displeased at being seen through by Joanna. When it came to important things—love, money, creation—human attitudes dwindle to remarkably few. She was pleased that Joanna was sharing her secret, and she was displeased that she was weak enough to want the sharing.

"I'm not remembering as clearly as I'd like," she said. "It was such a frantic time—between Lew and Gabe. Did I behave badly? To Gabe, I mean."

"You're asking me? Dear Evelyn, how would I know how you behaved? You didn't have me along, you know, on either of those adventures. My God, you're talking twenty years ago, about. I was probably more concerned with myself then. But, at a venture, I'd say you probably behaved no worse than anyone does in that kind of bind. How can you behave well toward a man you're ditching? If I know you, you did what you did as quickly as you could."

"Not mercifully?"

"There's no *way* to be merciful," Joanna said, refusing Evelyn the quick palliative she was seeking. "Any way you leave someone who loves you is the worst way."

Evelyn sighed. "I wish sometimes you were less wise and more comforting," she said.

"So do I. . . . But, listen, if you're seeing him today that means that he's seeing you. Obviously he's forgiven, which makes him as nice a gent as I seem to remember. He was nice, wasn't he?"

"Yes."

"If he remembers me, please give him my best."

"I will. Please don't feel depressed."

Joanna laughed. "I hope to God you didn't say that to Gabe twenty years ago!" she said.

Evelyn decided to walk. She lived in an apartment house on the East Side in the upper sixties. It was a typical November day: raw, overcast, possibility of rain or snow. Walking would put color in her cheeks, freshen her eyes. She looked for and found people walking in the streets, and that mentally reduced the chance of a mugging. She wanted to think a little more about the past. Joanna was right, as usual. There was no good way to break off a love affair. But had she ever really said she loved Gabe?

She had gone to bed with him. In those days, that meant something. What exactly *did* it mean twenty years ago? Evelyn found herself in one of those weird time zones where her own past seemed like something on the other side of the Roman Empire. Were things at all different? Or were they, unbelievably, cosmically different? She inclined more toward the "cosmic" view this time, which might have been due to her inability to fix the events of twenty years ago firmly in her mind. . . .

She had gone to bed with Gabe after Lew had told her about "the other girl." Sylvia . . . Sylvia Dacosta . . . Da Costa? . . . She never did get that straight. . . . She did remember that the family went back to thirteenth-century Spain. . . . A black cat appeared from around the fat side of a plastic garbage bag, stared at her, then suddenly darted across the street. . . . Oh, God, the mysteries of Sylvia Dacosta-Costa! There was a medieval chapel in Evelyn's memory where the Dacosta-Costas assembled to hold services in honor of the family's distilled blood. Black mantillas, goatees, and rings the size of walnuts. Actually, the family was in the business of buying animal glands all over the world to sell to pharmaceutical houses in the U.S.A. And Sylvia was nothing more glamorous than a textile designer—rather, an assistant to one. But none of these facts or fancies had come near the dark heart of her misery. As much as she would like to, now, she could not change or diminish what she had lived through.

She had fallen in love with Lew Pressman because he was clever and attractive and moved in an ambience brighter than anything she had known. Lew was her first lover, and there *was* some commitment in that. Not because of any moral view she took on the matter but because of things said, and done, and felt. And when Lew—solemn-faced, sorry-eyed—told her that there was this other girl, she set her own phoenix-fire of heartbreak. Only, she wasn't reduced to resurrecting ashes. She went on burning and burning, sometimes in the low flame of sorrow, sometimes in the blast furnace of jealousy. No use denying that she was jealous. She felt beaten by looks and class, even though she had never seen the other girl. Her pride was roasted daily on the spit of her imagining. Then she went to that June wedding and met Gabe Michelson, who was so nice, and she decided—yes, *decided!* there was no use denying that either—that if Gabe was interested, and if he went on being as nice as he seemed, she would have him for a lover.

Was it like that? Yes, she was afraid it was like that. Well, why be afraid? She had gone to bed with Gabe because she *liked* him. Of course, there wasn't much credit in that. She was incapable of going to bed with someone she didn't like. She had even wriggled out from under her own husband's body when she was at last ready to admit to herself that she didn't like *him*. . . . But there it was, the somewhat passionless decision to have Gabe Michelson as a lover because he was warm and friendly and very nice to be with . . . and because she needed the enjoyment and release of sex . . . and because she needed the one act she could imaginatively fling in Lew Pressman's face.

She could remember now, with a little flush of sensual remorse, how much sheer physical pleasure she had known with Gabe. Like most men, he began too quickly and ended too soon (so, for that matter, did Lew), but where she had been virginal and tremulously eager to please, she became a woman determined to *be* pleased. She remembered how she had imposed her own pattern on their love-making. She remembered how she had talked Gabe away from too much zeal, extended the minutes of anticipation, lingered over small sensations. . . .

Was it all a bag of whorish tricks, because she didn't love Gabe?

Because she was seeking revenge? Could that desire for revenge have washed off on poor Gabe? How could one really know? One was supposed to find such pleasure with the beloved—and, in fact, Gabe had become the beloved. She remembered his consideration, his sense of humor, his seriousness, his . . . well, his *integrity*. She could think of no other word for it. Gabe Michelson was an "integ" man. Evelyn smiled at her use of one of Joanna's made-up words. She remembered how he would try to skirt around certain topics because he didn't want to disagree with her, and how uncomfortable he would look when she would force the issue, and how, finally, sadly, he would take his stand against her, refusing to compromise his convictions. Adlai Stevenson, she recalled. They had argued about Adlai Stevenson. Gabe had said that of course he preferred Stevenson but that the man's rhetoric was ruining his chances, and she had said. . . .

What difference what she had said? She had enjoyed being with Gabe, had enjoyed sex with him, but all these pleasures proved to be only local applications around the deep knife wound she had suffered. That's the way it was, and all the wishing in the world couldn't make it otherwise. When Lew had gotten in touch with her, had asked to have lunch with her, she had agreed—stupidly, hopelessly curious! It wasn't going to work out with Sylvia Dacosta-Costa. He didn't, in fact, *like* Sylvia. The whole damn clan was sealed into its own juice like a can of sardines. And Sylvia was definitely one of the clan. Get this: He was expected to go into the family business! His business training at Wharton would be useful! . . . "I told them that I had a job in the movie industry and that I liked my job very much, and they looked at me as if I'd grown another head. . . . God, you can't imagine what a relief it is just to sit here and talk to you!"

She was at Fifth Avenue. Up ahead, she could see the break in the avenue made by the Plaza. The day was uncompromisingly overcast and chilly, and yet, perhaps because of the nastiness, all the more inviting to interior pleasures—restaurants, movies, museums—places that would enclose and enrich whatever friendship or intimacy a woman and a man might have to offer each other. She was glad to be going to this rendezvous. Nothing could have dissuaded her from going, just as nothing could have dissuaded her from leaving Gabe and going to Lew about twenty years ago. Lew thought he had loved another, and he had discovered that he didn't, that he loved *her*. Just as she had thought she might love Gabe, but didn't, she had loved Lew. In Lew's presence, she felt rise up in her all the bright and endlessly exciting possibilities that she hadn't felt with Gabe.

That's the way it was . . . but try as she might she couldn't fix the Algonquin precisely in that time. She remembered going there with Gabe to celebrate the publication of Jeff Singer's book of poems, but the occasion floated vaguely over all the hurts and elations and terrible uncertainties that had marked those years.

7

Because Gabe had never eaten there, they had lunch at the Plaza. Gabe asked for a table with a window overlooking the park. Evelyn ordered the crabmeat-tomato salad, and Gabe, on consideration, ordered the same. It seemed light enough to manage after the bad scheduling of his morning's tour.

The stone wall that defined the south end of the park looked black in the damp grayness of the day. There were still some leaves on the trees, but the wide sidewalk on the park side of the street was matted with a carpet of wet, brown leaves. Gabe felt caught in a soft net of time. He didn't feel there was the slightest inevitability in this meeting, but his compliance with its happening was so complete that he felt relieved of all compunctions. Evelyn felt different. Now that she was sitting next to Gabe Michelson, she did feel a sense of inevitability. She couldn't have predicted this, but it seemed to her that the drift of her days had been waiting for some hand out of the past to reach into her life and draw its looseness together in just such a compelling way. Sitting here, now, with Gabe, made it impossible to imagine it having happened in any other way, with any other person.

Gabe told Evelyn about his peculiar morning. He told her how he had been fooled by the laggard light into sleeping several hours beyond his habit. He told her that the stringencies of law school had changed him from a sleep lover into a sleep hater. Once awakened, no matter how groggy, the bulldozer of his conscience would push him out of bed, into his clothes, into his study for an early look at whatever needed looking at.

He then told her about his stroll up Seventh Avenue, his coffee-shop breakfast, the young couple he saw conspiring to out-maneuver the world, and the strange sensation he experienced when he counted himself among the city isolates who inhabit such coffee shops on cold Sunday mornings. Evelyn wanted to know what sort of feeling that was, and he told her it was a feeling of disconnectedness, of suddenly seeing one's obligations as options. Did he feel his obligations heavily? Evelyn wanted to know. Gabe shrugged and asked what man of his age, with a family, still-growing children, a profession, didn't feel his obligations heavily? He assumed, however, that there were men who disappeared into their obligations after a time. The costume became the skin. He didn't think that had happened to him as yet.

Evelyn liked the way he described himself, his life. She liked his immediate assertion of who he was and what he recognized. This was very much like the Gabe she remembered. None of the I'm-extraordinary-take-me crap. Nor was there any hint of the misunderstood husband or burdened father. He wasn't pretending that he didn't like his life, and that made whatever he might like in Evelyn White all the more valuable.

She asked Gabe if he remembered Joanna Hopkins, and Gabe said of course he did, that Joanna was *her* writing friend. Jeff Singer was his and Joanna was hers. Evelyn told him that Joanna never did pursue her writing career. She ran an employment agency in the city and was quite successful at it. She had talked to Joanna this morning, mentioned this meeting, and Joanna had asked to be remembered. Gabe asked that he be remembered to Joanna. Wasn't it true that one usually kept one friend out of the past? So many were lost, but usually one remained.

They talked about friends, and they talked about their work, and whenever they seemed to be coming close to their marriages there was a pause and a veering away, as if some undefined courtesy must continue to be observed in the newness of their relationship. And because they both seemed to guess instinctively where best to move and what best to avoid, the pleasure of the afternoon increased. The intimacies they had known didn't interfere with the acquaintance they were forming. Yet the intimacies were there. Neither could pretend that the intimacies had happened to two other people. The mixture of nearness and distance seeped into the talk and the passing minutes like a mild drug, loosening inhibitions without killing awareness, enhancing time without obscuring its passage.

After lunch, they went to the museum. Did Denver have an art museum? Yes, it did, and a very nice museum it was, with a fine collection, perhaps the best in the country, of pre-Columbian art. But, to a New Yorker by birth, there was only one real museum of art, and that was *the* museum. The hogs! They'd bought up everything in sight when the money and pride were there. Would something like this ever come about in today's New York? Probably not. Certainly not. More important than the necessary money would be the necessary sense of permanence, and if anything characterized the city Gabe had walked through this morning it was the spooky, pervasive feeling of impermanence.

Evelyn declared that they would look at only what he most wanted to look at, since he was the returned native. Gabe said he would most like to look at the Rembrandts. Good! That's just what they'd do, then. If there was time, and if they weren't exhausted, they would look later at the new Lehman wing. So they sought out the Rembrandts. Gabe asked Evelyn if she came often to the museum, and she confessed that she did not. When she heard of some special exhibit, she would go. Gabe was sure it would be the same with him if he still lived in New York. Still, the knowledge that it was there added a kind of richness to life, he supposed.

"Isn't life in Denver rich?" Evelyn asked.

"I guess you'd have to define richness," Gabe answered. "If it's skiing and sunshine and open sky and the outdoor life, you're a millionaire. If you value other things, there's a gnawing sense of being undernourished."

"I take it you value other things," Evelyn said.

"Yes, I do," Gabe replied, "but you have to keep perspective. We're talking about choices 95 per cent of the rest of the world would wonder at."

"I know," said Evelyn, "but did that ever make a difference?"

"None at all."

They were now strolling through rooms, pausing to look at whatever caught their attention. Actually very little was catching their attention. Their attention was centered on each other, and great art was passing at the outer edges of their fields of vision. They had wandered into the Impressionists—Cézanne, Monet, Renoir—and Gabe's field of vision was unconsciously gladdened. Evelyn was too intent on the interior view to much notice. . . .

"What happened at the Algonquin?" she asked.

Gabe turned and looked at the woman he was with. He smiled an evasive smile. He wasn't sure how the question was intended. She had changed so little. The same reddish-brown hair. Did she apply something to color out time? The same wide mouth, a little lined but every bit as appealing. With no warning to himself, or Evelyn, he leaned toward her and kissed her appealing mouth. Then he looked around the room and saw there were two people at the other end. He shrugged. It was a quick, experimental kiss, reaching out to touch some long-absent object to see if the nerve endings remembered it. It came so quickly that Evelyn could do nothing but receive it passively, in surprise. A second later, her heart gave such violent assent that she felt an actual pain in her chest. Not knowing what else to do, she took Gabe's arm and pressed it to her hurting side.

Gabe said, "Nothing happened at the Algonquin—nothing except that I knew it was over."

"Did I say so?" Evelyn asked, not looking at him.

"No."

"Then how did you know?"

"Do you really want to know?"

"I'm almost afraid to say yes, but yes, I do want to know."

"Well . . . let's see . . . there was a strain between us. You said there was another man. You said you didn't know if you'd gotten over it. Some doubt! You married him. Lewis Pressman. We had drinks there, and we toasted Jeff's bright future, and we decided to stay for dinner, and you were so happy for Jeff. You celebrated the daylights out of Jeff's success. . . ."

"Was that wrong to do?"

"No—but you celebrate to the extent that you feel like celebrating. I wasn't feeling very festive, and you were obviously as festive as hell. That told me everything. That told me that you had moved into a life that didn't include me at all."

"Oh, Gabe."

"Yes, Evelyn."

When they left the museum, they went to a nearby hotel and had a drink in one of those dim lounges. Museums are tiring. Add a potent cocktail, and a layer of insulation forms around the senses. Reality is muffled.

"When do you have to go?" Gabe asked.

"I don't have to go at any time," Evelyn answered.

"Do you want to have dinner with me?"

"Yes, Gabe, I want to have dinner with you."

"Do you want to spend the night with me?"

"Yes, I want that, too. Do you?"

"Isn't a man supposed to want that at all times, with anybody attractive?"

"Oh, I don't think so, Gabe. That's the convention, but I don't think it's true. And anyway, I wouldn't want it to be true with me."

"Well, it isn't true with me either," Gabe said, "I've never gone to bed with a woman that I didn't feel something serious had happened."

"Have you gone to bed with many?"

"Surprisingly few, if what I hear and read of the current track record is true."

"I meant after your marriage," Evelyn said.

Gabe didn't answer immediately. He turned his head slightly, away from Evelyn.

"You didn't like that question, did you?" she asked.

"I guess not. I guess I feel you don't have the right to ask that. I'm wondering why I feel that way, and I guess the answer is that there's still some resentment left in me. Is that surprising? It shouldn't be. Big hurts last a long time. Since I'm guessing so much, let me guess that not much time has gone by in the last twenty years that you didn't appear in one form or another in my thoughts. That shouldn't be surprising either. You're very much part of my past. Lesser people than Evelyn White have come back to mind from time to time. But I want you to know, Evelyn, that there *is* some resentment left. I want you to know that if we spend the night together, there may be a vengeful young man keeping us company. And I also want you to know that this is absolutely insane, my telling you something like this. But let me take one more guess: I guess I've arrived at a time in my life when what I am left with is as important to me as what I will enjoy. . . . There was only one occasion since my marriage, to answer your question. It turned out to be very unpleasant."

"Are you afraid this will be too?" Evelyn asked.

Gabe covered Evelyn's hand with his own. "No," he said, "it can't turn out unpleasant. It can turn out to be many things, but not unpleasant."

"Why do you think so?"

"Look, I've been doing all the talking," Gabe said. "You tell me."

"It can't be the same for both of us," Evelyn said. "We start from such different places. It couldn't be unpleasant for me because of how I'm feeling."

"Yes," said Gabe, "that sounds about right."

Evelyn would rather have gone to her apartment than to Gabe's hotel, but she understood that in the area of relative cautions Gabe had priority. Not to be able to answer an emergency call from home might be just the unpleasantness neither thought could occur.

They went to Gabe's hotel after leaving the bar, and they made love with a ruby neon light from across the street reminding them of the room with its narrow view of the Hudson. Gabe was neither hasty nor vengeful, and Evelyn was neither controlled nor controlling. Gabe stayed with her until that concentric rush swept in from every corner of her body, making her gasp his name over and over. In that excitement, he, too, gave way. There was no need to pretend to more than they felt, and what they felt was a total abandonment to feeling.

The question of how they would arrange that in their lives would have to wait until morning.

8

Gabe didn't take a chance on his internal light meter. He left a request at the desk to be awakened at seven. By eight, he had showered and shaved. By nine, he had finished breakfast. Between nine and ten, he reviewed the material in his portfolio. Several minutes before ten, he presented himself at the offices of Fairmont Enterprises, Inc., which were situated high above Fifth Avenue, with a northward view of Central Park. He was asked by a secretary if he would like some coffee while waiting for Mr. Sinclair. Gabe declined and turned to the view.

It was a bright day. And cold. An amateur meteorologist, Gabe had consulted the synoptic map in the *Times* to see if his guess was right. It was. A cold front had swept through sometime the night before, clearing out the messiness that had gathered in advance of its passage. It was not one of those Canadian polar outbreaks that drops the temperature twenty or thirty degrees, but it was a clean, distinct air mass. Visibility as far as the Bronx, and the rivers on either side of the island glittered in the sunlight. Below, just in sight, was the Plaza. That complex little shiver he had had to contend with all morning started up again, but he cut it off once more, opened the latch of his briefcase, and took out the papers he would need. He thought of his client, Harry Curtis, whose image, Gabe had discovered that same morning, worked powerfully against the virus of distraction.

"What I want, Gabe, is a very clear idea of what those fuckers in New York are expecting to get for their money," he had instructed. "I don't want to waste half a year and have them come up with a contract I'm not going to sign. See that *they* understand what they're getting. I don't want them telling me later that I'll have to spend a hundred thousand to get things into shape. I'm selling what *is*. See that they understand that."

Harry had all the attributes of a self-made man, including that of a case-hardened suspicion. He gave on points, he was not ungenerous, he conceded the rights of others, but when he detected some smartass tactic designed to screw him, it was war to the death. Then he didn't merely want to win, he wanted to annihilate the other sonofabitch. He wasn't all that big an operator—yet—but observant businessmen in Denver had learned that there was usually more profit in yielding to Harry than in opposing him. It all had to do with the self-image he had created—tough, smart, fair—and Gabe saw Harry Curtis as, ultimately, a very rich man, one whom universities could one day touch for large sums of money. Men with a strong self-image were like that. The portrait was as yet incomplete, but the pencil sketch of Gabe Michelson as legal counsel to that potential fortune was not displeasing. It suited Gabe's conception of a fully ripened career: a psychological-legal relationship with a single, powerful client. . . .

"Well, Mr. Michelson, we fixed you up a nice, brisk day for your New York visit."

Gabe turned and shook hands with Arnold Sinclair, who was a stocky, balding man. He spoke with a slight regional accent that Gabe couldn't place at first. He thought it was Boston, but Mr. Sinclair later corrected him. It was Chicago.

"Well—I'm a New Yorker by birth," Gabe told him.

"Are you? Well, then, there's not much I can tell you about our fair, bankrupt city."

"Just how it got in this shape."

"That's easy," said Mr. Sinclair. "The question is how the hell is it going to get out of it. . . . Mr. James will be joining us in a few minutes, but we can get down to business as soon as you like."

They got down to business. Mr. James, one of the firm's executives, joined them shortly after. As Gabe had anticipated, they wanted to see all the tangibles of their proposed purchase—properties, lands, inventories, liens, titles, taxes—and Gabe had prepared duplicates of all the records that could possibly be of interest.

They spoke until eleven, and then agreed to another meeting on Wednesday. The Fairmont side seemed satisfied with the kind of information they were receiving. They wanted to be filled in more thoroughly on zoning regulations, and variances, and the present direction of growth. They would leave all that for Wednesday, at which time they hoped Mr. Michelson would be free to have lunch with them.

Gabe stopped for a bite to eat, and then he returned to his hotel. There were several messages in his box. One from his sister, who had of course been informed of his visit and where he would be staying. She asked that he call her at home at his first opportunity. There was a note from Evelyn: *Please call*—and the number. The third was from Laura Singer. It, too, gave a telephone number, and the message: *Call as soon as you can. Please! It's urgent.*

When Gabe walked into his room, he surveyed the folded, tucked, tracelessly neat scene. Not a hair, not a wrinkle of evidence in all its smooth neutrality. The innocence of things! Gabe thought he detected a fragrance in the general moldiness, but on second thought he took it to be something retained in himself, rather than the room. He had been dealing with the secret taste of Evelyn in his mouth and the secret scent of Evelyn in his nostrils all morning.

She hadn't stayed the night. Gabe wasn't sure how he felt about that. They had both become ravenously hungry by nine, and that was the immediate and practical excuse to get out of the hotel. They'd had dinner in an East Side restaurant that Evelyn knew to be open and then had walked to Evelyn's apartment house.

"I'm not going to ask you up," she had said. "You have an important business appointment tomorrow."

"Come back to the hotel with me," he had said, more than half in jest.

"No."

"Why?"

"I'll keep you up half the night—and God knows what would happen in the morning. Get a good night's sleep. Be fresh. Think of me."

"Will you think of me?"

"No. Not at all. I shan't give you a thought. I never think of the men who make love to me. . . . Gabe, go away now, so that I can start not thinking of you. Will you call me tomorrow?"

"Of course. When?"

"When you get up."

"No. I won't do that. I don't want my head confused first thing. I'll call you after twelve sometime. Give me a time and a number."

"I'll telephone your hotel and leave the number," she said.

She had done that. Gabe was touched by the ruse she had used. The next day's contact, even at a remove, became the charm against dissolution. He shared the fear that the first touch of reality would make it all vanish.

Perhaps he hoped it *would* vanish. Perhaps that's why he had experienced that secret moment of relief when it became certain that she wouldn't spend the night at his hotel—a relief immediately followed by a throb of terror. Perhaps Evelyn herself was afraid of what such an action would mean. Perhaps she didn't care enough to commit herself completely. Perhaps it was the old reserve all over again. Could he accept her reason that it was based on solicitude for *him?* That might only be an excuse. On the other hand. . . .

Riding back to his hotel in a cab, he had caught himself at that point, had given himself a rough, internal shake. *Stop it!* Time had to make a difference! Jean, Pam, Andrew, a career, the erosions and accumulations of time, all of it had to make a difference. And it did. His feelings were solidly weighted with knowledge of the years. And it didn't—because the feelings that were weighted were exactly the same. He wondered what Evelyn would say if he could by some miracle transfer to her the muddle of his feelings. It was his guess that she would understand. What were all those cautions if not the signals of understanding? ". . . *No, go back to your hotel. . . . Be fresh. . . . Think of me. . . .*" Yet she phoned the hotel to leave her number. Caution, understanding, *and* the other thing! . . . If there was one difference he could be sure of, it was the mutually acknowledged need to act. He had obligations. Grown-up people accepted the sanctity in that.

He phoned Laura Singer first. He was fairly certain of the purpose of her call, and although he resented it, particularly after that cavalier dinner with Jeff, he knew it would only prey more and more on his mind until he answered this appeal.

The phone was picked up on the first ring, making him even more resentful of the way people took his dependability for granted. Of course, it may not have had anything to do with him at all, Laura might just be hovering around the phone these days, but he was deeply in the mood to dislike this involvement.

"Gabe, how wonderful to hear your voice! How's Jean? The kids?"

"They're fine, Laura. It's good to hear your voice too. It's been a long time."

"Much too long. Jeff told me he had dinner with you. . . ."

"Yes."

"Then you know something, I'm sure."

"I know something."

"Gabe, I wouldn't mind so much if it weren't so ridiculously *conventional*. I've always given Jeff credit for having an original mind. I think you know that. But he's acting the complete, aging fool, and the thing that burns me up is that there's no one but me to tell him he *is* being a fool! Did you say anything to him?"

"Say?"

"Yes, *say*. You just now admitted that he told you about it. Did you make any attempt to point out to him what an idiot he's being?"

"Why should—?"

"Because you're an old friend, that's why!"

"Laura, Jeff and I have been virtually out of touch for almost five years."

"Does that absolve all past connection, all responsibility?"

Gabe was seeing Laura more clearly as she lashed at him with her words. He could see her high, rounded forehead, which she kept so prominent with that flat, tight hair style. He could see her large, brown eyes, the one feature of her face that received cosmetic care, and that lavishly. Egyptian. Nefertiti. And always the jewelry to match. And always slightly zany, in Gabe's eyes, but in every way the kind of woman the young Jeff Singer was bound to marry. Laura's disguise was the kind Jeff needed to hide the mortal sameness. But husbands and wives wash and undress and get up in the morning. What was so amazing was the swiftness with which Laura had asserted her old, fierce self. From one word to the next, she was suddenly Laura: demanding, arbitrary, punishing. Seeing her accurately once again, Gabe felt his resentment drain away. Such a woman was all the more pitiable with her power gone.

"No, Laura," he said, "I don't feel that the past connection is absolved, but do you think it would have done any good to point out what he already knows?"

"What makes you think he *knows* it?"

"Well, if he doesn't know it, then he's set up a pretty strong defense against knowing it. Have you considered the advantage in letting him make a fool of himself?"

"What do you mean?"

"If it doesn't work out—and you seem convinced that it won't—then to whom will he have to turn when it's over? If I know Jeff at all, he's not a man to endure loneliness."

The silence that followed made Gabe think Laura was considering his words, but then he heard a catch of breath, and the voice that followed was almost unrecognizable. He had never heard Laura speak but in her own, rapid, uninflected way. The voice that came at him now was as jagged and lacerating as broken glass. ". . . *And what makes you think that I would want to take back that silly, pathetic, dried-up, old bastard! Will you tell me that! Why should I sit quietly and take this shit! Because women are stupid beyond belief? Because Jeff Singer has his permanent little harem of silly young bitches who sit at his feet and wet themselves when he inscribes one of his hopelessly out-of-date, out-of-print books? Did you know that he PAID, out of his own pocket, for another thousand to be printed up? Just so that he could pass them out to hare-brained little whores like Cynthia! I'm twice the poet he ever was, and he knows it! THAT'S why he wants out! Men won't look at me because I'm OLD, but pathetic wrecks like Jeff Singer will go on attracting young girls because women are so colossally DUMB!"*

Gabe was silent as Laura sobbed. He tried to imagine such an outbreak from Jean. Unimaginable! Jean never would. And Evelyn? He felt a visceral scald at the thought of Evelyn.

"Laura—"

"Talk to him, Gabe."

"Will you listen to me?"

"Yes."

Gabe told her that it would do no good. If there was anything that Jeff was prepared to hear, it was that he was making a fool of himself. Jeff had alchemized that foolishness into pure gold, and to tell him now that it was worthless would be to outfoolish Jeff. Even as he told her this, Gabe knew that it would be used against him. . . . *"Your own friend, Gabe Michelson, says you're a fool!"* . . . Oddly, it didn't matter. Gabe recognized that this old friendship had reached the "change of state" Jeff and he had discussed in the restaurant. They would probably go on being friends—or maybe not—but in any event nostalgia and past respects had crumbled away through the rub of fear and change. Jeff was a man fleeing himself. He told that to Laura, and that seemed to mollify her a little. He asked her if she would be so angry with Jeff were she to learn that he had become ill. Well, to a Jeff Singer the loss of creativity was premature death. Was it any wonder he was running amok? Gabe said he was surprised that Laura was not the first to recognize this. Could she expect good sense from a man in a state of hysteria? It would be a test of *her* superiority to see if she could help him through this. Gabe said that he agreed that it couldn't last, and the only thing she and Jeff would be left with was the way she had behaved during the crisis.

Laura sighed. "Gabe, I've been so hurt," she said, with something of her old monotone restored.

"I can imagine," he said.

"You've been so patient with me. I can't thank you enough. You're right, of course. Will you come and have dinner before you go back? You must, you know. After all these years. I won't forgive you if you don't."

"I'll certainly try."

"And Gabe. . . ."

"Yes."

"Don't say anything of this to Jeff."

"All right."

"I see that pride is my only salvation," Laura said.

"Yes," Gabe agreed. "Perhaps both your salvations."

He remained sitting on the edge of the bed after his conversation with Laura. He didn't feel the least elated about having placated her raging sorrow. His wisdom had a self-serving smell to it. He wondered if he had arranged the order of these calls so that he might find the moral strength to cancel the last. He hadn't known what to expect from Laura, but that combination of lamentation and spleen had surprised him. The lamentation most of all. He couldn't have imagined such a display from Laura, but, then, he had never seen her really hurt. And scared. Did Jeff have the right to inflict that on Laura? How the hell could anyone know? No wonder the courts had backed away from the whole question.

Still, he hesitated before making the next call, knowing that the shade of gray he had been left with would be deepened near to black when he talked to his sister, Ruth. Laura had touched him only from a distance—he couldn't make her sorrow intimately his own—but he was already feeling the deep, scouring pity that contact with Ruth always evoked. The truth was that he tried not to think of his sister too often, and the distance of two thousand miles had helped considerably in his secret dereliction. His mother had always leveled that silent, double-barreled blast at him. Deserting the family, mother and sister, one in her age and loneliness, the other in her tragic mistake. Was there any truth in that? Probably some. That offer from A-1 Trucking might not have appeared so attractive if it had not been seen against such a dismal background. But it *was* attractive, and he had offered to bring his mother out to that different life and fair climate as routinely as he had made his telephone calls, and she had always countered with, "That's very nice of you, Gabe, but my place is here"—meaning, of course, that his was too, if he had even a spark of family feeling. But there had been Jean, and Jean had had her say in the matter. . . . *"You can't allow such things to influence your decision, Gabe. If they eventually need your help, you'll be in a better position to give that help if you improve your career. . . ."*

The power of logic. The pull of responsibility. The push of loyalty. The shove of emotion. . . . *Ding dong bell, pussy's in the well.* . . . Gabe saw Evelyn's smile, and he felt again that visceral scald. He picked up the phone and dialed the well-known number. . . .

"Ruth—Gabe."

"Gabe! Wait a minute. . . ."

He could hear the baby crying in the background. That would be Naomi, the latest, the third, the newest Ehrlich. Gabe thought of Arthur, his brother-in-law with those large, limpid eyes and that strong, useless body, and that clarinet. What an amazing *shmuck!* He bought records of chamber music with the clarinet part missing, so that he could sit there in his Yonkers apartment and pretend to be the youngest member of the Budapest. So why didn't he become a musician? Because he wasn't good enough. He wasn't even good enough to become a member of the Westchester Symphony Orchestra when he tried out for that. And why didn't he stay in his family's hardware supply business? Because his father and two brothers had paid him off to get the hell out. And what had he done with the money? He had pissed it away in a fancy-food catering business, about which he knew nothing, but *nothing!* He had read an article somewhere about such a business in California, so he had decided to go into preparing very expensive, catered dinners for Scarsdale matrons. Oh, yes, he fancied himself something of a gourmet cook. The only thing he'd left out of his addled considerations was the cost to himself of preparing the food, and the packing, and the delivery service, and the spoilage, and the advertising costs, and fifteen thousand dollars out of the thirty his family had given him to be rid of him had flown away before the first dinner was delivered. . . .

"Gabe! How are you?"

"Fine, Ruth. And you?"

"Okay. How long are you going to be in the city? In your letter you said you were coming, but you didn't say for how long. . . ."

"I'm not sure. A few days."

"Then you will have a chance to come out?"

"I honestly don't know, Ruth. I have a very busy schedule. I'll try. Tell me, how are the kids?"

"They're fine. . . . Well, Naomi may have to go into the hospital for a few days. Infectious diarrhea. The doctor thinks she'd be better off in the hospital. How's Jean and Pam and Andy?"

"All well. . . . What's doing with Arthur?"

"He's all right. Right now he's working for a friend of his."

"Doing what?"

"I don't know exactly. It has something to do with coin-operated machines. His friend leases them and services them."

"You mean . . . like washing machines?"

"No, the kind they use in amusement parks, bowling alleys. . . ."

Yes! If there's a choice between the practical and the ridiculous, be sure that Arthur Ehrlich will be ass-deep in the ridiculous! . . . Gabe didn't trust himself to speak immediately. What rotten tricks time plays with traits we love! He was remembering Ruth as a girl—in her middle teens he remembered her best, after their father had died—taking over the house, quite literally, so that Bessie Michelson could step in and run her deceased husband's upholstery business until it was liquidated. Ruth began her role in life at fourteen or fifteen, never once, that Gabe could see, desiring anything better. Perhaps she wasn't the brightest (she couldn't be, marrying Arthur!), but she was surely the best, with her unfailing cheer, her true unselfishness. Having been the beneficiary of her bounty for so long, Gabe was grieved to sickness to see it wasted on such a vapid-eyed idiot as Arthur Ehrlich. But perhaps such unthinking goodness was bound to find its counterpart in unthinking ineptness. On the other hand, there was the old rage at seeing her so misused. Gabe had choked back a thousand times the urge to blurt out what was in his heart: *"Why don't you get rid of that jackass!"*—but this time it was out before he had fully committed himself to the words.

"I can't," Ruth said.

Since he had gone this far, failing to find the wise caution that had always checked him in the past, he decided to see it through. "Why not?" he asked. "Because of the children? I can't help believing they'd be better off without him."

"Then you know nothing, Gabe," his sister said.

"That could be. Tell me something."

"The children love him," she said. "I don't know what they'll think of him later in life, but right now they adore him. He's a grown-up child, and he makes their lives heaven. He doesn't even know he's doing it."

"And you?" Gabe asked.

"I have four children," she said.

"That can't be a life!" he berated her. "You're a woman! You need a man as well!"

"I guess if I really needed one, I wouldn't have stayed with Arthur," she said. "I've had lovers, Gabe."

If she had told him she had taken to robbing banks, he couldn't have been more astonished. Ruth! Lovers! His imagination had to perform an Olympian leap to cover the distance. His assumptions about Ruth had been all wrong. She may not have been able to prevent her life from taking the course it had, but that didn't mean there hadn't been revealing lights along the way. It was the revealing lights Gabe had left out of his surmises. For an instant, he thought of telling Ruth about Evelyn, but caution finally asserted itself. Ruth had enough to cope with.

"Does Arthur know?" he asked.

"Of course not! That would destroy him. I only tell you, Gabe, because I know how upset you've been about Arthur, about me, about our life. I could have had better luck, I know, but I have a feeling things will work out. I'm probably crazy to think so, but I have confidence Arthur will finally blunder into the right thing."

"I hope to God you're right," Gabe said devoutly.

"I want very much to see you," Ruth said. "I told the kids their Uncle Gabe is visiting from cowboy country."

"I'll get out there," Gabe promised. "I'm not sure what day, but I'll get out there before I leave."

"Tell me, Gabe, is it something big you're here for?"

Gabe told his sister about the transaction, and he could almost feel the old machinery of vicariousness begin to hum. There was no bitterness in Ruth that she hadn't married a man more like her brother. She was too busy taking pleasure from her brother's high-level doings.

He continued to sit on the edge of the bed after his talk with Ruth. He looked at his watch. It was now one-thirty, and with a little start of alarm he calculated it to be three-thirty in New York; then, with a start of comic relief, he remembered that he *was* in New York. Was that lapse an unconscious wish to be transported back to the safety of Denver?

Look, for crying out loud, you're not committed to anything! So you went to bed with Evelyn White. Think of it as settling a score.

Think of it as a happy fling with all sorts of nostalgic ribbons tied to the trophy. What trophy? What the hell was going on in his head? What the hell was he really thinking and feeling? Was he just aching to get Evelyn back in bed—in which case, hurrah!—or was there a good deal more going on? . . .

He picked up the phone again and dialed the number on the green slip. . . . "May I speak to Evelyn White, please?"

"May I ask who's calling?"

"Gabriel Michelson."

"Just a minute, please."

His heart put on quite a riotous performance in those few waiting seconds. "Hello, Gabe," he heard—and he had a much better idea of what was going on.

"And how are you?" he said.

"Fine. . . . How did it go?"

"My business? I thought it went well. It was my impression that things have been moved a little further along toward a profitable conclusion. How do you feel about me today?"

"I feel very good about you today. I feel so good about you today that I've thought of little else. I wonder whether I'm going to see you sometime today."

"If I have anything to say about it, you are. Will you have dinner with me?"

"Yes."

"Where would you like to have dinner?"

"I couldn't care less."

"Here's a regional oddity for you. Out my way, they say, 'I *could* care less,' and they mean the same thing. I don't remember your favorite foods. What? Chinese? Italian? French? I remember the Armenian restaurants. Did you favor that kind of food, or did we just happen to go there?"

"I really don't care, Gabe. Chinese. I know a very good Chinese restaurant. Szechuan. Do you like Szechuan cooking?"

"I think so. I'm sure I must have had it. What am I going to do with the rest of this day? We've already been to the museum. . . ."

Evelyn told him about exhibits at the Guggenheim and the Museum of Modern Art. She reminded him of The Cloisters. She recommended movies she'd seen and liked. She rolled out a royal carpet of possible pleasures, and he understood that they were making love by phone. What was this but the tenders of love? Gabe recalled how, once, at a visit to the dentist, he had breathed in the nitrous oxide, listening to the young, half-amused dentist explain that the nerves hadn't been deadened at all but, rather, that the gas was making him forget the pain from second to second. As he had done then, Gabe now shrugged away the explanation and took a deeper breath of the gas.

He managed to doze for an hour. When he awoke, the narcotic effects had dissipated. All co-ordinates of time, place, and circumstance came together in sharp focus. He knew he would be meeting Evelyn as soon as she was done with her day's work, and that they would go somewhere for a drink, and then they would go somewhere else for dinner, and then they would go either to a movie, or to a play if tickets were obtainable, or directly back here to make love. Along with a deepening dread, Gabe experienced an absolute explosion of lust. It went off in his groin and flew everywhere—fingertips, the roots of his hair, his very teeth—and once again the moist lining of his mouth gave out the taste of Evelyn, and the cells of his nostrils released the scent of Evelyn. He tried to recall if he had been so physically enthralled twenty years before, but memory offered him nothing to compare. Sex, like pain, had a diminishing coefficient in time. And if it didn't, what difference? Last night's bursting pleasure wiped away the past, even while it used it to excite and enhance and powder over with dream dust every touch and turn.

He had arranged to phone home after the first full day of business activity, so that there would be much to tell. The giddily perverse thing was that he was *eager* to talk to Jean. One doesn't lose the habits of a marriage because of recent betrayals. Or was it a betrayal? Evelyn White was no casual thing. Could he plead that in his defense? . . . *Careful, Michelson, be very careful. You have no experience in this. Scruples can be worse than stupidity when you're on unfamiliar ground.*

He picked up the phone and engaged a succession of operators to complete the Denver call. It was almost three o'clock—one o'clock, Denver time. All of Jean's classes were in the morning, the first one at nine, then two right after that, leaving her free by noon. She was home well before one, took a nap, was refreshed and ready for Andy's boisterous home-coming. . . .

"Hi. . . ."

"Gabe?"

"Uh-oh. You sound fuzzy. Were you dozing?"

"No. Wait a second. Just give me a second. . . ." He heard her sigh, could almost see her shake her head. "Oh-h . . . how are you? *Where* are you? Why are you calling now? I was expecting your call sometime in the evening . . ."

"I know," Gabe said, "but I may have dinner with Jeff Singer again this evening. I'm not sure yet. He's supposed to call me and let me know. I might as well tell you this now. . . ."

Gabe told Jean about the Singer episode. Jean said she was not at all surprised—rather, she was surprised it hadn't happened long before this. Gabe told her about Laura's abrasive desperation, and this, too, was more or less as Jean would have anticipated. That fierce, free spirit of Laura's had always struck Jean more as a literary conceit than a real-life attitude. . . . "This is all very interesting, Gabe, and I want to hear more about it, but why is it that you haven't said a word about the other thing? Did it go badly?"

"I guess I'm not saying anything about it because it went so well," he said.

"Well, tell me!"

He told her. He told her there would have to be at least one more meeting, more likely two. He would have to leave himself pretty much at their disposal, so that it would surely take all of this week, and probably would spill over into next. He hoped it wouldn't, but he had a strong feeling that if he let it ripen on the vine few days he could pretty much wrap up the deal in this one trip. At any rate, much would be accomplished. No doubt he would have to return to New York after Curtis had time to digest it all. . . .

He was covering bases like an old pro, giving himself present time and providing himself with time in the future, none of it an outright lie, all of it tainted by the perfidy of concealment. . . . He told Jean about his sister, Ruth, and her husband's latest venture, into coin-operated machines. He even told her about his sudden, incautious outburst, advising Ruth to dump the fool, admitting it was a stupid thing to say, interfering in other people's lives always being a guaranteed clinker. . . . "But you'll never believe what Ruth said to that. . . ."

"What?"

"She told me she knew she was destined to stay with Arthur because she'd had other men, had lovers—"

"What?!"

"Can you believe it?"

"Who? Ruth? . . . *Ruth?*"

"My sister."

"Gabe, you have got to be kidding!"

"Is Ruth the one likely to invent such a thing? Would I invent such a thing about Ruth? She said that's how she knew she had to stay with Arthur. Her fourth child."

"My God!" Jean breathed in astonishment. "Never in a million years!"

"I promised I'd try to get out there," Gabe said.

"Of course," Jean said, still bemused by incredible news.

It was a replete telephone call. There had been much to tell, and that was why he had picked up the phone at such an early hour. Jean was glad that he had called. When they said good-by, she had given approval to all time spent in the gathering of such rich news and fine accomplishments.

Gabe felt expansively, dangerously free.

9

Evelyn White had few superstitions. She knew she was a Gemini, that Frank Moore was a Sagittarius, and when the opportunity presented itself, she would find out Gabe's sign. But such tags weren't seriously considered. They were of no more significance than broken mirrors or phases of the moon. She had long since passed the stage of believing that there was any connection between what one did and what one received. For every Nixon caught, there were thousands who went their vindictive ways, making the lives of others miserable, accumulating the world's goods far beyond their talents or deserts, and who were carried to their graves in a sea of flowers. Villains prospered, and the blameless seemed to attract stinging, green-headed flies. Nothing in the past was a sure warranty of the future—but there was a fleeting instant between past and future, between dreams and consciousness, that she did heed.

In that nebulous, no-time zone between the sleep she was leaving and the day she was greeting, Evelyn thought she could make out at times, at times only, an uncolored, isolated truth in her life. Not *all* the truth of it, but the one part that had been working its way to recognition. Like the morning she had lain suspended in the heartsick knowledge that she didn't love Lew and never would again, hoping the knowledge would dissolve back into the dream it seemed so near to being, yet knowing that it couldn't be willed to sleep, that she would carry it into the day, the week, the rest of her life. In that no-time zone between sleeping and waking, Evelyn had her sibylline moments, seeing her future in the nature of the vision she was given to see.

On the Monday after the Sunday with Gabe, she was awakened, as usual, by the first, soft summons of her bedside alarm. She reached out and pressed it shut, then lay unthinking, turning momentarily back to sleep as one turns back for some forgotten item, gloves or keys, and then she turned to that corner of her mind that was filled with Gabe Michelson. She experienced nothing at first except a vague affirmation, but in another instant she saw clearly his black hair and his smiling face, and she received a shock at the enormous tenancy of his image. It dispossessed everything else. It had moved in overnight, occupied all the rooms, changed all things, slightly or greatly, according to their complementary value.

Fully awakened, she thought fully of Gabe, and she placed her hand over the place where he had kissed her. She caught her underlip between her teeth in a half smile, half moan of remembrance. She let her fingers linger caressingly where he had entered her, and her hips arced upward in anticipation of another such entering. Lord, keep her from becoming what she knew she could become when the craze was on her! Lord, keep out of her eyes that look that transmuted everything into an unspoken, smoldering invitation to bed. I'm an older woman. I have a son. Gabe is a man with responsibilities, with business on his mind. Lord, please help me to measure out what I feel in a sensible way.

The phone rang while she was dressing. It was her mother calling from Coral Gables. "Evelyn—" she heard, and was at once seized with alarm, fearing the dreadful news she more or less waited for from week to week, ever since her parents, in fine shape for their age, in full possession of their faculties, had liquidated all capital, holdings, much furniture, and a lifetime of associations, and had bought a condominium in Coral Gables. Old friends of theirs had moved there. "Come, it's a nice place," urged George and Hilda Ostrow by picturesque card and by telephone. So, two years ago, in the spring, they had started the long, tremulous business of tearing up their rooted lives. By autumn, they were in Florida, and that winter—"like a sign from heaven," her mother had said—Bernard and Norma White were spared the polar weather that punished half the nation. But even sun-cured and

82

content, they were old, older, and a telephone call from one was always a possible pronouncement on the other. "I tried calling you last night," her mother said, "but there was no answer. I called about seven or eight—after dinner it was, I remember—and then the Ostrows came over, and that was that. You know George when he gets started—"

"What did you call about?" Evelyn asked. "Is anything wrong?"

"No, nothing is wrong. I wanted to talk to you. I didn't hear from you in a couple of weeks. . . ."

Evelyn felt a cold confirmation of what she had been refusing to admit to herself. The evidence was there when she had visited last spring: in the number of times her mother asked the same question; in the way she spoke of Evelyn's brother, Bob, making references that made it uncertain whether she knew that Bob was no longer living in New York, that he had moved to Los Angeles five years ago. And the evidence had increased throughout the summer and fall, with odd areas of forgetfulness, remembering with accuracy the minutiae of thirty years ago and not remembering last week's telephone call.

"I telephoned you last Sunday," Evelyn said.

"You did? Evelyn, no, I don't think so. You know, everybody is trying to give me a good case of senility, but, please, I haven't gone that far yet. Last Sunday? You're sure?"

Evelyn was as sure of the call as she was of the cruel lack of purpose in insisting on it. She had done this for a time, *insisted* that her mother make the effort to get things straight, counting it a kind of sun-struck torpor that she had become so mentally sloppy. But now she saw that it was useless. She heard in her mother's voice the shaky terror of uncertainty. Evelyn felt a burn of fury against a God that would allow such a thing to happen to a woman who had lived with such pride of person, whose diligence in love had been the tender joke of friends and family. . . . "If I ever forget the date of my own niece's birthday, I call up Norma. She'll know."

"Well, I thought I did," Evelyn said. "I was preparing for that big convention last week, so it's very possible I got things mixed up. Tell me, how's Dad?"

"He's fine. He's standing here, he wants to talk to you. Have you spoken to Jay?"

"A couple of days ago."

"And?"

"I think he's doing wonderfully well," Evelyn said. "He sounded bright and confident and full of beans."

"What did I tell you!" said her mother—and Evelyn felt a wild impulse to reach out and embrace her. Dying in the Florida sun, she could still love. Seeing the temple of her worship fall apart, she could still celebrate. "I told you he would be all right," her mother went on. "You were so afraid he would get homesick, that he wouldn't get on with the others. . . ."

That much was accurately remembered. Evelyn *had* been afraid, and she had expressed that fear to her mother. The news of Jay's almost swaggering self-confidence was old by now, but it wasn't *that* old that she couldn't share the joy of it again with her mother. It made her want to share even more with her mother.

"Mother, do you remember Gabe Michelson?"

"Gabe Michelson? The name sounds very familiar. Wasn't he a friend of Bob's?"

"No, he was my friend," Evelyn said. "You remember I met him before I got married to Lew. He was a lawyer. He had just passed the bar. A big, strapping fellow with black hair. I met him at Dotty Nathan's wedding. We dated a whole summer—"

"Oh, yes, yes, yes! I remember now. I liked that boy. Very friendly. Very courteous."

"I met him quite by chance at the Algonquin hotel. He's living in Denver now."

"Married?"

"Of course. He has two children."

Evelyn heard her mother make a soft noise. Regret? Warning? Evelyn wasn't sure which. Norma White's instinct had been keen where Lew Pressman was concerned. She had never really trusted that one, found too much play-acting in his attentions. And although she didn't mind her daughter having Frank Moore for "company," she had already expressed her opposition to anything permanent. Not that she minded his Irishness, or the fact that he'd been married before (so, indeed, had Evelyn, but it wasn't Evelyn's *fault,* the breakup of that marriage), but, rather, the very same thing that Evelyn herself had come to fear. Norma expressed it differently. She said, "He's a very charming man, but I feel very sorry for his wife. What'll be left over after taking care of himself won't be very much."

"So what about Gabe Michelson?" Evelyn's mother asked.

"Nothing, really," Evelyn said. "Just the coincidence of meeting him after all these years. He looks just the same. A little heavier. We had dinner and talked about old times."

"Well, it's always nice to meet an old friend," her mother said, but her words cast a somewhat different meaning: *"What's the point if he's married?"*

"Mother, I think I've fallen in love with him!"

Evelyn would very much have liked to say the words, but she very much didn't. That's all her mother would need to brood over while knitting on the shaded west porch of their apartment. She said instead, in a half mocking way, "He told me I'm just as attractive now as I was then," and saying so assuaged a little her need to proclaim the new, large thing she was carrying.

"Well, that's very nice, but I don't need Gabe Michelson to tell me that," her mother said, a little offishly.

Evelyn laughed. "You may not need it," she said, "but I do. . . . Let me say hello to Dad."

Evelyn said good-by to her mother, then spoke to her father, who wanted to know when she would be visiting again. He wagered the weather was lousy in New York and boasted of the balm in Coral Gables. A bit later, he whispered, "Your mother is getting a little forgetful." Evelyn said she knew, and cautioned her father not to make a thing of it. "I know, I know," he said. "And what difference does it make. All time is one in eternity."

There was an increasing poignance in each contact with her parents, because time insisted on loading the same amount of baggage onto their increasing frailty. On this occasion, Evelyn was able to dilute the poignance, because time had called a temporary halt to its ruthless proceedings while waiting on developments in the Evelyn White case.

Most of the morning was spent arguing with the woman who was doing the "Children Around the World" series. Doris McAuley. A regular. That is, as regular as any contributor to the ten-to-twelve magazine. She usually submitted an idea for a series—or an idea was submitted to her—and the work and pay went forward from installment to installment.

The manuscript for the first two issues—to be run after the new year—had come in. They covered England and the Continent, and they were done with Doris' usual competence and style. The next two issues—running into the spring—covered Latin America and Africa, and Evelyn had read them at first with puzzlement and then with downright rejection. She had sent a note to Doris, requesting that she come around to the office so that they could have a talk before continuing with the series. She had set the date for the meeting after the conference, not knowing, of course, that she would have so momentous a weekend to reckon with.

Evelyn found herself reckoning with it every second of the morning. The intensity of her preoccupation made visible in the very near distance the things that would cross its path. She would have to call up Gabe's hotel and leave her office number. *He* promised that he would return the call sometime in the early afternoon, after he had concluded his legal business. He said he suspected it wouldn't go into lunch—but what if it did? Those business lunches could last well into the afternoon, particularly if the lunchers had barricaded themselves behind a rampart of booze and good fellowship. That might mean three or four in the afternoon before she heard from Gabe. She could see her nerves stretched across that impossible gulf of hours, thin filaments of impatience sagging in exhaustion. And, of course, Frank was sure to call sometime during the day. He was not a faithful caller, but depend upon it that he would call today. And what would she tell him? She didn't know what she would tell him. She would leave that to the improvisation of the moment. Would she, now? That would be a fine piece of perilous stupidity. Better to prepare *exactly* what she would say, instead of weaving an elaborate web of nonsense she could neither substantiate nor remember. She could say she was coming down with something, was rushing home to tea and aspirin. Crap! She was a lousy liar, and could no more make herself sound ill than fly. Why not the truth, then? Old friend in the city after a ten-year absence, and she had promised, as an old friend should, to leave her evenings free for the next few days. Free? How free? Free of the past, of the present, of clothes, of prudence? Well, she would say no more than was necessary, but she would say what came most naturally, and what came most naturally was the truth.

In the office, she consulted her appointment book, and she was reminded of the Doris McAuley appointment. She didn't feel like a long, tortuous argument with Doris, and she didn't see why there should be such an argument. It was perfectly clear that Doris' political slant had tipped her overboard. She could be a flaming communist, as far as Evelyn was concerned, but using a grade-school magazine as a forum was simply idiotic. Evelyn asked herself what Gabe would think and say about something like that, and she recalled with a flush of satisfaction those Adlai Stevenson arguments. Gabe would be on her side in this. Gabe would sensibly point out that blaming Western imperialism for the belt of starving children around the world was just so much propaganda in an empty pot. Was the Soviet Union or China sharing their grain with the less fortunate? Ah, but—she could hear Doris answer—that was not the Marxist solution. Precisely! But would you want to get into that kind of elaboration with American ten-year-olds? Even if the magazine was willing to take a polemical chance on some issue, it wouldn't be this, *like* this, *about* this. It was too simplistic. It was too pointlessly controversial.

Frank Moore, of course, would be all on Doris' side. Frank would say that it was just such temporizing bullshit that had kept kids starving since the beginning of time. *Now* was never the moment, and that's why the future never came, and that's why a nice, deep, bloody trench had to be dug right across time. Frank would say that if Don Marshall had any mind or balls, he would run the damn' series and be ready to lose his shirt. *His* shirt. Evelyn recalled that Frank wasn't quite prepared to lose his own shirt when it came to a choice between spending Saturday evening with her and getting his promised chapters in a day or two late. She had thought him right in his decision, and had made no fuss about the matter.

Doris arrived promptly at ten—clear-eyed, no make-up, and all primed for the issue and the argument. She was a not unattractive woman, in a scrubbed, ascetic way, but Evelyn had always experienced a slight nervousness in the presence of those eyes. Either

Doris didn't look at you at all, or once contact was made she remained locked onto yours with a moist, fierce tenacity.

"Doris, thank you for coming in," Evelyn said. "It's about the Latin American and African sections. It's political propaganda. You know that."

"Did you mind my mentioning that large areas were experiencing drought?" Doris asked.

"Of course not. It's true."

"Why isn't it just as true that the policies of imperialism in Africa and Latin America have contributed to the misery of millions? Is that true or isn't it?"

"I don't know if it's true, Doris. It may be. It's also true that live infants were sacrificed to Moloch. Would you tell that to a ten-year-old?"

"If I were writing an article about that period in human history, I would," Doris said, her eyes having fastened onto Evelyn's.

"Suppose you were convinced that such information would traumatize a ten-year-old, give him or her bad dreams; would you still insist on the purity of your principles?"

"You're making a ridiculous comparison," Doris said, boring in at her with those set eyes. "There *are* children being sacrificed, and we *do* know the causes."

"Please don't say 'we,' Doris. I'm not at all sure about the causes. What I am sure of is that this country makes large, regular shipments of food to these distressed areas. I didn't find any mention of that in your manuscript."

"I'd be glad to put that in if you'll run the rest as it is."

"No, I can't do that," Evelyn said. "Leaving the historical truths or untruths aside, we're still left with the question of whether such information can be absorbed into the young lives we're dealing with. Not that children aren't starving—you're saying that they are, and I certainly have no objection to that—but you're also saying that in some direct or indirect way it's *their* fault—the fault of our young readers."

"Say their country's fault."

"That's problematical to begin with, and you can't spell out such contingencies to kids of that age."

"So the most expedient thing is to drop it altogether?" Doris asked.

"We live by expediencies," Evelyn said.

"Please don't say 'we,' " Doris observed ironically.

"Oh, come on, Doris, you do too! Do you go around telling the unadulterated truth to everyone you know?"

"I try. Don't you?"

"No, I don't try," Evelyn replied. "I try to spare feelings."

"So you lie?"

Evelyn knew she was getting angry, a little out of control, so she took several long, cooling seconds before answering. She said, "I don't think I deliberately lie, Doris, although I'm sure I've done that too, on occasion. I guess it's a question of attitude. I don't think it's my intention to deceive, but I do try to avoid injuring others."

"How about trying to avoid injuring children a few thousand miles away?" Doris retorted. "If ten-year-olds were told how it might be done, they might want to do it. I know it's not the expedient thing, but it might do more good than all your food shipments and expedient lies. At least it would prevent the ten-year-olds from discovering later in life that they'd been made to participate in the sacrifice to Moloch."

And so it went, back and forth, Evelyn determined she would not lose patience with Doris, while Doris remained fixed on her ideology with burning-glass intensity. It occurred to Evelyn even while they argued that each knew what the other meant. At least Evelyn was certain she was understanding Doris' point. Doris was saying that a break in the dreadful continuum had to be made, and while Evelyn could agree with this in principle, she recoiled from the practical consequences. She understood that so many millions were doomed to live unspeakable lives in order that certain economic privileges might be maintained, but she also felt that effecting real change would bring on the horrors of war, revolution, which in terms of human suffering might exceed—oh, certainly exceed!—anything she could now see or imagine. And perhaps more important, she wanted her life with its pleasures. She would vote and contribute and petition for change, but she had no heart for carrying Promethean fires. She was certain that time and fury would one day topple it all, but she could no more change her own priorities than look at another human being with those Doris McAuley eyes.

Finally, Evelyn broke off the futile contest by falling back on her authority. "I can't accept it this way, Doris," she said.

Doris maintained that inhuman stare for a few more seconds, and then turned away to the tryptich of photographs at the other end of Evelyn's desk: pictures of mother, father, son. "I know you can't," Doris said.

"What do you mean, you know?"

"Just that. I knew you wouldn't let it pass."

"Then what?" Evelyn asked.

"Then I'll change it," Doris said.

Evelyn slumped in her chair and stared wide-eyed at Doris. "Why did we have to go through that dance?" she asked.

"So that you wouldn't get off scot-free," Doris said. "So that you'd have a clear idea of the difference between what I think and what you publish."

Evelyn looked sharply at Doris. "It sounds like you had it in for me," she said. "Me in particular. Is that true?"

Doris smiled faintly. Now she was in her non-staring stage. Not a glimpse. "It doesn't matter," she said.

"It does to me," Evelyn said. "Would you tell me, Doris . . . please?"

"You're so completely bourgeois," Doris said.

"Just that?" Evelyn asked. "I was never sure what the word meant. How can one word describe such a variety of people?"

Doris said, "Every time I look at you, I think of *The New Yorker* magazine and perfume ads."

Evelyn felt a resurgence of her resentment, both at the truth and the falsity of the description. She read *The New Yorker,* and she was conscious of perfumes—and the ads—but to define another human being by such foibles was as narrow as the most narrow-minded bigotry ever to come out of Tobacco Road. Evelyn remembered that Frank Moore had once chided her in a similar way. She had done some shopping with Frank for company, and he had remarked that she handled her charge plate and checkbook as a Catholic handles beads and crucifix, with loving familiarity and blind faith.

"I'm sure that wasn't meant to flatter," Evelyn said to Doris.

"Nor to insult," Doris said, looking, for once, a little remorseful. "I really didn't mean it disparagingly, Evelyn. I guess I'm a little jealous. You're a very sophisticated woman."

"The hell I am!"

"You seem that way to me."

"If I were," Evelyn said, "I'd be better able to handle situations like this. . . . Doris, have you ever read *The Other Island?*"

"What is it?"

"A novel."

"I don't read novels."

"You might try this one," Evelyn said. "It's written by Frank Moore, whom I happen to know. He's a very good writer, and I think you'll find his ideas very close to your own."

"Do you have a copy of his book?"

"I'll see that a copy is sent to you."

She had lunch sent up, which she often did, being often busy and rarely willing to undertake the lunchtime crowds. Knowing Gabe's schedule for the first half of the day, she was fairly certain he wouldn't be attempting to contact her around lunchtime. He would probably, deliberately, considerately, avoid her lunchtime. So she couldn't be said to be *waiting* while having lunch, or she pretended to herself not to be waiting. But pretending not to be waiting was as futile as pretending she hadn't been rattled by that morning's interview with Doris McAuley—or that there hadn't been a motive other than an intellectual one in recommending Frank's book to Doris.

She could feel herself sliding into another of those awful crises of confidence. Was she the calculating bitch Doris saw her to be? Was she grabbing for Gabe Michelson without a thought of consequences to him, to others? Was she trying to arrange something between Frank and Doris?—another of her "ditching" projects? Happiness and assurance were draining out of her. Her fingertips and toes were ice-cold, and she could feel her stomach declaring a state of siege. Hadn't it all happened too quickly for there to be any lasting reality in it? What could Gabe be thinking and feeling except a week's worth of fun with an old flame? And why should she think and feel about it any other way but that? Why had she allowed herself to fall headlong into such a state?

She had practically emptied herself of all feeling. She had passed from love to lovelessness, and in her sudden panic felt that long-dormant, miraculously activated nerve go dead. She could evoke Gabe's image easily enough, but it was as if the nerve carrying that image had been shot full of novocain. Nothing. No sensation. She had merely talked herself into a condition—God knows why!—perhaps because she had been unconsciously longing for the condition, and with the first excuse had allowed the bubble to burst and drench her with sweet excitement. A child's game.

She munched half her sandwich, tasting nothing. She sipped some coffee. She began to reread Doris McAuley's manuscript, making the deletions and suggestions she had promised to make. But she was still waiting for Gabe's call. She had no choice but to wait for it. She couldn't fly out of it this time as she had done the last, borne on the wings of another love. There was no other love. There was Frank Moore, who was charming and interesting and difficult. . . .

Gabe's call came, as such calls did, when her attention had at last wavered between the dominating thing and the tight marginalia she was penning to Doris McAuley. The phone on her desk rang. Her heart humped like a frightened cat. . . . "Call for you, Evelyn." . . . "Who is it?" . . . "Mr. Michelson." . . . "Okay—how are you, Gabe? How did it go?" "I thought it went very well," he said—and the same image that had appeared to her before in deadness was restored to life. His voice echoed none of the panic she had been feeling.

Frank called at five.

"Did you turn your chapters in?" she asked.

"Such as they are," he said. "When do you think you'll be finished?"

"Frank, if you're going to ask me to have dinner with you tonight, I'm afraid I can't."

"Jesus!" Frank swore, with a short, explosive laugh. "My prophetic soul! You know, just as I was dialing, I said to myself that today, *just today,* there will be fourteen different emergencies in the life of Evelyn White. I'm not happy with what I turned in, to tell you the truth. The truth, Evelyn, is that I'm not at all happy with that dung heap I turned in. I read it over this morning, and I felt like throwing up. It's precisely because of what you dared suggest might not be adequately resolved in the second-rate, amateurish mind of Moore. I knew the thing was in trouble, and yet I went ahead with it because I had promises to keep, which is about the dumbest thing I could have done. Why can't you have dinner with me?"

Evelyn told him about the old friend who had come to New York from Denver.

"Man friend?" Frank asked.

"Yes."

"I don't like that. Why an old *man* friend? Who is he? What's his name? Were you ever in love with him?"

"Stop it, Frank."

"How come you never mentioned him before? I thought you had at one time or another told me about everything and everybody of any importance in your life. This man from Denver can't be important. Tell him that you must cancel until tomorrow. I'll let you see him tomorrow, but it is extremely important—vital!—that I see you and talk to you and have some friendly fingers put together the pieces of my chopped-up heart. See?"

"I can't, Frank."

"Shit you can't! You sure as hell *can,* if you give it a second's compassionate thought. Who is this turkey that you can't put him off for one lousy day?"

"Now, look, Frank, this thing has come up unexpectedly. I didn't anticipate it. I made a promise because of it, and I intend to keep my promise. So don't be childish—"

"Ah, now, lady, spare me that!" Frank broke in, his voice taking on the deep, sardonic growl of an insulted Moore. "Don't pull that *maturity* bullshit on me! I'm not being childish. We've been together for two years now, fair weather and foul. I call you up in a crisis—and I mean crisis!—and you tell me I'm being childish for trying to draw on whatever little credit I might have in the White establishment. I'm not being childish, Evelyn, you're being the cold-hearted bitch!"

Evelyn felt herself weaken under this onslaught. She knew if she got in touch with Gabe at his hotel and told him that an emergency had come up, that she couldn't see him tonight, he would be understanding, not fuss, make it for tomorrow, harbor no suspicion or grievance; and it was precisely because this was so that she steeled herself against Frank. He *was* being childish. He was touching every stop of pity and obligation. He was demanding that his needs be satisfied first—and she was certain there *was* no overwhelming need—just Frank being his arbitrary, selfish self.

"No, I won't be coerced, Frank," she said. "I'll have lunch with you tomorrow."

"You will, huh? Well, that's very kind of you. Give my regards to Mr. Denver, and tell him I hope—ah, fuck it! One last time—will you please do this for me?"

"No, I won't, Frank."

"Everything may depend on it."

"Oh, stop it."

"I'm serious."

"Stop it, Frank. You're upset and you want me to console you. Okay. I understand that. But *please* understand that I, too, may have obligations that take precedence over that particular function."

"All right, Evelyn, have a nice time."

He hung up very softly, not the furious whack she was expecting. It was the first time Frank had lost such a contest with her. She wasn't at all sure what it would do to him, but she felt in her own perseverence the first testing in what might prove to be another long, costly contest.

10

Mr. Sinclair left the message at Gabe's hotel, asking that he be at the offices of Fairmont Enterprises, Inc., at nine, Wednesday morning. Gabe was there a few minutes before the hour, took his northward view from the window. The Bronx was not visible this time. A high-pressure area had settled over the East Coast, capping the crud, giving the air the look of a well-used exhaust filter. Gabe tried to recall when he had seen a day like this in Denver. Never, that he could recall. Plenty of pollution there, but with the mountains for background you could always see where the top of the stuff was. Sometimes, when there was a northwest flow, you got a good mixing, but then you also got a distinctive whiff from the stockyards to remind you where you were.

Evelyn was with him constantly now. She had completely anointed his body with her own, and even in utmost depletion any thought of her brought on the beginnings of that tumescence that had become the emblem of their reunion. It was embarrassing. Not that it had reached the point of showing, but carrying around that involuntary semiswelling was subverting to his composure, his clarity, his dignity. He had told that to Evelyn, and she had given him a delighted smile, taking his arm and squeezing it against her. No, it wasn't funny, exactly . . . it was marvelously, deliciously *magical*. It made her feel like Glinda, the Good Witch of the . . . West? . . . North? Anyway, she was thrilled to know she had the power to bewitch Gabriel Michelson. But the power could only work when there was correspondence, affinity, something. . . . For every bewitcher a bewitchee. . . .

It was stupid to have spent Monday night at Evelyn's apartment. He couldn't be sure at this point whether her persuasion had been greater than his resistance, or whether his resistance had been a pushover for the slightest persuasion. He was curious, naturally, wanted to see her life in its actual setting, wanted to sample the taste of permanence with Evelyn, not for serious reasons, things hadn't advanced *that* far, but just to see. Still, what folly! How could he have explained a whole night's absence from the hotel? Slept at Ruth's? Would Ruth back him up? Would Jean ever think of questioning him if he told her that he had spent the night at his sister's house? No, probably not, *assuredly* not. But suppose something had happened? The hollow-eyed specter of trying to reach a husband and father who wasn't there. It was stupid! Of course, nothing had happened. All the healthy, occupied Denverites were doing their various, engaging things. No messages of sudden calamity. . . .

Astride his loins, she had leaned forward and kissed him, eyes closed, an almost sorrowful look on her face. . . . "Why do you look so sad?" . . . "Because it's so good and you'll be going away. . . ."

The first note on the impermanence of things. The first little salient pushed into territory they had silently, mutually agreed not to enter. But there could be no silence when feelings mounted up, grew topheavy, toppled over. And there could be no mutuality when feelings proceeded at different rates, as they must, since they were different human beings, since the conditions of their lives were so different. . . .

In the morning, Evelyn had made breakfast. He had awakened at his usual six-thirty, was not the least surprised at finding Evelyn White beside him. He had slept uneasily. Dozed, really, having kept the knowledge of his danger with him through the night—and the personification of that danger was Evelyn. She, too, had stayed with him through his shallow sleep, and therefore he wasn't surprised to find her there beside him. She must have sensed his waking, turned around, and claimed his body in a burrowing half sleep.

She was up in a few minutes after that, made breakfast, looked at him searchingly from the other side of the kitchen table, her eyes full of the questions she feared to ask.

"You didn't sleep well," she said.

"Do I look tired?"

"A little. It was too nervous-making, being here, wasn't it?"

"Not being here . . . just not being there—in case."

"I know," she said. She held out her hand. Gabe took it. "I'm not going to say anything now. I'm not going to tell you how I feel with you looking at me from across this table. . . . When do you meet with your people again?"

"Tomorrow," he said.

She raised her head, released his hand, busied herself with a piece of toast. "I feel all shuddery inside," she said. "I'd like to tell you about Doris McAuley, but not now. I'd also like to tell you about Frank Moore."

"Who's Frank Moore?"

"A friend."

Gabe smiled. "A lover?"

She was silent.

"Evelyn?"

"I don't know what the correct word would be," she said. "We don't have good gradations in the English language. Whatever *it* was, it is no longer."

"My God, Evelyn, I hope you know that you don't have to explain such things to me. Don't you think I know how impossible it is to be alone, and how unsatisfactory most relationships are? I can't be jealous of your past. Don't forget, I had to get over that a long time ago."

Evelyn's eyes glistened with tears; the wings of her nose grew pink. She looked toward the window. A tear escaped and fled downward to the corner of her mouth, where she wiped it away with a napkin.

"I'm sorry," she said.

"Don't be."

"I'm not crying about the past," she said. "That would be too stupid."

She was forcing his hand. It would be feigning too much obtuseness not to respond. "Are you crying about the present?" he asked.

Evelyn took a deep breath and picked up her toast again. She said, "Sunday, Monday, this is Tuesday. . . . Since several decades have already gone by, we have at least a century ahead of us. Go see your restaurant biggies and work out a terrific deal for your client. I must go to work, and you must go to work, and we still have time without end."

Since Fairmont was a publicly owned company, Gabe had discussed with Harry Curtis the possibility of a stock offer in partial payment. Harry had agreed in principle to 25 per cent of their stock. Gabe had also forewarned Harry that the New York people would probably offer no more than 29 per cent in cash to stay within the IRS limits of an installment sale. Sinclair and James had showed a modest appreciation that these financial factors had been anticipated and that they would be spared bickering over obvious matters.

Again, as Gabe had anticipated, things had gotten sticky on the multiple-of-earnings question. Harry had given Gabe some room for negotiation, but he had set a minimum of twelve times the earnings for the sales price. Gabe mentioned fourteen. Mr. James gave him a cold look on that and shook his head very decisively. "I'm afraid we're not thinking alike on that," he said. "We had in mind eight." This, too, Gabe had expected, and he had brought with him two city maps and two sets of statistics, each five years apart, demonstrating business and population growth in the areas of Harry's properties. He showed them the locations in relation to the contemplated new highway, the new Performing Arts Center, and the mushrooming suburb on the eastern side of the city. Mr. James thought they could persuade the board to go as high as nine, but Mr. Sinclair continued to look gruffly dubious.

Gabe was certain he could boost them to ten fairly easily. He knew he could probably do it right now with a show of force. They wanted the deal. They were only bargaining. They must have looked thoroughly into the growth conditions in Denver. He knew he could finally strike a bargain at eleven, and that he would be able to move Harry one notch down to expedite the deal. He did some rapid calculations in his head. That one-integer difference amounted to almost two hundred thousand dollars—easily worth another trip to New York . . . easily a sum to make a man's lawyer hesitate.

"I don't think we're hopelessly apart," Gabe said, "but far enough to make a consultation with Mr. Curtis necessary."

"How long is that going to take?" Mr. James asked.

"Well, if I'm lucky, I can get in touch with him today," Gabe said. "I'm not too hopeful about that. Mr. Curtis is moving around a lot these days, looking at properties."

"We were hoping to conclude something today," Mr. Sinclair said. "We've done a lot of research. We have a lot of experience in these transactions, and we've found that extended negotiations are directly proportional to negative results."

Gabe compressed his lips and nodded. He felt like smiling. They were trying to browbeat him. He remembered Evelyn's smile when he had told her about the effect she was having on him. He borrowed her smile for the one he had just aborted. He, too, was feeling his power. He knew his client. If he went home empty-handed, telling Harry that they were unbudging on money, that he had told them to shove it, Harry would clap him on the back and still pay him a fat fee for true representation of the Curtis interests.

"Well," Gabe said, "I had no idea we were working against that kind of deadline. I'll get back to Denver in three or four days—Mr. Curtis had some other business in New York he wanted me to look into—and I'll let him know that the lines of negotiations are very short."

"But that will only delay matters," Sinclair said.

"Yes, it will," said Gabe.

"That's what we were trying to avoid."

"I'm sorry about that," Gabe said.

"Well, why don't you try to get in touch with Mr. Curtis by telephone?"

Gabe was patience itself. "I will try," he said. "Since the whole matter seems to be so pressing, and if I'm lucky enough to get hold of Harry, I'll let him know that it's a take-it-or-leave-it offer—"

"Now, just a minute," Mr. James cut in. "It's not all *that* pressing. We're talking about a large sum of money, and we wouldn't want Mr. Curtis to feel pressured. Get in touch with him. A day or two isn't going to make a difference. See what he has to say to our offer. Try to get back to us at least once more before going back to Denver."

Gabe walked out onto Fifth Avenue feeling more than a little cocky. His life had offered few opportunities to call a bluff. The cream of the coup was having two such confident hands to play with. Another rarity! Knowing that, for Harry Curtis, projecting the right image was just as important as obtaining the right profit had allowed him to play the other hand with just the right casual assurance. No wonder the successful were so successful. No wonder winning teams won. A realist, Gabe credited nothing to mystical forces, not even Evelyn's long-distance sexuality, but he did believe in the power of intangibles, the charm of charisma. FDR and JFK. Go explain the orchestration of a smile, a gesture. In one way impossible, in another quite easy. The untouchable assurance of a destiny. A supreme willingness to subordinate everything to attaining one's goal.

He walked toward his hotel unsure of the rest of the day. He had left it open that he would have dinner with his sister this evening. A look had passed over Evelyn's face when he had told her that yesterday morning, but she had drawn back from protest with almost imperceptible quickness. *Almost.* He had noticed it, and she had seen that he had noticed it, and the next look was a subtle reassurance that he had no need to worry. She wouldn't make his life uncomfortable. How could she have conveyed that in a single glance? Gabe didn't know how, but he did know that she had. Of course, he could be mistaken about it. Or if not mistaken about the glance, then about its guarantee. He suspected the strength of her resolution would decline quickly. Suddenly the Fairmont victory vanished, and he saw himself holding two other hands, neither of which gave him anything like the confidence he had exhibited a short time before.

He continued his walk south on Fifth Avenue, holding off full recognition as he had held off full recognition of Evelyn in the lounge of the Algonquin. His mind still occupied itself with the changes on the avenue. He looked into foreign banks, foreign tourist offices, airline offices, bookstores. Was it any different from the Fifth Avenue he had left ten years before? Yes. Definitely. The cachet had been badly rubbed. Somehow the distance between shop and street had disappeared. Maybe it had to do with new architectural methods, but the shops seemed to be spilling into the street, or perhaps the street was invading the shops. . . .

Would he come back to this city? For *any* reason? To live where? In one of those East Side apartment houses, gasping after lucrative clients in order to pay for every overpriced service and necessity? Why on earth should he want to do that? Such a move argued either the hairshirt or hedonism, neither of which had ever been his fancy. And yet he longed for something. He longed for the city in his head, if not the city around him. But that was really no more than longing for one's youth, for those cosmic novas of the spirit that would suddenly take fire when there was still room enough in one's time.

His room and his time were all spoken for. Weren't they? He had done his hitch in the Army. He had gone to law school. He had met Evelyn White and had envisioned a life with her. She had left him for another, and shortly after, he had met and married Jean Bernstein, who was studying art history at Hunter. They had a child quickly, and then another child two years after that, because Jean wanted her child-bearing-and-caring years done with in time to leave her a life worth living. There had been an almost fanatic determination in that, and they had lived like domestic athletes, trained by textbooks and current theories, the pediatrician their coach, the changing of infant necessities their schedule of games. Then the Denver opportunity, and the surprisingly little resistance from Jean. Why not Denver? In her usual fashion, Jean had gathered all she could find on Denver, from libraries, from government agencies, from Colorado itself, and she had learned that it was a high place, a dry place, a place of many good schools, many good hospitals, many scenic wonders. . . .

Jean. . . . Gabe at last allowed himself to think of Jean. Jean, who had gone back to school for a graduate degree in art history. An M.A.? Well, an M.A. was practically a defunct degree. A Ph.D., then? We'll see. . . . Jean, whose touchy skin had improved in the Denver climate. Jean, who had finally found a style for her kinky hair, a moderate Afro, which he had to admit was becoming. Jean, who began the second rearrangement of their lives with the same assumptions and efficiencies that had begun their marriage, finding another house that would give her the extra needed room for isolation and quiet. Jean, who still managed to know everybody else's schedules and progress, asking the pertinent questions, doing the efficacious things. It was admirable. It was a minor miracle. The only trouble—the only unspoken and scarcely conscious trouble—was that he didn't love her, hadn't loved her for years.

Was that true? And if true, did it matter? Does an athlete have to love his teammate to strive with him, to care for him, even, if necessary, to die for him? Did it matter whether he loved Jean or not, if what he *did* feel for Jean drew from him knee-jerk loyalties and responsibilities? *Did he truly not love Jean?* He had thought not for a long time. He had thought not when Evelyn White was only a vaporous patch in his past, something that thickened or thinned according to the unpredictable temperatures of memory. Didn't he love Jean as well as any man loves his wife after so many years of marriage? How the hell was one to know? There was no way of measuring the thing, because there was no way of being sure what it is. What he did know was that a certain kind of spontaneity fell dead when it encountered the image of Jean. He worried about her, he planned his life to convenience hers, but spontaneity fell dead whenever it made contact with the flesh of Jean's personality. Not Jean's *flesh.* They could still be a pair of make-out artists in that department, but the sudden expansiveness of self that is sometimes experienced in contact with another did not take place in the presence of Jean. It had not always been true. There had been moments . . . unless the moments he remembered were illusory hills placed by himself in the plateau of his days. If it hadn't been true always, it had been true for a long time.

That was the truth of Jean that hadn't even occurred to him when he had listened to Jeff Singer's banal tale of a new life. That was the truth of Jean that served as background for the colorbursts of self he had been made to feel in this week of Evelyn White.

But wouldn't it eventually be the same with Evelyn?

And would he allow whatever he felt to finally matter?

He left a message at Harry Curtis's office that he would be at his hotel until four o'clock Denver time, please to return the call.

Then he phoned his sister, Ruth, and asked if tonight would be okay. She said, "Wonderful! The kids have been so looking forward to their uncle, Gabe. They want to hear about the cowboys."

"Cowboys!"

"You know."

"I'll try to remember some of the stories I read when I was a kid in New York," he said.

He then phoned Evelyn. "I'm trying to work it out so that I can remain over the weekend," he said.

"Please try very hard," she said. "I'm making plans."

"Not too elaborate, dear," he cautioned. "The more anticipation the more disappointment if it doesn't come to pass."

"Would *you* be disappointed?"

"That's why I mentioned it," he said. "That's why I'm trying for it. Because it doesn't mean a thing to me one way or the other."

"You called me 'dear,' " she said.

"Shouldn't I have?"

"You're going to your sister tonight, aren't you?"

"How did you know?"

Evelyn didn't answer that. She said instead, "I don't call you 'dear' in the endless conversations I keep having with you."

"No? What do you call me?"

"Darling. . . . Darling Gabe. . . . Gabe darling. . . . Do you mind?"

"No, I don't mind."

"Would you say that 'darling' is more advanced than 'dear'?"

"Evelyn, you haven't answered my question."

"About how I knew about your sister? I just knew. You had that 'not-tonight' tone in your voice. I ought to know. I've been using it myself."

"Do *you* think it's more advanced?" he asked.

"Darling? Oh, yes! By far. But that's all right. I prefer words being a careful gauge of feeling."

"Now you're being foxy."

"Yes, darling."

"Well, darling, I *am* going to my sister tonight. I must, and the sooner the better. Then I can look forward to the rest of the time with you. If, that is, you don't have other plans."

"Oh, Gabe, when it crumbles, it crumbles, doesn't it?"

"What does?"

"All defenses. All caution. I want to say all the things I'll be sorry for."

"Why should you be sorry for them?"

"Because if they're not returned, measure for measure, I'll probably go into mourning."

"You shouldn't be so dependent on words."

"But I am."

"What would you like me to say?"

"Guess."

"Evelyn—"

"I know, I know, I know," she hastily interrupted. "You must proceed a responsible step at a time. Well, I owe you some advantage, and I want to say it anyway, for my sake, not yours. I'm in love with you, Gabe. Don't let it make the slightest difference in your life, and for God's sake don't let it depress you, but there it is."

After a moment's silence, Gabe said, "I don't feel advantaged. I don't feel burdened. And I don't feel depressed. What does that leave?"

"That you return the feeling?"

"Do you understand why the words weigh more heavily on me than they do on you?"

"Of course."

"When will I be able to see you tomorrow?"

"For lunch? For dinner? Shall I take the day off?"

"No, don't do that. We both need some ballast."

"Dinner, then?"

"Yes," Gabe said. "With great pleasure. As soon as you're finished with work. Say when and where we'll meet. . . ."

The phone rang a little after six o'clock, just as Gabe was about to walk over to Grand Central to get a train to Westchester. It was Harry Curtis.

"I just got in the office," Harry said. "What's doing?"

"We're haggling over money now," Gabe told him. "Actually, I think it's going quite well. They made an offer, and then pretty quickly boosted it. They started out with a multiple of eight. They saw I wasn't listening, so they quickly went to nine—"

"Gabe, I told you twelve," Harry said.

"I know you did, and I told you then it was an unrealistic figure. If you won't move on the twelve, Harry, I'll get in touch with them tomorrow and tell them so. I think that'll break it off, but that's up to you."

"What's your idea?" Harry asked.

"My idea is to let them stew for a couple of days. They want your properties. They're not going to let go of them easily. What you've got is perfect for their operation. As far as tying new construction into the contract, they're willing to offer rights of first refusal. I don't think you can reasonably ask for more. I feel they're still bargaining. I'm absolutely confident they'll go to ten on their own, and I would hope to make an agreement at eleven, which I think is a fair price. That comes to over two million, Harry."

"Are you sure they'll go to eleven?"

"Not absolutely sure, but I have a feeling they won't let it get away from them at eleven once they've gone to ten."

"When do you think you'll know?"

"I've got a hunch that if it hasn't broken off by the end of the week, we can get a deal at eleven early part of next week."

"How's the weather?"

"Lousy," Gabe said. "Cold and dreary. How's it there?"

"I just came in from nine holes. It was over sixty in the sun. What are you doing for entertainment?"

"Oh—meeting old acquaintances."

"Would you mind staying the weekend, if it goes that way?"

"No."

"Okay, Gabe, if you think they'll eventually go to eleven, sweat it out. But don't call me back and ask me how I feel about ten. I'll take eleven only for your sake."

"For *my* sake!"

"Because you're working hard. Because your efforts deserve respect."

Gabe smiled. "Okay, Harry, anything you say. Thanks."

"Stay dry," Harry said.

Gabe hung up, feeling as he did one incredible night last

spring, at one of those infrequent poker nights, when it seemed he had been appointed agent to a run of luck that was as eerily un-Michelson as it was profitable. He stayed in with pairs and won. In a betting duel, his jack-high straight beat Bruce Warren's ten-high straight. Twice he fattened two pair to a full house. Those alien cards passed through his fingers without his experiencing the slightest sense of identity. He was an amused witness at a kind of raree show, where all those hands had been programmed for the evening by a fate that had mistaken Gabe Michelson for someone else. Now, too, he felt himself, in part, a volitionless agent of events that had been programmed to work out in this way and in no other.

Gabe got up from the bed, where he had been sitting, and went to the closet for his coat. In those few steps, he caught a sudden glimpse of just how much he had contributed to each of the hands that had been played since Sunday evening. . . . *Not the same game at all!*

Ruth had done some preliminary rearrangement in the hope she could persuade her brother to stay overnight. She had set up all the kids' beds in one room, leaving one of the bedrooms available for Gabe. But the apartment was like an unsavory stew, thick with all kinds of leftovers—broken toys, broken furniture, soiled clothes —and a smell that made Gabe feel that all of it had been simmered for years in sour milk. And even that wouldn't have deterred him from spending the night for Ruth's sake—he'd spent uncomfortable nights before—but the fear of finally letting fly at Arthur was too imminently real to risk it.

For a man in Arthur's position to have stayed the same meant getting fatally worse. How old was the *schlemiel* anyway? Surely his early forties—although he had the kind of skin and eyes that go to the grave still touched by divine innocence. Others could seam and shrivel, but Arthur moved myopically through the years as moist and fresh as a morning flower. He was not merely nowhere: he was *permanently* nowhere. Too late to study anything (although it was really too late for that from birth), too late (if he had any brains or conscience) to venture into anything new, he talked about his pinball-machine nonsense as if he were a surfeited millionaire dabbling for the fun of it. There was, he claimed, big money in pinball machines. Not in keeping them in repair—which was what he was helping someone else do at the moment—but buying them and leasing them and collecting the coins out of the coin boxes. Some of the new, electronic ones got to be very popular, and he (Arthur, the Renaissance man) knew a little something about electronics, and he had an idea he'd like to try to patent. . . .

It dawned on Gabe, with a grieving heart, that his sister had played the loyal wife once again in luring her lawyer brother out to the house for a little free legal advice. Well, he'd give the advice, and his payment would be a polite but adamant refusal to spend the night. He'd felt at first that he was being too thin-skinned to refuse on grounds of mere distaste, but since Arthur had set up the *quid pro quo,* he'd take it, mournfully but gratefully.

"I may be mistaken about this, Arthur," he said, "but I seem to have heard somewhere that the real money in pinball machines is in the hands of racketeers."

"I don't know," Arthur said, shrugging. "Maybe. There are racketeers in everything. That doesn't bother me. If I could get a patent, they couldn't touch me."

"Get a patent for what?"

Arthur explained his idea. It was a horoscope pinball machine. You play it like an ordinary pinball game, but you set it at your zodiac sign, and at the end of a series of pings and flashes a ticket comes out predicting your future. "But isn't there something like that already?" Gabe asked. Arthur had researched the whole matter. There was something like it but not an electronically controlled, up-to-date machine.

"But what is it, exactly, that you would want to patent?" Gabe asked again.

"The idea," Arthur said.

"Of a pinball machine?"

"Of the pinball horoscope."

Gabe swallowed his mounting fury. He had done that so often during the evening that by this time it was like the thickness of phlegm in his throat. If the fool had stopped to think for a moment, he would realize that there was nothing patentable about any aspect of the whole, sorry mud-pie of an idea. Surely even

Arthur must realize that horoscopes and zodiacs and pinballs had been around for at least as long as Arthur Ehrlich. Surely the rawest common sense would have warned one away from so bootless a quest. Gabe glanced at Ruth in a searching, admonitory way, as if to ask why she hadn't put a stop to this latest futility, but what he saw in her eyes made him put a halt to attitudes and judgments. He saw understanding and sadness and narcosis in her eyes. What he saw made him at last touch bottom in the long, downward drift of hope. He saw that his dear, loyal, life-giving Ruth had taken on for preservation's sake the coloration of the clown she lived with. Her head tilted slightly at a listening angle, and her naturally healthy complexion seemed to be rubbed with the same dream-patina of innocence that had been the mark of the man she had chosen for husband.

So Gabe said nothing of what he knew and what he felt. He said he would look into it when he got back to Denver and write Arthur a letter advising him on the possibilities of patenting his idea. Ruth nodded contentedly at the suggestion, evidently finding in it enough time and muddle to dissipate this latest hope into harmlessness.

And later, traveling back to the city on a late suburban train, Gabe pondered deeply the question he didn't dare ask when he had had those few minutes of opportunity with Ruth. Arthur had gone to the children's bedroom to read them the stories that had become his custom each evening. There was no point in asking why she put up with it—he already knew that—but he did want to know how much of a sense of loss she lived with. Hers must be enormous compared to his own—or was it not a matter of quantity at all, but only the temperament that made it possible to accept one's losses, great or small, and go on living one's life as if there was something inevitable in its design?

Ruth began to reminisce as soon as they were alone, recalling the house on Pelham Parkway, and how when they were kids he would take her to the movies on a Sunday afternoon, coming back in the late afternoon for hot cocoa. From there, she went to the apartment they had moved to after their father died—and it became clear to Gabe that this deliberate evocation of the past was a cheerful plea to stay away from the incurable present.

Gabe walked from Grand Central Station to his hotel. Six or seven blocks. It was almost eleven-thirty. Not late, and yet the same spooky feeling he had felt Monday night, when he had dinner with Evelyn and walked with her to her apartment house on the East Side. There was some vehicular traffic, few pedestrians. People arranged their lives so that certain areas could be avoided after nightfall—this, evidently, being one of them. How different when he had lived here, rushing anywhere at any time, purpose out of mind, the subterranean crisscrossing of the city, and always the feeling of movement and population and safety. This was a deserted city. The desolation of it made him move more quickly until he reached Fifth Avenue.

Fifth was no better. It was just as deserted. Even the street lighting seemed dimmer than he remembered. The vehicular traffic was lighter here. Naturally. Fifth Avenue was one way south. Those who had come to the city for pleasure this evening were out of it by now. Those who lived in the city were immured in the safety of their apartments. There was a very definite sense of danger in these dark and empty streets; but even more than the possible physical danger was the sense of abandonment; the feeling that he had experienced on the subway when he was going to meet Jeff Singer; the coming change of state; the removal of humanity and love from the vast transience of the city. The only difference was that he was no longer a disinterested voyager catching an exotic whiff of history that was not his own. He felt no closer to the city itself, but the mood of transience it generated fed into and upon his own.

He brought this mood with him into the hotel room. He switched on the television set, looked for a minute or so at an old movie he knew he had seen years before, one of those standard wagon-train epics with Gary Cooper; and then he turned the dial from channel to channel until at last he switched it off. It was almost midnight. He wouldn't dream of phoning Evelyn at this hour. She would be asleep. She had a job to which she must go tomorrow morning. It was not in his nature to impose his own fugitive terrors on others. But wouldn't this be just the kind of gesture Evelyn would welcome? Might she not be hoping that all the turbulence of this eventful week might prompt him to do what it was not in his nature to do? Wouldn't the impulse be explanation enough?

He went to the phone, dialed 9 for an outside call, and then Evelyn's number, which he had written on the cover of the Manhattan directory. The connection was made, the signal sounded once, twice, three times, four, five, and he gently replaced the phone. Asleep? Not awakened by the phone ringing? Was that possible? It wouldn't be for him. The sound of a telephone ringing would jolt him wide awake at the very first ring. That was Gabe Michelson, not necessarily others. Evelyn? Conceivably not Evelyn. What did he know of the pattern of her sleep? A light sleeper? One of those who plunged into sleep as to the bottom of an ocean where no sound or light could penetrate? What did he know about Evelyn that he should assume with such certainty that she was simply not at home?

He dialed again, allowed five rings, and then replaced the phone again. He knew as surely as he was sitting in this room that Evelyn was not asleep in hers, and the certainty started up a brushfire of suspicions. Was this all a week's diversion in the life of Evelyn White? A repetition of the first experience? No! Out of the question! That was much more sentimental and unlikely than anything Evelyn had actually done, said, or implied. Good God, she was a divorced woman, with a son, with friends, with relatives, with an ex—or not-so-ex—lover, or perhaps more than one lover, or perhaps none at all. But, in any event, her absence from her apartment could be accounted for in more ordinary ways than he could imagine. Staying with a friend—possibly just to talk over the troubling business of Gabe Michelson re-entering her life. Staying with a relative—as he was supposed to be doing. And suppose neither of these things; suppose she was with her present or former lover? Would that falsify everything she had said to him? Of course not! The gestures of love continue far beyond its secret death. Who should know that better than he?

And with each cool application of reason, his fever mounted. He remembered Jeff Singer again. He remembered Jeff's words of many years before. He remembered almost verbatim, because their consequences gave them such memorability. . . . *"Proust, Gabe. Everything important in the world of men and women and time and love is to be found in Proust. It's particularly important for a lawyer to read Proust. You will know the human heart that much better, and that will make you a better lawyer. . . ."*

He had read Proust—slowly, impatiently, laboriously, and then with a growing appreciation of the sick Frenchman's genius—and he had finally to agree with Jeff's judgment. He couldn't be sure it had made him a better lawyer, but it did confirm the universality of the human heart. And now he was remembering Charles Swann and Odette, and that fateful evening when Swann missed the woman who wasn't his style at the Verdurins'. He had understood it before, but now he could almost laugh at the uselessness of recognition. He was jealous at the thought of Evelyn being with another man. He was left with a dry anguish at the thought of Evelyn taking away the tremulous, tender, perfumed, gorgeous gift of love. He sat on the edge of the hotel bed and gripped his knees and vowed that he would take a dive through that window before phoning again.

He phoned again. It was twelve-thirty. There was no answer. He took a shower and got into bed. Somewhere between an astonishment of grief and a profundity of self-reproach, he fell asleep.

11

"Do you really want advice?" Joanna asked.

"Which means," said Evelyn, "that you don't think advice is worth much."

"Is it ever? However—*do* you?"

"Say *something*."

"Have you gone to bed with him?"

"Yes. Does that make a difference?"

"Certainly it makes a difference," Joanna said. "Not the screwing itself, but the fact that you would let it go that far. Evelyn, you're not looking for some kind of moral justification in this thing, are you?"

Evelyn gazed out the large window. They were having lunch in Joanna's office, which was a very attractive office, looking as if Matisse had had a hand in it. Pale yellow walls and intense blots of color worked against that background in upholstery fabrics, hangings, and bric-a-brac. The employment agency occupied the top floor in one of those three-story brownstone buildings left over from the past century. There were four other interviewing offices besides Joanna's private office. Joanna's philosophy of "body snatching" was to seduce the potential employer as well as the potential employee, so she had made her office into a place of charm and privacy, with a round marble table, Scandinavian rugs, and elegant easy chairs. There was a coffee shop around the corner that made excellent hot lunches that the proprietor was willing to prepare on a tray and send over. A large picture window looked out on the side street, and an air-conditioning unit kept out most of the noise and dirt. Much more comfortable than most of the expensive restaurants, particularly around lunchtime.

"Why shouldn't I seek moral justification?" Evelyn asked, never quite sure where Joanna's sarcasms ended and her sincerities began. "There are lots of lives involved. Gabe has a wife and two children—"

"Has he talked to you about leaving them?"

"No."

"What makes you think he would?"

"I don't say he would. I'm just looking at the thing."

Joanna studied Evelyn for several long seconds with those gray-green eyes, then shook her head. "When is he going back to Denver?" she asked.

"It's uncertain. I think he's trying to extend the one week into two."

"Evelyn, what is it that you're looking at? Would you want Gabe Michelson to divorce his wife, leave his children, move back to New York, and marry you?"

"With my eyes closed—and very quickly—*yes*," Evelyn replied.

"That's asking a hell of a lot."

"If you have to ask, then, yes, I agree, it's asking a hell of a lot. But if it's something that wants to happen, then all those big things are details. . . . I keep coming back to the other thing: How many people will be hurt? Do I have the right?"

"Why Gabe?" Joanna asked, now genuinely curious. "I mean, you're a very attractive woman. You have only to sit still and men come to you. Frank Moore is a good-looking, intelligent, talented man. He can be a pain in the ass, I know, but who is not when you know him, her, anybody, long enough? But if not Frank, there'll always be someone else. Why take on these complications? Why Gabe?"

"Are you serious?"

"Of course I'm serious."

"You're seriously asking me why one man and not another? *You!* Why do *you* fall in love with the men you fall in love with?"

"Because I'm me," Joanna replied. "My love affairs are fantasies. You know that. I fall in love with a frog and make him into a prince. But I've always assumed that you were different. You see more clearly. You see what the rest of the world sees, not some illusion you create for yourself."

"I don't understand, Joanna," Evelyn said, shaking her head. "What you're saying argues the opposite of 'Why Gabe'? If I see more clearly, then I'm seeing *Gabe* more clearly, and falling in love with him *isn't* a fantasy, an illusion."

"I'm sorry, love, but I don't see it that way," Joanna declared. "If you see a man clearly, then you're halfway through loving him. At least you see the clay. Not that you can't love a clayey man, but if you have to hack your way through a jungle of difficulties, you might decide not to love that particular one."

"And you feel that such decisions can be made rationally?" Evelyn asked.

"You can pretend it's the birth and death of passion, but yes, why not? Isn't there always a split second, before you go off the diving board, when it's possible to turn around and crawl back on all fours? If you're off, you're off, and that's why I asked you if you really wanted advice. But, look, you decided not to love Lew, didn't you?"

"*I* didn't decide it. He decided it for me. He made himself unlovable."

"Somebody else married him," Joanna pointed out. "He made himself unlovable to *you*."

"You mean he could act differently to somebody else?"

"Perhaps not, but somebody else wouldn't see his behavior as you did. Or Frank Moore's behavior, which you tell me you see as a long, undermining operation. That's all I'm saying. You do see what *is*, from the start. I don't."

"Maybe that's why I've fallen in love with Gabe Michelson," Evelyn said. "What *is* is a very nice man. He's an 'integ' man, Jo. He has a sense of humor. It takes no conscious effort on his part to see me as another, complete human being. It seems to come naturally. He asked me did I want to spend the night with him in such a way that I knew he was thinking of *me*. He meant did *I* want to spend the night with him. Oh, I'm sure he wanted to get into bed with me—I'd be insulted if he didn't—but, for a real moment, his attention moved away from what he wanted to what I might possibly want. When he sat down next to me at the Algonquin, he asked me what I was drinking, and when I told him, he said he'd have sherry too. I don't know whether he likes sherry or not—he said he did—but he *asked*. It seems to me that his instinct is to find out what's special about my existence, which is *exactly* what I've done with every man I ever cared for. To find it returned for once makes me feel that I've been a good girl, and that God is at last rewarding me."

"And how hurt will you be if he goes back to Denver and stays there?" Joanna asked.

"I don't know," Evelyn said. "Plenty, I suppose."

"You'd better be prepared for it."

"I am."

She was. At least, she counseled herself, out of all the common sense and experience she knew herself to possess, to expect no more than obvious circumstances were likely to bring. Gabe's law practice was established in a city two thousand miles away, a very pleasant city where life was easier and much less expensive. Gabe was a man who took his responsibilities seriously. Gabe was a man who when faced with a choice between his own desires and the needs of those to whom he was responsible would undoubtedly opt for the latter. She compelled herself to look at these things as clearly and logically as she could.

Joanna was right, of course. The facts were overwhelming. Who in his right mind would expect a keystone to slip out of place and fall to the ground? All right, then, *expect nothing! . . . I expect nothing! . . .* The only possibility to prop against that crushing weight of reality was Gabe's own unhappiness. Was he unhappy? Unhappy, that is, with his marriage, with the mysterious Jean, whose formidable existence stretched across her imagination like the Rockies stretched across the continent?

But the one thing she must not do is mention Jean, hint at Jean, try in any way to put down Jean. Not only would that be a tactical blunder but a piece of gratuitous nastiness as well. For her own self-respect, she must avoid falling into that tacky trap. She knew nothing about Jean. The very thing she liked about Gabe now worked against her. She had admired the respect he'd shown: to her in acts of commission, to all that claimed him by the deference of omission; and therefore she must show an equal respect for his integrity. She knew nothing about Jean, or about Gabe's relationship with the woman. She must not assume that it was bad. It might very well be good. It might be wonderful. But could he have acted toward *her* as he had if it were wonderful? Yes . . . sadly, fearfully, humanly, yes. Men and women were not that different. She knew that it had always been possible for her to find diverting sweetness with another man even when she was still much committed to Lew. It just hadn't happened. There hadn't been that other man. Why, then, couldn't Gabe find diverting sweetness with her while in no way diminishing whatever he felt for his Rocky Mountain fastness? He could! He could—and probably did!

She spent the afternoon flailing at these ghosts between the solid bouts of work she had to get done. There was a pile-up of correspondence left from the convention. There was that proposal for a new series that she had promised Don to get into some kind of shape before the end of the week. This one was aimed at the junior-high level: career thinking in the light of today's world. It was Don's idea that a fresh look at real opportunities, and the lack of them, must be taken, and the information distilled in such a way as to be meaningful to teen-agers. Don was a sweetheart, and his ideas were generally good ones, but sometimes Evelyn wondered if in his sweet way he had any idea of the amount of work he heaped on others. Yes. Of course he had. That's why he was successful in his business, because he had good ideas and he knew how to get them carried out without exactly destroying the troops.

And she knew where to look for the stuff that was needed. She had sent away to the appropriate government agencies for the necessary information, and she had already received booklets. There were mountains before her. Damn mountains anyway! Well, she could do her work with other things on her mind. She had taught herself to do that during those last months with Lew, when he had simply moved into another life, leaving her to deal with lawyers and leases and apartments and explanations. She was the one who wanted out, wasn't she? Yes, she was. She had taught herself to divide a day into each of its hours—watertight hours, each sealed off from the others. And she could do it now, although it was harder, wanting something being much more wearing than not wanting something. It *was* wearing, having to shut so many doors that blew open in sudden gusts of fear and longing. How could she help but blame the source of the weariness, even though she knew it was not his fault? Still, when he phoned early in the afternoon, confirming that he would be spending that evening with his sister, she had forgotten the weariness, the awful speculations, the half-resolved resolutions, and had somehow shrunk all the immensities into an inane exchange about the relative significance of "dear" and "darling."

Stupidly, she felt better. Unreasonably, she hoped he would phone again—and when her phone did ring at about four in the afternoon, she was sure it was Gabe—but it wasn't; it was Frank.

Two summers before, Evelyn had spent her vacation at a beach resort near Montauk, on Long Island. One week with Jay, one week with Joanna. It was really a nice arrangement: tennis courts on the grounds, kitchen facilities, sun decks, and a few shuffling, sandy yards from the apartment to the wide, clean, dune-crested beach. She had chosen the place to entice Jay, who was rapidly becoming a tennis nut. . . .

"But who am I going to play with?"

"Well, me."

"Oh, Mom!"

"I mean until somebody real comes along."

Actually, she had conned herself into believing she gave Jay a fairly decent game, until she learned that her son gentled his ground strokes and practically emasculated his serve to keep from frightening her off the court.

But Jay had agreed to come, and he had a marvelous time that week, meeting another kid who was his match, and more, on the court, and who had a sister, which sister and the two boys went to places where rock bands played every night. Jay returned to the city after the week, joining his father, who was going to some posh place on the Carolina coast for more tennis. Life was really simple for people with a passion. Musicians went to Tanglewood. Dancers went to Jacob's Pillow. Tennis players went to wherever there were courts. Of course, money helped. Some people stayed in the city and roasted—which the tall, boozing gentleman pointed out belligerently to the other, more muscular gentleman at the party Joanna and she attended during the second week. The party was in East Hampton. Joanna had friends there, had contacted the friends, and was invited, along with anyone she cared to bring, to a big literary bash.

If several people hadn't intervened, Frank Moore would probably have wound up with a badly damaged face. He was no match for the other man, who was obviously younger, and chestier, and cleaner-living. But Frank wasn't backing off. They were on their way outside the house to settle the matter when a couple of Frank's friends interceded and talked the younger man away and Frank into another drink.

One of Joanna's friends finally got around to introducing Frank Moore. His novel, *The Other Island,* was scheduled for publication in a month, but some of the trade reviews were already in, and they were good. Frank Moore was at that enviable moment in life when one's future seems to promise nothing but acclaim for one's past. But as Evelyn was shortly to learn, Frank Moore was the kind of man who could be toppled from his precarious perch by a nudge from either side of fate. He drank to celebrate good news, and he drank to quench bad news, and drinking provided him with a personality that was impervious to both good and bad. When he drank, he was transformed into a knightly defender of that other man who dwelt so peerlessly in his head. Not the man *himself,* because the man himself wouldn't get so drunk and insulting and ridiculously touchy, but the spiritual bodyguard of that man, ready to start punching for his ideas and ideals.

"I suppose that was a typically idiotic performance," he said to Evelyn, claiming her arm and steering her toward the veranda, where there were Japanese lanterns.

"I wouldn't know," she said. "I don't know what's typical."

"Well," he said, "I can assure you that not only was it typical, but *quintessentially* typical. Besides which, the sonofabitch would probably have slaughtered me."

"Then why were you marching out there so eagerly?"

"Damned if I know. It's a good question. Honor? Do you believe in honor?"

"Obviously not your kind."

"Naturally. Terribly old-fashioned, my kind of honor. I don't believe in it myself, to tell you the truth. I guess what I do believe is that certain people haven't got the right to certain opinions. That isn't a question of honor, is it? That's just being an intolerant, howling nuisance. I apologize. I apologize to you, particularly, because I have a feeling that I would greatly value your good opinion."

Belligerence and charm. He wanted to know if there was any chance of seeing her tomorrow, the day after, anywhere, anytime, and she told him, quickly and regretfully, that she was expecting the arrival of friends tomorrow, that she would be spending her time with them. . . . The embarrassing thing was that she felt sure that she had been invited along with Joanna at Joanna's request, but that it was toward *Joanna* that Frank Moore was supposed to be directing his charm. Joanna had mentioned that the party was given to more or less celebrate Frank's impending publication, and Evelyn secretly believed that Joanna had known of these arrangements beforehand and had accepted a week with Evelyn White because it would bring her closer to a desired meeting. Joanna had looked with interest at Frank, but Frank, after a look, had looked only at Evelyn, and it seemed to Evelyn that her only move was to side-step the whole thing as adroitly as possible.

But Frank now stood between the light of the room and the lantern light of the veranda and waggled his glass before her in some sort of signal.

"If you're asking me do I want a drink, the answer is no," she said.

"No, I'm not asking you that," he said. "I'm trying to indicate, in my pride-saving way, that I understand it's *this* you're saying no to. I'm trying to indicate that I understand you don't relish the company of sloppy drunks."

That was true enough, whether it was her prime motive or not. She hadn't even thought of it—she had been too busy thinking of basic diplomacies—but now that he mentioned it, yes, she *didn't* relish the company of drunks, however interesting or charming. In fact, she had a mild horror of drunks, having had the childhood experience of her family's sorrow over a great-uncle's strange and shameful disease. For a long time, she thought it was some internal, rotting thing against which he had to swallow that amber medicine; and when she learned that the medicine was the disease, she conceived a lifelong contempt for those who took such medicine when they weren't even sick.

"I'm drunk at the moment," Frank said, "but I'm not *a* drunk.

I'm sure you've heard it before, but in truth I can leave it alone.
I'd like to prove that to you, if I may. Do you live in New York?"

"Yes."

"May I get in touch with you there?"

That seemed fair enough. Why shouldn't she? Just the promise
of sobriety had produced a sobering effect on Frank Moore, and
she suddenly saw, behind the obscuring veils of Joanna's priority
and Frank's drunkenness, an attractive man.

"If you will do me a favor," she said.

"Name it."

"Joanna Hopkins has read your novel and admires it greatly.
She's been looking forward to talking to you. Could you do that
without making it appear managed?"

"You mean the lady you were with?"

"That one."

Mr. Moore smiled. "And suppose," he said, "that I find your
friend Joanna the true companion of my soul?"

"Then you'll be acting soberer than you look, and showing
great good taste."

"Because Joanna is really the more sensitive, much more beautiful person—right?"

"I happen to think so," Evelyn said.

Frank nodded over his still swaying glass with monkish solemnity. He said, "All in all, I find women a finer breed. I've been
told, by women, that I'm a fool for thinking so, that female aggression just comes in a different form, but until I'm convinced by
my own experience I'll refuse to believe it. . . . All right, Evelyn
White, you give me a telephone number where you can be
reached, and I will do as you ask. I guarantee satisfaction. If
Joanna even hints at being set up, you call me a lousy amateur
when I phone, and hang up. And I *will* phone. Depend on it."

Later that evening, Evelyn saw Joanna engaged in deep conversation with Frank Moore. And Frank demonstrated his competence by not even glancing at her once the rest of that evening.
She felt a little piqued at the thorough way in which he carried out
his promise, and was more than a little surprised at his call the
following Monday.

They started going out. Ironically, Frank's enthusiasm for films
was equal to that of Lew's. She told him so, and he replied that he

hoped she was not the kind who judged an art form or an idea by its devotees. Very unfair, that. Like blaming God for the quality of his worshipers. She said that she hadn't blamed or thanked God for anything in years. Had he? Frank shrugged away the question of God in a way that made Evelyn feel that he'd been shrugging away the question his whole life.

Whatever his judgment on God, his judgment on films was informed and copious. So they went to many films. Old ones and new ones. And she enjoyed movies more with Frank for company —much more than she had with Lew. He pointed out things she had never looked for in films. His feeling for the great old ones approached reverence. Oddly, he didn't care for the stage at all. He said it was a different thing entirely—all an actor's show—and he didn't particularly care for actors. Liked them when their talents were made subsidiary to the whole, but found them offensive when they strutted all over the stage. So they went to many movies, and they went to poetry readings at the Poetry Center, and they went to jazz concerts in the Village and elsewhere, and had, all in all, a fine time together.

In a sense, they were neighbors. They both lived on the East Side. She in the sixties, Frank in the eighties. "Come to my place," he had said the first time they dated, and Evelyn said no. "Am I not sober?" he asked. She laughed and asked if he thought that that was all that was needed. "I also had the idea that you liked me," he said. "I do," she said. Now he grinned. "And that, too, won't get it?" She told him to stop looking for a combination. As far as going home with him, and all that implied, she would do it if and when she felt like it.

She felt like it long before she admitted to the feeling. She had been to bed with only one man since Lew, a married man, and she hadn't been too pleased with the aftereffects. She wanted to know Frank better. She wanted to feel more secure about his drinking. And when she did know more, felt more secure, she did go to his apartment. Frank embraced her and kissed her and succeeded in making her very desirous. Then he had a drink. It was the first drink she'd seen him take besides the one cocktail, or the one glass of wine, he allowed himself at dinner.

"Why that?" she asked.

"Because I'm afraid of what might not happen without it," he replied.

"Is that a problem?"

"Darling, I don't know what the problem is. Whether I drink from fear of the other, or suffer the other from drink. But allow me this indulgence, at least this once. I want very much to be the complete man with you."

She allowed him the indulgence. She went on allowing him the indulgence every time they made love, because she understood that Frank Moore's fears were many and deep, having to do with God and manhood and his crucifying need to be better than he was. There was so much to care for in Frank that she could easily see a life consumed in doing so. Perhaps she had been waiting for a reason strong enough to prevent its consuming hers.

Frank claimed he had gotten the tickets from his Boston aunt, who had bought them long in advance and who was obliged to spend the evening with the sick friend who was supposed to have accompanied the aunt to the opera. It sounded too devious to be true. Evelyn could see the pride-saving nuts and bolts in the construction. Just to have telephoned her after losing his last appeal would have been too humbling, but the excuse of a windfall gave a nice veneer of magnanimity to his ego.

The opera was *Don Giovanni*—and Evelyn recalled once saying to Frank that a Mozart opera would be a welcome change from the jazz groups he blithely assumed made the only music fit for modern sensibilities.

She wondered what she would have said to Frank if Gabe hadn't decided to make that visit to his sister. *Said*—because what she would have done was no longer a matter of doubt. She would be with Gabe every minute of the day and night he would allow her to be. She'd feign the excuse of sickness, of an emergency call to Coral Gables, to be with Gabe during the hours of her working day. Jittery as she was with immediate desires and coming crises, she would probably have blurted out the truth to Frank. She would probably have told him that the old friend was an old lover, a new lover, the lover celebrated in song and story. She would probably have asked Frank to understand and support her condition, because while he had his writing—and she had always supported *that*, hadn't she?—she had only this waiting love. . . . Good God, would she say things like that to Frank? She devoutly hoped not! That's all both their prides would need! Frank would dive into the nearest bottle, and she would retire into a mental nunnery of remorse. No, she wouldn't have said anything like that. Common sense and vanity would always save her from such extremes. But she was running scared. And perhaps the interval of an evening with Frank was what she needed. Perhaps she would be able to say something to Frank that was neither confession nor contrition, but just the right words that would give him to understand everything all at once, and would make him the wise counselor, the good friend. . . . *Some chance!* . . . *Some bloody chance!* . . .

No, he hadn't gotten those tickets from his Boston aunt. He had probably paid scalper's prices for tickets to *Don Giovanni*, and the impulse to say no to Frank, no to this gesture, shook her badly. She saw herself falling into the same follies and cruelties that had scarred her conscience in the past. She saw herself doing again what she had once done to Gabe—and suddenly, *shiningly*, the occasion presented itself as an omen of the future. *If she behaved well, fate would be good to her!* . . . Oh, Lord, let her not fall into the humiliation of horoscopes and tea leaves! But she knew she must go with Frank this Gabe-less evening. Fate and signs aside, she must try to behave decently. She had lived long enough to know how long regret could live with you.

She agreed to go to the opera with Frank, which necessitated rushing back to the apartment to change into something appropriate, which made dinner first out of the question. They agreed to grab a quick bite separately and then have something after the opera. They met in the lobby. Frank looked a little puffy-eyed. Evelyn knew he'd been drinking—not compulsively, that would ruin everything, but just enough to put a merciful haze around the crisis of the past few days.

The performance was magnificent. There were even a few moments when Evelyn could forget everything. She envied Zerlina. She wished *she* could ask forgiveness so effortlessly. A sure sign of her nervousness, such sentimentality. And after the opera, they went to a nearby place for dinner.

"I'd never seen it before," Frank said. "I was impressed. I confess I was impressed. I particularly liked that business at the end: the Don saying no even though he knew there'd be hell to pay. And then—immediately after, all that merriment. I wish there was something like it in my racket. It takes so *long* to get from grief to happiness in prose. . . . How come your Denver friend gave you the night off?"

"He's visiting his sister in Westchester somewhere."

Frank glanced at her. He had ordered a martini, and he fingered the sides of the glass as if it were a prayer of comfort in braille. "I'm surprised to learn there's a sister. I thought you were all he had in the world. Why didn't his sister provide him with the necessary cheer?"

"Because his sister is his sister, and I'm a friend. . . . I thought this was going to be a pleasant evening."

"Hasn't it been?"

"I sense a rapid erosion."

They both became aware of the narrowing margin of tolerance: the unspoken rights of lovers in each other's private lives. Love *was* an abrogation of freedom, no matter how much one raged against it, and the ease with which one reclaims one's freedom is a measure of love's decline.

"When does Birnam Wood go home?" Frank asked.

"What?"

"I'm thinking of poor old Macbeth. May I make a statement? I care for you very much. Love is probably the right word. I think I can say quite definitely that love is the right word. You may regard love as being something other than what you've seen from me, but that doesn't mean a damn thing. We all have our prejudices about love—and our hang-ups in expressing it. I wish I could say that for the sake of not losing out—let me finish, it won't be much longer—I wish I could say that for the sake of not losing out I'm about to become a different sort of man, but I know damn well I'm not about to become a different sort of anything. I've tried. You have no idea how much I've tried. You have no idea how much my behavior with you represents a compromising Moore. Christ, I've stopped drinking! This"—he indicated his martini glass—"is nothing. Just something to hold onto. But I'm not going to become a different man. The ego is set. I know I ask a lot, but I also try to give a lot—patience, I'm almost through—I don't think you can say you've found life dull with me. And there *is* a great deal of dullness in life. I think life would be dull with Mr. Michelson—"

"How do you know his name is Michelson?" Evelyn interrupted.

Frank examined his glass acutely. "Because you told me his name was Michelson," he replied.

"No, I didn't, Frank. I didn't mention his name at all."

"But you did," Frank said without looking up at her. "Not tonight, perhaps, but earlier in the week—when was it? Monday?—you said Gabe Michelson. . . . As a matter of fact, I think his name came up once or twice before this auspicious week."

"Never," Evelyn said, also incapable of a direct look, already hurt and embarrassed and angry and a little scared at the direction of her thoughts.

"How can you be so sure?" Frank asked.

"Who, Frank?" she asked. "Joanna?"

Frank opened his mouth to protest, then closed it and nodded his head. "Yes," he said.

"That I didn't expect," she said. "From you—or Joanna."

"Shouldn't that prove something?" he asked. "Yes, I cared enough to make inquiries. Let's get married, Evelyn. Let's do it quickly and spare ourselves sorrow."

"Frank, I couldn't. I'm in love with Gabe Michelson."

"Well, of course I knew that," Frank said. "I recognized the tune you were playing. But you'll fuck up your life, dear Evelyn. Mine as well. You know, you amaze me. You're so level-headed in so many ways, and yet so error-prone in the vital ones. Lew Pressman was a bad mistake, and now you're about to make another."

"You're much more like Lew than Gabe is," Evelyn said.

"You're wrong. Lew brought you nothing but the fish heads and bones of his life. I bring you the best that's in me. I may steep it in bile at times, but I bring you the best that's in me."

That was true. She had seen him with others and knew how completely he could disguise himself in civility or sarcasm, but he had always revealed his true being to her. Fears and elations. For a quick, experimental moment, she imagined the possibility Frank proposed. Gabe would go home. God knows if she would ever hear from him again. She would marry Frank. Close her eyes and marry Frank. Inwardly, she opened her eyes and saw the difference. Gabe opened her to herself in ways that made her want to sing for joy. Frank closed off access to her own being by the ever-increasing needs of his.

"There's nothing I can do about the way I feel," she said, rather lamely, even having lost her anger at the conspiracy she had uncovered.

"And you feel that strongly?" he asked.

"I'm afraid so."

Frank looked away at something behind her for long, silent seconds. "You might have pretended otherwise," he said at last.

"What would be the point?"

"Oh, I don't know," he said. "You make such a big deal of feelings. You might have spared mine."

It was almost one in the morning by the time she got back to her apartment. The whole thing had renewed itself again, and they had talked and talked. She understood that Frank was asking to have the poison removed from his wound, and it became impossible to refuse. She compromised. She said she was feeling this way now, please to give her time, to see what would happen in a week, a month, and the possibility that she might be mistaken in her feelings salvaged Frank's a little. She was getting older. She had learned to suspect the virtue in complete honesty—as she had tried to make clear to Doris McAuley. Her instinct was to be honest, but her experience reminded her of long and unpredictable consequences.

There was no way of reaching Gabe. She would have given much for a minute's exchange with Gabe. But he might as well be on the moon. He was at his sister's home. There was no number, no name—not that she would have dared call even if she had that information. She looked at the telephone and listened to its dense silence, feeling an instant's intense hatred against the whole unmanageable mess of love.

12

The Fairmont people contacted Gabe on Thursday. Mr. Sinclair told him they were reviewing the whole thing—would his other business keep him in New York over the weekend? It would. Good. They proposed another meeting on Monday, at which time it was Mr. Sinclair's guess they'd come up with a firm offer that Mr. Michelson could take back to his client.

Gabe telephoned Jean before she went off to her class.

"It's going to spill over into the weekend," he told her.

"Oh, damn! I was hoping you'd be home by the weekend."

"Anything special?"

"No, nothing special. I miss you."

"Well, that's good to know. Are you sure there's nothing else?"

"Alice Kirschner called to invite us to dinner Saturday night."

"Aha!"

"I told her if you came back in time."

"You call her again and tell her I will not be back in time but that you will be coming under your own, free-wheeling, husband-less power."

Jean said she wouldn't, and Gabe said she would, not to be absurd, that the Kirschners invited the Michelsons largely because of Jean, and Jean said that was even more absurd, and Gabe laughed and said that at this distance it was a little too expensive to argue the point. They'd settle the true nature of the Michelson-Kirschner axis when he got home, but, for the present, assume that there was at least as much interest in Jean as in Gabe, so she was to get her ass over to the Kirschners' and enjoy an evening of Alex Kirschner's whiskey sours and high-level art talk. Jean said she didn't remember the last time she'd gone to a dinner party without him, and she thought it would give her all kinds of strange feelings. . . .

"Nonsense," Gabe said. "You've resumed a career, and you're going to be interested in people who don't necessarily interest me, or whom I don't interest."

"That's just not true," Jean said, a little edgily. "Don't try to make me feel guilty. You've always been interested in art."

"Yes, I have," he admitted. "That doesn't necessarily mean that I'm interested in artists. Just as you've always been interested in my career but rarely interested in my clients. For which I don't blame you. Some of them have been clods of the first magnitude. Harry Curtis, for one, who you said you always pictured with a meat cleaver in his hand. . . . What the hell are we talking about, anyway? . . . Listen, how are the kids?"

"Fine. Andy took a haircut."

"Mazel tov!"

"You'd never tell the difference."

"It's a concession," Gabe said. "Maybe it'll lead to smaller and better things. And Pam?"

"We had another fight. She's being impossible."

"I know. Christ, I wouldn't want to be growing up in her world. . . ."

"Gabe, we've got to have a talk about her."

"We will. Do me a favor, Jean, and make a truce now. We'll have a big Geneva conference when I get home. You and me and Pam and Israel. . . . By the way, Jeff was in touch with me again, asked me to have dinner with them Saturday. Listen, have a good time at the Kirschners'. Give them my best. I'll call up again on Sunday—around noon, your time—tell the kids I'll be calling then—I want them to be there so I can say hello—okay?"

"Okay. . . . Gabe, why is it you never say anything about your big deal? How is it going?"

"I think it's in the bag."

"Are we going to be rich?"

"No—but richer."

"Oh, how nice!"

"Stay well."

"Good-by, darling."

The weather was turning threatening again. Gabe consulted the *Times* weather map and saw that the complicated system that had caused all sorts of havoc along the Gulf states was working itself north. Potentially the worst kind. That kind had a habit of stalling as soon as it reached the ocean, charging up again, and then plunging north, dumping half the Atlantic on the eastern seaboard.

Gabe had followed weather maps since high school. One of his teachers had been an amateur meteorologist, and he had taught his hobby with infectious enthusiasm. It seemed to Gabe that the synoptic picture had indeed changed over the years. Polar air masses were reaching southern latitudes they hadn't reached before. He wondered if the planet was indeed about to be visited by another ice age. *About!* Say in five thousand years, which was immediate enough in geological terms but distant enough in human terms to make it all rather academic. Still, he felt a pang of valedictory sorrow. Good-by coffee shops. Good-by ski slopes. Good-by General Motors. Good-by spring flowers and autumn foliage. Good-by all the people who would have shopped at Macy's or Denver Dry Goods. Good-by to the latest generation of Michelsons, who had either trekked south or perished. Pam and Andrew were safe, but it was through his daughter and son that Gabe felt an even stronger pang of cosmic grief.

Could the universe be indifferent to the extinction of its finest, most fouled-up flower? Was it possible that millennial miracles of blood chemistry, the human brain, DNA, the tough, loving, pumping heart, and the questing soul—all of it might one day perish in a slight axial wobble that would bring down a blanket of ice a mile thick over Saskatchewan and Cleveland and Sioux Falls and New York and Paris and Peking? What was the purpose in having created such an extraordinary instrument of cosmic contemplation only to have it exterminated in an accident? Was there really no better economy out there than that? Was there really no master love from which human love was copied that would lift a single, concerned finger to safeguard so precious a piece of work? Even if only a museum to preserve the best samples? If there was no more concern for man than this, then why not seize the slightest, latest increase of whatever, from whomever?

Gabe sat on the edge of the bed—his spiritual headquarters during this eventful week—and distracted himself with these large, philosophical thoughts. They were real enough, in one sense, but in another they were a laughable attempt to put some comforting distance between himself and the problem that had entered his life. He recognized in his imagery an attempt to put the problem on ice, or under it. . . . But if it was only a *problem,* then the solution should be fairly simple. If he was thinking solely in terms of *problems,* then there was nothing to do except let this thing play itself out over the next few days, and then fit the memory of it into the remaining years of his life.

He would have to do that—that is, he would have to, somehow, get at his true feelings, and on the basis of that begin to act in a way that would make their future, or lack of it, known to Evelyn. But the afternoon hours slipped by in the same way that his thoughts slipped by, and he finally went out into the gray day to buy some small, choice gift to bring to Evelyn in appreciation of the dinner she was preparing that evening in her apartment. Something exquisitely appropriate. Something that would express the gratitude of a man who had . . . had what? been exquisitely laid? For he had been that. There came to him an image of Evelyn leaning down to him with a cry of such measureless pleasure that what happened in the next few seconds could scarcely be called an orgasm. More like the milt that flowed from male salmon in mating grounds. A near-fatal emission. Worth dying for? And had he never achieved such feeling with Jean? Not for a long, long time. Their sex had been hedged with difficulties for so many years that cohabitation had become more a matter of compromise than passion. Does she feel like it? Do I feel like it? Shouldn't she make the first move? Shouldn't I? The years of daily drag when the kids were growing up, when fatigue was the only feeling that either of them could honestly admit to. That long, deadly period when Jean's dissatisfaction with mothering and domesticity took the form of sexual hostility, challenging him before intercourse to explode her out of unhappiness, weeping after intercourse for the impossible gratification it didn't bring.

Was this peculiar to Jean? Of course not. A whole industry had grown up talking, analyzing, treating, pictorializing, permutating, dehumanizing, and making a fucking fortune out of this very thing. And therefore would it also not happen to Evelyn, to Evelyn and him, should he by some unimaginable working out of circumstances find himself living with her? No doubt. The marvelous thing happening now would become hedged with its own difficulties, and sex on a weekly basis—three? two? one?—would have to take its cue from something other than the gasping newness of body and the stolen sweets of sin.

Try to get all that in a single gift! Gratitude, caution, sadness, gladness, doubt, a desire for permanence within the fear of goodby. The only thing he could think of was one of those perfectly round wooden balls that came apart in a dozen different pieces and could be reassembled in only one way. Still, he had to get *something*. . . .

He went to a bookstore and looked at the large, expensive art books. Extraordinary color work, like having Vermeer or Cézanne in the original. One of those books would be perfect for *Jean,* not Evelyn, and so he bought one, the Vermeer, for Jean. He was pleased with his purchase. Jean would love it. He must also remember to get something for the kids before he returned. He was glad that his original mission had been so fruitfully diverted. It would have been a sorry moment, arriving home having completely forgotten to bring mementos from his trip East, his absence from home. But Evelyn? What for Evelyn? Never mind the omnibus gift. What would be nice for Evelyn?

Gabe began to think of Evelyn. Not of ice ages, or of seizing the day, or of sex, but of Evelyn. He thought of her brown hair and her brown eyes and her special smile. He thought of the clothes she wore, and of the way she went out to him. She embodied his past. She was restaurants and movies and plays and museums and parties and torpid Sundays rescued from death by a sudden, surprising idea. Why? He didn't know why. Because her nose was set precisely where it was. Because she had once left him for Lew Pressman, closing off a promise that had withered and withered but never died. And was not all this incredibly romantic nonsense? Yes, it was, but it was also true, as true as Arnold Sinclair's business maneuvers, or Jean's striving toward self-realization, or his own, gnawing sense of responsibility. There was no final feeling. There was only this—and this—and this—and this—

So Gabe bought two bottles of wine on Sixth Avenue—one red, one white—each with a distinguished French label. And then he went to a Fifth Avenue department store and asked the saleslady to recommend a really nice perfume, something that had been around for a long time, something classic. Then he returned to his hotel, took a long, warm bath, dozed for a while, then started to read the paperback book he had bought in the bookstore. It was *The Good Soldier,* by Ford Madox Ford—A Tale (so it said) of Passion. He had once asked Jeff Singer to make a list for him of books he should read. *The Good Soldier* was one of Jeff's recommendations, one that he had never gotten around to.

This is the saddest story I have ever read, it began.

At five o'clock, Gabe dressed, left the hotel, and took a taxi to Evelyn's place.

He gave Evelyn the package containing the wines, which she unwrapped, exclaiming, "My goodness!" Then she unwrapped the smaller package and stared at the blue box for a long, incredulous moment, did something funny with her lips, and then turned her back to Gabe and walked quickly to the window. She was crying—or struggling to keep from it.

"That bad?" he asked, knowing something had touched a nerve. "The lady in the store said it was pretty classy stuff. You can exchange it, you know."

Evelyn shook her head. "Things are getting a little overwhelming, that's all," she said. "How did you know this was my perfume?"

"I didn't."

Evelyn turned around, walked to Gabe, gave him a quick kiss. "Thank you," she said. "Everything is beautiful. Wine and perfume. Je Reviens is what I use. Wait—" she went into the bedroom and brought back a bottle—"see. . . . Tell me how you knew. Did I mention it? Did you recognize the fragrance? Or did you ask someone?"

"Who would there be to ask?" Gabe said. "You did mention Joanna Hopkins, but I wouldn't even begin to know where to find her. Your ex-husband, Lew Pressman? Pure coincidence. Happy coincidence."

Evelyn set down her gift. She put her hands on Gabe's arms, and he embraced her. "Sit," she said.

He sat. She went to the kitchen and returned with a tray containing glasses and a shaker of martinis. She poured them each a drink. "What shall we drink to?" she asked. "To us," Gabe said promptly. They sipped their drinks, and then Evelyn told him about Wednesday. She told him she had gone to the opera with Frank Moore, because Frank had somehow obtained two precious tickets, probably at ridiculous prices, and although she didn't feel like going she felt that she must. "And why should you not go?" Gabe asked—and there was something in his asking that saddened her immensely. . . .

"Anyway," Evelyn continued, "Frank mentioned your name during the evening. I knew that I had never spoken your name to him. It couldn't have been a case of absent-mindedness, because you're on my mind every minute, just about, and I would have been very conscious of speaking your name to Frank. Frank finally admitted that he had gotten in touch with Joanna Hopkins, to whom I *did* speak about you. Now you come and present me with my own perfume, and I begin to feel that I'm in a very small boat in a very choppy sea. You know, last night, after I came back here from the opera, I sat in the bedroom and stared at the phone for about fifteen minutes. If plastic had feeling it would have let out one small ring of pity."

"What time was that?" Gabe asked.

"About one."

"I must have rung you about four or five times twenty minutes before that," Gabe told her.

Evelyn's eyes grew large. "From where?"

"From my hotel."

"But you said you were going to your *sister's!*"

"I was. I did. But I didn't want to spend the night there. I came back to the city. If plastic had hands, your phone would have wrung your neck while you were staring at it. *I* wanted to, for your not being there at that moment. . . ."

Evelyn got up from the sofa and held out her hand to him. "Come make love to me," she demanded.

"Now?"

"This instant!"

Gabe set down his glass and went with her into the bedroom. They took off their clothes and chucked them anywhere. Then they made love. Nothing leisurely. Nothing various. She was as ready for him as several hours of prelude could have made her. They joined their bodies in the most natural way, and their bodies cried out with almost brutal quickness. It was this brutality and quickness they both seemed most to want. Not the languor of sex, but the dumb, thrusting relief of it. A little later, they both began to talk.

They talked for a time in the bedroom, and then Evelyn got up and went into the kitchen to prepare the steaks and salad. Gabe joined her there. They talked about their lives.

Evelyn told him about Lew Pressman, his strange, unpleasant ways, and their divorce. She told him about her son, Jay. She told him about Frank Moore, and how Frank had brought her the color and craziness of a creative life. It had been exciting to be with Frank, she wouldn't deny that, but it was also a high-wire act. Frank was one of those reformed drinkers who put the terrific burden of equilibrium on the people near them. One is always conscious of danger, even when things are going well. But she had never loved Frank. She wanted Gabe to know that. . . .

"And if you had?" he asked.

"I just never did."

"But if you *had?*" Gabe persisted. "I hope you don't feel that you have to explain your life to me."

"Not explain, just tell. And now you tell me something of yours."

Gabe told her about his children. He told her that he loved both his children, but in different ways, and the way he loved his daughter was perhaps a little more afflicting than the way he loved his son. Perhaps it was the early and chronic conflict between daughter and mother that brought about the father-daughter tie. Anyway, Pamela was pretty, clever, and a trial, even to Papa. She carried her barely begun womanhood like a torch.

Evelyn asked how old Pam was. "Seventeen," Gabe told her, and Evelyn remarked that he was mistaken about the "barely begun" part. She said that her own "womanhood" reached back so far and so deep that it was like trying to find the underground springs of a brimming lake. Gabe nodded, said he was sure she was right about that. Pam had loved various things at the age of six—not excluding boys—with a possessiveness and passion out of all proportion to her size. Anyway, now she was seventeen, and her doings with boys were absolutely scary. Not that she might lose her virginity—he assumed she'd already lost that—but the impenetrable fog surrounding those telephone calls and parties and the dying responses to the merest questions. "Sometimes I get the feeling that that generation is protecting mine from eating of the tree of knowledge. Of course, I realize it's all *appearance*. That maddeningly glazed look, as if explanation was useless, as if any kind of communication was hopeless. And, you know, they know *nothing*. They're onto no way of living that assures happiness or prevents heartbreak. And sometimes, when they don't know they're being watched, you catch a look of such perplexity and fright that you know that nothing has changed. All the old questions remain."

Evelyn listened and nodded, not far from the same experience with her own Jay. She said, "Not once in all the years I was married to him did Lew and I ever talk of such things. I often wondered what was wrong, and now I see that nothing much was wrong, only this, only the fact that we never really *talked,* we only gossiped. About who had influence and who not. About stars and starlets. About vanities, not people. . . . Oh, never mind, I don't want to get started on that. . . . What about your son?"

"Andy is fifteen. Sometimes he's a baby, sometimes he's a purposeful young man. He takes after his mother. He's really very bright. He wrote a composition for his English class on entropy. He reads Isaac Asimov. I wasn't even sure what entropy was. . . ."

They had dinner in the dining area, adjacent to the kitchen. Evelyn had put on a robe—a blue velveteen robe. Gabe had put on his clothes after their love-making. He had even begun to fuss with his tie, which Evelyn had snatched from him with a little cry of, "Oh, my God, I won't have you wearing that after making love to me!" Gabe smiled and wanted to know why not. "Because it makes me feel it was some sort of reverse business engagement." Gabe laughed and agreed.

They were talking as husband and wife might talk. Gabe looked at Evelyn, and she returned his look, closing her eyes briefly and nodding, indicating that she had guessed his thoughts, and that words couldn't make matters more plain or less intricate.

"And Jean?" Evelyn asked, at last.

Gabe shook his head. "What shall I say?" he said.

"Can you say anything?" Evelyn asked.

"I don't know what I feel," Gabe said. "I have to go back and find out. I think—*think,* mind you, I can't be certain—that I wouldn't be here now if I cared for Jean enough. I know that sounds easy, possibly cheap, but easy and cheap things are often true. Anyway, I think I would have stopped before this if there were strong reasons to make me stop. I feel very content sitting here with you, talking."

"Don't you talk with Jean?"

"Of course I do." Gabe turned away from Evelyn's eyes. He knew it was time to say the crucial things. He knew that if he didn't do it now, he wouldn't do it at any time between now and his departure. "Evelyn, I'm not on bad terms with my wife," he said. "We do have a life. We do help each other. Sex is no more problem with us than it is with most people who have been married as long as we have. Sometimes it's good, sometimes not. We have done many things for each other, and there is that accumulation of indebtedness. All those complications obscure whatever it is I mean when I use the word love. Do I love Jean? I don't know. I truly don't know. I don't know what word to give to the responsibility I feel for her life. Am I happy? No, I'm not. I've known that for a long time too. Jean gives a great deal of herself to me, to the kids, but she gives only out of her own understanding of what is needed. What do you do with a generosity whose imagination is nothing like your own? You say, 'Thank you,' and dig a small grave for your starved gratitude. . . ."

Gabe fell silent after that. Evelyn reached out and touched his hand. "Please tell me more," she said. Gabe shook his head. "No more," he said. "I really don't want to say anything more now. I'll be going back in a few days. I'm almost certain I'll be coming East again. I don't know exactly when, but my guess is fairly soon. I'll be bringing an offer back to my client. He'll look it over, and then I'll be coming back with a counterproposal and a little leeway to conclude something. . . . It makes me happy to be with you. I like making love to you. I like talking to you. You make me aware of myself in many nice, bright ways. So what shall we do . . . ?"

"What indeed shall we do?" Evelyn echoed.

"Let's be lovers," Gabe said.

"No," said Evelyn.

"I know," said Gabe. "Of course not. A selfish thing to ask. What shall we do? I love you. Nothing I've said is canceled by it, but I do love you. Did you want to know that?"

"Yes. Very much."

"Look at me," Gabe said.

"I can't," she said. "Please, Gabe, I'm hurting. Say something hopeful. I feel like a beggar."

"Don't feel that way, darling. I'm going back to find out what I can do with my life."

"All right," Evelyn said, getting up abruptly and gathering the dishes from the table. "I promised myself I wouldn't do this, and here I am doing it. Gabe, go home and do what you must."

"Does that mean you don't want to see me again—I mean, while I'm still here?"

Evelyn's back was to him. She carried plates in both hands. She halted and lowered her head, looking like a figure in an allegory. "I want to see you," she said, continuing on into the kitchen. "Listen," she said, raising her voice slightly, "I want you to know one thing. I won't live with unhappiness for long. It's not in my nature. I'll love you only as long as there's more joy than sorrow in it. If it goes the other way, I'll find a way out."

The Singers had moved to this so-called "middle-income" housing project shortly before the Michelsons had moved to Denver. They had been on a waiting list for several years—although at this point it was difficult to imagine why anyone should have *waited* to live here. It was just south of the Washington Square area. Gabe vaguely recalled the hope that this area of the city would be reclaimed by an infusion of middle-income money and middle-class influence. But it seemed to have become only another fiefdom in the savage land. Gabe had to wander about a bit to find the right building. He saw uniformed guards at the various entrances. He inquired of one where to find the building number he was looking for, and he was directed to the right place.

He had to buzz first. "Gabe?" came the voice. "Right," he said —and the door release buzzed. He rode the elevator to the fourth floor, and there rode with him the ghost of old Saturday-night parties. Laura was waiting for him at the opened door of the apartment. Laura, with that same open, rounded forehead and her hair drawn back and fastened with the same severity. Gabe observed that that hair was now streaked with gray. She held out both hands to Gabe, and when he took them she proffered her large, hot face to be kissed. He recalled her strangely unmelodious perfume as he breathed it once again. It was a dry calculation of an odor. An *intellectual* perfume, if there could be such a thing. As he was drawn into the apartment, he took in the quick evidence that time had not been as kind to Laura as it had to Jean, or Evelyn White, or even himself. The lines on either side of her mouth had deepened, repeating themselves in a diminishing pattern of sister lines. The same fretwork around the eyes. Nor were the eyes as fiercely challenging as they once had been. They looked at him with covert inquiry.

Jeff took his coat and give him what Gabe took to be a look of ironic pity. . . . *Sorry you had to get mixed up in this, old man!*

They went into the living room. It was a room lined from floor to ceiling with books, and in that it bore a resemblance to the apartment Gabe remembered, the one just off Queens Boulevard. Nostalgia fastened softly onto Gabe's heart. His chest and nostrils inflated with a longing for his own past. Not that there had been anything to recommend it but hard work, heartbreak, and disappointment, but it had been *his*, and he felt toward it as tenderly as a father toward a neglected child. The days of digging into fat textbooks, looking out a window to see that snow was falling, or that pale, young leaves had unfolded. The sense of incalculable wealth in knowing there was at least as much time before as behind. That resource had been taken by time, and just to remember it was cause for a session of sweet grief. The Singer living room restored those years, and Gabe would have liked to embrace the Singers and magic them into happiness, just for the part they had played.

"What'll you have to drink?" Jeff asked, obviously in an entirely different mood.

"Anything."

"I don't have anything. I have scotch and bourbon and vodka and gin—tell me what you want."

"Scotch," Gabe said. "Soda if you have. Water is fine too."

Jeff nodded and went to the lovely system of shelves and cabinets attached to one of the walls. There was something stronger than irony in Jeff's attitude. Jeff was holding himself in, clearly an unwilling party to this conference. Suddenly nostalgia and melting good will vanished for Gabe, and he, too, resented being here, where he was at best only half wanted, having to play whatever thankless role would develop out of these hostile forces. He had told Evelyn that he couldn't be with her on Saturday evening, that he had promised the Singers he would come to dinner. She had looked at him unbelievingly, woundedly, unable to comprehend why he would *choose* to be with others. He told her of the crisis in the Singer family and his involuntary involvement. Quickly her look had changed to one of resignation. There was his own life: his own past, his own friends, his own responsibilities. God knows he would rather be with her! But there was no use in trying at this late date to reform himself into selfishness. When Jeff had contacted him at the hotel and said that Laura wanted him very much to come to dinner, he could no more have said no than cut his throat. It was an unhappy thing, a fruitless thing, but his presence was called for, and he had virtually no experience in turning away from that kind of moral demand.

"Now," said Laura, when they had all settled down with drinks, "I want to hear all about Jean and the children and living in the Rocky Mountains."

Jeff raised his eyebrows and rolled his eyes. "Nothing less than *all*," he mocked.

"*I* want to hear," Laura said without looking at Jeff.

Gabe said that they weren't exactly living *in* the Rocky Mountains. They were living on the plains, to be exact. He showed them recent photographs of Pam and Andrew, which he kept in his wallet, and Laura exclaimed over their size and beauty. Laura got up and went into another room, bringing back a recent photograph of Emily. The girl had always looked like Jeff. This photograph gave even stronger evidence of the resemblance.

"There's no question who her father is, is there?" Laura remarked.

Jeff snorted. "God!" he exclaimed. "I never doubted Emily's paternity, if that's what you're trying to say."

"I'm not trying to say anything," Laura returned icily. "I'm just pointing out a resemblance."

Jeff rubbed his forehead vigorously and shook his head. He said, "Come on, Laura, let's cut this shit. You had Gabe come here for a reason. I agreed to be part of it, although I'm damned if I know what you expect Gabe to say or do that will make a difference."

Gabe felt heartsick. The frail hope that this might not be a completely disagreeable evening was blown away in that gust of brutality. He felt sorry for Laura, and he felt his own banked resentment against Jeff flare up into fire. Whatever had happened in the past, whatever it was he wanted, there was no need for *this*.

"You see," said Laura, smiling at Gabe, still in possession of her controlled monotone, "this is the new Jeff Singer. A regular little street tough. He's learned how to let it all hang out, all the aggressions, all the frustrations."

"I recommend it to you," Jeff said to Laura. "It would do you a world of good."

"No, thanks," Laura said. "I don't feel it necessary to cover my failures with mud."

"Oh, you admit to having them—failures? Good. That's a beginning. It's the first time I've heard the admission, that I can recall."

"That's not true, Jeff," Laura said sadly, a little *too* sadly, Gabe thought. "I've always admitted to my failures. How often did you tear one of my poems to shreds, and I just took it. How often did you say 'sentimental,' 'academic,' 'trashy,'—and I just took it. Went away and read it over, when I could manage to stop crying, because Jove had handed down the Word on something I had done. I read my poems over with *your* eyes and burned them, seeing that they were no good. Oh, I've accepted my failures. Don't dare say I haven't. But tell your friend, Jeff, what you did when—I won't even talk of criticism—but when my praise of one of *your* poems was lacking something in holy awe. Tell him some of the things you said—"

"You misunderstood me," Jeff said, looking neither at Laura nor Gabe, but at some invisible thing at his side that was filling him with disgust. "You *always* misunderstood me. Did you really think that such vituperation was aimed at your insignificant poems? They didn't merit it. They weren't important enough. It was *you*. Your poems were a means at getting at all your other failures. Your failure as a woman. Your failure as a friend. Your failure as a mother. Your failure as a human being—"

Gabe, who had been sitting in an armchair, got up abruptly. He realized he was still holding his glass, and he thrust it away from him, as if he was in urgent need of a refill. Then he said, "Jeff, please—"

"Yes, Gabe?" Jeff pounced, as if he had actually been trying to goad his friend into some kind of protest.

"Cut it out," Gabe said.

"You expected something like this, didn't you?" Jeff asked. "What did you think was going to happen? Why do you think she had you come here? She's probably exhausted everybody in New York, so she had reserves brought up from the West."

"That's a lie," Laura said quietly.

"That *is* a lie," Gabe said. "And you know it. May I have a refill?"

"With pleasure," Jeff said, crawling out of the sofa—if that's what it was!—in which he was buried. Gabe realized then that part of his horror was caused by that ridiculous thing in which Laura and Jeff were reclining. *Reclining!* Imagine saying such things to each other lying there like a pair of decadent Romans! Yet there was no other way to arrange the body in that rectangular acre of upholstery! Laura lay curled in one corner, and Jeff had been stretched out in the other. Tearing each other apart in such luxuriousness! "Here you go," Jeff said, almost thrusting the glass at him. He didn't burrow back into that thing, though. Perhaps Jeff himself had become aware of the surreal nightmare in howling mortal insults from such postures. He went to the window and pretended to look out.

Gabe sipped his drink standing. He would have liked to set this glass down somewhere, get his coat, and walk out of both their lives. Why, indeed, had he been called in to mediate this ugliness? Did they really want his opinion? Did either of them hope to find support in his presence? None of these things! He suspected it was his long absence. He was *their* past. Arguing in his presence, they

were able to restore the fullness of lives they felt had been betrayed.

"Well, Gabe, say a little something," Jeff said. "You're a lawyer. Friend of the court and all that. You have a duty."

"Come off it, Jeff," Gabe replied. "I'll say a little something,
since you're so hot for it. I don't understand Laura's terrible
crimes. You may not want to live with her, that's one thing—and
I'm sure as hell not going to pass judgment on that—but I don't
understand where all these failures come in. As a woman, as a
friend, as a mother—"

"You didn't live with her," Jeff said.

"Ah, but you did," Laura put in. "So give Gabe a for instance.
How did I fail as a woman?"

"Do you really want me to go into that? It would sound a little
too clinical."

"You don't frighten me, Jeff," Laura said. "I can get clinical
too. It takes two to tango."

"Christ!" Jeff moaned wearily. "The simple truth is that you
don't like to fuck, and I do. The simple truth is that you don't like
to laugh, and I do. The simple truth is that you don't like to live,
and I do."

"The simple truth," said Laura, "is that you've found someone
who is willing, for a short time, to adore you as you want to be
adored. Someone who thinks you're the unsung William Butler
Yeats of our time."

"What's wrong with that?" Jeff asked. "Sounds good to me."

"There's only one thing wrong with it," Laura said. "You don't
believe it yourself. You don't want to accept what you've made of
your life. You're looking for compensations you don't deserve.
How long do you think it will last with your Cynthia? She's just a
younger excuse for the poems you can't write. More sooner than
later she'll run out of hosannahs. What will you be left with, Jeff?"

Jeff turned around and faced Laura. "If that's the case, why do
you want me to stay?"

"Because I've lived through it with you," Laura answered. "I'll
never be contemptuous of what I know. Believe me, Jeff, she'll be
contemptuous of what she discovers."

Jeff moved away from the window. He went to the hall closet
and took his coat and hat. Gabe could scarcely believe what he

was seeing. "Jeff—" he began, but Jeff was unhearing, busy putting on his clothes. Standing at the entrance of the room, he said, "You may be right. If you are, I'll never forgive you. If you're not, I'll never forgive you. So you see, you can't win. . . . Gabe, I'm sorry. This was not my idea. But it worked out well, your being here. Everything that needed saying got to be said. You can go home knowing you've performed the office of a friend."

Gabe felt a rush of fury. "That's a contemptible thing to say!" he shouted at Jeff. "Don't be such a goddam fool!" But Jeff had turned around and slipped out of the apartment.

Laura didn't even turn her head. She sat moist-eyed and motionless, staring straight ahead. If one could talk of winning, she *had* won. It had served her needs as a woman to tell the truth. It had served Jeff's needs as a desperate man to lie.

Gabe ate dinner with Laura, because to leave her at such a moment was beyond him. They talked of Jeff, of nothing but Jeff, the ruin he was bringing on himself, and it was almost as if they were sketching a rough draft of his obituary. Laura said that she would never take him back as a man but only as an object of pity, and there was something in the way she said it that made Gabe shudder. A Cassandra pronouncing Jeff's doom—and it didn't take much prophetic power to see how right she was.

Later, at the hotel, Gabe stretched out on the bed and closed his eyes, thankful to be alone. He had very little to do with what happened, only a witness, but he knew that the wracking weariness he felt had come from fighting his own case, not theirs.

13

Evelyn took the East Side Drive to the Triborough Bridge. On the other side of the bridge, the Grand Central Parkway. Past La Guardia Airport.

"Things have been done here," Gabe noted.

"Yes," said Evelyn.

She was driving. She had rented the car from an agency not far from where she lived, picked it up on Tuesday morning, drove it to Gabe's hotel, drove away with Gabe and his luggage. She had told Don Marshall the day before that she wouldn't be coming in that morning. She was in the fortunate position of not having to explain her infrequent absences. She didn't count hours on the other side of her job, and Don reciprocated fairly.

"Are you sure you want to do this?" Gabe had asked.

"Positive."

"I wouldn't want us sitting in the car like a pair of stricken birds, making phony cheeps of cheerfulness."

"I'm not happy saying good-by to you," Evelyn had said, "but I'm not stricken. You'll be coming back. You *say* you will. Will you?"

"Without question."

"Then it's not good-by."

"It's not good-by."

They drove past La Guardia and out toward Kennedy. Gabe's flight was at eleven-thirty. It was only ten o'clock. They could still talk without the sense of using up the last of a dwindling supply. Weaving through the streets of Manhattan toward the East Side

Drive, Gabe had told Evelyn that the business that had brought him East had been productively unconcluded. The Fairmont people had made an offer that Gabe was pretty sure his client would accept. But they wanted to make the payment in a somewhat larger percentage of corporation stock than he had supposed, and this would probably give rise to some haggling. That part of it was up in the air. He wanted to talk to an investment counselor he knew in Denver before making a recommendation to his client. In any event, another trip East was a certainty. He couldn't say exactly when. Probably after the holidays. Thanksgiving, Christmas, and New Year's telescoped the weeks. The only thing that counted in the business world at that crazy time was retail sales.

Evelyn told Gabe that her son, Jay, would be coming home for the holidays. School started again rather early in January. She had thought of the possibility of flying back with her son when he resumed school, which would bring her that much nearer to Denver; but St. Louis, she saw on the map, was as far from Denver as it was from New York, almost . . . and besides there wasn't a reason she could think of that her son would accept. He would see it all as some kind of maternal nervousness, and that would be as welcome as a case of hives.

"And if you did come to Denver . . . what?" Gabe asked.

"I don't know. You tell me."

"I can just imagine," he said. "You stay at the Brown Palace or the Denver Hilton, and there'd be the usual secretive this and that. No, thank you. I get depressed just thinking about it."

Evelyn drove past Shea Stadium, the old World's Fair grounds, and Gabe recalled aloud the first World's Fair, the one in '39. He had been even younger then than his son was now. He recalled seeing the actor Edward G. Robinson strolling through the grounds. He had stared in recognition at this sinister man, and the man had given him a very pleasant smile. Now Edward G. Robinson was dead. And so were Humphrey Bogart, and Gary Cooper, and Clark Gable, and Robert Taylor, and Betty Grable, and Groucho Marx. . . .

"Are you trying to tell me something?" Evelyn asked, after that roll call of the dead.

Gabe laughed. "No, I'm just jittery about time. Normal pathology in men of my age."

"Would you do me a favor?" Evelyn asked.

"Anything."

"If when you get back home and you find that it's all been a pleasant interlude, or a dreadful mistake, will you take the trouble to tell me that quickly?"

Gabe didn't answer immediately. He looked out the window of the car. They had come to the self-same bottleneck that funnels into the airport. In all these years, nothing had been done to open up this maddening blockage. He thought of how unanswerable Evelyn's question was. It was both a pleasant interlude *and* a dreadful mistake. And it was neither. It was, if anything, dreadfully serious. He longed for the plane, solitude, a chance to be high above all attachments, so that he could see them in the cold, thin, clear air of reality. Insane! There was no reality in air you couldn't breathe. The only reality was the thick, polluted minutes that pushed you to some decision. Of course, a crash would be its own, definitive reality.

Evelyn thought: Well, so I did the wrong thing again. I swore I would give him no ultimatums to take home, and I've done just that. I swore it would be a cheerful occasion, letting him see my strength, letting him see the cool control of Evelyn White in crisis, and instead I've given him half an ultimatum and half a broken heart. Damn him! Damn me! Damn everything!

"I take back the request," she said. "Forget it."

"Don't be mad," he said. "I feel exactly as you do. Do you really suppose that I could see it as either a pleasant interlude or a dreadful mistake by the time I get home?"

"No."

"If only things could be clearly right or wrong."

"They're not," she agreed—and after a few seconds of silence said, "I have a second favor to ask: rescue us both from the gloom I've created."

"You expect a lot from me."

"Yes, I do," she said. "You're so much more resourceful than I am. I'm full of admiration. The years have done good things to you. You have more intelligence and compassion than I remember. You're mature. You're a terrific lay. I love you. Goodby."

"All right," said Gabe. "Today is Tuesday. I will phone you at your apartment on Friday, five o'clock Denver time, seven New York. Don't worry if you can't be at home at that hour. I'll understand and try another day, another time. I will need some time for my business, but during the early part of next week I will write you a long letter in which I will reflect on time spent with Evelyn White. You're a terrific lay too, you know. Is it nice to say that to a woman? In many ways I'm still a very old-fashioned man. If Friday, seven o'clock your time, proves to be the best time for you, then that's when I'll call you regularly. I may also call you at odd hours, at your office, at home. I will keep you informed of the progress of my New York business, and when I might be coming East again. I'm told I have a nice epistolary style but that I do tend to embroider. Don't, for God's sake, feel you have to answer in kind. If you're economical in letters, then by all means be economical. Above all, be yourself. Someday—did I tell you this?—someday I intend to compete with your friend Frank Moore, and write a novel. Like everybody else, I believe I have a fascinating world to bring to life. I love you, too, Evelyn. Please don't do that, or we'll have to drive into one of those airport motels and I'll miss my plane and that will be messy. Am I rescuing us from gloom . . . ?"

"My hero!" said Evelyn. "Yes, yes, yes! Please go on saying things like that!"

Gabe went on saying things like that: about his office in downtown Denver, about the letters he would write, about the difficulty he had in keeping his eye on the ball in tennis . . . and they drove into the airport. Gabe refused to let Evelyn park the car and accompany him to the terminal. The mood of gloom had lifted from both of them. Life is an ongoing process, and he had made it an ongoing farewell.

They kissed cheerfully, and Gabe picked up his luggage and walked into the terminal.

14

Evelyn no longer trusted her own Christmas selections where her son, Jay, was concerned. Shirts, sweaters, sporting goods, even *jeans* had become subject to such strange mutations that the wrong choice had begun to appear more like an insult to one's religion than a mistake in taste. Evelyn admitted to herself—and to Jay—that she was totally in the dark. She wouldn't take a chance on *shoelaces*. So what did he have in mind for Christmas loot?

"Well," he said, "since you ask, there is something I'd like, but it's kind of expensive, and I was wondering . . . well, you know that stereo set I've got, it's supposed to be putting out thirty watts, but I took it to a store near the school, and the guy there told me it wasn't even putting out *twenty*. So what I thought . . ."

What Jay thought was that he'd like a new, powerful receiver, but he realized that would be too expensive for just one of his parents, so he was wondering if maybe they could get together on this single gift, instead of the separate ones they usually got. . . .

As fate would have it, Jay was growing to look more like Lew all the time. He was even now bigger than his father, stockier, but with Lew's springy hair and Lew's deep-set eyes. The color of the eyes, and the mouth with its large, surprising smile, were hers. When Jay was still a child, Evelyn had wondered what an increasing resemblance to Lew would do to her feelings. The resemblance had increased and so had her feelings of love, protectiveness, and selflessness. *Not* possessiveness. She did not want to possess him. She could draw happiness from his progress at a distance of a thousand miles.

Jay was very much on his own now, and his vacation days in the city no longer had the old structure of a private school in Riverdale, hours of homework, the known apartments of friends, the times and activities that co-ordinated with her own. He was a college man. He claimed his privileges with decent deference, but he did claim them. He told her who he was going out with and approximately where, but to her question, "Any idea when you'll be home?" the answer was, "No idea, Mom." To her terror-stricken queries about streets and subways in the vampire hours, he made a little grimace, gave a little shrug, said that this is where he lived, where *she* lived, and what could be done about *that?* But he did throw her a sop by saying that he was a native, knew the badlands, knew when to take a cab instead of the public conveyances.

"I hope you understand, dear, that I'm not checking on you in any way," she said.

"I understand."

"It's just that . . . well, I sometimes wonder why you don't get together with your friends here," she said.

Jay shrugged, looked away. "I dunno," he replied. "I mean, you know, no particular reason."

"Are you uncomfortable here?"

"No-o."

Now he was putting on his mask of filial patience: veiled eyes, faint smile, vagrant interest in distant corners of the room.

"You know, I don't have to be here," Evelyn pointed out.

"Don't have to *be* here!" he said, looking at her critically. "What are you talking about? This is where you live, isn't it? Besides, I'm not ashamed of you, you know."

It had never occurred to her that he might be, but she asked him what happened at those other places, the places he found more congenial. He said that nothing happened, except that . . . some of the guys had their own places, some of the girls had *their* own places, and things were just more convenient that way. Nobody was in anybody's way. Evelyn wanted to know if there were *none* of his friends living with parents, and Jay said sure there were . . . some.

"Do those parents get in the way?"

He shook his head, was silent, gave evidence of guarding a secret, a condition he seemed reluctant to share with her. "All right, Jay," she said sadly—and that sadness reached a place her questioning had failed to reach. "Mom," he sighed, going limp in resignation, in the superfluousness of this spelling out of things, "how do I know when maybe *you* may want to be alone?"

"Alone?"

"I mean—with *somebody*."

Evelyn stared at her son for a long moment. The mystery of the loved one's mind at last revealed. All the questions she had left shrouded had been examined by her son in the common light of day. The mother was a woman, an attractive one; and Jason Pressman, freshman, knew what happened to attractive, divorced women even when they happened to be one's own mother. Evelyn raised her eyebrows, opened her mouth, tried to smile, tried *not* to smile, tried to find some expression to meet this utterly simple, hopelessly complex crisis.

"Is that why you stay out so much?" she asked.

"No."

"Did anybody tell you I was seeing someone?"

"No, it's nothing in particular," Jay explained. "It's just a general thing. I mean, I don't want your life to come to a halt just because I'm at home. . . . Incidentally, I'm going to stay at Dad's place for a couple of days. You knew that, didn't you?"

"No, Jay, I didn't know that."

"Do you mind?"

"No, of course not," she said, her heart feeling as though it had been wrapped in dirty burlap, weighted with rocks, and dumped into a cold, dark lake. She asked, "Was it Dad who suggested I be left alone occasionally?"

Jay shrugged again, and again he studied those distant corners. "No," he said. "Dad simply said he'd like me over at his place for a few days—that it was only fair for everybody if—you know—at this time of year—people have parties, see friends—you know. . . ."

The only thing that Evelyn knew with any certainty was that she must let Jay off the hook. At this point, Jay could never reconstruct who said what, and it would be pointless to insist that he try. Jay may have hinted something to Lew, which Lew would be quick to pick up, and then would have confirmed, or embellished—

who knew what? Or Lew may have hinted at something to Jay. But for what purpose? To lure Jay away from her during the holidays? Perhaps a more permanent luring? The opening gun of a campaign to subvert her image in Jay's eyes?

But why should Lew do a thing like that? He had access to Jay. He had never shown signs of that kind of moral ugliness since their divorce. If anything, the opposite: co-operative, concerned, congenial. Then, what? She didn't know what, but she must take the trouble to find out. Once discovered, these things mustn't be allowed to continue a day longer than necessary. Look what happened between Lew and herself. Not that she feared that kind of break with Jay, but the thought of any diminution filled her with dread.

Darling,

It's been a month. Only a month! I feel as if you left Kennedy in Noah's ark, and that there's been enough time to sail around the world four or five times. You might have made a stop here, you know.

Gabe, if I could only have you for a day! I don't mean HAVE you. I wouldn't touch you. I wouldn't let you touch me. I would sit you down somewhere—this apartment or your damn hotel—and talk and talk. I'm much in need of your good will and wisdom. For the first time in years, I feel disadvantaged by my femaleness. My son, Jay, is home for the holidays, and I find my life heavily in want of male maturity.

I think my son is assuming I have a lover. He should know! I do have a lover—about a million miles away! No, I don't mean that. You're really quite close as long as I can write these letters and look forward to my once-a-week telephone call. That sounds like a complaint too, doesn't it? I don't mean to complain. I hope you understand that this is not a complaint but a cri de coeur. (See how I remember my French!) I feel I'm not being as clever and far-seeing as I should be. I'm feeling very vulnerable. Am I losing Jay? I think if you were here you would tell me what to say and what attitude to take. I'm jumping all over the place. I seem to lack coherence—which is, I think—I HOPE—not my usual condition. I really don't know what to do, but the thing that bothers me more is that I don't know what to FEEL.

Shall I be cool? Let it wash over? Shall I express what I'm feeling to Jay? Shall I tell Jay about you? That's what I'd like to do, but I believe that all he wants from me at the moment is the favor of keeping my problems to myself.

What do you think? You're a father. Tell me.

Love,
Evelyn

"Are you alone?" Gabe asked.

"Yes. . . . Gabe, did you get my last letter?"

"I did."

"Disregard 90 per cent. I apologize. I was slightly hysterical."

"Does that mean that all problems are resolved?"

"Are you kidding?"

"I assumed not," Gabe said. "I wanted to give you some advice."

"Bless you! Give!"

"I think your last paragraph was the smartest one. Be cool. I know that's an easy thing to say, tough to do, but it's the wisest. Let it wash over. Don't burden Jay with your problems. Don't tell him about me, particularly if he seems to be getting close to his father. Don't shove him. . . . And, other than being torn apart by wild horses, how are you?"

"So much better for hearing from you. And you?"

"Going along."

"Do you miss me?"

"The rhythm of that missing has changed," he told her.

"Oh? What does that mean?"

"When I first got back," he told her, "I spent much time reconstructing everything. But there were also times of the day and night when I didn't think of you at all. Now I find that the rises and falls have leveled out. You've become more a part of my day. Does that mean I'm taking you for granted?"

"I don't know what it means, Gabe. I'm not sure I like it. If you take me for granted, I'm afraid you'll find you can do quite well without me. Can you?"

"No, I'm not doing quite well without you. If I were, I wouldn't be conniving like a thief to get back East."

"Is that what you're doing—conniving?"

"I am."

"I take that to mean that it's not a sure thing, your coming back

152

East. Why should you have to connive? You told me that the conclusion of that big deal absolutely necessitated your coming back East."

"Did I use the word 'absolutely'?"

"Absolutely!"

"Well, then, absolutely I'll be coming back East. I tell you that both parties are still very much interested. I tell you that the thing is going forward."

"And everything else?"

"Like what?"

"Your family? Your life?"

Gabe told her that everything was as one might expect it to be. Jean was deeper and deeper into art history. He prayed each day that his children wouldn't break their legs skiing. The weather was extraordinary. He read of the catastrophic blizzards that were sweeping across the eastern half of the nation. Just the other evening, he saw on TV an apocalyptic scene of a lone skier sliding along Wall Street—or was it Madison Avenue? Was that a prophecy? Perhaps it was time to think of relocating. Shouldn't she talk to her boss about skipping away from the leading edge of the new ice age while there was still time?

In her dream, she was with her parents, only they were not in Coral Gables. They were all staying at some other place, a beautiful white house near some body of water. There was a tennis court to one side of the house. Jay was playing tennis with Lew. She could see them playing although she was in the house, and somehow their playing was part of the confusion and lethargy surrounding her choice of a dress. Her mother said the yellow one, and took it out of the closet like a saleslady, holding it up by the hanger, letting it drape over the other arm. It was a low-cut, old-fashioned thing, ridiculously inappropriate. She knew her mother wanted her to look dazzling, because there was going to be a dinner dance and she might meet a young man. She was so filled with the oppression of having to go through that "hunting" period again that it brought on her period. She looked in the mirror and saw the telltale rings beneath her eyes. The dream grew shallow, and she knew that she couldn't be in that phase of her life again if Lew and Jay were out there playing tennis. She turned to Gabe, who was on the other side of the twin beds, packing a suitcase. He shook his head, saying, "I don't think it's my place to say." Then she caught that terrible look between her mother and Gabe, and she knew that they were having an affair. Her sobbing woke her.

Dearest Evelyn,

You see, we still use the Metropolitan Museum cards for our Xmas greetings. Yes, the Xmas madness is just as intense at this elevation as it is at sea level. You might just as well pretend that you're not in a flood or a hurricane. I say this, I'm sure you agree, yet here we are both sending gifts. Thank you, darling. It's as handsome as can be, this desk set, and if anybody asks I intend merely to say it's from New York, which will mean nothing to anybody and everything to me. I hope you like what I sent you.

I've promised myself to get it all on this card, and now I see I must begin telescoping my message. My feelings have undergone another change. It's no longer a reconstruction or a leveling out, but a vacuum. Not my whole day, not my whole life—I would be lying to say so—but a portion of all my days, and consequently my life, is spent wanting your presence. If I could explain it meaningfully, I would, but I can't. I've described the feeling as best I can, but my analysis is as yet incomplete. When I can get it all together, you will share it with me.

Do you understand, Evelyn, how careful I'm being in what I say? I hold my right hand with my left, figuratively speaking, to keep myself in check. I will not allow my feelings to run ahead of reality, although they do strain, which may be why I feel so tired much of the time. I'm almost out of space. My client is vacationing in Hawaii. When he returns, after the new year, we'll begin serious discussions apropos of N.Y. Would you still welcome this partridge? I, too, need reassurance. . . .

Love,
Gabe

She had sent a Christmas card to Frank Moore, received none from him, which added to the general melancholy. This was surely one of the most wretched Christmases she could remember. Joanna was departing for her seasonal visit to family in Vermont.

"I'd love to go with you," Evelyn said, half in jest.

"Isn't Jay with you?" Joanna asked.

"Yes—if you can call it being *with* me."

"What's the matter?"

"Oh, I don't know. Jay's being the young man about town these days. Between my trying not to be in his way and his trying not to be in my way, we're about ready to start biting. He's suddenly become conscious of my sex life, such as it isn't. I have the feeling Lew has put a bug in his ear about me. For the first time since we split, he's having Jay at his place. I don't know what it is, but I have a very unkosher feeling. Can you think of a reason why Lew would want to undermine me with Jay?"

"No," said Joanna. "Jay's discovering his father, that's all. What the hell, look at all those glamorous contacts. Maybe he's fixing Jay up with one of those movie queenlets."

"Yes, I've thought of that," Evelyn said. "I suppose that's the father's traditional role, but with Lew I always fear something decadent."

"Oh, don't be silly. Lew's got his *shtik,* but he's not crazy."

"I know. . . . When are you leaving for Vermont?"

"Tomorrow."

"Tomorrow! Well, *bon voyage!* Weren't you going to tell me?"

"Well, you know I go about this time every year."

"Yes, I know—but you usually call before leaving."

"Oh, I was going to call you. . . . Listen, Evelyn, I don't know whether you were serious or not about wanting to come with me, but I'd advise against it. If you're feeling down now, you'll be ready for a wraparound vest after a day in sleepy, creepy Vermont. I can endure it because we light a big family bonfire with old feuds, but it would drive you up the wall."

"I suppose," said Evelyn. "Well, have a tolerable Christmas."

"You, too. I'll be in touch with you as soon as I get back. That'll be before the new year. Incidentally, have you got any plans for that?"

"Not a thing."

"Maybe we can get together and huddle against the storm."

"Yes," said Evelyn, "that would be cozy."

As she was expecting, Lew got in touch with her. He had made it his custom to pronounce in person his benediction for the new year. It was his shriving time, his annual show of good will. In various ways, he had made known his feeling that he had been more sinned against than sinning in their divorce, so that his Christmas/New Year's greetings always had something faintly forgiving in them. Never strong enough to give Evelyn cause for mirth or accusation, but just enough touched with injury to leave her mildly depressed. This year, there was an immediate, practical reason.

"I've looked into that component Jay wants," he said. "They're all over the lot in price, but it's going to cost somewhere between three and four hundred dollars. Is that all right with you?"

Evelyn was shocked—and angered. Jay had no *right* to decide on that kind of a Christmas gift. Why not a little two-seater Mercedes while he was at it! Wasn't one supposed to accept with thanks whatever one was given? She resented the rich boy's arrogance in Jay's behavior, and then she realized that the aggregate of Jay's Christmas loot came to that anyway.

"I suppose," she said.

"I wouldn't expect you to pay half," Lew said as if he had read her mind.

So that was it! All part of the same damn conspiracy! When they had given each other gifts in the past, it had been a matter of personal taste and love, but hard cash would reduce the whole thing to gross measurements. Well, let it be. She wouldn't play that game.

"Lew, is this something you'd like to buy Jay on your own?" she asked.

"I wouldn't mind."

"Good. Then do. I'll get him something else."

"He said he wanted only that one thing."

"I know he did, but I don't like the idea of a requisition list for Christmas—or for any occasion."

"Don't get sore," Lew said. "It's truly what he wants. He was very concerned about the whole thing, about how you would feel. He asked me first if I thought it would be okay with you."

Evelyn's quick, defiant fortification came crumbling down in a dust-filled billow of silence. Her eyes filled with tears. What the hell was the matter with her, anyhow! She felt a spasm of hatred against Gabe for having taken from her so much self-assurance.

He had made her whole world an uncertainty, and she was seeing the worst in everything.

"I'm sorry, Lew," she said. "I'm not sore. It's just that—well, things are happening, aren't they? I'm assuming that you're getting to know Jay better, and that's fine—"

"Evelyn, do you want to talk about Jay?" Lew asked quite seriously, and his asking made her realize that that was precisely what she did want to talk about.

"Yes," she said. "Let's talk about Jay. Of course, you realize—"

"Evelyn," he interrupted again, "I don't mean talk about him *now*, over the phone. I had something a little more serious in mind than that. . . . Look, I'm having a New Year's Eve party at my place—do you have any plans for New Year's?"

"Yes," Evelyn said quickly, although she didn't have any plans, couldn't imagine what sort of invitation Lew was preparing to make, felt it safest to invent a very occupied New Year's Eve.

"Well, then, perhaps we could arrange to have dinner one night," Lew suggested.

That, too, made Evelyn uneasy. But why uneasy? If they were going to talk about Jay, then they had to put aside an hour or two of some day. Sheer mechanics. It was just that dinner with Lew seemed to be announcing a new era of co-operation, a different direction, and she had enough to cope with at present.

"Couldn't we make this sometime after the new year?" she asked.

"Why not before?"

"Well, then, could we go somewhere for a drink . . . say about five-thirty?"

Lew gave a little laugh. "Are you afraid to have dinner with me?" he asked.

"No, not afraid," she said. "It just doesn't seem necessary. I'm surprised you would have the time."

"To talk to you about Jay? I would have the time, Evelyn. You know, ever since we parted, you've acted toward me as if I had moral syphilis. I don't think there's any call for that. Do you find me so disagreeable?"

"No, Lew. I'm sorry if it comes across that way. I thought you were just making an occasion so we could talk, and I wanted to indicate that the occasion could be small. That's all."

"All right, then, let's have a drink at five-thirty," he said. "How about Thursday?"

"Yes, Thursday would be fine."

They agreed on a place they both knew.

She felt like a surly fool. Worse, she felt she had suffered a serious loss in that exchange with Lew. She had given away with both hands her best advantages. She had always maintained a balanced judgment for Jay's sake, never saying a word that would prejudice the boy against his father, and now here she was full of resentment and self-pity, behaving in a way that gave Lew grounds for scolding. For there *was* something insulting in the way she had brushed aside his suggestion for a meeting. If she allowed her frustrations to spill over everything, she might just as well say good-by to everything, the things she had as well as the things she longed for.

And yet how strange it was that Lew had been on the point of inviting her to a New Year's party. *His* New Year's party? That is to say his and—what was her name?—*Sara*—his and Sara's party? Funny how names that at one time would have been removed like warts in Hollywood's crazy ethnic operating room were now lucky charms. . . . Evelyn found herself wandering back and wondering if the supposed awfulness of her marriage had been no less a prejudice. Were things really that bad? Should she have accepted Lew's invitation? If Sara wouldn't have minded, why should she? She imagined herself in that proposed corner with Lew discussing their son, smiled at benignly by long-haired, pretty Sara, and again she felt the old recoil. What the hell was that if not decadent?

Perhaps it never even occurred to Lew that his New Year's party might not be the ideal place for such a conversation. Now Evelyn was remembering more clearly, and she recalled the gradual transformation of their life together into a cheap imitation of a royal court. Those last few years, in one way or another, they were either holding court or attending someone else's court. Small parties, large parties, somebody's house in Connecticut, somebody's penthouse apartment with a jeweled view of the city, a block of tickets to a new movie opening. It was like living with Henry VIII!—only, without the Thomas Mores and Erasmuses, just those strange little courtiers of moviedom.

Thinner, grayer, and yet more youthful-looking than when she saw him in that theater lobby. He wore a striped business suit, a blue shirt, a gorgeous tie. He looked more the executive than the swinger. Another metamorphosis? Or was this something he had put on for her sake—for the sake of their "serious" talk? You just couldn't tell with Lew.

He was amazed, he said, at the changes in Jay. The kid seemed to have taken a giant step. Didn't she think so? Yes, she agreed, there'd been great changes, so much more self-reliance, much more mature.

"But something not to your liking?" Lew asked.

"He's gotten a little withdrawn," she said.

"Every action has a reaction," Lew said. "Moving toward something means moving away from something else."

"Is he moving away from you?" she asked sourly.

Lew smiled. "That depends on the starting point," he said. "Almost any move Jay would make would seem to be away from you. Not so to me. Do you see what I mean?"

Evelyn nodded. She did indeed see. He was right. The only movement Jay could make would be away from his mother, since it was his mother who had wanted and had taken full possession. Acknowledging the rights of the father was a fine, free gesture of the heart when the heart was completely unthreatened. But how well would she do fighting a rear-guard action, forces in disarray? How would *Gabe* handle this? What difference? Gabe was not a woman.

"You and Jay are closer now, aren't you?" she asked.

"I would say so," Lew said without any smugness. "I'm not quite sure how it came about. We had an easy time of it when I visited him at school. He showed me around. He said the food in the dorm was garbage, and I suggested we have dinner there. I wanted to see how bad it really was. It was pretty bad—I mean, what you might expect—but I told him it was considerably better than Army food. I suppose it was because I ate there, that I found the food passably lousy, all that sat well with him. Also, he chose to do a movie review in his expository writing class, and I was able to give him a few ideas. . . . I guess he felt he'd discovered a new human resource."

"I'm glad of that," Evelyn said.

"Are you?" Lew looked at her with humorous skepticism.

She was forced to smile. "I suppose I'm a little put out," she admitted. "But I do see the advantage for Jay. I really do."

Lew nodded. He said, "Evelyn, I've never pumped Jay about you. I never wanted to put him in the position of a double agent. But the fact is I've been curious about your life. I know that there's that writer, Frank Moore—is that going anywhere?"

"No," she said.

"Is there someone else?"

"No," she decided to say, knowing that whatever she hoped to retain in the way of pride and love depended on her keeping the Gabe thing to herself. She had told Joanna because she was in the habit of telling Joanna everything, but since then she had developed superstitious fears. The more exposure the more risk—or at any rate the more need for explanation. Silence, always, was a beautiful pearl.

"Then you must be having a lonely life," Lew said.

"Not too bad. I'm busy."

Lew nodded, leaned back, regarded her with an expression she wasn't sure she was making out in this undersea light. Why did these places go in for this dim romanticism? Maybe people liked it. *She* might under other circumstances. The stretching seconds of silence began to sag. Why was Lew being so peculiar, starting up in that way, then falling dumb? What had she said? . . . *Not too bad. I'm busy.* . . . Was that the wrong thing to have said? Was there some insult or innuendo she wasn't hearing in her words? She was getting as jumpy as a cat. No! She had said *nothing* that could be taken in any way other than the way it was intended! She spoke again, raising her voice: "Nothing. I manage to keep busy."

"Yes, I heard you," Lew said.

"Good," she said. "I had to try the words again to see why they produced such a strange reaction."

Lew said, "I'm just sitting here trying to put together the right words."

Evelyn felt as if a brutal hand had reached into her body and seized her heart. She could feel the blood drain from her face. Now she was thankful for this muffled light. Lew's strangeness fell into place. . . . *Jay had decided to live with his father, and he had left it to Lew to tell her so.*

"I don't remember you ever having trouble with words," she said.

"I usually don't, but this is different."

She sat there waiting. She was in a chamber where Lew's next words would mix with the cocktail air and brew the fumes of her death. But she wouldn't wait a second longer! She wouldn't allow him to do this in his own sweet time!

"Has this to do with Jay?" she asked.

Lew shook his head. "Nothing to do with Jay," he said.

She closed her eyes and began to breathe again. She felt slightly faint. She took a sip of her drink, began to revive.

"Evelyn," Lew said finally, "I don't know how much longer Sara and I are going to last. . . ."

Evelyn's eyes grew large. The last words she had expected to hear! She had imagined Lew sitting so pretty with his long-haired, lovely Sara, making contacts, contracts, movies. . . .

"I'm sorry to hear that," she said.

"Yes, well . . ." and he began to tell her about the life she had wondered about, not deeply, not for long, but nevertheless wondered.

She would, he said, find it amusing, or ironic, or God knows what, considering their own history, that Sara's moral view of life made his own look like basic Bible. She wasn't promiscuous—that could be understood in today's climate—but just *ambitious*. . . . "Well, I'm ambitious too, as you know," Lew said, "but I had no idea what the outreaches of ambition could be. Everything is relative, and what you found excessive in me looks like timidity to someone else."

It was Sara's belief that everybody had a price or a vice, and that any part could be obtained, any advancement attained, as long as you took the trouble to discover and then gratify the right person's craving. "I tell her she's got an essentially romantic view of life, but she insists she's a realist." It was this, Lew insisted, that was the most disturbing thing about his young wife. She was not unintelligent, she was not without imagination, but both intelligence and imagination had been so incredibly corrupted that it seemed to have arrived at a weird purity. Maybe the Eleusinian rites were something like this. Every indulgence a purification. . . .

"But what does she *do?*" Evelyn asked, helplessly, hopelessly fascinated. "Just sleep around?"

"Well, that, yes," Lew said. Then he shook his head. "If it were only that. She wants *me* involved."

"You mean . . . switching . . . that kind of thing?"

Lew shook his head again. "I don't know exactly what kind of thing, Evelyn. After a point, I no longer cared to go into it. What I do know is that things have come to a bad pass. Maybe that's why I've been able to go out to Jay the way I have. I'm finding in my own son some degree of normal affection."

For the first time in years, Evelyn felt something for Lew outside the almost automatic reflex of distaste and suspicion. She wasn't sure what it was she felt. Perhaps only a little bit of the satisfaction one gets in seeing someone served his own bitter medicine. But that was immediately followed by shame and remorse. Two perversities don't make a virtue. Well, then, *friendly?* Yes. She felt friendly—or at least a little friendlier—toward Lew. Was it possible they could be friends?

"And through Jay . . . you," Lew said.

"What do you mean?"

"I mean I think of you," Lew said. "I mean I think of you quite often. . . . Look, I realize that my life will never have much appeal to you, but we did live together for a long time, and I'm able to judge better now what those years meant to me. They meant a great deal. *You* meant a great deal. I'm finding out at this stage in my life that people have a certain weight in the human scale, and it doesn't much change with time and distance. I would like for us to be friendly, Evelyn. It's not for Jay's sake. I'm making this appeal for myself. When I think of you, I think of you with longing. All right, that's my business, but I would like us to be friendly. Fit me into your life in whatever way is convenient. It would be the easiest thing in the world for me to find random bed partners—I think you know that—but that isn't what I want. I don't expect that you would think of me in the same way—I doubt that you've thought of me at all—but *do* think of me, Evelyn. I feel very much alone, despite everything you assume about my life. And you tell me *you're* alone. If you can think of me in a friendlier way, then let's see each other more often. Let it be no more often and in no other way than suits you, and if it gets to be no more than an occasional dinner, or a cocktail, fine!"

Jay was already in the apartment. She knew that before opening the door. The music throbbed in the cloistered air of the hall. Why no one had complained yet was a mystery. Maybe her neighbors understood it was vacation time for college men. But why did he need such volume?

Would Sara welcome the noise, the freshman ways, the husband's son? Would Jay appeal to her Eleusinian appetite? But there would be no gain in it, and gain was everything, according to Lew.

Jay turned down the volume as soon as he was aware of her presence. "Hi," he said. "Hi," said Evelyn—and despite her determination not to, she added, "Jay, do you ever think of the neighbors?"

"Was that loud?"

Dear God, he looked so much like Lew!

"A bit," she said. "I suppose the dorm rocks with hundreds going all at once."

"Nobody hears it," Jay said.

"A deaf generation," she said.

She put into the oven the meat loaf she had prepared the night before. In a half hour, they were eating.

"I've never been to Dad's apartment," she said. "Do they have an extra room?"

"Extra room! They got about *five* extra rooms. And about five bathrooms. Maybe only three. God, an apartment like that must cost a fortune! Is Dad that rich?"

"I guess he is. . . . Do you like Sara?"

"Yeah, sure."

"Do you get along with her?"

"Sure."

"All right, then, you'll be going over there tonight, and you'll be staying for the weekend. Then you'll be back here on Monday, and your flight is on Wednesday. Let's talk about what you're going to need to take back with you, because I want to get things over to the dry cleaner so you'll have them in time. . . ."

She had waged an internal struggle, and she had decided she would do nothing, say nothing, about Jay's stay with his father. It was only for three days—three nights—and it seemed to her that Lew had made those confessions so that there would be no deception. This was the way his life was, and he couldn't help it, but his son was his son, and he would know how to protect what was valuable to him.

At least she fervently hoped that's the way it was. She couldn't take a stand against that. She couldn't say to Jay, "Your father told me horrible things about his present wife, and I beg you to cancel this visit." If she said such a thing, she would violate what was surely meant as a confidence and put both Jay and Lew in a position where they would have no choice but to draw tighter against the clawed world of women.

But there was no misinterpreting what Lew meant. He meant he wanted to begin a love affair with his ex-wife, and Evelyn, alone in the apartment, Jay gone, sitting propped against pillows in her bed, put both hands on top of her head and pressed down against the swelling astonishments of this life. She had told Lew, yes, they could be friendly, friendlier, but that was all, if she understood him correctly, because she wasn't entirely sure she was absorbing what he was saying. . . . God knows what she had said! It had come spilling out of her in frantic quickness, wanting only to end that long, sincere harangue and get away. She could think no further than getting away and *thinking!*

And when she had gotten away and had thought and thought, she found herself immovably stuck between head-shaking astonishment and nervous laughter. She didn't know what to make of it. No, not true . . . she did know what to make of it. Lew's lovely, golden-haired wife was what she was, and because of that Lew had conceived a hunger for his former wife. Was that impossible? No, not at all. And what did she feel about it? She didn't know what she felt about it. She felt stuck between high astonishment and nervous laughter. She wanted to phone Gabe and tell him all about it. . . . *What do you think about THAT, my distant darling?* . . . That's what she wanted to do: she wanted to tell Gabe about it, share it with him, astonish him with it, *threaten* him with it!

15

As promised, the Michelson family went skiing that Saturday. They skied for two hours in the morning, and then had the traditionally awful hamburgers and chili in the chalet-type cafeteria amid the thunderous thumping of ski boots. Everybody had acquired a quick sun and wind burn around the goggles, making them appear a family of bright-plumaged, white-eyed polar birds.

Pam particularly, in her new yellow jumpsuit, her mirror glasses raised and resting on her Jean-type hair. In complete repose there was nothing special to take the eye. She appeared to be a healthy, attractive girl. But her face, her hands, all of her, was seldom in repose. She had fifteen shades of surprise, twenty of joy, and several hundred to reflect disappointment. For her father, it was as varied and intricately harmonic as a symphony. There had already been boys who had hurt her, and aside from the quick murder that had stirred in Gabe's heart, there was the slower astonishment that any male, at any age, in any degree of sanity and vigor, would not lose heart, head, and entrails to Pamela Michelson on first sight. How strange that having diapered the child, seen her in every stage of puling messiness, he should find her now possessed of every ancient female mystery.

Jean's outfit was powder blue. Her face was marked by those little islands that cold bleached into her skin. She was trimmer now than when he had married her, nineteen years ago. They would celebrate their twentieth anniversary in July. There were crosshatches at the corners of her mouth and eyes, and the flesh around her neck had taken on a vertical looseness. But she was trim. There was a scar on her left breast where a benign tumor had been removed, but the shape of her breasts remained unimpaired. She could reduce her food intake as decisively as turning off a faucet. She never slumped. It had always seemed to Gabe that she had willed her posture and the condition of her body. He had seen her do it. He had seen her train her will with the devotion of an artist and the determination of an athlete.

"I made the last run in eight minutes," Andy declared. "From the top."

"Thanks for telling us," Jean said. "Are you trying to break your neck?"

"I've only fallen once this year, and that was when some turkey flopped all over me."

"Aren't you the hot dog!" said Pam.

"What's your record?" Andy challenged.

"I don't go in for records," Pam said aloofly. "Just a slow and sinuous beauty, catching the rhythm of the mountain."

Andy's mouth hung agape and his eyes swooned.

"It took me about twenty-five minutes to get down the last time," Gabe said. "My sinuous beauty caught the rhythm of the mountain in slow motion. When you're over the hill, you like to enjoy the scenery."

"Listen to him," said Jean.

"You're *not* over the hill," Pam said with a little grimace. "You think *you're* over the hill? God, I know kids whose fathers sit around with bellies full of beer, watching television like zombies. If they had to bend over to tie their shoelaces, they'd die of a heart attack."

"You're really in great shape, Dad," Andy concurred. "You can still beat me in tennis, for God's sake!"

"That's just trickiness," Gabe said. "You're the better player, basically. But all right, I won't argue. I'm in great shape and hillwise I'm nowhere near over." He looked at Jean, who gave him a silent accolade. Paternity triumphant! "Listen, while we're on the subject of hill-climbing, I might as well announce that I have to go to New York again."

Jean gave him a narrow look. "When was this decided?" she asked.

"Friday," said Gabe. "I called up the people in New York and we got together on the second week in March."

"But why didn't you tell me that last night?" Jean asked.

"Because it slipped my mind completely," Gabe said. "Maybe I was trying to repress it."

"Dad, take me!" Pam suddenly blurted out. "Oh, please, Dad, I haven't been back in *years!*"

"Don't be ridiculous," Jean cut in. "Dad's going on business. It's not a pleasure trip."

"But I won't be in the way," Pam pleaded. "Dad, you know I've been *dying* to get back to New York!"

"School," said Gabe.

"You won't be gone for long," Pam argued. "And even if I do miss a couple of days, or even a week, it won't make the slightest difference. We're doing nothing in school anyway. Everybody in my class is just waiting to graduate. Dad, that can be my graduation present! I swear I won't expect another thing! Please!"

Gabe looked at Jean. Jean shook her head slowly, admonishingly. He was not to entertain any notion of yielding to Pam. Gabe understood that he was being asked to support Jean's authority in this. Pam was being too petulant and self-concerned, and she must be put in her place. Sweet Jesus, what a tiresome battle! But even as he deciphered Jean's look, he entertained a scene in which he would introduce Pam to Evelyn (chance meeting, planned magic), and he almost smiled at the pleasure that flowed from the image. Such an encounter hadn't occurred to him —why should it?—but now that it had, he was full of its odd, illicit appeal. They would get along, those two! They would be friends. Even if there were no Gabe Michelson in the picture, they would still be friends, because of like factors. Different things might set them off, but they came out to equal values of brightness. The quick scene was shattered by a quick stroke of remorse. Pam was *Jean's* child, for Christ's sake!

"Hey, how about me?" Andy chimed in. "I haven't been back to New York for as long as you haven't been back."

"You don't remember a thing about New York," Pam said, looking daggers at her brother. "You said so yourself."

"So what? I was born there, wasn't I?"

"Now, just a minute—" Gabe began.

Pam gave a violent twist of frustration. "Naturally, you would have to open your dumb yap!" she seethed at Andy. "You no more want to go to New York than you want to break a leg, but you would have to spoil it for me!"

"Pam, what on earth are you talking about?" Jean finally broke in. "An idea flies into your head, and it's already an accomplished fact. Gabe, will you please say something about this madness!"

"If you'll all keep quiet for a minute, I will," he said. "Pam, you can't go with me. Aside from the expense, which would be considerable—I only get reimbursed for my own expense, you know—and with meals and an extra hotel room—but that's all beside the point—the point is that I wouldn't be able to spend any time with you."

"I didn't ask you to!" Pam snapped.

"I know you didn't, and that's precisely why I'm saying no. I don't feature you sitting in a hotel room all the time you're there. You'll be running around all over the place, and I need a clear head. I can't spend my time worrying about where you are. No, Pam, it's impractical and inconvenient."

"Of course, there are no girls my age in New York," Pam countered. "They gather them all together at eight o'clock in the morning and put them in the dog pound. Thanks a lot!"

"In one way or another, you are determined to spoil every occasion we're together," Jean said. "There's absolutely no call for this. If anybody should go with your father to New York, *I* should. I have a professional reason for going."

"Knock it off!" Gabe cut in. "We'll *all* go. We'll all go this summer, if everybody is so keen on it. That's where we'll take our vacation. Okay?"

"Okay," said Andy.

Pam, slowly taking apart a plastic cup, nodded solemnly, not too displeased with this compromise but clearly drawing back into that defense she kept mobilized against her mother.

Jean's expression kept its distance. Gabe could see her carefully sorting out her accusations. *It wasn't her fault, this bit of nastiness!* She was right, of course, it wasn't her fault if her instincts inclined to cool reason whenever Pam became unreasonable. A different kind of love might have made her incline differently, but to accuse her of that would set off another of those wearisome arguments about "spoiling."

He knew he hadn't heard the last of it.

It started up again that same evening. They had again been invited to the Kirschners'. Alex Kirschner was head of the Art Department at school. Art history was subsumed by the general Art Department. Gabe had heard all about the Incivil War from the opening gun to the last battle, when General Kirschner had taken the defeated sword of Commanderess Bailey at the Tennis House. Helen Bailey announced her retirement, which was the signal of surrender. A reception was given in her honor, and the occasion marked the end of hostilities. What it all came to was that Alex Kirschner, chairperson of the department, had to fight off a secession attempt on the part of the art historians. He won in the end. Jean Michelson had resumed her school career at a time when the war was at its crackling best, had taken sides with the Kirschner forces, and had become an important aide-de-camp to Alex.

Alex was a cheerful, bustling man in his mid-fifties who spoke English with a blend of three or four root languages. Gabe thought he detected something Slavic in the occasional absence of prepositions, something cockney in the vowels, and something French in certain nasalities. It was known he had lived in England during the war. He was born somewhere around the Baltic, but for some reason he chose to be vague about exactly which country. In any event, he had brought to the United States in the late forties an irresistible international flavor and a small reputation as an abstract expressionist. One London critic had found strong echoes of Delaunay in Mr. Kirschner's color composition.

Alice Kirschner was a tall, blue-eyed, bony woman who had once studied under Alex. She could be seen most mornings jogging in the vicinity of the Botanical Gardens. Her family were among the early adventurers in Colorado, connected with the fortunes dug out of the mountains. She had only recently bought the mansion where these Saturday-night parties were held, so that she could have one studio, Alex another, and plenty of rooms for the five assorted children from the several different marriages preceding this union.

Alex didn't like parochial parties. He said he heard enough art all week. He cultivated the acquaintance of medical specialists, crusading politicians, writers, musicians, and other football enthusiasts. He was himself fanatic about the fortunes of the Broncos, watched every game, knew infinitely more than Gabe about the fine points of the sport.

There had been one of those marvelous buffet dinners that evening, with guests filling their plates and wandering back to the living room, which looked more like a corner of the Uffizi Gallery than a room in Denver. Someone had started a conversation about new housing developments along the front range and how it seemed impossible to stop the predators from bringing to Denver the same urban horrors that had befallen other cities. Naturally Gabe thought of Harry Curtis and felt a conflict of loyalty. Secretly he agreed, but he didn't agree with the view taken by Alex that there ought to be a periodic suspension of laws—not all laws, but some—so that people could be allowed to shoot sharks instead of being eaten by them.

"You're speaking figuratively, I hope," Gabe said, smiling.

"As a matter of fact, no," Alex replied. "I don't mean open season for everybody with a gun, but I do mean the death sentence for those who use the law to desecrate and pillage. No protection for legal gangsters. Third offense in drug dealing, up against the wall! This shocks you, Gabriel. I can see the horror in your legal eyes."

"It doesn't shock me, because I don't think you're serious," Gabe said.

"But why not!" Alex almost exploded. "I assure you, I *am* serious! We kill the enemy in war, and there isn't a moment's compunction. We allow ourselves to be eaten alive by law-protected mobsters, and for some reason our traditions require that we tolerate that kind of aggression."

Alex's theory of *ad hoc* punishments seemed to tap a not-so-deep reservoir of resentments, and others were quickly contributing their bit to the new dispensation. They weren't all for drumhead courts, but they did want a fiercer justice. One young man—an assistant conductor with the symphony orchestra—offered the recently published list of giant corporations that hadn't paid a dime in taxes. Why shouldn't such grand thieves get a grand sentence—say a thousand years! Another got off about the muggers and housebreakers who were in and out of jail like tourists. He suggested a fifty-first state, sealed off and autonomous, where all the creeps would learn to live together or die together.

Gabe listened and said little. He glanced at Alex Kirschner and saw that that chairperson was enjoying the war dance he had incited. Jean caught his eye and tried to indicate by her smile, by a slight shake of her head, that it was all nonsense, a parlor game, like charades, and that everybody would go home, lock their doors, and pay their taxes.

But Gabe wasn't feeling as indulgent as Jean. He was keeping quiet because he feared talking. His head was full of history. He didn't want to come on like a purple pamphlet, pointing out the results of recent and past lapses of the law. He didn't want to point out that whatever we lived with was paradise compared to a state that decides to escape the encumbrances of law. He didn't want to recite any of the platitudes, because he was himself half on the side of the vigilantes. He was feeling his own downward slide toward a rage of lawlessness.

And later, when they were driving home and Jean remarked on the silliness of the whole episode, he said, "Alex dotes on that kind of silliness. I've never met a man whose weather vane of principles was so well oiled. He catches every breeze."

"Oh, don't be silly."

"Am I being silly? I don't think so. Alex is an opportunist, a slick one, one who knows how to make advantage look like sacrifice, but nevertheless an opportunist."

"Don't take it out on Alex," Jean said stiffly.

"Take what out on Alex?"

"This morning's unpleasantness."

"Now you're being silly."

"Every time there's trouble over Pam, you run to another part of the forest to pick a fight," Jean said.

"Jean, I wasn't picking a fight. Don't distort. Your Alex Kirschner is not one of nature's noblemen, however much you'd like to think he is. He can be, and very often is, a hypocritical, self-serving little shit."

"And you're a fool for taking him so seriously," Jean retorted. "In some ways, Alex is a child. That whole business this evening was nothing more than a form of entertainment. He's a political moron. I'm surprised you don't know that. No one knows less about politics and issues than Alex Kirschner."

"I see," said Gabe.

"You see what?"

"I see that one is supposed to be very tolerant of Alex, forgive him his *shtik,* because he's a political moron. But he doesn't want to be treated as a moron, does he? What do you think would have been his reaction if I had said, 'Alex, you're a political moron, so why don't you stop talking nonsense'?"

"You have far too much intelligence and compassion to say a thing like that."

"Suppose I were to say to Alex that all of contemporary art is a gigantic hoax, and that laws ought to be passed to protect the public against such impostures."

Jean laughed. "Oh, for God's sake, Gabe! You *are* being ridiculous. If Alex is a political moron, that doesn't mean that you have to be an artistic one. I mean—well, you know what I mean."

"I'm not sure I do."

"Yes, I think you do know what I mean."

But Gabe was wound up. He went on to say what had been a long time on his mind. He said that it had become a sharp and persistent pain in the ass to accord Alex Kirschner all the respect in the world in his area of seriousness, but that one must always be ready to have one's own area of seriousness made the springboard of wit and whimsy for Alex's amusement. When Alex talks about art, there must be a universal hush of respect. When anybody else talks about anything else, it should be with a court jester's cap and bells.

Jean was silent. Out of the corner of his eye, he caught sight of her box of Benson & Hedges. He saw her reach gloved fingers toward the dashboard lighter. She remained silent through its seconds of heating, plucked it out at the click, applied the red ring to her cigarette. She opened the window on her side a crack to let the smoke be sucked out of the car. He detested smoke in the car.

"Nothing to say?" he asked.

"No," she replied. "I don't want to go on with the silliness about Alex. Alex is what he is. I've never tried to make him into anything else. That's his wife's job, if she had a mind to. He's a fine artist, and he knows more about art than anyone I could possibly hope to meet. I learn from him. If it makes you genuinely unhappy to be in his presence, then we'll arrange it so that you're not. Now why don't we talk about what's *really* bothering you?"

"What's that?"

"Pam."

"What's bothering me about Pam?"

"You would have liked to take her to New York, wouldn't you?"

"What would have been so terrible about that?" he asked. "It's been five years since she's been there."

"It's been five years for me, too. And Andy."

"Well, I said no to her, didn't I?"

"Gabe, she's getting worse and worse," Jean said. "She has to be put in her place. It's a mortal struggle to get her to do anything in the house. I don't like fighting with her all the time, but I have to because she feels she can always get support from you. You have got to stop pampering her. She has no sense of obligation. She knows that all she has to do is crook her little finger and she can get anything she wants from you."

"That is a crock, Jean, and you know it! You're talking as if I *did* say she could come with me. I said she *couldn't*. And I gave *reasons* why she couldn't."

"Yes you did, but I'm arguing about something else," Jean said. "I'm arguing about a principle. I'm arguing about a *tone*. You don't realize how permissive you've become with her. If I ask her where she's going on a Saturday night . . . like tonight . . . do you happen to know who she's gone out with? . . . where?—no, of course not . . . nor do I . . . and why on earth shouldn't we know? Suppose it got to be two, three in the morning, who would we begin to phone? Something terrible could happen, and we wouldn't know who to turn to. Do you think that's right?"

"No I don't," Gabe said. "I assumed you knew."

"Well, I *don't* know. She refuses to tell me. She says 'friends,' and dares me to pursue it further. It's none of my business."

"Jean—"

"What?"

"Stop it."

"Stop what?"

"Stop talking about Pam as if she were the bitch of the world. She's not. She's seventeen years old. How would you like to be seventeen years old in this world? I can't imagine it, to tell you the truth. What the hell must the world look like to a seventeen-year-old boy or girl, not a value that stays in place for twenty-four hours, no assurance of marriage as a career, or anything else as a career?"

Again Jean was silent. Again he understood her silence. She was saying that he was talking drivel. She was saying that he was trying to skirt around the main issue with a lot of abstract nonsense. And was he? No, not entirely. There were always degrees. Where did his abstractions end and Jean's seriousness begin? She refused to understand what he meant about Alex, because *she* understood Alex, and if she understood Alex why shouldn't *he?* She had made up her mind about Alex, had fit all those odd angles into place, and just wouldn't see that those same angles might bother and cut and tear the living flesh of someone else. She had decided that Pam had reached the limits of her seventeen-year-old bitchiness, and she was blowing the whistle. She didn't see it any other way. It never occurred to her that a different approach might be needed; that perhaps—just perhaps!—she might see Alex Kirschner a little less with her own eyes and a little more with her husband's; that perhaps what was needed for Pam was not sterner measures but a different kind of love.

"You know," Jean spoke at last, "I've grown very tired of competing against my own daughter. You never show me the affection you show her."

"Jean! For God's sake!"

"Don't act so shocked. It's true."

"The truth is, Jean, that you rarely seem to want affection."

"What makes you think so?"

"I don't know. Don't people have a way of making it known when they want affection?"

"Maybe you don't see it."

"Maybe."

"Maybe it's because I don't twine leaves in your hair and wiggle my tail."

Gabe snorted and shook his head. "No, you sure as hell don't do that. Want to give it a try?"

"It's not my style," Jean said.

No, it wasn't her style. Which didn't make her wrong. She was partially right about Alex, partially right about Pam, partially right about affections and pampering. Jean had very definite points of view about art and man, mothers and fathers, children and parents, and who was he to run down that definiteness, partial as it was? It wasn't so long ago that Jean's definite points of view were good and valuable things. He had needed them. He had accepted with gratitude the way she had ordered their world, giving him the time and room to start a career, arranging their lives so that whatever income there was was enough. He had acceded to her arrangements, because a definite point of view was a very handy article for hanging a variety of hats on.

And now what? No longer needed? Time for a change?

Lying in the darkness of their bedroom, Gabe shook his head over the futility of all this rationalizing. Jean was no better or worse than she ever was. He could have gone on living with Jean without any crisis of feeling if he hadn't gone to New York for Harry Curtis. And was it really a matter of better or worse? The curious thing was that all the years had brought him no closer to a final understanding of Jean. No more final understanding of her than of himself. There was only one year after the other, and the same standoff was played over and over in different settings and for different reasons.

And even if by some stroke of insight he should come upon that "final" understanding, would that make a difference? Probably not. It wasn't understanding that was at stake. Things wouldn't be made better by better understanding. There would still be feelings . . . the feelings that fell dead on contact with Jean . . . the feelings that revived on contact with Evelyn. They were important, but were they *that* important? Did it not all come down to a very simple arithmetic? Could he pay for Evelyn with Jean's unhappiness?

Christ, if that didn't sound like the soapiest of soap!

Yes, but wasn't that the trouble with everything that was less final than death and more severe than athlete's foot?

Go! Go, Gabe, to New York. Have a nice time. Enjoy yourself. See if you can manage to be a little less hypocritical and self-serving than Alex Kirschner!

16

Lew sent her tickets for the preview of a big, new movie. The screening was only for reviewers, distributors, and other 16-inch guns in the word-of-mouth world. Evelyn decided she would go.

The movie was another of those strangely disordered things, in which people make utterances that seem to have no cause and produce no effect. It took place in New York, and it concerned the seemingly unmotivated murder of a girl. Very graphic. The cross hairs of a telescopic sight tracking the girl as she walks to her apartment. The view is from an apartment-house roof, where someone has stationed himself with a rifle. Dead-center aim at the back of the girl's head. A truck moves across the field of vision. Clear again. The shot. Slow-motion death as the girl's pocketbook, packages, and presumably pieces of her skull go flying. Then several more people are introduced, anyone of whom might be the killer. The action centers on one young man, a Vietnam veteran, going to college on GI benefits. He is studying script writing for TV at one of the city schools. He does this at night. During the day, he has a job working for a wholesale florist. He has a girlfriend. The girlfriend loves him, prepares nice dinners for him, has sex with him about as graphically as the other girl had her head blown apart. Scenes of Vietnam. More slow-motion deaths—more in number and excruciating detail than any sane person would care to look at for whatever reason: art, entertainment, masochism, sadism, anything. He is the murderer, of course. He has murdered on the street in one of the New York boroughs as anonymously as he had murdered in Vietnam. He wants to write a script about it, and he killed once again because the sensation of all that murdering in Vietnam was beginning to fade and had to be renewed. It didn't prevent him from loving his girlfriend. It didn't prevent him from other normal, random acts of kindness. The movie was full of long silences, long close-ups of faces, so close that the very pores in the skin could be made out. Evelyn assumed she was supposed to be understanding something special from, or through, all this mute trickery. She didn't understand. *She did not understand!* Had the nerve of conscience died in the practice of slaughter? Was the audience being asked to understand and forgive trained killers who felt a periodic need of practice? The young man is not discovered, although it's made clear to the audience and the girlfriend that he is the killer. The girlfriend runs away. (Evelyn White applauds silently.) The young man writes his TV play. It is produced and is a great success, naturally. In it, the cross hairs of a telescopic sight show up, and a Vietnamese woman carrying a child is murdered in slow-motion flight. . . .

The screening had taken place in an old TV studio on Broadway. Some of the audience had been invited to a further celebration in the apartment of one of the movie executives. Not Lew's apartment. Fred Davenport's, whom Evelyn remembered from the old days. *She* had been invited. In the beige-colored, raised-print invitation that had been mailed to her was inserted another invitation, delicate, in script—cocktails, the address, the apartment number.

The studio where the screening took place was fairly large, and after the film Evelyn looked around for Lew. She didn't have to look long. Evidently he had been looking for her. He motioned from the aisle. She moved out.

"Are you going to Fred's place?" he asked.

"I don't think so."

"Why not? Please do. There'll be lots of interesting people there. You don't get out that much."

Evelyn hesitated, then accepted. Why shouldn't she? Indeed she didn't get out much. Everybody she knew seemed to have dug into a spiritual igloo to hide against the wearisome, end-of-the-world winter. Joanna had practically disappeared from sight. She could be reached at her office, at her apartment in the West Seventies, but she was either exhausted, about to come down with a cold, or just getting over one.

But boredom and isolation in themselves wouldn't have broken her resistance against Lew and one of his parties. She didn't really fear Lew. His campaign to get her into bed was being conducted in such a low-keyed way that Evelyn half suspected he was enjoying these failures as much as he would have enjoyed a quick success. Probably more, if she knew her former Lew. Probably he was renewing his sex life with kinky Sara in these equally kinky versions of courtly romance with his former wife. Best, or most fortifying, of all was Gabe's call announcing he would be returning to New York. Paradoxically, that call made her feel free to enjoy the company of others. It was as if she had been passing through some kind of testing period, measuring her love in terms of loneliness and frustration. She took Gabe's call to be the terminating signal. He was returning. She could resume a normal life. She *had* to resume a normal life if she was to meet him as a normal woman, not some distraught creature full of constraints and accusations and God knows what!

The Davenport apartment was in the huge, curved building that faced the park. Evelyn had often wondered who lived in that citadel. She tried to imagine the rent as she had once tried to imagine the parallel lines that were supposed to meet in infinity.

Her coat was taken by a maid. Two steps down into a room large enough to lose a grand piano in one corner, and to have fifty people, more or less, standing around without crowding. Evelyn allowed herself to take in the opulence with sheer, dumb delight. Everything was glass and chrome and enamel white, with one enormous blue canvas on the wall. She knew one could be just as miserable here as in a two-room flat in Hoboken, but the mind had to work so much harder imagining why. *She* could imagine why. Hadn't she lived with Lew Pressman for almost fifteen years? But now she was a visitor, and for a visitor there was the botanical smell of captured sunlight and the mingled effluence of rare species.

Young men in maroon blazers passed around food and drink. Was that some kind of uniform they were wearing? Was that champagne? Yes. Of course. What else? Deductible expenses. Promotion costs. . . . *Gabe, I'd rather be with you right now. Practically anywhere. Would I? Yes, I would! Are you coming this time to make some important difference in our lives? It's possible to do that, Gabe. It's done all the time. Do you mind that I'm enjoying myself, just standing here and enjoying myself . . . ?*

Lew found her again. He was wearing a blue velvet tuxedo, bow tie, and one of those ruffled shirts.

"My goodness!" she said, looking at him admiringly.

"I'm sort of a semihost," he explained. "How did you like it?"

"The movie? Well, I thought—"

"You thought it was lousy," he concluded for her with a laugh.

"No, I didn't. Not at all—"

"That's a nice dress," he said, to ease her difficulty. "I don't think I've ever seen it. You probably have a whole new wardrobe I haven't seen."

"You're quite wrong," she said. "I probably have all the clothing you're familiar with. . . . Isn't Sara here?"

Lew looked at her with a small smile and shook his head. That look of his reminded her of the many slow scenes in the movie. Was it a new form of communication that hadn't reached her yet? . . . Her heart was given a sudden sharp wrench at the sight of Frank Moore. He was standing some distance away in a group of four or five. . . .

". . . She's in California," Lew was saying. Evelyn had to force herself back to Lew and the answer he was giving to her question. . . . *Sara . . . She had asked about Sara.* . . . "She's in a film," Lew was explaining. "At least I think she's in a film. That's what she went out there for. I'm not absolutely sure she got the part. . . . Have you spoken to Jay?"

"Last Sunday," she said. "He's fine. Haven't you spoken to him?"

"It's been a madness these last few weeks," Lew said. "I haven't had a chance to call him, but I did ship out that stereo equipment he wanted."

"From here? Why couldn't he buy it out there? It must have cost a fortune to ship."

"I happened to get a terrific discount. Very powerful stuff. It can blow the windows out of a cathedral."

Bribery, she thought. "He'll destroy his eardrums," she said.

"Nah. He's a sensible kid. . . . Evelyn, I have to circulate. I have to talk to some people. Promise me you won't leave before I have a chance to talk to you again."

"I have to go to work tomorrow."

"All right. I'll get back to you before you go. You're not going to leave right away, are you?" He looked at his watch. "It's only ten-thirty. Please stay another hour. Will you?"

"All right."

"See you."

Lew reached out, took her hand, gave it a squeeze. He moved off in his blue velvet jacket and ruffled shirt. . . . And there was Frank Moore coming toward her! As she glanced in that direction, she caught sight of another familiarity she somehow had missed before. My God, was that *Joanna!* Yes, of course it was! Twenty pounds less of her—at least!—but no one else in the world! Something jogged in her mind, and scattered drops of mercury shivered together in a single, shining mass. Joanna's strange taking off at Christmas, her recent inaccessibility, this new, *thin* Joanna, and Frank Moore!

Frank didn't hold out his hand, or make any gesture of greeting. He came up to her, highball in hand, saying, "It's hard as hell to get some bourbon around here. Nothing but champagne."

"Hello, Frank," Evelyn said. "I'm very glad to see you."

"*Very* glad," he mocked. "Just glad won't do."

"Well, I am," she said. "I sent you a Christmas card. I don't recall receiving one. . . . Are you here with Joanna Hopkins?"

"Oddly enough, yes. I had a helluva time getting her into this place. They insisted on one man one invitation. No tickee, no washee. I didn't think you'd be here. Knowing your ex-husband had something to do with this extravaganza, I was sure you wouldn't be here. But it was your good ex-husband who stepped into the breach and came to the rescue of his ex-wife's friends. There's nothing like clout. I love it. Lew probably saw the beauty in a full stable of Evelyn ex-es. Ex-husband, ex-boyfriend, ex-girlfriend—"

"Is Joanna my *ex*-girlfriend?"

"Oops. Sorry about that. Mistake. Just me."

"Are you my ex-friend?"

"Don't I even rate an 'ex'?"

"Oh, Frank, please. As far as I'm concerned—"

"What did you think of your ex-husband's latest?" Frank interrupted.

"It's not my ex-husband's," Evelyn replied, looking toward Joanna, who remained steadfastly engaged with the same group of people. "He's not the producer or director. He's on the business end of things. And please don't cut me off that way."

"Oh, my goodness! A coal from Newcastle! Look who's talking about cutting off— Incidentally, were you the one who gave a copy of *The Other Island* to Doris McAuley?"

"Yes. Why?"

"She told me somebody had sent her a copy, she wouldn't say who." Now Frank grinned. "But she did eventually tell me that she got her bread writing articles for a certain school magazine."

"But how did she find you?" Evelyn asked.

Frank didn't answer that. Instead he said, "I just didn't know if you were capable of a little long-distance pimping. Offhand, I would have said no, but we never know what we'll do when we're under the gun."

"What do you mean by 'pimping'?"

"Oh, you know, throwing Doris my way to see if she'd stick. A diversionary tactic."

"Frank, go away," Evelyn said, turning away.

Frank put out a hand to detain her. "I apologize, if an apology is in order," he said. "Maybe you honestly thought we'd make a team. We did for a couple of weeks."

Evelyn glanced at Frank, her curiosity greater than her anger. She was appalled, amazed, at the idea of Frank and Doris, but she also felt a little guilty, because there had been that notion playing around in the back of her mind at the time. Yes and no. A little warfare of conscience. In the end, it had been only a fly-buzz she had brushed away. The truth—if that commodity ever came in usable form—was that she had sent Doris Frank's novel because she was sure Doris would enjoy it, and because she had been genuinely pleased to boost Frank's work. But she didn't want to say all that, or even part of it, because there *had* been that little impurity, and Frank had all the insight in the world when it came to spotting the slightest malign design.

"What do you mean, 'made a team'?"

"You wouldn't expect me to kiss and tell, would you?"

She tried to imagine it. She tried to imagine dry, no-cosmetics, politically passionate Doris McAuley. . . . Well, why not? She would probably go at it with the same intensity that she gave to world revolution. God, she could use some intense sex herself. . . . Oh, who *cared!*

"Why are you telling me this?" she asked irritably.

"Why are you asking?"

"Frank, what's between you and Joanna?"

"You never answered my question," he said.

"What question?"

"How did you like the new movie . . . *Sharpshooter?*"

Evelyn looked closely at Frank. Cloudy eyes. He was drinking again, heavily. And there was a heedless aggression in him, the same aggression that had made him risk being badly beaten by a younger, stronger man. This was Frank's aggression turned against a woman, a woman he had cared for and who had ditched him. Wasn't that Joanna's word: *ditched?* Well, she had, hadn't she? It was getting to be, if not the story of her life, at least a few sizable chapters. And it didn't suit her at all. She wasn't that way. Or was she just kidding herself, as Frank kidded himself about not being an alcoholic?

"How *you* liked it seems more to the point," she said. "That's why you're here, isn't it? Are you reviewing movies regularly now?"

"More or less," he said. "It takes my mind off important matters. How I liked it? I did. I thought it was good, frankly. Frankly, I thought it wasn't bad. Which I'm sure wasn't the case with you. If I remember your taste in flicks, you probably thought it was a pretentious bomb."

"What I thought is not important," she said.

"Come, come. I wouldn't say that."

"I know you wouldn't," she said. "I'll say it for you. You've told it to me often enough. No, I didn't like it. Yes, I did think it was a pretentious bomb. I don't like to sit through a couple of hours of torture. I am, to tell the truth, sick and tired of having to drink a bucket of blood as part of the price of admission. Or be made into a voyeur, whether I like it or not. . . ."

She went on, her anger making her ride high on a wave of eloquence. It didn't happen often, but when she felt herself being cornered meanly and unfairly, she could strike back in style. Frank had positioned himself deliberately between her and Joanna, physically blocking her view, using his long, loose, more than half-drunk presence as a symbolic comment. His glass was empty. He was probably dying for a refill. But he continued to stand there, asserting something that was at once childish and ominous. All right, he had been hurt. She had been instrumental in that hurt. But she had never mentioned the word love. He had never spoken of permanence, and she had never hinted at any such wish. What did he think she wanted to do with her life—make herself into a plump pillow for Frank Moore's literary and sexual woes? Lew with his slow serenade. Frank with his crucifixion kit. God damn these men anyway! *Including* Gabe, who was somewhere on the moon, endlessly packing a suitcase!

"Pissed off, aren't you?" Frank said.

"How did you ever guess?" she snapped. "Frank, why don't you get yourself a drink?"

"Where's the Denver flash?" he asked.

"Frank, please!"

"All right, dear enemy. You *are* my enemy. People who hurt me are my enemy. I have never been able to outgrow that childish notion."

"Then I feel terribly sorry for you," she said. "For all your championship of the real world and the underdog, what you really want is a sanctuary. One place where you can't be hurt. Who isn't hurt, Frank? The only way not to be hurt is to be perfectly still, and I'm afraid the both of us are movers."

"I got a contract for my new book," he said.

"Congratulations. I'm glad. Believe it or not, I'm glad."

"A big advance, dear Evelyn. The biggest I've ever gotten."

"It doesn't hurt me, Frank. You are not my enemy. I'm not in competition with you. Why do you want to pick a fight with me? You can't. I don't want to fight with you. I wish you happiness and success, but I'm afraid of you."

"Why's that?"

"Because you came here with my friend, Joanna, and now you're standing here doing what you're doing."

Frank looked into his glass, smiled, straightened his shoulders. "You're right," he said. "I need a drink."

He walked off.

Evelyn took advantage of Frank's temporary absence to walk over to Joanna. There were three people with her now—another woman, two men—and they all smiled at Evelyn, as if to welcome her into this circle, whoever she was.

"Hello, Joanna."

"I was just waiting for a chance to get over to you and say hello," Joanna said. "Would you excuse me?" she said to the others, and moved away. Evelyn followed, surveying her friend quickly. From a distance, Joanna had presented only the slender outline of her lost poundage, but closer up Evelyn could see a haggardness beneath the heavy make-up—heavy and professional. Joanna never did, never could, do that kind of a job on herself. Joanna moved around islands of people, seeking, Evelyn assumed, some safe corner. She stopped at last before one of those maroon-jacketed young men and helped herself to another glass of champagne.

"So what did he tell you?" Joanna asked.

"That he liked the movie," Evelyn said.

"Did he tell you about his book contract?" Joanna's eyes wandered unhappily around the room.

"He did. I'm glad for him. He doesn't think so, but I am."

Briefly Joanna's eyes touched Evelyn's. They were tired and fugitive eyes. A quick scene came to Evelyn. She recalled a late-fall day when she and Joanna had driven back to New York from a visit to Joanna's cousin at West Point. The sun was going down, setting off a golden blaze above the foliage. Joanna was driving that old convertible Plymouth with the patched roof. She looked out at the splendor and wondered aloud if a scene like that, a tropical fish, an orchid, every visual wonder, could possibly be sheer accident, the creation of an indifferent eye. Joanna confessed not to believe so. She said things that well done required a planner and a plan. It had stayed with Evelyn because it was the first and only evidence Joanna gave of some belief . . . or if not belief, a reluctance to give it all over to helpless, hopeless chance. The incident gave a touching preciousness to the friendship, making Evelyn feel she had been entrusted with a tender secret.

Still not looking directly at her, Joanna said, "He got in touch with me the first time when you were starting up with Gabe Michelson. He wanted to know what was going on. All I could tell him was what I knew: Gabe Michelson . . . an old boyfriend. Then, after, something happened, he never told me what, he just got in touch with me again. He came to my place and drank himself into a stupor. He's been on the sauce pretty steadily ever since. He's about three quarters through with the book he's working on. He stays at my place during the day, when he's capable of working. He says he can't work at his place. He says the stink of failure has infested all the rooms. God, do I ever know what he means! He was certainly welcome to share the cuckoo nests in my own rooms."

"And does he get anything done at your place?" Evelyn asked, recalling that Frank had once asked her if he could use her apartment during the day.

"I think so. You can always tell when he's managed a few pages. If he hasn't had a drink by the time I get home, then he's done something. If he's sloshed, it's for the opposite reason. He says he has to pay for each day with a minimum quota of words, and if he hasn't paid his remittance he has hell-fires to quench."

"Frank Moore would have hell-fires to quench with or without words," Evelyn said.

"I take it he's said the same things to you?"

"More or less. Joanna—"

"Yes, Evelyn, yes. . . . Yes, probably, to almost anything you're about to ask."

"Vermont?" Evelyn asked.

"Yes," said Joanna. "He went with me to Vermont. He stayed in a motel in Rutland. I shuttled between my parents and Frank. God, he was sick! I had to take him to the hospital while we were there. He got a roaring case of the dt's. They would only release him if I signed for him. Like a lost parcel-post package. I had to promise that I would see that he got help. It's incredible how afraid he is of shrinks. He's afraid they're going to steal his mind, his creativity. . . . Am I going on too much?"

"No, dear, but I know about Frank Moore."

"Well, then. . . ."

"You've said everything but the most important thing," Evelyn said.

"Oh, there's the middle-class Jewish princess talking. What's the most important thing?"

"Why are you being so hostile to me?"

"Am I? Maybe because I don't want you to start crowding me with 'the most important thing.' You have no claims on Frank— I mean, you don't want any, do you?" Joanna had settled her vagrant eyes on Evelyn's earring. Her head tilted slightly to one side, and she kept her tired, decorated, gray eyes fixed on Evelyn's pearl earring. "Or are you getting ready to reclaim him?" she asked. "It would be no problem, you know."

"Meaning that you don't feel secure with Frank?" Evelyn asked.

"I wouldn't feel secure with gentle Jesus."

"Then why do you want it? Why are you doing it?"

"Because, all things considered, it's better with someone than alone. You know, dear, *I* was supposed to meet Frank Moore in Amagansett, not you."

"And you've been mad at me ever since?"

Joanna's eyes moved the short distance to Evelyn's. She shook her head. "I haven't been mad at you. Frank went for you. You couldn't help that, nor I, nor he."

"But why have you been staying away from me now?" Evelyn asked. "You know you have. You haven't had that many colds."

"Why do you think?" Joanna asked.

"Because of Frank? He doesn't want you to see me? I can't believe that. He wouldn't be that childish."

"Wouldn't he, though! But no, on the contrary, Frank has been insisting that the old friendship resume."

Evelyn felt she had been pressing against a masked surface, looking for the concealed hollow space. She thought she felt it now, beneath her hand, and that one more push would tear a hole. She hesitated. Did she want it torn? Did she want to see what was concealed there? The foreboding that had begun to gather around Joanna's absence drew closer. There was something here she must prevent, but she knew she was powerless against two such formidable people. The same fear she had expressed to Frank seized her again, only this time with stronger fingers.

"Why do you let him use you this way?" Evelyn asked.

"I'm using him," Joanna replied.

"Is he capable of sex?" Evelyn asked.

"Rarely."

"Are you in love with him?"

"I'm in love with something, Evelyn. I don't know. Whatever it is must have another name. Does it matter if the result is the same? . . . Evelyn, I want to get back to Frank. He's going to pick a fight soon if I don't get him out of here."

"Am I going to see you again—ever?"

"Yes. Of course. Leave it to me for the present. Be patient. All right?"

Evelyn nodded. What else could she do?

She decided she would wait just long enough to see if Joanna could get Frank out without some awful incident. Lew was going about his business with the agility and reserve of a professional boxer. She found herself wondering what she could do to help in the intricate operation. That was a laugh! As if she didn't have enough of her own problems! She caught Lew's glance several times. He signaled her, nodded, but didn't for a second break contact with the person he was talking to. Probably a big distributor, or an important reviewer, or maybe a new executive in Lew's company. There must be many new executives by this time. She had read somewhere that a merger was being considered—or was it one of those conglomerate purchases? As she watched, Lew broke away, walked quickly over to her, put his hand on her arm, said, "Please don't leave before I have a chance to talk to you. If only briefly. I have something important to tell you. I'll be through there soon."

As Lew left, one of the group that had been talking to Frank and Joanna came over to her. This was the younger one. Early thirties was Evelyn's guess. He had a handsome face, intelligent, but hard. He introduced himself, holding out his hand. "Eliot Klein," he said. "You're Evelyn White. I've already asked. Are you in films or around them?"

"Neither."

"Good," said Eliot Klein. "I'm around. Collaterally. I work for the agency that's going to do the advertising on *Sharpshooter*."

"Then you must be very pleased," she said. "It has all the ear-marks of success."

"Maybe," he said. "Personally I thought it was a stinker. Please don't say I said so."

"Oh, I won't. I agree with you."

"I'm glad you do," said Eliot Klein. "Not that I'd find you less attractive if you didn't, but it's nice to be confirmed. I'd thought we'd gone far beyond that kind of post-Vietnam traumatic crap."

"Is that what you thought was wrong with it?"

"Yes. Didn't you?"

"No," Evelyn said. "I'm afraid my complaint is much less so-phisticated. I didn't think it made much sense."

"Well, of course not. I agree. It didn't. I mean we've been through all that so many times that the imagination simply has nothing to go on. It's stultifying."

Evelyn tried to conceal her perplexity from her companion. She didn't know what he was talking about. She was experiencing the same arrest of understanding with his words that she had experi-enced with the film. Was the Vietnam horror *passé*? Is that what he was saying? Was he saying that a national nightmare was not to be revisited because it didn't fit current jargon and attitudes? *Such a hard young man.* She wondered what his sport was. He probably had more than one. Handball? Wrestling? He seemed not to have an ounce of excess on him—flesh or sentiment.

"Movies mystify me," she said, thinking of Frank. She looked around to see if she could locate Frank and Joanna.

"Are you here with anyone?" Eliot Klein asked.

"No," she said, finding Frank and Joanna, and noticing that Joanna had taken Frank's arm and was trying to lead him away from a conversation.

"Why don't we cut out of here and go over to your place for a drink?" she heard her companion say as she saw Frank rear his head in a familiar way. The words ". . . *the fucking garbage you use for a brain* . . ." cracked out like a loud slap in the face. Evelyn saw Lew turn and move in that direction. Joanna was now pulling on Frank's arm. Frank stood his ground for a few more seconds, then turned and bulled his way through the crowded room, Joanna following. The insulted man was shaking his head pityingly. . . .

"What?" Evelyn said, turning to Eliot Klein.

"I said," he said, "let's get out of here and go to your place . . . or mine."

"Why should we do that?" she said, just to give herself time, just to let settle back the sudden uprush of fury that had almost spilled up and over, like a boiling pot. "What for?"

"What *for?*" he said, smiling amiably. "Just for the good clean fun of it."

"I don't know you," Evelyn said.

"You should," he said. "I'm worth knowing."

"I don't think so," said Evelyn. "I don't think I'd like to know you one second longer. Go away from me, or I'll make a second scene."

Young Eliot Klein shook his head, rather like the man bellowed at by Frank Moore, dispassionately, pityingly.

Evelyn didn't wait for Eliot Klein to move. She looked, spotted Lew, then walked away without another word.

"Lew—"

"Excuse me," Lew said to the man he was talking to. "Yes, Evelyn—"

"I must leave now," she said. "Please. I'm dead tired. We'll talk about whatever it was some other time."

"But I don't want you going home alone," Lew said. "What was the matter with your friend . . . Frank Moore?"

"I don't know, Lew. . . . Look, I *live* alone. I go home alone all the time. Please do forgive me. I'm not feeling well. Some other time."

"Will you take a cab from here?" he asked.

"Yes, I will. Is that the important thing—that you didn't want me to go home alone?"

"No, it was something else."

"Some other time," she said.

"All right, Evelyn. Take care."

In the taxi, Evelyn closed her eyes and tried to deal with her crisis. This was not like her at all. She wasn't given to hysteria, but her heart seemed to have enlarged to three times its normal size and its pounding filled her chest, her head, everything. She wanted to cry. She wanted to make whimpering noises. She was so full of anger that she could almost feel her fingers curve toward some anonymous, collective throat. No, *not* anonymous. Eliot Klein would do just fine! That smooth, inhuman, cold-blooded *creature!*

She opened her eyes and took a deep breath. Enough! Nothing so extraordinary. It was just the pile-up of things. Joanna and Frank. That seized her again in its cold, ominous grasp. There *was* something dreadful about it, and she was implicated in the dread. She was very near to panic. She felt she was living in a madhouse—she who had always looked on the "madhouse" cliché as a soap bubble! She recalled the young black girl she had seen standing naked in the street several days before, in the morning, on Sixth Avenue. The poor thing had on some rag of a coat, but the coat was open, and beneath the coat was nothing but her flesh. Her eyes were glazed and people walked around her quickly, quickly, as they would around a lamppost or trash bin. Even then the word "madhouse" hadn't occurred to her. This was New York. She had lived with the changes from year to year, but she had lived toughly and hopefully, waiting for the mass shudder that would convulse the city and shake it out of its paralysis.

But it was a madhouse. People were mad, and that's why it was a madhouse. The smooth savagery of an Eliot Klein, who singled out a woman for a night's sexual feeding as a tiger would a sheep, licking it pleasantly once or twice before crushing its skull. Lew, looking as stylish as a toreador in his blue velvet tuxedo, making a few passes at the bulls in his arena, coming over to say a few seductive words to his ex-wife. Joanna, in her new make-up, disastrously deep in an affair with Frank Moore. Not a love affair—no distortion of language could give it that name—but a terrible coming together of two people who had need of each other's troubles. And Evelyn White, who was waiting, waiting. . . .

17

This time, Gabe arrived in a mild, sooty, twilight glow. He took a
taxi from the airport. Not to the same hotel. Time had undone the
fading charms of the old place. He had made a reservation in advance at a newer hotel. It was more expensive, but Harry was not
one to balk at petty costs.

It was Saturday. He had planned to come on Sunday, but his
own meteorological check had made him investigate the possibility
of a Saturday flight. There was a big front bowling in from the
Pacific, and either it would be all over Stapleton Airport by Sunday or it would drop dead in the mountains. He decided not to
take the chance. He had an appointment with Mr. Sinclair and
Mr. James on Monday morning. He had arranged to have dinner
with Evelyn on Sunday evening. All of it—cold front, Evelyn, the
Fairmont people—crowded uncomfortably in his imagination. He
needed a little time to take out his clothes, to settle into the
city.

He had told no one among family and friends of his coming except Evelyn. He would have to speak to Ruth, of course. If she
found out that he had been East and hadn't contacted her, he
would be inflicting needless sorrow on his sister. As for the Singers
—he had had one letter from Laura, mailed to his office, which address he had left her, at her request—and that letter informed him
that Jeff had moved out for good. . . .

He telephoned to ask when it would be convenient for me to have
him come pick up his things. I said anytime, but he insisted that I

not be there when he came. He said it would be best for both of us
if we avoided another session. Thus ends twenty-five years of marriage. Not that I have all that much to say for the institution, but I
do feel betrayed in my deepest beliefs in the human spirit. Over the
years, I have seen Jeff protect his pride and dying talent with some
pretty shabby tricks, but I didn't think it possible for him to fall to
the level of a dime-store Faust, making such a cheap bargain with
fate. I shall start another life. I shall go on. The fool knows he must
support me, which gives me all the more freedom to begin to make
my own career in poetry. I have already contacted several people
who have read my work, and who are interested in me as a poet,
not as the wife of Jacob Singer. Not "Geoffrey." Did you know
that? He didn't like the distinguished name of Jacob, so he changed
it long before you and I knew him. I should have known when I discovered that that there was a fatal flaw in his character. Well,
enough! When you come East again, please contact me. I hope you
come with Jean. I would love to see her.

Just in case, I'm going to give you Jeff's new address and telephone number. Are you surprised that I have it? Don't be. It's much
in keeping with the Jeff Singer neither of us knew. He may pretend
to a new life, but he doesn't want to sacrifice any valuable old contacts. Someone might want him for a reading, or an anthology, or a
penny's worth of praise. He asked me to forward such inquiries. . . .

Gabe reread the letter in the muffled room of his hotel, sitting
in an armchair, half listening to the hum of the air duct, half listening to the sound of Laura's voice in the words she had written.
She had every right to her Joan of Arc act. The tears and the pain
were as real as the years could make them, but something in the
rhetoric sketched in a podium, a lectern, footlights. She was herself giving a kind of reading, even in a letter like this. Well, so
what? Who was not conscious of his style while still in control of
his language? Lawyers and poets made very different use of the
language, but the long experience of being judged, of *wanting* to
be judged, made them both semiprofessional performers.

*. . . I shall start another life. I shall go on. The fool knows he
must support me. . . .*

Gabe looked at the words one more time, seeing Laura strike
the pose appropriate to them, and at the same time he was aware

of the heartbreak that no posturing or rhetoric could diminish. Laura had always been an unlovable exotic, and even when circumstances had forced him to act her advocate, it was more in the nature of an abstraction than a reality. A sense of fairness had put him on Laura's side, but he could only come so close, and then her strange severities put him off. Her hair, her unfragrant perfume, her large, brown, slightly crazy eyes. He could credit Laura with all the emotions, but he could not pity her with the roots of his being.

Jeff was another story. Jeff's defects fell well within the range of Michelson affinities. He was out of sympathy with the man, but he knew how little it would take to be *in* sympathy again. Jeff contained great portions of his past, because Jeff had become for Gabe Michelson the universal against which one measures personal experience. They had never coveted each other's gains. There had always been a sameness in their responses. Like coldnesses and like warmths. Even in that last, dreadful scene, it seemed to Gabe that he and Jeff had argued over the head of Laura rather than about her. Laura mattered, of course, but it was not solely for her sake that he had expressed sorrow and disgust. It was more for Jeff's own sake. It was to prevent a blinded and panicked friend from doing himself some permanent harm. He could have left Laura without all that savagery. That savagery would come back to haunt Jeff, and that haunting would lead to worse self-mutilation.

Gabe wanted to talk to Jeff, to see him. His curiosity about Jeff had reawakened the moment he was certain he would return to New York, and it had grown with every passing day. While the return remained in doubt, the Singers didn't occupy his mind at all; but when the second trip was confirmed, Gabe began to think of Jeff, trying to imagine Jeff's new life. It became more than curiosity: it became a mirror image; he thought he might see something of himself in Jeff's accommodation.

The information Laura had given him in her letter was practically an omen. He had said to himself that he would not get in touch, that Jeff wouldn't welcome the contact, but he knew that he would. It was part of the pattern of events that had made him come a day early.

"Hello." A woman's voice. Cynthia?

"Is Jeff Singer there?"

"Yes. Just a moment."

"Hello—"

"Jeff—it's Gabe—Gabe Michelson."

"Gabe! Are you in New York?"

"Yes."

"Wonderful! How long? Where? What are you doing tonight?"

"Nothing in particular. I was—"

"Come, then," Jeff said. "We're having a few people over. It'll be nice. Let me give you the address—"

"I have it."

"How so?"

"Laura."

"Ah. . . . Have you spoken to her?"

"Not yet."

A pause, then: "Come. I'd like you to meet Cynthia. She wants to meet you. And I want to see you, of course. Will you?"

"All right."

Gabe considered the possibility of getting in touch with Evelyn and taking her with him. That would be an announcement, a commitment. Well, a partial commitment. Providing, of course, Evelyn was available. No, it would be a mistake, even if she was available, willing to come. There must be just the two of them when they met again. He must test his feelings purely, and not unconsciously conspire to be tripped toward some decision.

"It was lucky you found us in," Jeff said. "We're usually out Saturday night. . . . Cynthia, meet an old friend, Gabe Michelson. We met on the handball courts of De Witt Clinton High School, in the Bronx, several million years ago, when the earth was still warm."

Cynthia put out a hand and Gabe took it. She wore hexagonal eyeglasses. She was blond, pale, not particularly pretty. But she smiled a smile that explained a good deal. Gabe immediately thought of Evelyn. It was not an Evelyn smile, but it had its own wry charm. Cynthia wore a pair of beige slacks and a blouse. "Come in," she invited, turning around and walking into the living

room. There was a tough sensuousness in her movements. . . .
This is my body. Like? Look, then. No? Fuck you. . . . But he
could be mistaken in all these silent surmises. God knows he had
been mistaken in the past!

Jeff took his coat and hung it in a foyer closet. Gabe walked
into the living room, where a group of young people sat around,
as young as Cynthia, *her* contemporaries. Students too? Jeff took
over and went around in a circle, introducing, "Ann . . . Richard
. . . Maggie . . . Gary . . . this is Gabe Michelson, a very old
and dear friend. . . . Sit down, Gabe. What'll you have? Scotch,
right? Scotch and soda. . . ." Jeff went to the tables where the
bottles stood and prepared the scotch and soda. He went on talking—a little compulsively, Gabe thought: "Our friendship has survived distance, time, and, worst of all, or best of all, different
values. . . ." He handed Gabe a highball glass. Gabe took it and
noticed with a shock of distaste a smear of lipstick on the rim. He
turned the glass, said nothing. He had wondered how Jeff would
pull this off. Jeff was obviously going to make a production of
their friendship. He was going to be wise and witty and probably
untruthful. That "different values" was already a slight veer into
fancy. How different? Their values weren't all that different. Possibly a little defensiveness on Jeff's part. The girl introduced as
Maggie had lovely, dark eyes. Cynthia sat on a hassock, that same
smile on her pale face. It suddenly struck Gabe that there was a
good deal of attentiveness beneath that Da Vinci smile. . . .
"And do you know why our friendship has survived?" Jeff went
on, finding a place on the sofa, sitting down opposite Gabe, and
looking at Gabe rather critically, for all the affection. "Our friendship has survived because neither one of us is mean-spirited, narrow, parochial. Right, ol' buddy? We both believe there's more to
life than our specialties. Gabe believes in the importance of litera-
ture. I believe in the importance of law"—he smiled—"or at least the
right interpretation of the law. We respect each other's gifts. Isn't
that so, lawyer Michelson?"

Gabe said, "You're the gifted one. I'm just a plodder."

Jeff made a face. "That's what I mean by respect," he said. "I
happen to know different. He's not a plodder. He's a practicing
humanist. He's a man who tries to squirt a little justice into the

monstrous machinery we call law. . . . You might be interested to know that Gabe makes his home in Denver. . . ."

They were interested in that. There were the usual questions about Denver. He knew what fascination a city like Denver held for New Yorkers. Much more foreign than Paris or London. But he soon discovered they weren't all New Yorkers. Maggie, the girl with the large, dark eyes, was from Detroit. Richard, the young man with the scraggly beard and clever look, was from Scranton. Cynthia was originally from Florida. The other two were natives.

The conversation turned away from origins. Gabe learned that Maggie worked in the garment industry. She tried on new outfits, because her size was just right and she could tell the designer what alterations to make before going into production. Richard worked as a junior editor in a big publishing house. Ann was married to Richard. Gary, a Viking with a blond beard and blue eyes, knew everything there was to know about cameras, and he worked in a big discount shop on Lexington Avenue. How did they all come to know each other? This way and that. Through school, through marriage, through the purchase of photographic equipment. Gary and Maggie were, presumably, lovers. Jeff Singer was poet-teacher, and Cynthia was his pale and enigmatic mistress.

They went back to the conversation they'd been having about the prospective closing of Radio City Music Hall. Richard offered embellishments to his first idea. He had proposed a refurbishing of the place into dozens of small theaters, where each evening—or maybe only a few times a week—the city's criminals would be invited to talk about or act out their particular violence or vice. Muggers would be guaranteed an average week's haul for their participation. Instead of injuring their quota of victims and adding to the general terror, they would take part in a city-sponsored encounter session, talk about their backgrounds, give a demonstration of their street techniques, come to know their potential victims at a personal level, and take away enough loot to make it all worthwhile. Prostitutes would come with their pimps, and they would talk about the more arcane aspects of that relationship. There were easily available figures on the nightly cost of these depredations to the citizenry, and wouldn't it be worth that same cost to remove the nightmare, make the streets safe, and provide an entirely new form of entertainment?

Gabe was reminded of his evening at the Kirschners'. Life was becoming Orwellian. Some wanted counterviolence, some wanted to absorb into society the horrors afflicting it, like this kid, Richard, whose idea was, of course, not being advanced seriously, but even in its absurdity there was a degree of thoughtfulness that spoke to the imagination. It was not *totally* absurd. Gabe's own mind was already working on the legal niceties of such a fantastic scheme, figuring what kind of legal immunities could be worked out to allow both the community and the criminal to co-operate without violating every law on the books—which meant that his own predilections were firmly on the side of the absorbers instead of the counterpunchers.

Absorbed, indeed, for it must have been some time before he noticed Cynthia, noticed her eyes, which had the look of having examined him for long seconds. She smiled at him. She kept her lips closed when she smiled, one corner of her mouth skewed slightly, giving an effect that was at once mocking and kind. Jeff, too, was looking at him, as if challenging him in his maturity and long friendship to find in this scene the moral club that he, Gabe, had come to find; that he, Jeff, had *invited* him to come and find. Each spoke to him differently in their silent ways, and Gabe was able to make out the true and terrible pathos in the life of his friend Jeff Singer. It was not the difference in years, the betrayal of Laura (who might not, after all, have been betrayed), nor even the spectacle of a failed poet trying to coax his half-charred phoenix to rise, but, rather, the hopeless disparity of experience. He could see it now in Jeff's age-creased, defiant, yet self-doubting eyes. These young people, Cynthia included, were cut off from Jeff's experience and therefore couldn't share in its poignance; just as Jeff was cut off from their future and therefore couldn't share in its vision. Oh, sad! If Jeff's art had been great and prolific, Jeff might have attracted sacrificial virgins right into his grave; but his art had been neither great nor prolific, and this Cynthia was no sacrificial virgin. She would leave him in time, and exactly for the reason that Laura, the sibyl, had foretold. Cynthia would finally gauge his limitations and be contemptuous of them. Cynthia would not have the lifetime of effort before her eyes to make her compassionate and forgiving. She would leave him for the reality of his age, as he, Jeff, had seized her for the hope of her youth.

And later, in the kitchen, where Cynthia had gone to prepare coffee and where Gabe had gone to get a drink of water, it was as if this pale young woman had read all his thoughts.

"Have you seen Laura?" she asked.

"Not yet . . . but I did get a letter from her a couple of weeks ago."

"How's she doing?"

"I gather she's doing well."

"I told Jeff she would."

"Does Jeff worry about it?"

"Of course. Did you think he wouldn't?"

"I didn't know. It was a bad scene at the parting. I happened to be there."

"Jeff told me," she said. "He thinks a lot of you. He values your good opinion. I hope you'll go on being his friend."

"I'm here," Gabe said simply.

"Yes," said Cynthia. "I'm very glad you are. Jeff needs his friends."

"Who doesn't? But why in particular?"

"Because," Cynthia replied, throwing a quick look at the doorway, "his last book of poems has been turned down everywhere. Last week it came back from some dinky press out West. They had the damn thing for more than six months. It was as if someone had punched him in the stomach. It knocked the wind out of him. He couldn't speak all day."

"Ach!" Gabe groaned. "I'm sorry to hear that."

He *was* very sorry to hear that, not only for the crushing rejection to Jeff but because it made his gloomy vision that much more immediate. Cynthia said they were good poems, the best he'd ever written, but Gabe understood, as did this girl, that the best Jeff had ever written was neither for posterity nor today's fashion. Cynthia was already in the process of amelioration, and it was clear to Gabe that she had none of Laura's training or experience.

Then Jeff entered the kitchen and said, "Talking about me?"

"Yes," said Cynthia.

"Don't," said Jeff.

"All right," said Cynthia, and walked out with a tray bearing a coffeepot, cups, and saucers, leaving Gabe and Jeff alone.

"She had this apartment before I moved in," Jeff remarked inconsequentially, not looking directly at Gabe. "Did I tell you she has a son?"

"No."

"She has. Seven years old. He's living with his grandmother right now in Ventnor City, out on the Jersey coast. It's very nice. I've been there. Nice place for a kid to be growing up. The seashore. . . ." his voice trailed off.

What a mess! Worse than anything he had imagined! A seven-year-old boy! How long would such a balance of imperatives weigh in Jeff's favor?

"Did she tell you about my book?" Jeff asked.

"Yes. . . . I'm very sorry to hear it."

Jeff propped his butt against the counter and looked up at the ceiling. He said, "There is out there a world of faggotry and malevolence that is beyond the reach of even the most hellish imagination. I, for one, cannot imagine it. . . ." He looked at Gabe. "The fact is," he said in a hoarse voice, "the fact is that I'm through with poetry!"

The rest of the evening passed in an uncomfortable haze for Gabe. The talk turned to summer plans. Richard and Ann and Gary and Maggie all had bright ideas about backpacking through Europe. Jeff and Cynthia had no such plans. Jeff and Cynthia would undoubtedly stay in the city and hotly await one catastrophe or another.

Gabe had already cut himself off from the fortunes of these people. They were all nice, and he wished them well, but they were neither his children nor his peers. He was really an intruder here. Even Jeff had been removed to a new distance as a result of this evening's visit. He had never thought of himself as Jeff's savior, but he had always felt himself linked to Jeff's fate. Jeff was of his generation, and he had always counted on Jeff's survival powers to confirm his own. Now he realized that Jeff would not survive, that Jeff was going down to a bad defeat, and he felt his own vulnerability because of it.

They had dinner in the same Italian restaurant where he had dined with Jeff. He asked Evelyn if she had ever been there before. She said no. Gabe said that was one of the differences between New York and Denver. In Denver, a restaurant this good would be known to everybody who could afford it. In New York, it could lie undiscovered for generations.

They had another drink, then they gave their orders. Gabe recommended the veal parmigiana. Evelyn said she wasn't too fond of cheese. "Everything is good," he said. She ordered the piccata.

They were nervous. He had phoned her midafternoon, and immediately sensed the effect of the overwrought weeks. The seal of infatuation had been broken, and the air of the world had seeped in. There was tentativeness. Each waited for the other to set the tone. There was a mutuality of fear, and this drove them both to retreat behind a flurry of banalities. . . . "I'm staying at a different hotel." . . . "You sound no nearer over the phone." . . . "Is everything all right with you?" . . . "Will I be able to see you tonight?" . . . "Is that a serious question?" . . . "Tell me everything—all at once!" . . . "Save it for tonight." . . .

He had walked to her apartment early in the evening. When she opened the door, she was dressed for the evening, a dark blue dress, a simple gold band for necklace, her face made up in her fashion, her reddish-brown hair shiningly in place, her hands held out to him. He took them, stepped inside, kissed her.

"I've made us a drink," she said. "To help get over this moment."

"Is it a bad one?" he asked.

"A nervous one," she said.

He nodded. No use denying it. They had lived apart so intensely that coming together disturbed the special intimacy of their separation. Gabe felt that their feelings were trapped in layers of different density, and neither knew what movement was needed to blend them. They silently acknowledged the difficulty of the moment, had their drink, went to dinner.

During dinner, they were able to relax a bit more. Evelyn told him about Frank Moore and Joanna Hopkins. She expressed to him her fear of something destructive.

"Like what?" he asked.

"I don't know," she said. "It's bad chemistry. Two unstable solutions—if that's the way to put it."

He nodded. "Who concerns you more?" he asked.

"Joanna," she answered promptly. "I don't think Joanna can harm Frank any more than he can harm himself. Not so the other way."

"Have you warned her?"

"Yes. No need to. She knows."

Gabe waited a few moments to see if she would say any more. She was silent, tasted the veal, looked at him with an expression of disbelief.

"Good?"

"Divine!"

"I always take you to good restaurants," he said.

She nodded. He felt a desire to reach under the table and put his hand on the softness of her thigh. The thought of it caused a sudden stir of lust. She looked at him and smiled, and her smile seemed to acknowledge that stir. . . . *It must be over,* he thought. . . . There was too much inertness. If they could have fallen into such difficulty in so short a time, then last November was nothing more than a sexual flare-up, made possible and quickened by the accident of having known each other before.

"Is yours good?" she asked.

"Oh, yes. You wouldn't think it so difficult to do, and yet I've tasted nothing like it elsewhere. I think all you would have to do is learn how to crisp the top just this way. . . . Shouldn't there be limited responsibility in friendship?"

"What?"

"I'm back to Frank and Joanna."

"Oh. I lost you for a moment. I don't know, Gabe. Limited if you feel limited. I feel terribly involved in this."

"I know what you mean. I guess I feel just as involved in the mess Jeff Singer is making of his life."

"Oh?"

"Yes—did I tell you about this before?"

"When do you mean?"

"In November."

"No."

"Probably I was afraid to mix the two: what was happening to me—to us—what was happening to Jeff and Laura. . . ."

He told her about Jeff and Laura, Jeff and Cynthia. He told her that Jeff had moved in with a young woman who had a seven-year-old son, and that the scene he had witnessed last night had all the earmarks of an unraveling, unstoppable tragedy. It would be different, he said, if Jeff had arrived at a point in his career where such antics could be absorbed into his accomplishments. A second round of notoriety might even make people take notice and applaud, might even renew interest in his poetry. But when there's only been one publication—and that practically stillborn—then there's a loss of dignity and the sickness of despair.

Evelyn listened sadly to the sad tale of someone she once knew. Gabe filled her glass from the wine decanter.

"We both have writing friends in trouble," she said.

"It would seem so," Gabe said. "Only, yours is about to have a considerable success, you tell me."

"I don't think that will make much difference," she said quietly. "You told me we had gone to the Algonquin that night to celebrate the publication of Jeff's first book of poems. You said that was the night you knew it was over between us. . . ."

"Yes?"

"Is that why we're here now, to round out everything?"

"What do you mean?"

"Jeff's success, Jeff's decline. The end of our first love affair . . . now this."

"What on earth are you talking about? Are you trying to tell me something?"

"No, dear Gabe, I think you're trying to tell *me* something this time."

"What am I trying to tell you?"

Evelyn was silent. Gabe looked at her profile. She had tipped her head away from him. He knew that he could end it right now— or that it could end itself by allowing these attenuating seconds to play themselves out. Had he been secretly arranging such a scene? But *why?* Why should he have arranged the means of getting back East, if it was only to wring a few farewell tears from both of them? Or was it something else? Did he want to take one clear last look at what he was losing before settling into his loss? Well, here it was. It was all but lost. He knew he could come on strong, snatch them away from this crisis, pump cheer, assurance, the rich red blood of desire back into this dying body, but he felt powerless to make such a move. He remembered Evelyn saying that there was nothing better than fun. . . . *Nothing is better than fun!* . . . Perhaps. Fun would be a hell of a lot better than what was happening right now—*but it wouldn't be more important!* Nothing was more important than finding out what was at the other end of this slow, airless journey.

They both knew it. Gabe couldn't be more certain of it than if he had spoken his thoughts aloud. It was there in the tilt of her head, in the delicious food she had left on her plate, in the little stalling play with the tines of her fork. They remained motionless in the seconds that sagged. . . .

"Evelyn—"

"You said, 'last night,'" she put in quickly.

"What?"

"You said you had visited Jeff and his girlfriend last night."

"Yes?"

"You told me you were coming on *Sunday.*"

There was no point in making up stories. The truth of his feelings—and hers—was the only thing that mattered. "Yes," he said. "I came a day early because there was a chance of being snowed in if I didn't get off on Saturday. When I got to my hotel, I wanted to phone you, to tell you that I was here, but I decided against it. I decided I needed some time in the city by myself, to see how much *was* the city, how much was my state of mind, how much was separation from my family, how much was anticipation of sex with you. Also I wanted to see Jeff, I wanted to see what was happening to him. . . ."

"And?" she asked.

"And what was happening to him was terrible."

"And you don't want the same thing to happen to you," she said.

"It couldn't," he said. "I'm not Jeff. I wanted to see if I could recognize any of my motives or feelings in him, his in me, but it's all different. No comparison at all. Do you know what I think? In these last few minutes, we've begun living our lives without each other. How does it taste?"

"Rotten," she said. "But I'll live."

"Of course you will! So will I. Nobody dies from that sort of thing. . . . Look, are you through with that dish of yours?"

"Very."

"Do you mind if we just skip dessert and get out of here?"

"Not at all."

They did that. Gabe paid the bill and they walked out of the restaurant, into a damp, chilly evening. For no particular reason, Gabe turned right and they walked to Houston Street. There was a playground of some kind on the corner. A tall storm fence around the playground. It was a dark, forbidding corner. Gabe stopped, reached out an arm, and drew Evelyn close to him. He could feel the deep shiver of her body.

"Yes," he said, "that's the way I feel too. I don't want to lose you. I would survive, but I don't want to lose you. There's no use trying to analyze why it's so, it's just so."

"What will you do?" she asked.

"What I have to," he said.

He knew that Harry Curtis had a deal on his properties as soon as he met with the Fairmont people the following morning. Mr. Sinclair and Mr. James were punctually present, and this time they were joined by a Mr. Joseph Dietrich, who was obviously the man to make final decisions.

They sat around a table in the same room where Gabe had enjoyed a northerly view of Manhattan on previous occasions. It was again a dirty day, with fog and soot.

"We'd like to buy your client's properties," Mr. Dietrich began. "I'm acquainted with the negotiations which have been going on. I think the two sticking points are the multiple-of-earnings factor and the rights of first refusal of future—"

"May I interrupt?" said Gabe.

"Certainly."

"My client has changed his mind on the rights of first refusal. He's no longer interested in that kind of contract work."

"Good, then," Mr. Dietrich said. "That should simplify matters. And I can say in return that we no longer insist on a stock transfer as part of the purchase price."

"A promissory note?" Gabe asked.

"Yes. We'll pay 29 per cent in cash on the final figure, and a promissory note for the balance over the next three years."

"That sounds satisfactory."

"Good. . . . Now . . . on the multiple-of-earnings figure: Why don't we just split the difference? Can we settle on ten-and-a-half after taxes?"

Gabe did a rapid calculation. That figure would bring the purchase price to slightly over two million. Twenty-nine per cent of that would be about six hundred thousand. Enough for Harry to begin throwing his weight around in Douglas County. With that kind of cash and notes from Fairmont for the rest, Harry would have nothing but smiles from his banker on any loans he might care to negotiate.

"That sounds fair to me," Gabe said. "I'll get in touch with my client and try to get an answer for you within twenty-four hours."

Mr. Dietrich got up and shook Gabe's hand. He said, "Arnold has a list he'd like to check over with you. Can you spare the time now?"

"Certainly."

Gabe looked at his watch. It wasn't ten yet, but he assumed that most of the day would be taken up with Mr. Sinclair. He would have to phone Evelyn sometime before noon and tell her that the day looked spoken for. He recalled the look of the morning streets when he and Evelyn had walked around the corner from her apartment house for breakfast. The air was chilly and heavily impregnated with river effluvia. But he had felt very much at his ease. Evelyn was in the midst of one of her brimming menstruations, and they hadn't made love, which was all right too. . . .

He and Arnold Sinclair began going over contracts, mortgages, accounting practices, current and pending litigations, indebtedness, liabilities, and all the flotsam that bumps against the sides of such negotiations but never sinks them.

18

Gabe was in touch with Harry Curtis late that same afternoon. The next day, he was able to conclude a purchase with the Fairmont people.

He continued working with Mr. Sinclair all day Tuesday, telling him at the start that he wouldn't be able to work with him on Wednesday. Perhaps they could conclude all this preliminary work by Thursday, so that he could get back home by Friday. Mr. Sinclair saw no reason why not.

On Wednesday morning, quite early, Gabe rented a car, picked up Evelyn in front of her apartment house, wound through the streets to the Midtown Tunnel, and by nine o'clock they were well on their way to someplace on the Island.

Evelyn hoped that he wouldn't be disappointed in this trip. She said the shore might not be so nice at this time of year. Gabe challenged that. He said he'd always found the shore best in the off seasons. The beaches were clean, and there was a flavorful melancholy not to be had in the summer. He said that was one of the things he missed most.

"Don't the mountains give you something like it?" Evelyn asked.

"They give me something, but not that," Gabe replied. "No, really, the mountains are grand. There are places in Denver where you come upon a view that takes your breath away. Particularly in the winter months, early spring, when there's still a lot of snow up there. The snow gives it definition. Late afternoons, in certain kinds of cloudiness, you get a blue so blue that you think it's going to run down the slopes in streams of ink. It's awesome, but it just doesn't speak to me the way the ocean does. I can see how it would speak to others. If you had them in sight when you began dreaming your dreams of specialness and immortality."

"Did you dream of specialness and immortality?"

"You bet. Who didn't? Didn't you?"

"Specialness, yes. I don't think immortality."

"Never?"

"I don't think so."

"My goodness, there must be something wrong with your apparatus," Gabe said scoldingly. "Didn't you think God had special plans for you? Didn't you believe that God would finally reveal His fine discrimination by exempting you?"

"No, I never did," Evelyn declared. "Rather, I never thought of it. I had my eyes fixed on a huge celebration that was being prepared for me, a super Chanukkah-Christmas love feast. I would meet the prince I was going to marry, and we would be given the mortgageless key to the castle, and a no-pay credit card to all the Fifth Avenue shops in the world."

"God, you are a materialist!"

"I know," she said sadly. "Much more so then than I am now. I've learned."

"Learned what?"

"What's worth."

Gabe waited a few seconds, then asked, "What's worth *what? What* what's worth?"

Evelyn pressed his arm and said, "If we're going to talk crazy, then it's every man for himself. You don't believe in your immortality any more, and I don't believe in my credit card. What's worth is what's worth."

"You're so right."

They stopped at a diner at about eleven, deciding that they would have a lot of whatever could be had so that they wouldn't have to trouble again until dinner. They had orange juice and ham and eggs and toast and coffee.

It was a typical diner, with a running counter for the solos and booths for the ensembles. Gabe and Evelyn decided they would sit at the counter. The woman who served them had orange hair two stories high, skin as pink-pale and soft as a rose petal, a thin nose, a small mouth, small blue eyes, and a small gold crucifix at her throat. She talked to them as if they had been coming in here at least three times a week for the past five years.

"Want those eggs over, hon?" she asked Evelyn. Evelyn said yes. "Want those scrambled wet or dry?" she asked Gabe. Gabe understood and said wet. When she served them, the woman said, "Enjoy," and then went on: "I'll bet you're going to look for a place for the summer, huh? None too soon. It's getting worse every year. Somebody who stops in regular owns a place in Sag Harbor, says March is the end of it. You haven't got it by March, forget it. That's Sag Harbor. Not even on the ocean. That's a nice blouse, hon. I like those loose-knit things. I bet you live in the city, right? You probably took the day off to look for a place. It's a good idea. It's the only way you can get anything. . . ."

Evelyn thought: *She has a marriage band. She has no children. She and her husband never went to a specialist to find out why, but she counts herself at fault. She prayed and then said it was God's will. Now she goes to the hairdresser once a week and has that thing sprayed and remounted. She cuts out recipes from* Family Circle *and tries a few experiments in sex with her husband to make up for their sorrow. Oh, I hope he's nice, her husband! I hope he, too, tries to make it up to her. . . .*

Gabe thought: *There's friendliness in Denver, too, but it's a different kind. They don't exchange lives as easily there. Which do I prefer? I prefer this. I guess this is exactly what I mean when I try to define the difference. This woman makes me feel a life, and there's a daily bounty in collecting lives this way. It enriches my own. I can see this woman going home to a Cape Cod. She has three children. The eldest is married. The other two are old enough to take care of themselves. Her husband works as a guard at one of the electronic plants on the Island. They watch whatever they watch on TV, have friends over on Saturday night, have two cars. Swann said that everything was a matter of style, and calling his own tastes fine and Odette's vulgar was only an exercise in prejudice. I'm happy sitting here with Evelyn. She feels this woman's life as I do. I feel a great enjoyment just sitting here with Evelyn, talking to this woman. . . .*

They drove to Montauk, parked in the public parking area, and walked along the paths fronting the ocean. The coast-guard station stood out specter-white in its gray surroundings. The middle of March rarely borrowed from the coming season here in the East. Much more frequently, the departing one hung around to play more than one unnecessary reprise. This day was more on the side of winter than spring, but everything that Gabe hoped to find was here. The luminous white underside of gulls, the cutting northwest wind, the green-gray-black ocean, the tough beach growths, spiny and bitter green.

Evelyn had prepared for the day by wearing her fur-lined leather coat. This time she wore boots. Gabe, who had only what he had brought, wore a business suit, overcoat, and dress shoes that were rapidly becoming caked with damp sand.

"You look sensible," he said. "I look idiotic in this outfit: a businessman beachcomber."

"Who's to notice?" said Evelyn.

"Well . . . you."

"You look fine to me," she said.

"Do I?"

"You sure do. Even in your raglan coat and Florsheim shoes."

"Why do you like me?" Gabe asked.

"It's true that I do like you," she said. "I also happen to love you. I don't know why."

"How about a kiss?" he suggested.

They kissed with cold lips, feeling insulated from each other by layers of clothing. They continued walking.

"Why do you like *me?*" Evelyn asked, after some seconds.

"I was waiting for that," Gabe said. "Let's not go into such things. If we do, we'll get around to subjects I want to avoid completely today. I would like this to be a day . . . of what? . . . Come help me: what would I like this day to be?"

"Perfect?"

"That's lazy. Have a brilliant insight about what I'd like this day to be."

"I'm not the one for brilliant insights. You are."

"Am I? Do you respect my intelligence?"

"Enormously."

"Do you? That pleases me very much. You couldn't have

pleased me more if you said I had the body and vigor of a twenty-two-year-old."

"God forbid!"

"Why God forbid? Wouldn't you like that? Don't you have a taste for the green fruit?"

"No, thank you."

"But why not? You got something against twenty-two-year-olds?"

"Not a thing. Love them in their place, but their place is not with me. They're too busy finding themselves to see much of anyone else."

"Would the same be true of a twenty-two-year-old female?" Gabe asked.

"Would it?"

"No, it wouldn't," Gabe admitted. "A twenty-two-year-old female is a woman."

"Would you like to go to bed with a twenty-two-year-old woman?" Evelyn asked. "Would the green fruitiness of it appeal to you?"

"They're scarcely green at twenty-two these days," Gabe said, "but in a generalized way, yes, I would like to go to bed with a twenty-two-year-old. That's in a generalized way. Particularly, no. I've conceived a great particularity for you."

"But suppose you found yourself with a twenty-two-year-old who gave every indication that she was willing?"

"Why suppose something like that? That's a dumb suppose. I *wouldn't* find myself with a twenty-two-year-old, because in all likelihood I wouldn't be looking, because in all likelihood I would be very preoccupied with the many preoccupations that preoccupy me, mainly you. You satisfy me greatly. Therefore I do not look."

"What a sweet cop-out!" Evelyn said. "Have a brilliant insight about sex."

Gabe sighed. "Okay," he said. "I believe sexual exclusiveness is a man-made thing. Nature intended promiscuity. I walk in the street and see the general outline of a bosom and a behind and there's an ancient ache in my jaw. But on the other hand I *like* man-made things. I like Florsheim shoes and raglan tweed overcoats. I like antibiotics. I like bridges. They're very handy for crossing rivers. I like exclusiveness. I like you."

"And—?"

"Love you."

Evelyn slipped her right hand into the left pocket of Gabe's coat. She made a fist and ground it into the palm of Gabe's hand, which happened to be in the same pocket.

Despite the large brunch, they stopped at the pier in Montauk for oysters and clams. Gabe said that shellfish in Denver was confined only to the autumn months, and was much missed the rest of the year by an old shellfish eater like himself. Evelyn nodded, vaguely imagining the mountain fishermen going off with their nets and things.

"Where would you find shellfish there?" she asked.

"God, these are marvelous!" he said.

"Gabe!"

"Yes?"

"Where would you find oysters and clams in Denver?"

"You have to dig very deep," he said.

"Liar!"

"Take some of the starch out of your New York provincialism," he said.

They ate dozens.

They made remarkably good time coming back to the city. They were slowed as they approached the city, but even so Gabe had the car back to the rental agency by five-thirty, leaving them a great stretch of time before they could decently go to dinner. The streets were jammed with the homegoing. A late clearing of the sky provided an hour of blue dusk instead of the usual quick plunge into night. Evelyn and Gabe had walked from the East Side rental agency as far west as Lexington Avenue, enjoying their feeling of truancy as much as they had enjoyed their trip to the end of Long Island.

Neither had said so, but the feeling had grown between them that they were playing a game of grown-up hooky, stealing time to enjoy whatever it was their fancy to enjoy. Half the fun was the illicitness. Evelyn had taken the day off with a bad conscience, knowing that the material on the "Vocations" project was flooding in and that she should be putting in night hours and weekends instead of making holiday with her lover. Gabe was appalled at his own dereliction in breaking into ongoing negotiations to have this day with Evelyn. They had started out in the morning, carrying with them the gritty lees of guilt, but by this time they were high on anarchy. They would do whatever they wanted to do, and the more scandalous to their sense of order the better.

Like the movies, since it was still too early for dinner. They went to a foreign film in which two different actresses played the role of one, and the handsome, goateed male lead seemed not to know that he was the victim of a *Doppelgänger* gag. No, that wasn't quite it: the two women were really various projections of his own lusts, but since he didn't succeed with either, the whole thing took on the aspect of a colorful wet dream. At least for Gabe it did. For Evelyn it was another of those moviemaker movies, full of lovely, arbitrary scenes. But it didn't bother her this time. She ate the scenes like pastel-colored Jordan almonds, sweet candy in the darkness, holding Gabe's hand.

Then they went to dinner at a French restaurant, one Evelyn knew. Since they hadn't reserved a table in advance, they had to conspire murmurously with the *maitre d'*. . . . ". . . *if this party doesn't show up . . . why don't you have a drink at the bar, and we'll see. . . .*" So they had a cocktail at the little bar, and then another cocktail, and another, and by the time they were shown to a table they were pretty well smashed on martinis.

"You told me," said Evelyn, "that you had only one affair since your marriage. You said it wasn't very nice."

"If I said so, why do you bring it up?"

"Because I want to get that out of the way. It bothers me."

"Why does it bother you?" Gabe asked. "You didn't even know or care that I was alive then."

"Don't be silly. *Now* I know you were alive then. I'm reconstructing a life. Tell me. If you tell me something interesting, I'll tell you something interesting."

"I'll keep you to that," he said.

"All right. . . . When did it happen? How long ago?"

Gabe sighed and tried to summon back to life an incident that was misbegotten from the start and mercifully dead in a very short time. . . .

She was, alas, the divorced wife of a client, who had called him up to say that she had some legal business she would like to discuss with him. He tried to make an appointment at his office, but she insisted on taking him to lunch. Well, to make a short story shorter, the good lady had other business in mind. She was a very good-looking woman—in fact, a downright voluptuous woman. Gabe said he couldn't claim any marital unpleasantness going on at the time. It was only and simply a highly desirable, excessively sexual woman making this blunt, perfumed, dream-stuff proposal. She said she was surprised that he hadn't noticed her interest before, when she was still married to Ed, particularly that evening when he had come over to discuss some business. Well, he hadn't noticed, and he seriously doubted that she had sent out any strong signals. She might have thought she had, but, then, women were always supposing vibrations in the air when all he had ever observed were the conventional nods and smiles. . . .

"Are you being a male whatsis?" Evelyn asked.

"No, I'm not being a male whatsis," Gabe said. "I think women are everything *they* think they are. But, look, if you'd rather I didn't go on with this story, I'd be perfectly—"

"Please go on! Now I've got to hear! So she seduced you. How? Where? Her place?"

"Yes. Her place. Her very own apartment. With incense and music."

"And was she voluptuous?"

"Oh, Evelyn!"

"Please!"

"She was a Turk's dream."

"I think I'm going to kill you," Evelyn said, eating her food very fast. Then she asked, "And why did it turn out to be so unpleasant?"

"Because the woman was a fool."

"How?"

"Evelyn, this is ridiculous!"

"Gabe, I promise you: no more. Just tell me that. Don't you see? . . . I've *got* to know how that woman was a fool."

"Her mental grasp was about ten miles short of her reach," Gabe said. "She had ideas about everything and knowledge of very little. She was an interior decorator, an expert on antiques, a gourmet cook, had the inside dope on Colorado politics, was consulted regularly by the Denver art museum on the arrangement of exhibitions . . . none of which, of course, was true."

"Oh, I feel so sorry for her," Evelyn said. "Don't tell me any more."

"With pleasure. Now you tell me your story."

"I feel *so* sorry for her," Evelyn went on, deep into some kind of rueful identification. "How terribly inadequate she must have felt!"

"From this distance, yes," Gabe agreed. "Close up to it, as I was, it was just depressing."

"And her voluptuousness disappeared?"

"Practically overnight. No amount of sex can triumph in such dimness."

"And yet I'm jealous of her," said Evelyn.

"I know you are," said Gabe. "I know that's why you asked. I know you had no story to tell me in return."

"How did you know that?" Evelyn asked, realizing that she didn't have anything to trade, that that one little passage before Frank Moore had receded so far from life that attempting to revive it would be more like necromancy than anecdote.

"And I could kick myself for letting you twist my arm," Gabe said.

"Darling, have one more insight," she pleaded.

"No!"

"Yes. . . . Why am I jealous of this poor woman and not of your wife?"

"I have no idea."

"Yes you do," she said, but didn't pursue it.

She was right. He did have an idea. It was a nebulous idea that had begun to collect in his mind even before she asked the question, but that wouldn't condense into form until he could examine it apart, alone, look at it steadily and whole, as he felt he must.

He conducted this examination after he had concluded his business with Mr. Arnold Sinclair. He now had a firm offer to bring back to Harry, and if Harry accepted it he would get in touch with Sinclair and tell him to go ahead with drawing up the final contract. His business in New York would be completed. Successfully. He would get a fat fee. Nothing to retire on but enough to make some pleasant changes in his life . . . in *all* their lives.

"All" included Evelyn, and with this inclusion he was brought back to the question he had brushed aside. Yes, he knew why Evelyn was jealous of that other woman but not of his wife. It was of the same order of feeling as he had experienced when he included Evelyn in his thoughts of the future. Evelyn had legitimatized their relationship, and in doing so she was forced to accord Jean her rights. But not that other woman. Jean had earned her right to respect as a wife, but that other woman was the eternal threat of sundering and chaos lying at the edge of order.

And Evelyn knew, too, why she was jealous of the other woman and not of Jean. The frozen fear within her had been thawing in their warmth and now had come to life to sting her viperously. She was her own threat. If that other woman, why not Evelyn White? If Evelyn White, why not some other woman? By abetting infidelity, she had sanctioned it. There are only two sides to a curtain, once drawn, and there was no human reason to suppose that she wouldn't occupy the other side of the curtain at some time.

But even that was not it. Infidelities like the one Gabe described could be dealt with, but how about the heart that could be moved from so many years of intimacy, loyalty, and appreciation? Gabe had never denied that there had been great appreciation for the patience and sacrifice and the large debt of small things a man and a woman living together can accumulate.

Was she offering something better than that? Now, *seriously*— because it was as serious as it could be—what demand could she make in the face of that indebtedness? What could she offer to weigh against that weight? Just love? Did she really value it all that much herself, that she could ask this decent man to tear up so many lives for the sake of it? She didn't know. She had thought she knew, but now she realized she didn't know. Her heart went out to Gabe in the painfulness of it. Now that it was imminent, she could see how much pain there would be, and because she had come to mean enough to Gabe to exact such pain, she felt it was almost possible to exempt him from the choice.

They paid a price for all that fun. The day of hooky had left them with a near panic of responsibilities. Gabe had announced to Jean that he would be returning Friday. There was nothing more to hold him here. On Thursday, he had his last, lengthy conference with Mr. Sinclair. It started in the morning, went on through lunch, and continued until late in the afternoon. He hadn't phoned his sister *once!* Unthinkable! Well, did he *have* to phone her? Who was to tell her that he had been to New York? The chances of her finding out were too remote to think of seriously. But good odds didn't relieve him of the guilt of dirty dealing. *Ruth,* for God's sake! She who had cheered on his life and good fortune with the steadiness of sunrise! So he must phone her. Don't think, don't brood, just do it!

He apologized to Ruth for not telling her in advance that he was coming to New York, but it had all happened with the unexpectedness of a ripening business deal. She could understand that.

"How are things?" he asked.

"All right."

"The kids?"

"They're okay."

"Ruth? What's the matter?"

"Oh . . . nothing."

"Tell me. Is it Arthur?"

Of course Arthur! Eternally and ludicrously and hopelessly Arthur! He had gotten into trouble with his coin-operated machines. Gabe had written a letter after the last visit assuring Arthur that his pinball horoscope idea was totally unpatentable, but that hadn't prevented the cotton-brained fool from going ahead with it, investing money in having machines built to his specifications, and then trying to get them placed. So far he'd had his tires slashed, his machines smashed, and nighttime calls threatening his life.

"Jesus!" Gabe whispered, feeling that this brother-in-law of his had raised misfortune to the level of high art. "He's getting out of it, isn't he?"

"How can he? All the money we've got is invested in those stupid things."

Sitting in a chair in his hotel room, Gabe squeezed shut his eyes and tilted back his head, rocking it slowly from side to side. This was disaster. That man was born with a deficiency of mind as others are born with a deficiency in the blood. He had none of the normal immunities. He was as susceptible to exploitation as others were to disease. He should be committed to an asylum for the helpless.

"So what are you going to do?" Gabe asked. "Is it a matter of food on the table, next month's rent, what?"

Silence.

"Ruth. . . ."

"I told him I would leave him," she said.

"It's about time!"

"I told him I would take the children and go away."

"And you should!"

"He said that I must do what I think right, that he would respect my decision, but that he had to fight for his own rights. . . . I don't know, nonsense like that. He feels he's in a war, and that he mustn't run in the face of the enemy. . . ."

"Ruth," said Gabe, "sooner or later you had to face the fact that Arthur is deranged. I don't know what to call it—I'm sure it has a name—but whatever it is, it is a source of constant danger to you and the children. It seems to me that Arthur is a man who was born at odds with reality. I don't think he sees things the way you do, or I do, or any normal person."

"I'm afraid that's true," Ruth said.

"All right, then," he said, knowing he could no longer avoid taking a hand in his sister's hopeless marriage. Naturally this would happen now, when he needed every scrap of his resources to do whatever had to be done, but the nature of the beast was recognizable by its stripes. The reality of his own situation became clear through the complication of Ruth's. "Tell me," he said, "what is the most important thing at the moment? Is it money? If I gave you a check for a thousand dollars—"

"Gabe—"

"—just to give you some mobility right now—"

"Gabe—"

"What?"

"I'm not going anywhere."

"Ruth!" he exploded. "You have got to leave that maniac!"

Perhaps, if she had to, but not now. If those gangsters killed him, they killed him, and that would be the end of it. But she couldn't leave him now for a very practical reason. She wouldn't be able to take care of her own children if she did. She would be paralyzed waiting from moment to moment for the news. Better to stay where she was. Better to let him fight this thing out on his own. His family knew about it. They weren't indifferent to her life, to the lives of the children. They were sending her checks now, regularly, every month, with the ironbound understanding that Arthur was not to be given a penny of it. It was set up in a bank account in her name only. . . . "You know," she said, "in a way you have to admire his courage. He's fearless. . . ."

Yes, thought Gabe, *lunatics often are.*

But there was something in Ruth's voice that arrested Gabe even as he sought to break into her sad monologue with a roar that would blow her and her kids out of that mare's nest. He listened more closely, and he could finally make out what she was saying. She was completing the process of making Arthur her fourth child. The red haze cleared from Gabe's vision, and he saw that Ruth was waiting out this latest and last of Arthur's futilities. Arthur's family and Ruth were now in league to build around the man that asylum for the helpless. Ruth would be in charge of the money. Nothing could stop Arthur from pissing away whatever money he had in his possession, but when that wreckage was complete Ruth would gather up the poor fool and put him away. She would hand him his clarinet, and he could tootle away the rest of his life. He was not to be trusted with anything. . . . "Maybe," Ruth said, "in a couple of years, when the kids are a little older, I'll start up a business of my own. Arthur can help me. I'll be able to keep an eye on him. Arthur's family said they would set me up in a hardware store in a good location if I would stay in charge. . . ."

"And you don't need any money now?" Gabe asked.

"No, Gabe."

"I'm going back tomorrow," he said.

"I'm sorry we didn't get together this time," Ruth said, but there was no real hurt or accusation in her voice. The critical turn in her own life had for once pre-empted her concern for others. "Give my love to Jean and the children."

"I will."

There was nothing he could do. Ruth's strange life had come full circle, and in a way there was something condign in her fate. She could have been much luckier—Arthur needn't have been such an extreme case—but the image of Ruth in charge of the drill bits and electric toasters was not an incongruous one. She would bring to it the efficiency and good cheer she had brought to everything in her life. If she could manage Arthur, a hardware store would be child's play.

But the fading of his imagined role in Ruth's life gave Gabe no ease. He had reached the stage where anything that happened, or its opposite, could be made into a comment on his own situation. If the burden of Ruth had looked like a familiar perversity of fate, then the relief of that burden looked equally perverse in the freedom it gave him to act.

There was, he knew, no point in looking for signs. Everything lay within.

Nor could he even leave Laura to her own fate. He wondered if he wasn't himself suffering from some kind of emotional disorder. Why should he feel compelled to get in touch with Laura? God knows he had never felt close to the woman, and she certainly had no need of him now; yet he felt he must be in touch with her this once before leaving the city. Weariness drained him at the thought of it. Natural attrition should have worn away the relationship to dust by this time, but precisely because it would have been so easy *not* to call, he felt he must. He was doing it much more for his own sake than hers. He was in training. He had slipped into the discipline of refusing to avoid the unpleasant.

Laura was, by her own estimation, a different woman. Jeff had done her a great favor. He had freed her to act. At last! Yes, she had succeeded in obtaining a job. She was giving a course in the evening at an adult-education center, three times a week. She loved it—*loved it!*—and best of all, she had made a host of new friends through it. She was proud and free! She was a different woman!

To himself, Gabe thought that she was not a different woman, that she still thought of herself and the world in the same shrill, romantic terms. But it also occurred to him that one's sameness in different circumstances was all the change one needed. Ruth had been forced to act, Laura had been acted upon, and neither had been destroyed. Far from it!

"I saw Jeff," he said.

"Yes . . . and how is he?"

Condescending! Patronizing! *Maternal!*

"He seems to be all right," Gabe told her.

"Good!" she said with bright beatitude. "It won't last, of course, but I'm afraid I can't any longer make that my concern. There has always been a strong undercurrent of self-destruction in Jeff. I suppose you knew that. Sometimes I wonder if I would have allowed him to drag me down with him if we had stayed together. I thank God that he made the decision for me. Tell me, Gabe, did he mention to you the book of poems he's had circulating?"

"No," Gabe lied.

"I was wondering if he had any word on that," Laura said. "I don't believe there's a chance of it being accepted anywhere, and for the sake of his reputation it's for the best. They were not good poems. You know, we're not in touch at all. It's just as well. I didn't believe that something like that could end so completely, but it has, it has, completely. . . ."

The growing distaste he felt at Laura's tone had reached dangerous proportions by the time he hung up. No, she hadn't changed. Or if she had, she had changed in ways that made her no more endearing to Gabe. Cold or warm, in fear or in self-styled nobility, she remained a woman alien to his own nature. He would never understand or like her. Knowing this, he had recoiled against telling her that Jeff had given up on poetry after that last rejection. He would feel a traitor to Jeff to be the bearer of such confirming news. Nor could he bear to add a cubit to the awful pride that had raised Laura up to these towering heights.

Evelyn said she would rent a car and drive him to the airport. Gabe shook his head. He wouldn't allow it. She had already taken off one day this week.

"It's time coming to me," she said. "There'd be no question if I were ill. This is as important to me as any illness."

Gabe nodded. "Yes, but—" he said.

"But what?"

"But you're not ill. We know the difference."

Evelyn gave in. They did know the difference. That's why they had found their time together so pleasurable; they recognized differences and similarities; they recognized sincerity and fakery; they sensed limits and feared excess. They sensed they had come to some kind of limit, and they feared the weariness that would result from excess. It was not that they'd had too much of each other, but they'd had too much of the high-strung playing that substitutes for permanence. That was what was so wearying: the strenuous avoidance of the middle ground of emotion; the fear of relaxing in each other's presence. To relax would be to take certain attitudes and decisions for granted, and as yet nothing could be taken for granted. Another morning drive to the airport would only cause a thickening of mood. They were not children. They understood the crankiness that follows festivity. They understood the danger of trying to draw from each other what the self could no longer provide.

So they had dinner at the same fish place where Evelyn and Frank had occasionally eaten. It was convenient, and fresh sea food was rarely available in Denver, no matter how deeply one dug. The place had a mercifully mundane look. Tile floor, no-nonsense tables, brisk service, nothing leisurely or candlelit. A good place to depressurize the week.

Gabe told Evelyn about his sister and her crazy husband. He said he was amazed how impossible it was to prevent some fools from acting out their follies. He never really could understand alcoholics, drug addicts, or limpid-eyed Arthur Ehrlichs, who was really an angel of imbecility. He never did anything out of malice, only wrong-headedness. Gabe said he feared in himself a low threshold of tolerance for aggravated otherness. Like Laura Singer, for instance. He mentioned that trial too, and how he had found himself being drawn back to all the old aversions after acting her champion in the Singer crisis.

"I just can't stand the woman," he said. "She's a person who takes no cues from the world. She lives sealed within herself as in a plastic bubble. . . . But what am I saying? I just complained of having the same trouble, didn't I?"

Evelyn shook her head. "Not the same problem," she said.

"How not?"

"Because you worry about such things. You're aware of them. I don't think Lady Laura is."

"Maybe you're right. . . . We should be talking of something else."

Evelyn closed her eyes. Gabe noticed the pouchiness beneath those eyes. Ah, yes, she was tired! He knew so little about her, only what she chose to tell him, and what she chose to tell him were selected bits that would not compromise whatever stage they had reached in their odyssey.

"Would you like to know what I'm thinking?" he asked.

"I'm not sure," she said. "I guess so."

"I'm thinking that I must never see you again unless it's to live with you more or less permanently."

"I like the more or less."

"I don't," he said. "I don't know why I said that. It dribbled out. I'm nervous. Are you nervous?"

"Yes."

"Yes," he said. "We should be. This trip has rubbed away the newness. It's all very serious, and it has to be, because I have to have very serious reasons."

"I do too," Evelyn said.

"Meaning that you're not sure now?"

"Meaning that I wouldn't be sure of my feelings if I thought a tremendous sacrifice was being made."

Gabe turned away from Evelyn, looked at the large open area where waiters and waitresses crisscrossed, carrying orders. He said, "I guess there's no getting around the tremendous part of it." He turned back to her. "I love you," he said. "I'm tired as hell right now, worn out from the strain of it, but I know I could be happier living with you than I ever was or will be living with Jean. It would be a tremendous thing for me to live with you, but it will also be a tremendous thing for me to divorce Jean. I can't help it. If you would want it not to be a tremendous thing for me to divorce Jean, then let's say good-by now. It can't be a small thing for me. I can go on living with Jean, because all the machinery is there, but if I come to live with you the machinery will have to be broken. I don't see it as a sacrifice, because I'd much rather live

with you, but I will have to live with the breakage, and so will
you."

"Yes, Gabe," said Evelyn. "I had more or less figured that
out."

"I like the more or less," he said. "Have you also figured out
how you feel about it?"

"No. . . . I've been thinking about it a lot. I've been thinking
about nothing else . . . but I still don't know how I feel about it.
Come home and sleep with me. I don't want to do any more
thinking."

Evelyn set the alarm for the usual time in the morning. They
both showered and dressed. Gabe had to return to the hotel to
pick up his luggage, check out, take a cab to the airport. He had
plenty of time. They went down into a sun-bright, chilly day.

"Let's have breakfast in that interesting place around the
corner," Gabe said, then asked, "Is *everybody* there gay?"

"Everybody," said Evelyn.

"Even the customers?"

"Not you and me, darling."

It was a surprisingly cheerful breakfast. They had both dreaded
a continuation of last night's heaviness, but something had buoyed
their spirits. Even as they talked of other things, each rummaged
through memory to see if they could discover what that something
was.

19

Early in May, Evelyn's brother, Bob, flew to New York from Miami. He was making a round-robin trip, having completed the first leg with a visit to his parents in Coral Gables, then proceeding to New York to visit his sister. Evelyn had been to see her parents just a few weeks earlier. A short visit. Just a few days.

She met her brother in the hotel, just off Fifth Avenue, where he was staying. "Wait down there," he said over the house phone. "I'll be with you in a minute."

"Did you talk to Mom's doctor while you were there?" Evelyn asked her brother.

"Yes," he said. "He said there was nothing to worry about. There's no way of predicting memory loss or the rate at which it will proceed. It's irreversible, once started. But that doesn't mean she'll become incontinent, feeble-minded, anything like that. It's just these . . . erasures in the tape."

"Oh, Bob! You make it sound like Watergate!"

Bob smiled and shook his head. "That didn't occur to me. . . . Evelyn, come on, be reasonable. Mom is almost seventy. That's not a great age, I admit, but neither is this memory loss coming on like a four-alarm fire. As soon as she oriented herself, she remembered everything. She knows where I am, what I'm doing, the names of everybody. . . . You know, it's not a calamity. She's in no pain. She loves her little garden. She has friends. Dad is being a sweetheart—considerate, loving—so what's with the hand-wringing?"

"I just find it monstrous that a woman with such lovely memories should have to lose them."

"How do you know how lovely her memories are?"

"Why, don't you think they're lovely?" Evelyn asked, shocked at the challenge. She wondered if her brother knew something she didn't. Nothing like a glorious love affair to make you slightly paranoid. "How could they not be? Anybody who has been that nice to others must have lovely memories."

Again Bob smiled, and shook his head. "Okay," he said. "In your own sweet way, you're as sentimental as Mom is."

"Am I?"

"You sure are."

"Do you think I deceive myself?"

"About some things."

"What things?"

"Other people," Bob said.

"Like you?"

"Like me. Like Mom. Like Lew. . . . Incidentally, that new film his company is putting out—*Sharpshooter*—that's going to make a pot of money. . . ."

"How do you think I was mistaken about Lew?" she asked.

"Why go into that?"

"It's important to me, Bob. At this moment, it's very important to me that I understand my miscalculation about other people."

He looked at her sharply. "Is it?" he asked. "Why?"

She told him about Gabe. Bob recalled more of a name than a presence. He must have been about eighteen or nineteen at the time, and rather fiercely occupied with his own life. She told him that it was all very serious, and that Gabe was in the process of doing something about it in Denver. She told him she was deeply disturbed at what this was doing to the lives of other people, and that each day became a moral battleground. . . .

"Who—or what—is winning?" Bob asked.

"I don't know who's winning, but I think I'm losing," Evelyn said. "I think I'm on the point of giving up."

"Giving up Gabe?"

"Yes."

"Does he want to be given up?"

"I don't know."

"Why don't you leave it to him to decide?"

"Isn't that what I'm doing?"

"Apparently not. You seem to be fighting it out here. I think you're trying to make up his mind for him, one way or the other. That's an old habit, Evelyn. You make up your mind what people are like, and then you decide how they should act."

"Oh, Bob, for God's sake! I can't stand this *glibness!* What's happening to you? *Shouldn't* I try to decide what people are like? *Shouldn't* I try to anticipate how they'll act? Don't you? Doesn't everybody?"

"No, everybody doesn't," Bob said, looking steadily at his sister. Not hostility, but not gentleness either. There was a reckoning in his dark brown eyes. The years of being the younger brother? The years, possibly, of being misunderstood? He said, "You were always sure you knew what I was like and what I would do, and you were mistaken. You thought I should be some kind of priest of purity, and it always disappointed you that I was more part of the world than that. Isn't that true?"

"I thought you had an unusual mind," Evelyn said.

"And now you don't?"

"I still do."

"Yes, but you thought I should apply my unusual mind in an unusual way," Bob said. "People are not always what they appear to be, Evelyn. I always had a materialistic, competitive streak in me, and for some reason you didn't want to see it. Take Lew: it amazed me when you woke up ten years later to the kind of man he was. Not that I think he's bad. He's not. He is what he is, but you thought he was something else. He's clever and ruthless, as he has to be, and a rather accomplished con artist. I saw that from the start. You didn't. You thought it was charm. You thought it was being sensitive to others. Well, he *is* sensitive to others, otherwise his system wouldn't work; but his sensitivity has very utilitarian limits. He doesn't use it much beyond those limits. I don't know this Gabe Michelson, but if you're in love with him, and if, as you say, he's in love with you, then for God's sake let him make up his own mind! Don't decide what's right or wrong for *him* to do!"

As she had feared, it was a mistake to unburden herself to Bob, but not for the reason she had imagined. He was not indifferent or uncomprehending, but something else. Honest? Was he right about the things he said? Whether he was or not, it was the last thing in the world she needed. Her self-confidence was bruised enough without this further mauling.

But was she really so prone to misread others? It would seem so. Look at Joanna. Look at Frank Moore. Could she have foreseen their getting together in this mysterious, sinister way? *Should* she have foreseen it? Were Lew's faults so easily detectable, or was Bob availing himself of the benefit of hindsight? Were there things about Gabe she wasn't seeing now, that she would learn to regret later, when it was too late, after so much uprooting and pain? What was it her brother was trying to tell her? To be less judgmental and therefore less exposed to the penalties of error? To take what was pleasurable and not examine its source or motives? God, where was she at? On one hand, Doris McAuley accusing her of sinking into a warm, ambrosial bath of self-indulgence. On the other hand, her brother accusing her of puritanical narrowness. On one hand, her former husband wooing her like a courtly gallant. On the other hand, young, creepy strangers like Eliot Klein offering a night of sexual acrobatics. This world was *unreal!*

As if that were something new! She knew quite well what the world was, but she had never before been so uneasy about her own place in it. She had never before felt so stripped of her moral and intellectual clothing. She was beginning to feel an inner nakedness and a shame at that nakedness. What had happened to that whole wardrobe of attitudes and convictions she had stored away with such smug assurance? Should she believe her brother, Bob, and put an end to expectations and judgments? But then, what does one refer to? The merest craving? I want this and this and this—and that's the whole circle of the universe!

No, she may be mistaken about many things and people, but she was *not* crazy! Gabe was decent and Lew was devious. Joanna was in deep trouble and Frank Moore was the cause. Bob was clear-sighted and she was scared. This world was in a bad way and so was she, but she must not abandon her sense of right and wrong, her messed-up kit of values, because if she did she would be left howling in a desert, and she was just too middle-class for such a fate!

"Sometimes I wonder if we're not both living out some kind of fantasy," she said to a two-thousand-mile-distant Gabe.

"I know," he said. "How long has it been?"

"About six weeks . . . this time. It began in November. That's six months. And we've had a grand total of ten days together!"

"Nonsense," Gabe said. "We've been together at least six months. Considerably more, if you count inner time. We write, we talk, we think of each other—which is a hell of a lot more than happens in most marriages. I know I've discouraged you from coming here. I guess I just don't like the idea of you sweating me out in some hotel room. I'm afraid of it. I'm afraid it will spoil something. . . . Listen, are you feeling different about things?"

"Gabe, I don't know. Yes, I'm feeling different. I told you once that I wouldn't live with unhappiness for long. I'm feeling unhappy. I'm not sure it's all because of you, but certainly a part of it is. This is going to sound ridiculous, but besides being my absent lover you're also my absent friend. Tell me, friend, what shall I do about you?"

"I think you should forget about me."

"Very likely! Does that mean nothing has happened? . . . nothing is going to happen? Why haven't you told me that before? I think that's something you should have told me."

"Are you finished?" he asked. "Something *has* happened. It doesn't matter what, since I'm still here and you're still there. But I have spoken to Jean. Listen, Evelyn, this may sound equally ridiculous, but I see now that the decision I make has to be valid whether you're there or not. I *want* you there, but I'm going to continue to live with myself, and I've got to know that I *can* live with myself, that I didn't do it *solely* for you. Does that make any sense at all?"

"Yes, Gabe. And if you decide that it isn't valid?"

"Then, I won't do it . . . but by that time it may be too late both for you and for Jean. That's the bind I've gotten myself into."

"You don't sound like you, Gabe," she said. "You sound shaky."

228

"I am shaky. Did you think I was some kind of fortress?"

"Yes."

"Well, you were mistaken."

"Oh, God, I know! I've been told I'm running up an Olympic record of mistakenness!"

"But do you see what I mean?" Gabe insisted.

"I suppose so. Yes. It's something that has nothing to do with love."

"Not nothing, just not exclusively. It isn't exclusively you or Jean. It's me, Evelyn. Darling, you go about your life. I do love you very much. I know it's absurd to say forget me, because you're not going to forget me, but try to go about your life without me. I'm working out what I must work out for my own sake. And you must go about your life for your own sake."

"This is insane," she said.

"I know it is," said Gabe.

"*You* must be the strong one," she said accusingly.

"Why?"

"Because I'm feeling so weak."

"My sweet and sexy Evelyn, I'm sorry I can't be as strong as you'd like. I wish I could be a tower of strength for both of us, but I never was able to bench-press two hundred pounds, try as I might."

"Let me come see you."

"When?"

"I don't know. Sometime in the next few weeks."

"What will that decide?"

"It may decide something for me."

"All right, then, come."

"I'll make arrangements in the next week. I'll call you up as soon as I know when I can get away."

"What a peculiar outcome after all we've said," Gabe remarked.

"I know," said Evelyn. "And I may change my mind about this, too."

"It wouldn't surprise me."

20

Gabe was no longer sure what would or wouldn't surprise him. His own thoughts and actions had become unpredictable, so why should anyone else's seem more certain? He didn't know what Jean was thinking. He didn't know because she didn't tell him. She told him nothing after what he had told her, and he accepted this silence as natural. He had no idea what to expect, but withdrawal and silence were recognizable preliminaries to anything that might follow. Jean had always responded to conflict by withdrawal and silence—and what was this if not conflict?

But surely it was something beyond conflict. Perhaps that's why he felt so abysmally tired and vacant: that she should have responded to this ultimate thing with the same refrigerator technique. Maybe she didn't think of it as "ultimate." Maybe she thought he was just confessing his sins, so that he could begin whatever expiation would be required, and then resume his normal life. And wasn't there a part of him that had considered this a distinct possibility? And wasn't there a part of him that reserved all finalities against the Jean that would be revealed in this crisis?

When he had come home this time, it was to tell Jean, as quickly and honestly as life would allow, that he was in love with another woman, that he wanted a divorce, that he wanted to marry and live with this other woman. But as life would have it, he was confronted with the exciting news that the art museum had opened an exhibit of the Armand Hammer collection. She had mentioned to him that it was coming, but he had probably forgotten. Now it *was* open, and she'd already seen it once, and it was a fabulous, fabulous collection, and they would both go early, that Saturday, the crush being tremendous, so they must plan to go as early as possible, and it was really a thrilling exhibition. Everything! Rembrandt, Van Gogh, Renoir, Rubens, Cézanne, Sargent. . . .

Of course, he mustn't spoil this exciting, joyous time for Jean. He had just concluded a big deal in New York, and she had congratulated him on his success, and now he must allow her the untroubled enjoyment of her life's passion. So they went early on Saturday morning. Pam had already seen it once, had other plans for the day. Andy was asked if he'd like to go, and he masked his indifference behind the pious fakery that some things a husband and wife should enjoy just by themselves.

The collection was as fabulous as Jean claimed. Not fabulous for a museum, but fabulous in the realization that one man had collected all of this, paid for it, owned it. Or had owned it. The brochure said these treasures would be taking their permanent places in various museums. Gabe found himself debating the morality involved in one man's amassing so much of the world's wealth that he could afford to buy himself this art kingdom. It was a relief simply to move moral debate away from the grounds that had become such a quagmire.

"Do you think anyone has the right to make all this his private property?" he asked Jean.

"Just as long as it isn't lost," she replied.

So much for that!

There was a gray, bleak Van Gogh that affected Gabe deeply. It looked like a walled-off enclosure in a prison yard, but it was entitled "Garden of the Rectory at Nuenen." Gray, gray . . . the trees, the landscape . . . and in the distance the pale yellow brightness of a sunset—or was it a sunrise?

"Do you like that?" he asked Jean.

"It's marvelous," she said, "but a little too morbid. I like the others better."

Yes, it was morbid. Maybe that's why Gabriel Michelson was finding such spiritual affinity in it. Jean knew that it was among the last paintings of the so-called "Dutch" period in Van Gogh's career, and that that eerie light that seemed to muffle its own refulgence, allowing very little of it to irradiate the landscape, was a harbinger of the eruption of color that would follow. Two such paintings—"The Sower" and "The Hospital at St. Rémy"—were across the room, and Gabe read appreciatively of "flame-like mobility of brushstrokes" and "controlled riot of contrasting colors." But he kept returning to the gray one in his tour of the room, trying to give a name to the feeling it evoked.

It spoke to him of lostness and familiarity. It looked like nothing he had ever seen, not that kind of familiarity but, rather, a reminiscence of mood. Finally he left the painting and joined Jean in the next room. More marvels there, particularly two portraits by John Singer Sargent. And there was the famous portrait of George Washington, evoking American history, bringing back to Gabe's mind an essay he had written in grade school, an essay on John Paul Jones, with a red, white, and blue cover, and a comment by the teacher that this was a well-written and imaginative piece of work of which he should be proud, which indeed he was, as were his mother and father . . . and Gabe at last located the mood in the gray Van Gogh painting.

It was the mood that had haunted him ever since he had pulled up roots from New York and had come to this high, sunny place. It was the familiar mood of lostness, despite the gorgeous weather, and the grandeur of the mountains, and the unhassled existence, and the freedom to walk the streets at night, and the glorious late-in-life sport of skiing, and the opportunity for his children to grow in an atmosphere free of fear. How could one not prefer all these things to the bankrupt mess the city of his birth had become? One did prefer it. He had reconciled himself to living out his years away from the filth and danger and expense. Good God, this was the century of uprootedness and mass murder! To have remained alive and well fed was to have drawn a winning hand from fate. As far as good fortune went, he was among the shamefully lucky few of the earth's needful billions. He had lived his whole life with a goodly share of the oceanic feeling, identifying with the misfortune of others, and yet this knowledge of relative blessedness left untouched the mood contained in the Van Gogh painting, the mood of lostness, the mood of a landscape unilluminated by a nebulous sun.

So the significant landscape was the interior one. Relative blessedness didn't feed a crumb to the absolute of self. He felt alien in this sun-bright land and probably always would. In this century of uprootedness, he had left his own roots by his own volition, and now, after ten years, he understood that one can leave a city but not a condition. By awakening love in him, Evelyn had awakened the sore consciousness of what he had been missing. He had been missing the condition of life the city of his birth had given him.

And if so . . . what? What did cities and senses have to do with Jean and Evelyn and the momentous move he was about to make? It was too easy to find reasons to justify desires. He had been looking for a tougher line of reasoning, one that would hold up in the future and on the other side of desire. He knew that he could have gone anywhere and lived rootless in this century of rootlessness if there had been enough love to make up for the loss. There hadn't been; that was the simple truth of it. You leave a city that will not allow a decent life, but you can't leave yourself, the self that was nurtured on those intensities and colors. There was a hunger in him for the deep colors that had been bleached out of his life, not by the beautiful sun of mile-high Denver but by the pale, Van Gogh sun of compromise he had created for himself.

When they left the museum and drove south toward the Valley Highway, Gabe said, "Jean, I must talk to you. . . ."

She looked at him as if she had a premonition of what he was about to say. "Talk to me about what?" she asked.

"About you and me."

"Yes, Gabe, about you and me. . . . Is there another woman?"

"Why do you ask that?"

"Because that's the way you sound."

"Yes, Jean, there's another woman."

In the hours and days that followed, he was to go over the bare simplicity of those few words and wonder if they could have been said differently, with greater sensitivity, with less directness, and he would come to the conclusion that since it was said as briefly as possible, it was said as well as possible.

They continued to drive in a silence that, second by second, enriched the irrevocable change that had come into their lives. Whatever happened, they could never be the same. They both knew that, and there was almost a feeling of awe to go along with the anguish.

Jean stared straight ahead, dry-eyed, her skin blotched by emotion. Gabe was grieved by the sudden, terrible isolation he had caused her. He was at once enemy and husband. The habit of years made him want to share her pain. The habit of years made him condemn himself for having caused it. He realized that he had always condemned himself for causing her pain, and while it was only a thin sliver of light in the massed thunderhead, it gave some small comfort to see it there.

"Please say something, Jean."

"What is there to say?"

"I'm sure there's something on your mind you could say."

"Who's the woman?"

"Evelyn White."

"Who's Evelyn White?"

"The woman I was going out with just before I met you."

"The one who threw you over for the movie producer?"

"That one."

"So that's the reason for all the business trips to New York."

"We met quite by accident."

"Do you expect me to believe that?"

It hadn't occurred to him that it might be difficult to believe, but now he saw that it might well be *impossible* to believe. Still, nothing he might invent would be more or less difficult than the truth.

"It's the truth," he said.

"And so what?" Jean said. "What do you want, a divorce?"

Nor did he expect to be confronted with that question so quickly. He understood this stiffness from Jean. She was holding him off, holding herself off, from whatever reaction lay on the other side of this shock. Did he want a divorce? No, he didn't want a divorce. He wanted something else. He wanted to slide out of his life with Jean and into a life with Evelyn by a kind of transitionless magic, but he recognized the wish for the gutless thing it was. That wasn't the way things worked in this life, or any life that had ever been arranged in the long, troubled history of man and womankind.

"I don't know," he said. "I guess, under the circumstances, I want to know if you do."

Jean turned away and looked out the window on her side. It was another lovely day. It was to have been a happy day. There was another long silence, and when Jean turned again it was to seek a handkerchief in the shimmering welter of her tears. She opened her pocketbook and found the handkerchief. She brought the handkerchief to her mouth, then began to weep, granting neither him nor herself any respite from this anticipated punishment.

Then followed silence and a cold adjustment to the new condition of their lives. He thought that Jean would make some arrangement in the house so that they wouldn't sleep in the same room, but he was mistaken. They didn't touch, but they continued to sleep in the twin beds, side by side. He thought that Jean would want the children told of the situation between their parents, but he was mistaken. She said nothing herself to the children, and by covert but powerful signals she indicated to him that she didn't want him to say anything either. Naturally the kids sensed something was up, but every time talk came near the central freeze, Jean shot him a look that warned him away from breaking it open.

She didn't want it in the open, that was clear. Gabe wasn't sure whether it was because of a bitterness she wanted to resolve in herself first or because she secretly hoped that another kind of resolution would obviate the necessity of telling Pam and Andy. Perhaps tell them when the crisis was past? . . . in an atmosphere that would make the telling less painful? Reconciliation? He wasn't sure. She wouldn't say. She said whatever was necessary to keep going the semblance of a family. . . . "I'm going to the cleaners today. Anything of yours you want me to take?" . . . "There's something wrong again with the checking account." . . . "I think you'll have to have the lawn mower sharpened if you intend to use it." . . . But in the privacy of their bedroom, she creamed her face, and read, and slept, and woke in the morning, and went through day after day in a heavy, unhappy parturition.

21

Jay told Evelyn that finals would be in the first week of June, and that he would be getting ready to leave for home right after. If it was all right with her, he would like to spend a week with his friend Mark before coming home.

"Where does Mark live?"

"Washington."

"D.C.?"

"Yeah."

"Well, sure it's all right, dear, but how are you going to manage all that? I mean, your things. . . ."

That, too, was all planned out. They were going to rent one of those U-Haul things and drive east to Washington. Mark's father worked for the government, and they had a big house in one of the nearby Virginia towns. Jay said he'd just unload the stuff for a week, then maybe rent a car for the trip to New York. He could get just his things in the trunk and back seat.

"I spoke to Dad about a car," Jay said.

"Yes? And what did he say?"

"Well, he said I wouldn't need one for the summer, but that it'd probably be a good idea when I went back to school."

"Yes, it probably would be," Evelyn agreed. "Did he offer to buy you one?"

"Well, he said he'd chip in. He said I ought to earn some money over the summer and pay for part of it myself."

Evelyn almost feared to ask the next question. She feared the

236

answer, and at the same time was accepting the inevitability of it. The shadow had been lengthening through the late winter and into spring. Lew and his curious, reticent attentions. The approach of vacation time for Jay. Her own unsettled and unsettling life. The recent development in Denver that gave to time another excruciating turn of the screw. She felt as if her days were acted out in the waiting room of a hospital where an intricate and obscure operation was being performed. The operation had been deemed necessary to her health, and she had given consent to it, but the wearisome surprise was how long it took, and that it could be performed without her being present.

"Does he have any idea where you might get a job?" Evelyn asked.

"He says it isn't absolutely certain, but he thinks his company is going to be shooting a film in New York this summer, and he's pretty sure they'll be needing extra hands. He thinks maybe I can get a job as an assistant to the guy in charge of building sets. You see, a lot of the scenes are going to be indoors—"

"Well, that's wonderful!" she exclaimed. "That's terribly exciting. Are you excited?"

"Yeah, sure, sort of."

Of course it was exciting. What nineteen-year-old wouldn't be thrilled to find himself on the set of a movie in the making? Like being invited on board the starship *Enterprise. . . . Oh, Jay, it was only yesterday that you were watching Captain Kirk and Mr. Spock warp out of their dangers for the umpteenth time! Now, just like that, you're a free agent, all over the country, choosing your friends and your summers and your parents!*

"But you'll be coming here to live, won't you?" she asked, her heart already fleeing in panic.

"If it's all right with you."

"Yes, it's all right with me."

"You see, if I went out and looked for a place, it'd probably cost me—"

"Jay!" she almost shrieked. "Why are you explaining? Haven't you always lived with me?"

"I thought. . . ."

"You thought what?"

"I thought maybe you'd have other plans."

"I have no other plans," she said. "And if I had other plans, you can be sure that you'd be the first to be taken into consideration."

"Okay, okay. You're my favorite mother."

"Thank you, I'm sure."

She hadn't seen Lew since that evening reception after the preview of *Sharpshooter,* which was as successful as her brother, Bob, thought it would be. Lew had been very much taken up with the publicity of that film and the activities surrounding the making of another. Probably the one Jay was talking about. But he did speak to her regularly, and when he arranged for one of those five-thirty cocktails at his favorite bar, she asked him why he hadn't said anything about getting Jay a job for the summer.

"Do you mind?" he asked.

"Of course not. I think it's wonderful. But some of my own plans revolve around Jay. I should think you'd know that. What I do depends on whether he's with me or elsewhere."

"I think we're going to have to stop thinking of him in those terms," Lew said. "He's pretty much on his own now."

"At nineteen?"

"He's mature," Lew said. "Don't you get that feeling?"

She did. Jay had taken his giant step. He was much more man than boy. Fine! But where does one go to take a short course on giving up a child? All she had to do was reach behind her to pick up a bag full of Jay's toys. And her knowledge was due in large part to Lew Pressman's seemingly forgotten derelictions as father. Well, he was making up for it now.

"Evelyn. . . ."

"Yes?"

"I have to go to Atlanta over the weekend. Come with me."

So here it was at last! A proposition from one's very own ex-husband. It astonished her that Lew would risk his ego in this way. There had been no talk of his actually leaving Sara, and making a weekend arrangement with someone younger and prettier and, best of all, *newer* than his former wife should be no problem for Lew Pressman. Unless the four years had made her new all over again . . . or unless he meant even a small fraction of the things he'd been saying about memory and regret. This last possibility made her decide to tell Lew.

"I can't, Lew. You see, there *is* someone."

"Oh? I can't say that surprises me. Who is he?"

"Strangely enough, someone you once met, just briefly. You dropped over to the old apartment on West End once and he was there. His name is Gabe Michelson. It was the time of Sylvia Dacosta—is that name spelled in two parts or one?"

"One," Lew said. "Yes, I remember Gabe Michelson. You did more than just date him, if I remember. You told me it was a heavy thing for a while."

"It was."

"And is again?"

"Yes."

"Is he married?"

"Yes."

"Still in New York?"

"Oh, no . . . no . . . he lives in Denver."

"Denver! Is that where he is now?"

"Yes."

"So there are problems. . . ."

"A few."

Lew nodded. Lew quietly and obliquely considered the situation, and then he said, "I hope this works out for you—but, still, why not come to Atlanta with me? It isn't as if I were a stranger. We do share a lot. . . ."

"I *couldn't,* Lew! You understand that. But, my God, *why,* Lew? Why me?"

"Why do you think?"

"I don't know. I truly don't. My own thought is that you would have preferred to leave our past just as far in the past as possible."

"That," said Lew, "is because your view of our past is different from mine."

Everyone's view of a shared experience, long or short, is different from that of the person with whom it is shared. Hadn't Gabe made that abundantly clear? Even the views held by each while in the process of sharing. Someday she might know what this time was like for Gabe, but right now his communiqués were like those from a battle front—terse, evasive—as though the sharing was more an obligation than a relief. She passed from tenderness to tension a thousand times a day, and then from that to a kind of existential sleepwalking. The *situation* had become the central reality, while the feelings that gave rise to it hovered above, insubstantially, like ghosts, sometimes vanishing completely, sometimes returning as thick and enveloping as fog.

"May I speak to Joanna Hopkins, please?"

"Who's calling?"

"Evelyn White."

"Oh, hi, Evelyn. I thought I recognized your voice. This is Denise. Joanna isn't in."

"Again?"

"Yes, again," said Joanna's office manager. "Listen, Evelyn, I'm glad you called. I was on the point of getting in touch with you. I know you're one of Joanna's oldest and dearest friends, so, please, let me speak frankly. Someone has *got* to try and get to her. This can't go on. I've been told not to phone her at home because that sonofabitch Frank Moore is there, but I don't know what's *happening* to the woman. I'm scared out of my wits!"

"Why?" Evelyn asked.

"Well, you've seen what she looks like, haven't you? And it's not only that. You know Joanna. She has never neglected business, no matter what was happening. To tell you the truth, things are going to hell around here. Joanna is the only one who can get some of these bastards to pay their bills. Something's happening to her, Evelyn, I swear. Maybe she's sick. I wouldn't be surprised. I mean, either physically or . . . some other way."

"I'm going to get in touch with her," Evelyn said.

"Please!"

Evelyn had done all her phoning to the agency since learning that Frank was staying at Joanna's place—at least staying there at times. She wouldn't have minded speaking to Frank, but the thing between Frank and Joanna had become so Byzantine in its secrecy and seclusion that she feared the possible effects of a wrong word. But it was clear now that it had gone beyond the respect of privacy.

She phoned. A small time-explosion burst in her head with Frank's impatient "Yeah!"

"Hello, Frank. This is Evelyn. Is Joanna there?"

Two or three seconds of considering silence, then, "How are you, Evelyn?" His voice sounded . . . different. She didn't know quite in what way, but different. Less aggrieved, perhaps. Less tense . . . an intonation she vaguely remembered. "Joanna isn't here right now," he said. "I believe she went out to buy a few things. . . . What's doing in your life, Evelyn? I ask Joanna from time to time, but apparently she doesn't know very much."

"I don't want to talk about my life, Frank. I would like to talk about Joanna's."

"Would you? Not mine?"

"Yours, too, if you'll permit it. Yours seems to be having quite an effect on Joanna's."

"Oh, I see," he said. "For that reason."

"Oh, Frank," Evelyn suddenly and unexpectedly implored, "you can be so wise and compassionate in your books. Why don't you save a little of it for the people who come into your life?"

He had no ready response to that. The silence that followed frightened Evelyn, because somehow the silence seemed to speak of a fright in Frank, too. His reply came from a corner and in a way that only increased Evelyn's anxiety.

"I'm leaving for California in a few days," he said.

"Is Joanna going with you?" Evelyn asked quickly.

"No," he replied; then, after a pause, "Could I see you once before I go?"

Evelyn recoiled at the idea. She distrusted his motives. She feared an attempted resumption. She feared anything that might carry the faintest shade of misunderstanding. But she couldn't afford such squeamishness now. All that seemed of secondary importance. The important thing was to get a firsthand account from Frank. And besides, there was still something in his voice that suggested all her calculations and guesses were wrong.

"All right, Frank," she said. "I'm going to be very busy today, but how about tomorrow? Lunch? Shall we make it early to avoid the crowds?"

"Don't worry about crowds," he said. "I'll make a reservation.

Let me buy you a classy farewell lunch. How about that place on Sixty-first . . . remember?"

"Yes. All right."

It was difficult to tell how deeply Frank was into the bottle. He didn't exhibit the usual flamboyant touchiness that signaled his serious drinking bouts. His eyes gave some evidence. They were puffy, covert—which, again, might be due to some other kind of stress. His hands trembled a little when he lifted his martini.

"Luck," he said.

She nodded, then said, "What's happening, Frank?"

"With me?"

"Yes, with you."

When he told her, she was able to understand much more. It explained the strangeness she hadn't been able to place. Frank had hit it. His novel, now complete, had received a big advance, had already been sold to a paperback house for one of those fairy-tale figures. He displayed an uncharacteristic uneasiness about that, which made Evelyn feel it was all the more fabulous—five hundred thousand? a million?—and there was also a movie. At least there was serious talk about a movie. That's why he was going to California. They wanted him to do the film script, and he wasn't quite sure whether he wanted to or not, so he was going out there to see for himself what variety of cat he'd be dealing with. As she knew, he liked movies, but he didn't very much like the people in them.

"But how wonderful, Frank!"

He looked at her and gave one quick nod. Evelyn understood: *You chump! See what you could have been sharing with me if you didn't go and get yourself reheated over some old flame!* She created a quick vignette of herself packing a set of new, apple-green suitcases for a fresh new life adventure in Hollywood—then immediately gave the picture a realistic semiturn and saw herself in a room, in a restaurant, in a hotel lobby, anywhere on God's apple-green earth, listening to Frank Moore rave on about this one's stupidity and that one's corruption.

Seeing Frank again gave her a clearer perspective of Gabe. It was Frank, really, who was the Prince of Indefinite Glories, and Gabe was the man whose proportions matched the self that Evelyn White had become. She thought of that day on the Island,

242

and the perfection of it cupped her heart in happiness. Frank would have changed sun, sea, air, everything, into scenery for his troubled soul. Frank always insisted on her seeing the world through his eyes. Gabe was willing to share it with her. One would have to love Frank's soul more than one's own, and she didn't, never had.

"Did you know that Doris McAuley was almost murdered a couple of weeks ago?" Frank said.

"No!"

"Yes. Our Doris inhabits a world of her own. Seems she was driving upstate and picked up a hitchhiker, all hair and backpack. Somewhere along the journey, he suggested she do him a small favor, one that wouldn't discommode either of them too much. The whole thing could be accomplished by just pulling into any one of the numerous side roads. She told him to get out, and he pulled a knife. Cool Doris slammed on the brakes, hopped out, and began running and waving to the oncoming traffic. Backpack took off. . . ."

"How do you know all this?" Evelyn asked.

"Why, Doris told me, of course."

"You're still in touch with her?"

"Oh, yes, we talk from time to time. Why do you ask?"

"Because I gathered from your remarks that night of the preview that it was a brief thing and—well—rather weird."

"Weird would be about right," Frank said. "Doris called me up and told me someone had given her a copy of *The Other Island.* She liked it and would like to talk to me about it. Would I care to come over to her place for a drink? Just like that. Ordinarily I would have said no to that kind of frontal attack. Usually when it comes from a woman, she thinks you know something she doesn't —either that or she wants to correct your appalling ignorance. In Doris' case, it was a little of both—and I guess that's why I accepted her invitation—she sounded interestingly in between. In any event, we had a drink, and another, and another, as you might imagine. . . ."

"And?" Evelyn asked.

Frank shrugged. "There's just so much you can do with the body," Frank said. "And I, you may remember, often have trouble doing merely what comes naturally."

"Was all this happening while you were with Joanna?" Evelyn asked.

"*With?*"

"You know what I mean."

Frank looked away. He maintained a long, withdrawn silence. Evelyn accompanied his silence, thinking that any urging she might do would only lead him to another diversion. Left alone, he might find his way to Joanna. She was right—although again from an odd angle.

"Well, I cared for you very much," he said, keeping his eyes elsewhere. "You might say I loved you, in my fashion. I suppose I still do. No *suppose*—I do! But I probably would have killed it in myself in time. Self-hatred is self-murder, and sooner or later I would have killed the Moore who loved you. I went to Joanna to talk about you, and I found myself an easy mark. Much too easy. . . ."

She might have sketched it all in her own imagination. Frank had made this appointment to flesh out the scene in fright-white and blood-red colors. He reminded her (she needed no reminding) of Amagansett and that literary cocktail party several summers before. Joanna had worked hard at not hating either of them because of what happened, but strenuous time put in for negative results is still a loss no matter how virtuously you look at it. Joanna had looked at it for a long time, feeling that she had something to offer Frank Moore and that her friend Evelyn White did not. Life being the hopeless perversity it is, Joanna really had nothing to offer. She only thought she did. Yes, she understood better than Evelyn what it was he was trying to do in his writing, but that's not what he needed, that kind of understanding. What he needed was what he wanted. He wanted Evelyn. He wanted Evelyn, with her smile and her perfume and her hair and her credit cards and her pure gut reaction to the things he put on paper. She was the sensible, charming world of his mother, who wished him success. She was the world he must enchant, astonish, and finally subdue by the great magic of his art.

"Why not Joanna?" Evelyn asked.

"Joanna knew too well what I was about," he replied. "She could see where and how it was all put together. Her remarks al-

ways had technical savvy. She thought that's what would be help-
ful, what I would appreciate."

"And you didn't."

"But not at all."

"And. . . ."

"And what?" he asked.

"And something else," Evelyn insisted.

Frank shrugged again. "She wanted to live her own frustrated
creative life through me," he said.

"Would that have been so bad?"

"Maybe not," Frank said. "But I didn't want it. I can't act as
anybody else's surrogate. It would fuck up my head."

"And. . . ."

"And *what!*" Frank snapped, turning on her with sudden anger.
"What's this legalistic bullshit? Are you putting in some training
for life with your lawyer boyfriend? Incidentally, do you plan on
going out there to live? There's the question of money, I should
imagine. If old Gabe's got his practice in Denver, he's not going to
be able very easily to set up shop in New York again. I've been to
Denver. Swell place if you like trout fishing and country western
at Red Rocks. . . ."

Evelyn kept her gaze on the slender center vase with its single
rose. When Frank slackened off, she said, "And so you were
mean?"

"What do you mean, 'mean'?"

She was silent, kept her gaze away for a few seconds longer,
then looked up at Frank. His eyes touched hers for a moment,
then turned away. His anger evaporated.

Yes, he had been mean. He had pretended it was Joanna's over-
zealous, too-intrusive interest in his writing, but that was only the
ready-made club she handed him to beat her with. He knew of the
long, close friendship between Joanna Hopkins and Evelyn White.
Evelyn had told him often enough. But even so, the vicarious punishment wouldn't have worked so well if Joanna hadn't been such
a willing, wanton victim. Jesus *Christ,* she wanted it! Why didn't
she tell him to go to hell? Why didn't she just kick him out? No,
she just took all that mindless, heartless abuse . . . "—and she
didn't even get a good lay out of it," Frank finished off, covering

with a small, shaky laugh whatever other sound might have expressed his sick remorse.

"What did you do to her?" Evelyn asked, her voice blanched with fright.

"You can imagine."

"Tell me."

"Oh, I didn't hit her, for Christ's sake! You know damn well what I did. I told her to write her own bloody novels, not mine. I told her not to be such a sacrificial slob. I told her that you told me she was in the habit of taking on spiritual cripples like me for the kicks in it. I told her lies, and I told her the truth, and I was trying to get at you through her—and I've given myself something to bleed over the rest of my life. I walked out not because I couldn't stand Joanna anymore but because I couldn't stand *myself*. Does that answer all your *ands*?"

"Yes," Evelyn whispered.

Later that afternoon, she tried phoning Joanna again, but even while dialing she knew it was useless. If Joanna was there, she wasn't answering the phone. Evelyn understood this determination not to be approached, but she knew she must not let it be. If there had been no Evelyn White, there would be no such situation, and however much common sense could be brought against such fatalism, it would have no effect on the guilt that had become as much a part of her consciousness as thoughts of her lover or her son. She had as much hope of separating herself from it as from a sick child. She was not the disease, but she was the one who might have done, or not done, this or that small thing to prevent its happening.

The next day, she phoned Joanna's apartment early, before starting out to her own office. The phone rang and rang. A little later, in her own office, she tried Joanna's agency. She spoke to Denise. Denise had heard nothing from Joanna.

"She's gone somewhere," Denise said.

"What makes you think so?"

"I took a cab to her apartment last night. It was about ten-thirty. I told the cabbie to wait for me. If I could have got my hands on her, I would have dragged her off bodily to my place.

But there was nobody there. I even managed to get hold of the super. He knew nothing of her whereabouts. No message."

"Denise—"

"What?"

"Are you frightened of something?"

"Petrified!"

"Why?"

"I don't know why. I just am."

Evelyn said, "I've got the telephone number of Joanna's family in Vermont. I'm going to give them a ring immediately and find out if they know anything. If I hear anything, I'll let you know."

She dreaded making the call to Vermont, knowing that no matter how cleverly she camouflaged her reasons she would give cause for worry. There was a WATS line in her office, so she needn't add the expense of long-distance calls to her other worries. Don was looking at her these days with sad, comprehending eyes. She was managing her work, but just. Don was aware of her state. People had problems, and Don had patience with human problems, but he seemed to be asking why she hadn't taken him into her confidence. Of course, it wasn't all that confidential—Joanna knew, Lew knew, even Frank knew—but she did wish to keep her job and her personal anxieties apart. Apart they gave her some kind of balance; together her life would begin to list badly.

She telephoned Vermont.

"Yes," said Joanna's mother, "she did say she was coming for a few days. I heard from her last weekend, and she said that she would come sometime this week. She wasn't sure exactly what day. . . . Is there anything wrong?"

"No, not at all," Evelyn hastened to reassure. "I rather thought she forgot about tickets for a play we both wanted to see. It's not important. Look, when she comes, will you tell her that I phoned. Ask her to call me at home. I can give her ticket to someone, but I wouldn't want to do it without her permission."

"Oh, you're quite right. Yes, Evelyn, I'll tell her that you called and ask her to call you back."

"Thank you."

Evelyn set the phone on its cradle. She felt limp. She felt like crying. She felt herself victimized by the excesses of others. Why should she be made to suffer because Frank Moore had a headful of sadistic hang-ups? Now that he'd made it big, he was taking off for other diversions, sick of his own vendetta, no doubt on his way to create new ones. And what gave Joanna the right to step out of friendship as if it were the waiting room in a bus terminal? They were, the two of them, heartless people, self-centered people, and neither of them deserved the concern she had wasted on them.

But she couldn't work herself into a proper state of self-vindication. Her overwhelming sensation was one of relief, but she knew that that relief had only anesthetized her guilt. About Frank, she could do nothing. He would give up nothing of his raging self to accommodate her, or any woman, and while she could feel sorrow for his self-destructiveness, she felt no regret at his going.

Joanna was something else. Evelyn was sick with the loss of Joanna, and that loss was connected with Gabe. She didn't love Frank. She couldn't help that, any more than Frank could help being what he was—but why should Joanna have been made to suffer for it? Joanna *wouldn't* have suffered if there hadn't been Gabe. Things would have happened differently but for Gabe. It was the quick, blind priority she had given Gabe that had brought about this turmoil. She didn't believe in moral retribution, but she did believe in penalties for error. She had made errors. She had been careless with other lives in the heedless flush of delighting her own. Now she felt a change in those priorities. She would be entitled to nothing unless she took care of her obligations as a person first. She was feeling a dishevelment of character that sought to hide itself and accuse others, while all her instincts demanded some kind of sternness, a rectitude. Not piety but decent self-denial. She must call Denver and tell Gabe that she would delay her visit. She must find her friend and restore her to the overweight condition of her self-esteem.

After work, Evelyn stopped at Bloomingdale's to buy some things. She needed hosiery. She needed some summer outfits. There never seemed to be enough time. Here she was without husband, lover, or child, and she was literally gasping for breath. What would she do when she gave up this splendid isolation? How would she manage, with others to consider daily? Oh, she'd manage all right! She could always stop working. Nonsense! If Gabe came East to live, he would come at considerable sacrifice, as

Frank had so devilishly pointed out, and her job wouldn't be a luxury but a bedrock necessity. Forget it. Don't think about things like that now. There's no use in planning a hypothetical life. If it became an actuality, ways would be found. If not, the fruitless strategies would be so many more specters to haunt her memory. . . . She looked at a print dress that reminded her of the summer dress she wore to that wedding a million years ago. She took it off the rack, went to a mirror, held it to herself. . . .

"That will look lovely on you," said the girl who appeared in the corner of the mirror.

"Yes, I think so," Evelyn agreed—and then looked again at whom she had mistakenly taken to be a salesgirl, a very pretty girl, which prettiness turned to recognition when the girl smiled an uncommonly attractive smile. The one ironic observation Evelyn had made about the girl Lew Pressman had married was that she had a smile very much like Evelyn's own.

Evelyn turned. "You're Sara Pressman, aren't you?"

The girl nodded. She had long, blond hair, very blue eyes, looked unseasonably sun-tanned. Evelyn wondered if she had just returned from some ambitious trip to St. Tropez or the Riviera. She also wondered if the girl knew of her husband's late campaign to make his ex-wife his mistress. She *must* know that there was contact between Lew and herself, if for nothing else, over Jay.

"You should buy that," Sara said.

"Perhaps I will," Evelyn said.

"We've never really spoken to each other," Sara remarked.

"No, we haven't . . . although I do know that you were recently trying out for a new film."

"Me?"

"So I was told."

"By Lew?"

"Yes."

The girl shook her head slightly, smiled, bit her lower lip. "No, I wasn't trying out for a film," she said. "I was trying out for a spot on a new TV serial. I didn't get it."

"I'm sorry," Evelyn said. "I'm almost sure Lew said it was a film."

"Lew says things," said Sara—then impulsively added, "Let's

talk, Evelyn. Can you spare a half hour? Do you want to buy that dress?"

"Some other time," Evelyn said.

They went to a nearby place and had drinks.

Lew Pressman's second wife told Evelyn that she had for a long time wished to make this contact. It wasn't that she felt either owed the other confidences or explanations, but being married to Lew Pressman occasionally wanted some corroboration. She had been married once before, to an actor, so the peculiarities of ego were nothing new to her. She was no rock of ages herself . . . but Lew . . . well, Lew—he did have oddities, didn't he?

Evelyn agreed that he did, but she nevertheless wondered whether they were the same oddities that had developed out of fifteen years of marriage to Evelyn White. Those oddities might have taken all kinds of hybrid forms by this time. Or the same oddities married to this lovely, seemingly *open* young woman might have an entirely different look. But Evelyn hesitated to venture too close. Sara didn't look like the ambitious harlot Lew made her out to be, but one never knew. At least one never knew from appearances, but if Sara was what Lew said she was, would she have used a chance meeting in this way? Evelyn was thinking of the coming summer, and the happy possibility Jay had announced. She was thinking that in this hazardous season of her life, she had best keep her eyes wide open and catch every whisper in the air.

"I'm at a disadvantage," she said.

"Why?" asked Sara.

"Because I don't know what Lew has told you about me."

Sara didn't hesitate to tell her, and there was something in her telling that made Evelyn believe it was all the truth. Sara told her that Lew had said that she, Evelyn, was a clever, capable woman, but that they couldn't get along because she had come to distrust and despise the world in which he moved. She looked on everyone in the movie business as a monster of deceit. . . . "I told him I didn't believe that," Sara said, "because, I said, it just didn't go along with the other things, but he insisted it had become a disease, to the point where you refused to go to movies or plays because knowing all the people behind the scenes spoiled it for you. . . ."

Evelyn listened as Sara told the strange yet familiar tale of Lew Pressman's invented worlds. She realized at last her one mistake about Lew: *he* was not the chameleon, but the small-time wizard who wrought chameleonic changes in others. She realized now that everything he had told her about Sylvia Dacosta and the medieval Dacosta clan was probably false, false in any objective sense, although God alone knew how it appeared in the then mind and chambered memory of Lew. She realized that she—and no doubt this young woman—had been alchemized by the same Pressman magic. But there still remained a nag of doubt. Who was telling the truth? By daubing every reality with his own colors, Lew almost succeeded in making the world as illusory to others as it was to himself. Almost. Not entirely. Now Evelyn felt she *had* to know, because her Jay had become one of the pieces in Lew's crazy game.

"Lew told me that you were very ambitious," Evelyn said to Sara.

"I suppose I am."

"He told me there was difficulty in your marriage because of that ambition."

"Really? There's difficulty all right, but I didn't think it was because of that. What else did he tell you? I knew, of course, that the two of you spoke on occasion, about Jay and things. Don't worry about anything getting back to Lew. You know, sometimes I get the feeling that I'm living in a dark corner of Dr. Caligari's cabinet. . . ."

So Evelyn told golden-haired, blue-eyed Sara about the sexual accounting attributed to her by Lew, with debits and credits instead of lust for motive, and Sara's eyes grew large, and her mouth opened in wonderment, and Evelyn was certain that this was another of Lew's invented worlds. Sara told her that she hadn't slept with another man—not *one!*—since she began going out with Lew, not to mention the time of their marriage, that sex didn't interest her all that much, and it was a lousy business tactic anyway, as no one knew better than Lew. . . .

She had little less than a month. She must think of a way of telling Jay that his father was not to be trusted. Perhaps Jay knew that already but kept it hidden among the other accumulated secrets of his life. Perhaps Lew was not to be trusted with everyone except Jay. . . . *Too dangerous! That was putting off her responsibilities again because life had become so complicated and full of heart-wrenching terrors.* . . . So what must she do? She must think. She must carefully and cleverly set about to . . . to . . . *do something!*

Evelyn sat in her solitary bedroom in her dressing gown, sipped some of the white wine brought to her so long ago by her vanished lover, and wept slow, bewildered tears.

She slept late into Saturday morning, decided to finish her postponed shopping that day. It was almost eleven by the time she went down, pausing in the hall to check the mailbox. There were several bills and a pale blue envelope with some kind of motif in the upper left hand corner. The Blue Goose Motel, it said. Vermont, it said. Her heart gave a fearful, premonitory turn as she recognized Joanna's cramped, backward-slanting script. Evelyn opened it quickly and read as she began her walk west toward the stores:

Dear Evelyn,

I was on my way to Rutland when I ran into a storm, hail and all, so I stopped at the glorious Blue Goose. It's so lovely here. This arthritic little desk shudders with every stroke of the pen. Through the window I see a yard or two of space and then a kind of hillside garbage dump, where the builders apparently threw all the odds and ends of this melancholy construction. I don't think I really wanted to go to Rutland anyway.

You may or may not know that Frank is on his way to California to become rich and famous. If you don't know, let me be the first to bring you the exciting news. He is. Fat contracts exploding like roman candles in Frank Moore's personal Fourth of July. I always like to imagine whether anybody's extravagant fate, good or bad, could have been foretold before its happening—or, having happened, whether that personality will be able to absorb it. What do you think? My own opinion is that he will manage quite well with wads of money and tight-jeaned students doing their dissertations on the contemporary novel. Yes, I think it suits him. Him I think it suits, to use Frank's own jive. It was bound to happen, because Frank's hang-ups are the world's, and sooner or later he was going to find a way of shrieking it loud and clear. He has in this novel. It's what Joyce called a "funferal." Something for everyone. And success will suit Frank because now he will see his boozing as a necessary salute to the bad world he has defined.

I'm sorry for the disappearing act, Evelyn, but that, too, was necessary. Doomed from the start, of course, like all my affairs, but I knew I was only a padded wall against which Frank could rebound. Maybe that's why I began starving myself. On the other hand, maybe not. Maybe I just wanted a little less of myself around. Less and less and less. . . .

All in all, I find it a sorry life. The truth is I'm sick of envy, sick with envy. Very simply, I don't want to be me. I want to be someone else. I want to be the woman who has written the book. I want to be the woman who is content in the body she has. I want to be the woman who wakes up in the morning and finds a face or a fact to smile at.

Well, how do you do that? I'm sitting here in this chilly, silly Vermont rabbit hutch, looking out on a scene that some exquisitely sensitive artist has designed just for me, and wondering how you do that.

Love,
Joanna

Joanna had not indicated the day of her writing in the letter, but the cancellation date on the envelope made it on or before last Thursday, which meant that Joanna should have been with her family since Friday, at least. Evelyn decided she would phone as soon as she returned from shopping. She would love to join Joanna in Vermont for a few days, but she couldn't. Could not! In fact, she would have to spend the rest of the day working on the "Vocations" series, which Don wanted out of the way before the end of the academic year.

The dress she had looked at in Bloomingdale's was no longer available in her size, so she walked to Fifth Avenue and looked into the shops there. She found an even nicer one in Saks, also a cotton print, but the colors more flattering, the style more becoming.

Since it was a glorious day, she strolled over to the zoo, sweated out the cafeteria line there for a wilted salad. But she managed to find a seat on the patio, and she was able to relax in sight of the seals and in the splendor of the sun. She saw a man who looked like Gabe bending over and talking to a boy of about three or four. She wondered if a child was possible for Gabe and herself. God knows she was still menstruating at a great rate, so biologically it *was* possible; but, then, she'd read all those horror statistics about the increase of birth defects with the increase of the woman's age. Besides—what nonsense! What on earth would they do with a child at their ages, in their economic situation, in this city?

But why *this* city? Suppose Frank was right? Suppose Gabe asked her to come live in Denver? Would she do that? *Would* she? What would there be in Denver for her? It was true that this city had become a nightmare, had been a nightmare for some time, and in many ways was becoming a daymare as well—but, oh, it was so immensely *her* city. But so what? People have left cities and nations before—had to—and probably her own ancestors had trekked from country to country in that two-thousand-year-old odyssey. But New York on a day like this! The blood-humming vibrancy of hours running into twilight, into nighttime, into all the wonderful things that one rarely did. She had had the opportunity to do them with Lew, and she had found that the wrong people can make a wormy mess of even the most Platonic apple. No, today was only a small, warm interlude in a reality that had grown rather nasty and frightening. Person had become infinitely more important than place—but whenever she thought of some distant, strange place, like Denver, she felt the chill of exile.

It was almost three by the time she returned to the apartment. She decided on a hot bath first, sinking tiredly into that luxuriousness, and actually tilting into one of those quick, happy dreams before snapping out of her dangerous snooze.

She slipped into a terry-cloth robe and went into the kitchen, where she kept her book of telephone numbers. She looked under H to find the Vermont Hopkins, and began reaching for the phone extension attached to the side of the cupboard when it suddenly erupted into a rude, startling ring. Her hand leaped away as if it had broken into fire instead of sound. She shook her head, expelled a sigh, then lifted the phone.

"I have a collect call from Denise Quinby. Will you accept the charges?"

"Who?"

"Denise Quinby," the operator repeated—and to the side of that voice, she heard another voice calling, "Evelyn, Evelyn—"

"Yes, I'll accept the charges."

That Denise!

"Evelyn—"

"Yes, Denise?"

"Evelyn. . . ." The voice floated high, and then seemed to come apart in the air.

"What is it, Denise?" Evelyn managed to get out, her heart already congealed in dread.

"I'm calling from a police station in Bennington," the woman sobbed. "Joanna is dead—she's dead—dead!"

22

Once, years ago, in those doleful, cradle-and-career days and nights, they had gone through a similar period of profound separation. Then, too, it seemed to Gabe that they were creating something, rather than destroying it. It seemed to him that they were arriving at the finest and truest divorce that man and woman could achieve. There's nothing particularly noteworthy in legally acknowledging a condition of mutual unhappiness and estrangement, but that's not what was happening between Jean and himself. The conch-shell roar of dailiness in which they lived was too intense, too *busy,* to be called unhappiness. The talk of teeth and bowels and bathing and bills was far too engaging to suggest estrangement.

And yet they both knew that they were as unmarried as two people living together could be. The fourth year? Pam was about three, Andy just toddling, he had begun working for that Wall Street firm, a nickel-and-dime existence; and Jean, who had wanted her children early, keeping a providential eye on the future, compared herself to the goddam spindle in the washing machine down in the laundry room: fixed in one place, turning this way and that way, immersed in a hot, dirty, soapy tub of maddening *work!*

He reminded her that she was the one who wanted children quickly.

She said she had no idea one had to go into penniless servitude *after* one became a lawyer.

He reminded her that he had made the immediate future clear to her. She just hadn't been listening.

She said that it didn't make a difference who said what, or what was true or untrue, that there was something mean and dehumanizing about this; that obligations, promises, and even love could all go to hell if it meant the death of her mind and spirit.

It was not entirely impossible that Jean would walk out of the marriage right then, leaving him with the children. There was that kind of tight-lipped desperation about her. Rightly or wrongly, Gabe thought of that time as the time when Jean's dislike, or enmity, or death of mother love, or whatever the condition involving Jean and Pam could be called, came into being. Andy was still a non-communicating, helpless thing. Pam was just old enough to add her bouncy little ego to all the other creatureliness that was butting Jean to death. She took to pinioning Pam's arms to her sides in a very firm grip and looking at the child with very furious eyes to make her understand that she mustn't, mustn't, *mustn't!* Jean never raised a hand. That would have been a fatal symptom of the death of the spirit she feared. But she did bring her anger down on the child in a way that amounted to physical force.

All right. In his eyes, not the crime the psycho-world made it out to be. He'd been batted around some as a kid, and he hadn't come away hating his mother and father. But what *was* a crime was the deep, cold vault in which all feelings were stored for unbelievably long months. It started with their sex life, which quite simply ended during the cold-storage period. Jean was tired. So was he. But tired people make love. If the tiredness comes from strain and monotony, it becomes an act of faith and renewal to conquer the tiredness through the physical act of love. But Jean turned on her side each night, and either was, or pretended to be, asleep in a matter of seconds. He knew that that quick plunge into oblivion was only another gesture of resentment. And he in turn resented the rejection, fiercely, because the warmth of bodies and the triumphant act of sex was all the triumph they could enjoy at that time. And of course there's always something ludicrous in an abandoned hard-on. It was only later, because of something Jean had said, that he realized it was precisely this element of humiliation Jean was invoking in her physical rejection. Because she felt humiliated herself. She admitted it wasn't his fault, but, then, *fault* doesn't really matter when two people find themselves caged together in such a demoralizing way.

The undeclared war brought about changes in behavior and mutuality that came close to a new state of being. They learned how to use words in a different way. Instead of referring to past intimacies or anticipated pleasures, they made the immediate moment and its needs the center and meaning of their existence. It was like working the pedal on a piano cutting off all reverberations. They fashioned a system that was a cold work of art. It became a challenge to their ingenuity to give the appearance of pleasantness with none of the feeling of it, and there was a glazed astonishment at how well it was working. He had the overwhelming demands of a novice lawyer to deal with. Jean had the brutal realities of life in an apartment house with two small kids to deal with. They became a pair of ambassadors who bring the language and manners of diplomacy to higher and higher refinements as their governments prepare some bloody horror.

Then it broke. Jean's mother, who had been living in Hartford with a younger sister, died, leaving a surprising inheritance. Apparently, there had always been that bank account of Mr. and Mrs. Bernstein. This besides the life insurance that Jean's mother collected when Jean's father died. Jean was an only child. It all came to about fifteen thousand dollars. Not a fortune, but enough to break the siege of need encircling their lives.

A day, or two, or three, after the news, they walked in that Queens park with the kids, sat on a bench in the sunlight, and Jean stared straight ahead with an almost blind intensity as her body shook with silent weeping. She reached for his hand, held it, saying that this nightmare must come to an end, that she had been demon-possessed, had been near some kind of a break, that she was sorry, sorry. . . .

They had resumed a more normal life, but it was a life altered from what each thought it would be. The intensity of the crisis had quickened latencies. Jean never lost control again, but, perhaps to insure this, she became a very ordered person. It seemed to Gabe that from that point on Jean began to organize everything toward the eventual resumption of a life more natural to her being. The time of their crisis became a symbol and warning. She must not be pushed outside the borders of her personality. She must be allowed to impose an emotional economy on the family so that she would have the room to resume her own interrupted development.

Gabe had tacitly agreed. It seemed a sensible compromise with expectations that were probably unreasonable to begin with. And it *was* a sensible compromise. There were no great conflicts after that. There were also no great joys.

Now they were back in that crisis again. *He* had brought it about this time. They had stopped making love. They had again arranged a domestic artifice where the business of life was conducted in a language designed to disguise reality. They were polite. There were automatic considerations, like Jean's hours at school, like Gabe's late snack after his Wednesday-night tennis, and there was now a much greater adroitness, since there were two other grown people in the house, from whom little could be concealed.

It had gone on for almost a month since he'd told her. He wondered whether she was simply waiting for him to make a move, and he himself wondered, having told her, why he *didn't* make a move. What was he waiting for? Why didn't she tell him to go? There was something in her behavior that signaled: *Wait!* And he waited, because he really hadn't the power to wrench himself out of this unhappiness without accounting for everyone's future—Jean's, Pam's, Andy's—and because, for reasons he couldn't define, he felt he owed Jean as much time as she needed, or wanted, or chose to exact from him.

But he noticed how the children had begun to look at each of them, at each other.

"The kids . . ." he said to Jean.

"What about them?"

"They know something is up."

"Of course they know," she said. "They've known before."

"Yes, but they're older now."

"Then they understand better that things go wrong between people," she said.

"If they understand better, then why don't we tell them what's gone wrong?"

"Because I don't know what's gone wrong! Why don't you tell ME what's gone wrong!"

He was silent. He couldn't tell her what had gone wrong, because it was too cruelly simple. He had fallen in love with another woman, that's all. But he couldn't bring himself to say it. He'd said it once, but to say it again, to bring it forth as his only and overwhelming reason, was to trivialize her life. He did indeed love another woman, but he loved another woman because he didn't love Jean, and he didn't love Jean because of that long and heavy history it would be unforgivable to trivialize. He had hoped that all of this would be present in her mind too. If it was present, she wasn't revealing it to him. If it wasn't, it would be too hopelessly snared in the brambles of time ever to disentangle.

"You know what's gone wrong," he said.

"I don't want the children told anything until we're absolutely sure what we're going to do."

"But I can't be absolutely sure *until* I've spoken to the children," Gabe said.

"Why? Will what they say make a difference?"

"It might."

"And do you think that what the children say will make a difference to *me?*"

"I don't know," Gabe said. "You're not saying anything. We go from week to week in the same polite refrigeration . . . like that time in Kew Gardens. I can't go on this way."

"Then don't go on," Jean said. "Just go."

But he didn't go. There was no place to go, except possibly to a hotel. But going to a hotel would announce what was happening more shockingly than any words could do. And they hadn't even begun discussions on the multitude of problems, decisions, agreements, disagreements, the whole miserable machinery of arrangement waiting to be wheeled on stage. And there was something else, the ineffable thing, the thing that couldn't be defined, the real reason for his waiting.

It had something to do with what Jean had become in this terrible time of waiting. She moved within a hard, invisible shell of anger, and she seemed to challenge him to find a way to penetrate that shield. She was utterly removed, and she blazed incandescently within the shell of her removal. She had asked him to explain what had "gone wrong," but there was no sign that the maladjustment had found any soft corners of sorrow.

This, then, was what had gone wrong. This need to arrange people and circumstances. She loved him. Or had. She surely loved Andy. She even loved Pam, in her way, but she had found no way of dealing with any manner of love but her own. Gabe knew she looked on it as a small price to pay for all the work and sacrifice she'd given to her family. And in a way she was right. And in another way she was fatally wrong, because in the long run the manner of love becomes love itself, and to live with someone who will not yield to another's manner of love can be worse than no love at all. It was this want of resiliency that had formed the shell of Jean's days and nights.

Gabe wasn't sure what he would have done if Jean had said, "Yes, I know I've had to have things my way, and I'm sorry about that. Things will be different from now on." Possibly he never would leave her, because the accumulation of other things weighed so heavily on him. But he could see how impossible it was for Jean to find this resiliency. She must preserve herself, as she had preserved herself in that time of crisis in Kew Gardens. She must not expose herself to the risky business of examining the causes of *his* unhappiness. And he understood that. He understood that she must not be invaded by a doubt that would shake her confidence in herself. He felt almost a proprietary interest in preserving that posture in Jean. He feared what might happen if she lost it.

And still he looked to Jean for some other sign.

But the kids had no reason to wait for more signs than they had already received. It was all very well to decide what was best to do, or not to do, for one's children, but one's children might have perceptions of their own.

Pam spoke first. It was Sunday. Jean was a volunteer member at the museum. She was on a committee that worked with the public schools in bringing to students the world of art. It was a sunny day, the kind of day that one should spend outdoors, but Jean was an impassioned servitor in her cause.

Andy had gone on a bike trip with friends into the mountains. Pam had been invited to a friend's house where there were an indoor swimming pool, an outdoor tennis court, a sauna, and other delights attending a six-figure income. The father, Pam told her father, was the biggest merchandiser of junk furniture in the city.

By eleven that morning, Gabe was in the back garden, mowing. Pam came out wearing a T shirt and shorts. She said something. Gabe shook his head, pointed at the roaring mower. Pam reached down and touched the metal strip to the spark plug, stopping the machine. She took him by the arm and led him to the roofed-over patio.

"Please have a seat," she said.

"Thank you."

"What's up?" she asked.

"Up?"

"Between you and Mom?"

"Is something showing?" he asked, thinking how often life tries to imitate art, assuming a stop to all other things while one finishes one's own scene.

"Yes, Daddy, something is showing. Has been for weeks. What is it?"

"A situation," he said.

"Are you and mother splitting?"

"I don't know, Pam. It's a possibility. . . . Look here, do me a favor, honey, no matter what we say now, don't take on like we've said anything. Okay? Your mother doesn't want you and Andy to know what's happening until such time as she's ready. I understand her reasons. It's something for us to decide before you and Andy get in the act."

"Okay," said Pam, "but may I ask *you?* Is there another woman?"

"Any evidence of that?" he asked.

Pam sat down herself on one of the bright-striped, plastic chairs. She said, "Usually there's someone else, isn't there?"

"Why not another man?" Gabe asked, quite curious.

"Because the likelihood is the other way," said his daughter.

"Why's that?"

"Because Mom gets what she wants from you, and I don't think it works the other way."

Gabe glanced at his daughter. "I'm not sure I know what you mean," he said.

"Oh, Dad!"

"No, seriously; I don't know what you mean by mother getting what she wants from me."

"I mean that this family is arranged to please Jean Michelson. Everything in the house reflects mother's taste, not yours. She's got *good* taste, but so what? Every vacation we've taken has been where Mom decided we should go. You don't even see it, but when anything at all comes up, you immediately find reasons why we should do it her way. Like the New York thing. You could have taken me to New York. What's wrong with taking a seven-teen-year-old to New York? It would have been fun. I wouldn't have been in your way, and you know it. Andy prefers to horse around with his friends. Mom didn't think it was a good idea, and you knuckled under."

"It wasn't quite like that, Pam. I happened to agree with your mother. There were too many problems."

"You would have found ways of getting around the problems if Mom had said sure, fine, have a nice time."

Gabe looked out toward the bushes at the back of the yard. The forsythia was badly in need of pruning, and he decided he would prune it no matter what happened. The forsythia required its own hygiene no matter what was happening to the Michelsons. The re-ality of separation followed immediately upon his thoughts about the forsythia. He was going to leave Jean, break up his marriage, probably go to New York. He had seen for the first time the shadow of pastness on this long and sacred commitment. His own daughter had made him see just how much he had withdrawn from participation in a life with Jean.

"Pam, are you saying we should split?"

"No, I'm not saying that. I'm just saying I see reasons."

"But suppose we do part?" he asked.

"Then you do. We'll all live."

Again Gabe glanced at his daughter. He noticed her freckles, a sure sign that she was under some stress. Her words sounded tough, unfeeling, but he could see that it wasn't all that casual a thing. Her words announced something else to him, and although he felt he should close off all talk of this now, in respect to Jean, he couldn't help asking the last question.

"Has the possibility of a divorce occurred to you before?"

"Oh, Dad!" Pam moaned, shaking her head. "Where do you

think I live, on the moon? And who do you think my friends are? Over half have divorced parents, and I think the other half are just waiting for it."

Gabe's gaze went back to the bushes. He nodded abstractly, but he felt a shudder of lostness. The landscape of his children's lives suddenly cleared for him, and he was given the sharp, painful image of statistics made flesh. Divorce rates, dwindling resources, drugs, marriageless unions, doubtful futures, the whole world that boiled on the pages of newspapers became the lives of his children. The surprise was not that his own children had found no immunity from it, but that he hadn't himself.

And if Pam knew, Andy would know. He wouldn't have believed Pam even if she had promised not to tell Andy. She had her own sense of responsibility, and Gabe knew that would call for independent action. She would tell Andy what *she* thought he should know. The things she had said to him revealed a different center of moral choices and necessary actions.

The next day, Monday, when Andy came to pick him up at the office, he asked the boy if Pam had said anything to him.

"Yes," he said.

"And?"

Andy shrugged uneasily. He looked unhappy. He said that it happened all the time, but he didn't expect it would happen in his family.

"Neither did I," Gabe said.

Andy was silent as they inched forward in the traffic on Colorado Boulevard. Gabe observed his son ride the clutch, a bad habit, something he had warned him against. But cars were no luxury to Andy. They were as much a part of ordinary life as pizza—or the possible divorce of his parents. Gabe supposed that Andy didn't live on the moon either, and had friends whose lives made up the statistics. He felt like reaching out and touching him, or bringing him close, closer, but awareness of the impulse brought awareness of the need, always, to bring Andy closer.

"Will there be enough money?" Andy asked.

"For what?"

"Well, you know, Mom isn't earning any money—I'm not—or

Pam—I mean, how are we all going to live? Will Pam be able to go to college?"

Gabe didn't know whether to laugh or cry. It wasn't crass. Andy was just a boy of his time looking squarely at the facts. But where was the heartbreak? Where was the terror of the world being split down the middle? He should feel relieved that his children were able to take such quakes without their inner walls crumbling, but he didn't feel relieved at all. He felt immensely sad.

"Andy, you should know this," he said. "Whatever happens, my first responsibility is to my family. There'll be money for Pam's college . . . and for yours."

"So you had to tell them," Jean accused.

"Not exactly," he said. "They told me. Pam did. As good as told me. She asked what was going on, and I couldn't bring myself to say nothing was going on."

"You could have said we were having a difficult time."

"I suppose I could have said that. Don't you think they're capable of judging just how difficult, and the nature of the difficulty?"

Jean said nothing to that. They were in the bedroom. Jean had taken a shower, and now she was dressing. He tried to remember if there was some engagement this evening, something she had told him about. She often accused him of forgetting deliberately. Had he forgotten?

"Are you going somewhere?" he asked.

"Yes," she said, turning around and facing him. "I'm going to the Kirschners' this evening. I didn't say anything to you because I know you don't want to go there—and frankly I have no wish for you to come with me. Do you mind?"

"No, Jean, of course not."

He was alone in the house. Pam was off doing homework at a friend's house. This was Andy's night to bowl. He belonged to a league. He bowled one fifty, one sixty, fairly consistently, and quite often swept over the two hundred mark.

The house was full of emptiness. It was indeed Jean's house, the one she had selected as lending itself to the architectural changes she had in mind. To put a skylight in here, to break down the wall there, to make a division here—and it had worked out very well, giving room for everybody, allowing each to pursue his studies and interests in privacy and quiet.

Gabe put a Mozart quartet on the machine and sat down to read a contract he would be presenting to a client tomorrow. The man was a contractor who made plastic parts for the aerospace industry in the city. He was buying up an adjacent piece of property to enlarge his own facilities. . . . It occurred to Gabe that he would have to contact the ABA and his old law school if he was going to make a move to New York. . . . *Oh, my God, how would all of it ever be arranged!* . . . Instrumental music never bothered him when he read. Chamber music formed a neutral background, sometimes rising above, sometimes falling below a subliminal level. Not vocal music. Operas, cantatas, *lieder*—they were out. The human voice was too involving. . . . He thought of phoning Evelyn, collect, so that a New York call wouldn't appear on the home bill, but he knew this would only be soliciting easy comfort. He mustn't begin to live any other life but this one. He must remain true to the words he had spoken to Andy about where his responsibilities lay.

It was not the first time he had deliberately pushed Evelyn out of his mind. Sometimes he wondered if this thing playing itself out right here had anything to do with a woman in New York at all. Evelyn seemed to be passing through some personal hell of her own. The letter he had received from her a week ago telling of the suicide of her friend was strangely devoid of any approachable grief. She was telling him in order to explain her postponement of that proposed trip to Denver, but it seemed not to be asking for any of the comforts one seeks from a lover at such a time. There was a tired, dry privacy in her words, and while they didn't exclude him they made no attempt to bring him in. He and Evelyn were fighting different wars.

At ten, the telephone rang. It was Jean.

"Gabe, I'm going to stay with the Kirschners tonight," she said.

"Yes?"

"Do you mind?"

"No, I don't mind, but what shall I tell the kids?"

"Just that," said Jean. "That I'm staying at the Kirschners'. I'm sure they'll understand. Tell them I'll be home tomorrow afternoon. Tell them anything you want. Surely there are no special explanations needed by this time."

"No, Jean, no special explanations. Does that mean that you don't want to explain anything to me either?"

"Over the phone?"

"I suppose that isn't the best way of doing it—"

"What is it that you want to know, Gabe?" Jean put in quickly, her voice high and sharp. "I don't mind explaining it now, over the phone. The Kirschners don't mind. Perhaps it would be just as well. I've been talking to my friends tonight, Gabe. That's why I didn't ask you to come . . . I wanted to talk to my friends . . . and they told me things I very much needed to hear. Would you like to know what those things were . . . ?"

"Yes, I would."

"They told me that I was quite a person in my own right. They told me that I was a *fool* for trying to preserve a marriage where the incompatibilities were so obvious and so deep. I *was* trying to preserve it, Gabe. I walked around for weeks bleeding internally, but I was trying to preserve it. They told me it was time to let go. They told me things that you never told me. They told me that I was competent and strong and talented. They told me that all the progress I had made was not because of you but in *spite* of you. They told me I had a future, an independent and meaningful future, quite on my own, a future that I've been making for myself all these years, Gabe, without any encouragement, without any assistance. . . ."

And Gabe could see Alex and Alice doing it. He could see them all, over their coffee, in that Uffizi living room, called in sudden emergency council to advise a fine, loyal friend. How unlikely that it should be happening this way, over the phone, through the agency of Alex and Alice Kirschner. And yet how right! The Kirschners *were* the difference. That Jean could find comfort at this moment with the Kirschners explained why she could never find comfort in him, why he could never find comfort in her.

But he didn't dislike the Kirschners now. He liked them for being Jean's good friends at this time. He liked them for telling Jean the things they had told her, for they were true things. She *had* made herself strong and competent and talented, and he hadn't exactly encouraged her in the effort. He hadn't encouraged her, because he had never been able to reach that secret part of her where ambition was understood and joy could be shared. There was no one to blame for that.

". . . and so, Gabe, what's the point in going on a day longer?"

This was what he had been waiting for. Without putting it into words, he had known all along that the signal of release must come from Jean. He had known all along that he could never leave until he could see Jean's future as well as his own.

"Yes, Jean," he said.

23

Another of those summer mornings when yesterday's heat seemed to have kept the streets oven-ready for the next day's baking. The sun hadn't yet cleared the roofs, but its contact on Evelyn's back as she walked toward Second Avenue had a soft savagery in its push, urging her on to her marketing before the swelter really started. But even with the day hopelessly committed to another round of inhuman heat, it was still morning, and while there was scarcely a breath of freshness in it, the chemical composition of the air had not yet thickened to its full, summer mix. Separate smells could be distinguished: river smell, traffic smell, garbage smell, and, coiling like a tendril through the others, a dusty, asphalt, watered-down-city smell that was as sweet and reminiscent as penny candy.

She had debated the alternate benefits of dinner out and dinner at home, and had decided on the latter. It would have been much easier on her not to spend the day preparing, but dinner at home would have the mark of permanence in it. Gabe's plane would be arriving at about four. Clearing the baggage and getting into the city would make it near to six. He would only have time to wash his hands and they would be rushing out to dinner. All of it suggestive of that former transience, which she didn't want at all.

She still hadn't made a complete adjustment. She was still living her former life, worrying about Jay's almost daily contact with Lew, now that that job had materialized. At least she wouldn't have to worry about that situation at the moment, because Lew and Sara had gone to California for the last two weeks in August, and Jay was living at Lew's apartment. There was something contaminated in it, but Lew was Jay's father, through her own, willing body, so who was she to complain of influences? Lew was a liar, but not insane. He was staying married to Sara, at least for the present, and the mere fact of a reconciliation of some unimaginable sort made things seem less sinister. Evelyn guessed that Lew and his pretty wife would never have children of their own, which gave Jay a special importance. She recalled reading somewhere that each man has in mind a place that he must come to with clean hands. Perhaps Jay was Lew's.

Part of her plan in having dinner at home tonight was having dinner out tomorrow, Sunday, with Gabe and Jay. She had at last told Jay about Gabe. "Oh," he had said, nodding judiciously, as if the man, whoever he was, had only waited upon a name. "Okay," he had said when she told him that Gabe was coming that week and that she would like Jay to meet him.

No resentment. No sense of displacement. Only a faint smile, as if some prescient wisdom had been confirmed. And also something else in that faint smile, something a little heart-chilling, something that in looking back tasted like condescension. Yes, there was definitely something like condescension in her son's smile. His generation looking at hers and seeing the persistence of a certain kind of error. Was that what it was? Could there be that much coolness in Jay's contemplation of his mother? She was afraid so. Jay was bursting into maturity, a condition that allowed only brief, backward glances of toleration.

Which, she supposed, was as it should be. After all, she would become in the not too distant future Mrs. Gabriel Michelson. Or maybe Ms. Evelyn Michelson. Or maybe continue as Evelyn White, for the sake of business connections she would have to, want to, maintain. Oh, definitely want to! Even if they didn't need the money—which they certainly would, if, as Gabe said, the best he could hope for would be a job in someone's law office or in some corporation's legal department. How on earth would she pass the hours of the day? Poring over cookbooks? Doing volunteer work? Talking to friends? *What* friends?

Evelyn walked a half block down the avenue and entered the cool supermarket, thankful for the neutral atmosphere of dampness and vegetables. The manager, a solemn-faced man with a mustache, held up a hand in greeting. She waved back. She liked Mr. Newhouse. His flirtations were harmless and ego-boosting. He was, as Frank Moore might have said, quintessentially New York with his sentimentality and cynicism. He had told Evelyn that she was the woman of his life, his Ann Sheridan, his Lucille Ball. He had offered to run away with her anywhere—Hong Kong or Wyoming. He had told her if she ever wanted anything special to come to him. So she went to him and said she wanted veal scallops, very tender, for someone she felt very tender about. Mr. Newhouse offered to kill the tender bastard, and told her to do the rest of her shopping and then come around to the meat department. She went to the vegetable section and examined the green, bursting bouquets of broccoli, suddenly full of thoughts of Joanna. . . .

She had gone to Vermont for the funeral, had learned enough of the facts to be assured of a lifetime of ghastly little vignettes to shuffle around in her mind. Joanna's letter had described the place vividly enough, and her own mood in that place, but she had left it to Evelyn to figure out for herself when it was that she opened her veins in that rickety, mildewed bathroom (for that's how it was reconstructed), then wandered into the other room, fully clothed, to lie down on one of the two lonely beds and let her unwanted life pulse away. There was that letter to read and read for the unmistakable clue that this is what she would do after she had addressed, stamped, and posted the envelope. The lady in the motel recalled that the lady in 4A (why A?—there was only one floor) had brought her a letter and had inquired when there would be a mail pickup. She recalled telling the lady in 4A that she was indeed lucky, because the mailman usually came by a little before three, and it was almost that, although he might be delayed because of the storm. . . .

They say all suicides are a form of revenge. Against whom? Evelyn White? Frank Moore? The world? Life itself? Evelyn automatically took the blame. If it were not for her, Joanna would still be alive. She didn't want to hear arguments to the contrary. She had merely informed Gabe of the event. She had thought of writing Frank through his publisher, but decided against it. No matter how she phrased it, it would come out sounding like an accusation against him, and it wasn't Frank she accused, but herself.

She had lived with that guilt for weeks. No doubt she would live with it the rest of her life. She couldn't imagine beginning a life with Gabe after this, and she had been on the point of writing him and telling him so countless times. Her own mood was one of death, and that was not the dowry she wanted to bring.

But even in the worst of it, doom-encrusted with grief, there was still the Evelyn who wanted happiness with Gabe. She accepted each morning's diminution of sorrow grudgingly, but she accepted it. She told herself that she was without character, totally unadmirable, but she knew that she was already in the process of limiting her culpability. She knew that the only way to deal with life was to reject death. And, finally, she knew in the deepest part of her that it was *not* her fault, that she was not to blame for Joanna's having run out of alternatives, that if it hadn't been Evelyn White it would have been someone else who would provide whatever circumstances surrounded the end.

Having rid herself of mindless self-blame, she found herself left with something that would probably prove more enduring because it was more truthful. She was left with the reality of Joanna's death. The vitality and unrealized art of Joanna Hopkins was scooped out of Evelyn White's life, because circumstances had made Evelyn Joanna's friend. No one knew better than Evelyn how large and gratifying Joanna's life could have been. Some little chemistry had worked against a ripening of first-rate things, and Joanna had always been contemptuous of the substitutes.

This is what Evelyn knew, and she would have to live with the knowledge of both: the woman Joanna was and the woman she could have been. It was not a happy fate. Death rid Joanna of that fate, and bequeathed the memory of it to her friend, Evelyn. But, day by day, Evelyn made the unoriginal discovery that death itself is irrefutable, but that in the persistence of silence there begins to grow an answering eloquence.

By late afternoon, everything was ready. She had only to put what she had prepared in the oven. She looked at the kitchen clock: it was almost four. Gabe's plane would be making its approach. She had offered to pick him up at Kennedy, but he wouldn't hear of it. There were so many things to talk about—so *many* things! It was frightening. She didn't feel in the least bridal.

But she did feel right. She thought of Gabe's face and felt in herself a great welcome to that image. She knew he would be bringing enormous problems, but after they had dealt with those problems, she would very much like to sit down and begin to tell him . . . everything!

24

Gabe walked out of the terminal building and signaled for one of the waiting cabs. The driver stepped out and took Gabe's bag, which he slid in beside the front seat. A young man, Gabe noted, with glossy brown eyes and a glossy brown beard, tight-knurled, like the marble beards of Greek statues. Gabe got in, and in a moment they were winding their way out of the John F. Kennedy Airport. This cab didn't have the wire-laced shield of glass. Gabe leaned forward and examined the name on the license: *Mark Shapiro.*

He leaned back and smiled to himself. He thought of that first cab driver and that fifty-thousand-dollar medallion. Fifty thousand dollars! Were Jewish families in New York putting their sons into the taxi business? *My son, the cabbie!* Well, why not? A big investment. The young man up front was not that much older than his own children, and Gabe knew from his own children that futures were looked on differently now. The professions were no longer looked on as the Eretz Yisroel of the Diaspora. Israel was Israel, and it was fighting its battle of survival in a more conventional way. Jewish kids in America smoked pot, strummed guitars, wore beards, and blended into Kansas wheat fields or foothill campuses. Some of them. Others wanted to go completely around history and arrive at the beginning. . . .

"Is it as hot as this in Denver?" asked Mark Shapiro, cab driver.

"Not quite," said Gabe. "How did you know I was from Denver?"

"The tag on your bag."

"Oh . . . well, it's hot all right, but not like this. It's very dry."

"I'll bet," said Mark. "That's one town I've never been to. I'd really like to go there. I'm looking around for a place to do my graduate work. Are the schools good there?"

"So I'm told," Gabe said. "What's your field?"

"This'll sound crazy, but I can go with either psych or lit. I majored in psychology in my undergraduate work, but I got my best marks in my lit courses. Boy, I wrote good papers!"

"But haven't you got a heavy investment in this cab?" Gabe asked.

"Me? Nah. This isn't my cab. I don't own it. I just drive it a couple of days a week to make a few bucks. Friend of mine owns it."

Gabe examined the license again and saw his mistake. It was another bearded face. This, then, wasn't Mark Shapiro. But what difference? Let it stay.

"Wouldn't you miss New York?" Gabe asked.

Substitute Mark Shapiro half turned and glanced over his shoulder. "Would you miss a cancer?" he asked.

"I see," said Gabe.

That would teach him to philosophize on five cents' worth of evidence!

They came to the inevitable funnel around Jamaica Avenue, and the young man honked and swore and swooped like any good New York cabbie. The air that poured through the open window felt like the exhaust from some vast machine.

Gabe thought of Pam. He had said to her that she mustn't think of transferring East from the school in Los Angeles where she had enrolled, but he fervently hoped she would. Not necessarily to New York. Indeed, he preferred *not* New York. The idea of Pam roaming around Morningside Heights or the Village gave him cold shivers. But there were so many schools around the city, good ones upstate, or Connecticut, or Boston. . . . He imagined himself taking a shuttle flight to Boston, he and Evelyn, spending the night at one of those old hotels on Commonwealth Avenue, spending the day with Pam somewhere along the Charles

River. . . . Yes, and how about Andy? Where would he be? . . . And how about Jean? . . .

He cut off his thoughts. He had learned how to turn valves in his mind. One thing at a time. It was extraordinary. The future, which had looked to be such a placid sweep of sameness, had to be parceled out a day at a time to keep the complexities from flooding.

Was that good or bad? Gabe wasn't sure. In recent mornings, when he woke up in the hotel room, which he had moved into provisionally, he would lie for several seconds in the darkness and the air conditioner's hum as in a chemical suspension, feeling that the slightest jar of reality would restore his former life, which had not been unbearable, which he had slipped away from (it seemed at times) almost by accident. And even when all the immediacies were enormously in place, he was still left with a vague wonder. Were such consequences intended?

No they weren't. Not *intended*. They happened a step at a time. As did his first love affair with Evelyn. As did his marriage to Jean. As did the growth of his children. As did this flight East. It was as real as anything else in life—and as fantastic. Perhaps if Jean had been hateful? But she hadn't been hateful. She had been, only and always, Jean. Why couldn't he have gone on living with that? He could have. That was the remarkable and sometimes frightening thing. *There was nothing inevitable in all of this!* He would perhaps be more comfortable with some sense of inevitability. It's so relieving for criminals and lovers to say: *"I couldn't help myself."* But Gabe Michelson was left with the distinct impression that he *could* have helped himself.

Which made it all a very conscious, deliberate thing. That was the fact to be faced: it was all conscious, all deliberate, and he wasn't sure he would ever get over letting something of this magnitude happen without the blessing of inevitability.

But, then, so much had happened without that blessing.

Like what?

Like the assassination of Presidents. Like mistaken wars. Like Watergate. Like men and women playing at sex as they do at volley ball. Like things running out in this exhaustible earth. . . .

Ach! What nonsense! Whom was he kidding? He preferred one woman to another, and it became more and more possible to have his preference. But no! He was not that way! He had never been a man to reach for whatever he wanted simply because he wanted it. Then, what? What was behind all of this?

"To tell you the truth, mister," suddenly piped up substitute Shapiro, "I'm thinking of taking in Europe before I go back to school. That's one of the reasons I'm driving this hack."

"That's a good idea," said Gabe.

"Although I realize I may be a little too late. Italy's going Communist, and the buck is going right through the floor."

"That's true."

"Still, I'd like to go."

Yes. He should go, because everything was changing. Michelangelo's "David" would be the same under a Communist regime, but some connection would be lost. . . .

The taxi went through the Midtown Tunnel and entered the city through that relatively quiet side door. There was no sense of homecoming in Gabe, but he did feel again the slow ferment of possibility. He had thought that this would be the moment when he would have to deal with a burst of anticipation or the enormous weight of sin, but he felt neither. He felt, instead, the solemnity of occasion.

This was much closer to it—this feeling of solemn occasion. It had all been deliberate, all conscious, but the morality that he thought would finally demand a strong sense of inevitability had not made that demand. He had lived through all the changes, and without his really knowing that it had happened, his life conditions had become his morality. It was no longer something apart. That's why things had happened as they had happened: because he had known for a long time that a man like him must have a very strong sense of rightness in the few vital contracts that remained.

"Here we are."

Gabe gave him a handsome tip. "That's toward your European trip," he said.

"Hey, thanks!"

Gabe carried his bag into the outer vestibule, set it down, and looked for the button marked WHITE. He pushed it.

"Gabe!"

"Yes."

The buzzer made a festive little racket, and Gabe pushed through the door.